THE AMBASSADOR

Also by Peter Colt

The Andy Roark mysteries

THE OFF-ISLANDER
BACK BAY BLUES
DEATH AT FORT DEVENS *
THE AMBASSADOR *

* *available from Severn House*

THE AMBASSADOR

Peter Colt

SEVERN
HOUSE

First world edition published in Great Britain and the USA in 2023
by Severn House, an imprint of Canongate Books Ltd,
14 High Street, Edinburgh EH1 1TE.

Trade paperback edition first published in Great Britain and the USA in 2023
by Severn House, an imprint of Canongate Books Ltd.

severnhouse.com

British Library Cataloguing-in-Publication Data
A CIP catalogue record for this title is available from the British Library.

ISBN-13: 978-1-4483-0767-8 (cased)
ISBN-13: 978-1-4483-0791-3 (trade paper)
ISBN-13: 978-1-4483-0790-6 (e-book)

All Severn House titles are printed on acid-free paper.

Typeset by Palimpsest Book Production Ltd.,
Falkirk, Stirlingshire, Scotland.
Printed and bound in Great Britain by
TJ Books, Padstow, Cornwall.

For Cathy, Henry and Alder

AUTHOR'S NOTE

William Healy Sullivan was the Ambassador to Laos from 1964 to 1969. His policies in Laos were a source of irritation for many in MACV-SOG. For me, that seemed like a great plot line for an Andy Roark novel. My fictional Ambassador to Laos, Gordon R. Stevenson, is a character created from my own mind and is in no way meant to be a thinly veiled version of Sullivan. Any incidents that are depicted, opinions stated, the appearance of Stevenson are purely fictitious.

ACKNOWLEDGMENTS

I have the easy job. I write the story, the manuscript. The following people turn the often misspelled, grammatically flawed manuscript into a novel.

CME who reads and tirelessly edits the manuscripts and offers advice. TFA who listens to countless story ideas and provides much needed advice. There is a small group of people who read the initial manuscripts and keep me honest about Andy's world and time.

My editor at Severn House Rachel Slatter who provides much needed editorial guidance.

Penny Isaacs who edited the rough edges off the manuscript, concealing from the world most of my literary flaws.

The good people at Severn House who worked hard to ensure that this book found its way into your hands.

The incomparable Cynthia Manson, my agent, without whom I literally could not do this.

ONE

October, 1985

I was sitting at the bar in the Harvard Club nursing a scotch and soda. It was nice as bars go, dark wood and dim lighting. The last time this much mahogany and teak had been used in construction in Boston, it was to make ships to fight the British. There were heavy leather wing chairs scattered about the joint. There were small, dark wood tables too. A couple of the bigger tables had a combination of wing chairs and love seats. The carpet was a deep red. The place spoke more of class than money, which meant it was expensive. I was fortunately spared Groucho Marx's philosophical dilemma of not wanting to belong to any club that would want me as a member. I had finished my degree at night school, and I was most definitely not Harvard Club material.

I was dressed to fit in though: loafers, pressed khaki pants, Oxford shirt with a tie that might have been a school tie or just a collection of slanting red and blue lines. I was wearing a blue blazer with brass buttons; it had come from Brooks Brothers, and it did a good job covering the snub-nose .38 in a holster in my waistband. There was a large folding Buck knife in my front right pocket and a speedloader holding five extra hollow point .38s in the left. You could take the boy out of Southie . . . well, you know the rest.

People like my people don't go to Harvard. We worked in the factories, the mills, crewed on their whaling ships and fought wars for the people that did. That was the way it was and would always be. The natural order of things. I had no complaints. I would have made a pretty bad captain of industry, but I had been a pretty good soldier once.

There was a large doorway to my left leading to the Boston Room, where you could order beef Wellington and the appropriate wine. It also led to the front doors. The large door behind me led to a grand staircase. Beyond that, there was a great hall type of affair with a giant granite fireplace and more wood paneling. Less classy places would call it a function room. Here it was named after some dead alum whose name I missed. Inside some pompous windbag was holding forth, giving a speech that I wasn't being paid enough to listen to. Actually, I wasn't being paid anything yet. The pompous windbag in question was Ambassador Gordon R. Stevenson, the man whose dime I was drinking on and who had invited me to his club to offer me a job I was sure that I didn't want. It wasn't that I had anything against earning money, I just didn't want to take his money. We didn't know each other, but we had some shared history.

I had a third of a drink left when there was the sound of sustained applause from the great hall. This didn't seem like the type of place where people would wave cigarette lighters in the air looking for an encore, or cry out for the band to play 'Free Bird'. I was confident my prospective client was going to come walking through those doors in a few minutes. I wasn't sure how long it took an Ivy League-educated retired Ambassador on a lecture tour to get through a crowd of fans.

I started to take a sip of my drink but stopped. Standing in the doorway to my left was a woman. She was tall and blonde with long legs and high heels. She was wearing a simple but expensive-looking sheath of red material. She had straight, platinum-blonde hair, bangs on her forehead, and a nose that plastic surgeons were paid a lot to imitate. She walked over to me and rested a hand on my arm, red lacquer on her fingernails to match the dress.

'Excuse me. You look like the type to have a spare cigarette on him.'

'I do if you don't mind unfiltered Lucky Strikes.'

'Anything. I just sat through a god-awful speech without a drink or a cigarette.' She was probably thirty but except for the small, fine wrinkles around her green eyes, she could have passed for a co-ed. I fished out a pack of Luckies, shook one loose, and offered it to her. She took it, nodding her thanks. I took my battered Zippo out and lit it. She held my hand in hers as she pulled the flame to the cigarette.

'You aren't a member here, are you.' She was stating fact, not asking questions.

'What gave me away?'

'Your hands, they have a little too much history on them.'

It was true. They had small scars and calluses, the types of things that happen when you have been in a few fights or carried guns your whole adult life. If she had been on my other side, she would have seen my right ear, which was missing most of the lobe after an angry Vietnamese Army colonel shot it off. He was trying to kill me and either he had been a bad shot, or I had been really lucky. That was six months ago, and it still itched a little.

'Don't tell anyone, but I work for the university undercover,' I said.

She smiled at me, bright rows of pearly white teeth. 'Doing what?'

'I am responsible for ensuring that the god-awful speeches are sufficiently boring to meet the school's quota.'

She laughed. 'Well, I assure you this one fit right in. I should know, my husband is the speaker.' She smiled at me, and I was reminded that this wasn't the first time that I had walked into an ambush.

'Mrs Stevenson, I presume . . . you aren't what I pictured the Ambassador's wife . . .'

'You envision someone older, dumpier . . .' I had, but I wasn't going to admit it. 'I am the second Mrs Stevenson.'

I was spared further chance to jam my loafered foot in my mouth by the arrival of the Ambassador and an Ivy League type who might just be thirty. The Ambassador was an older version of himself from the covers of *Newsweek* and *U.S. News & World Report* that I remembered him being on ten or so years ago.

He was tall with a cleft chin and grey hair that was fashionably long across his forehead but never approached his collar in the back. He had a bushy, gray, not-quite-handlebar mustache that seemed more at home on a cigarette-selling cowboy than a man trying to sell his memoirs. He was broad through the chest with just a hint of softening at his waist. He looked like a man who spent a lot of time riding horses or captaining sailboats.

Next to him was a young man almost as tall. The younger man obviously went to the same barber and took it so far as to have the same haircut. Fortunately, he didn't have a mustache. He was lanky and narrow-hipped and I got the feeling that he had never been inside a public school in his life. When he spoke, I was sure of it.

'Mr Roark, I am Bradley Lawrence, the Ambassador's aide-de-camp.' It was an interesting choice of job title. I was pretty sure that he wasn't working for a general officer, nor were either of them in the military. Maybe he was uncomfortable being a male secretary, or maybe the old man saw himself as an Army officer. To each their own. 'We spoke on the phone.'

'Yes, we did.' It had been a short conversation, asking me to meet here, dress appropriately. I love a good challenge.

'May I introduce Ambassador Gordon Stevenson.'

The Ambassador had been waiting for this and stuck his hand out. We shook and he squeezed it hard enough to let me know that he was still fit at his age.

'Mr Roark, nice to meet you. Let's sit down over there.' He gestured to a table in a discreet corner with a love seat and two wing chairs. 'Brad, Mr Roark and I are going to talk. Get him another and get Honey and me our usual.'

'Yes, sir.' Brad the ADC dipped his forehead, and I was half expecting him to click his heels like some sort of Prussian cavalry officer.

I followed Stevenson and Honey to the table. They took the love seat and sat thigh to thigh. Lucky Stevenson. I sat in the wing chair that would let me see the room and the two doors. Brad the ADC drifted over and was soon followed by a waiter bearing a tray of drinks. He handed the Ambassador and Honey matching martinis. I bet they even had monogrammed robes. Bradley had what looked like scotch on the rocks.

'Mr Roark, I understand you were in Vietnam?' Stevenson's voice was deep and spoke of a lifetime of giving orders.

'Yes, sir. I was.'

'You were Special Forces.'

'Yes.'

'MACV-SOG?' His eyes were blue and cold and locked on mine. Military Assistance Command Vietnam – Studies and

'Look, sir. He's an asshole. Insubordinate, flippant, and in the few years I have known him, a colossal pain in the ass.' Stevenson nodded in agreement. 'But he is also – and I can't believe I am saying this in front of him – tough, smart, and probably just the guy you need right now.' I wasn't used to being showered with such high praise from Brenda.

'You left out handsome and charming.' Maybe it was the Harvard Club, it brought out the charming romantic in me.

'No, I didn't, and don't push it.' Brenda had long, honey-colored hair, and once – after my car had been blown up – she insisted on clearing my apartment in case the bad guys were there waiting to finish the job they had botched. If I hadn't been a little drunk, a bit sad, and kind of blown up, I would have asked her to stay the night. She might have taken pity on me. She might be mad at me now, but she was there for me even when I was hell-bent on making bad decisions.

'Look, sir, there are guys who might have his background, there might even be some who might help you, but he is the guy you can get.'

I am not sure if it was Brenda's argument or Honey's efforts to calm her husband, but he took a sip of his martini and looked at me. 'OK. I don't know why I am surprised that he would be a bit of a cowboy. Hell,' he boomed with sudden bonhomie, 'he might just be the type of son of a bitch I need.'

Jesus, he went from bad to worse in the blink of an eye.

'Mr Ambassador, why don't you tell Roark your problem. Maybe he can help.'

Leave it to Brenda to overestimate my abilities.

He looked at me, trying to assess me or my sincerity, took another sip of his martini and spoke. 'I have been receiving threats. Death threats.'

'Someone has been sending Gordon these awful letters,' Honey chimed in. Her hand had moved from his thigh to his forearm.

'OK, is it some random nut or a crazy? Another Hinckley type?' The attempted assassination of Ronald Reagan was still a recent memory. 'The FBI, Special Agent Watts, they are good, and they have resources that—' I started to say.

Stevenson cut me off. 'He's one of you.'

'Excuse me?'

'He is one of you, one of the SOG cowboys.'

'Andy, the letters indicate that he might be a Special Forces guy. Like you. From Vietnam.' Brenda cut in smoothly, interjecting a bit of rational calm.

'Oh . . . OK.' That explained why Watts had set up the meeting. It also wasn't that far off. I knew a lot of guys, myself included, who, after a few drinks, had expressed a desire to go to the Ambassador's residence in Vientiane and 'frag that motherfucker'.

'Mr Roark, we're worried that it is possible someone holds a grudge from Vietnam against the Ambassador.' Bradley's voice hit all the notes of prep school and the Ivy League. Princeton or Dartmouth would be my guess. 'Like any great man,' he actually called Stevenson that, 'the Ambassador has his share of detractors, enemies; even some who might send threats. What worries us is . . .' He paused, trying to find the right words.

'You're worried that someone who is experienced and skilled enough to pull it off is sending the letters,' I finished for him.

'Yes, Mr Roark, that is it. Most people aren't a threat, but one of your SOG cowboys looking to kill me because of some misperceived grudge from the war, well, that is worrisome.'

It was the way he said 'SOG cowboys' like he was saying 'deviants' or something else unseemly. I had served with the finest soldiers in the free world, they were my brothers, and there were too many whose names were on the black wall in Washington. Him . . . he was, at best, an asshole. But it was his patrician tone and manners that made me want to punch him in the nose. Instead, I drained my scotch and soda in one pull and stood up.

'Thanks for the drink, Mr Stevenson, but I am not the man for the job.' I bowed toward Honey and couldn't make eye contact with Brenda Watts. Maybe someday she would get used to my being a disappointment.

I walked out of the bar, out of the club, and my fists didn't unclench until I was a block away. When they did, I fit a Lucky in my mouth and lit it, the smoke filling my lungs, calming me down some.

TWO

It was a good night to walk back to my apartment, cool but not yet cold. Only the first few leaves had started to fall. The fall rains and carpet of browning leaves weren't far off. If you have never walked from the Harvard Club down Commonwealth Avenue to the Public Garden at the height of fall, you should. Between the tall trees and stately brownstones, it rivals anything in Paris or London . . . well, almost anything. But it is still nicer than New York.

I had good reason to hate the Ambassador. Those of us who ran Recon in Vietnam did. He had ruled over his Ambassadorship in Laos with an iron fist. Our missions were constrained to a narrow corridor in Laos, which meant that the North Vietnamese Army knew we couldn't go outside that corridor, which meant they could concentrate on the likely areas that we would try to use as LZs. Anything outside of that box had to be cleared through the embassy in Vientiane.

If that weren't bad enough for Recon missions, it was disastrous for Bright Light missions, when teams would charge in to help other teams in trouble or try to rescue downed pilots before the NVA could get to them. Those were situations where speed was critical, and the Ambassador, not wanting anyone else to play in his little 'kingdom', would deny missions or just take so long to approve them that they were moot. A lot of good men – SOG men or brave pilots, aircrews trying to save our asses – were killed. It was one thing to lose guys to the NVA. It was war, and they were good soldiers. It was another to lose them because some bureaucrat made up his own arbitrary rules.

More than a decade later, it still left a bad taste in my mouth. I could still see the red dust swirling in the heat and humidity at the Launch Site. It was my team's week on Bright Light duty, which meant a lot of waiting. When word came in, we would throw on our gear, run to the birds, pile in and go full tilt toward gunfire. We'd all been in the shit and knew how much it meant to the guys on the ground knowing there was help on the way.

It had been a slow week. We were almost done, ready to rotate back to the Forward Operating Base and start preparing for a Recon mission. We were killing time leaning against rucksacks on bunks. The screen door burst open and one of the guys who I was in training group with popped his head in. 'Red, you'd better get your team ready. We have a bird that went down.'

'Shit, how bad?' He was already gone. I was on my feet, and my One-One was already moving without being told to get word to our Montagnard mercenaries to get ready. I threw on my web gear, slung my ruck over one shoulder, and grabbed my CAR-15.

My One-Two was also experienced and took my gear, telling me to go get the brief. I handed him my rucksack. I knew he and the One-One would have the team ready to go. I hustled over to the Operations shack, the screen door slapping shut behind me, reminding me of summers in Southie. Kids exploding out of screen doors to go play stick ball or run around or just cut loose.

'Red, we have a downed pilot. There was a team in trouble,' the Operations officer said. He continued, 'The team was picked up, and they are on their way out. We had an O-2 get hit and go down.' An O-2 was a light observation plane carrying a pilot and sometimes a Covey Rider.

'Shit.'

'He was flying solo, no Covey Rider.' That was something, at least. Covey Riders were Recon men who ended up riding shotgun with the FACs, using their experience as Recon men to help teams in trouble. 'We are trying to get a fix on the wreck, and we have a call into the embassy in Vientiane. Hopefully the Ambassador isn't playing golf.'

'Do they have commo with the pilot?'

'He made one transmission on his emergency radio at 1300 hours.' That was twenty minutes ago.

'Where did he go down?' The captain pointed to a spot on the map. It was at the edge of our operational capabilities. The choppers could get there and back, but there wouldn't be a lot of loiter time. That wasn't what concerned me. The downed airplane was well outside of the box that the Ambassador let SOG operate in. It would be like pulling teeth to get clearance from him.

'Sir, how soon until we can go?' The captain looked at me, and his face was grim.

'Red, we're still waiting for clearance.'

'Sir, we are wasting time. Let me and my guys get in the air. We can make time, and if the clearance comes through, we will be that much closer.'

'Standby, Red. Hang in there. Clearance is coming but you know . . . the Ambassador.' I didn't know him personally, but I had heard of him. He was so protective of his little patch of Southeast Asia that he had been known to delay giving approval to missions just to send us 'cowboys' a message. That was if he didn't deny them outright.

I looked at the maps of where the pilot went down, looking for LZs near but not too near the crash. I listened with half an ear as a different Covey circled the area, trying to make comms with the pilot. Covey reported hostiles in the area. A couple of A-1s came on the net. It was fascinating listening to them make their gun and bomb runs. After the extraction chopper, they were my favorite bird in the sky. Though the Cobra Gunship was a close second.

I looked at the maps making mental notes. My One-One came in and I started going through LZs and routes with him. The whole time I was watching the clock as minutes dragged by, and then an hour. The Ops officer was sick of my questioning looks, and eventually we went down to the flight line to wait by the birds. There was only so much looking at the maps that we could do.

Later still, the sun was on the downhill slide for the day. There was no way, even if we left then, that the birds would get us to the pilot before dark. The Ops officer walked up the hill to the flight line. I gave him a lot of credit for that. He was a captain and could have found a junior guy to come deliver bad news.

'Hey, Red. You and your men stand down. We're losing

daylight and we don't have clearance from Vientiane. The boss says to call it for today. We will try for first light if the weather cooperates.'

'Fuck. Sir, there's a pilot alone out there in the jungle. Almost on top of the Ho Chi Minh Trail.'

'I know, Red. It sucks, but those are the orders. Get some hot chow and get some rest. You guys will launch first thing tomorrow.' He walked off down the hill. He was a decent sort, the captain. It didn't take much to see that this didn't sit well with him either.

The next day, we finally got clearance from Vientiane and launched at the crack of noon. We had watched the minutes crawl by, turning into hours, and just when everyone was thinking of heading back to the hooches, we got the order to launch. Everyone had grown impatient and ill-tempered with the waiting.

We rode on the birds toward the downed pilot that no one had heard from in almost a day, wrapped in our own thoughts. The LZ we had picked was as close to where the wreckage of the Cessna O-2 had been spotted as we dared put in. The O-2 was a good spotter plane, but it was unarmed and unarmored, carrying only smoke rockets for marking. Only the great skill of the pilots kept them from getting shot down; that, and luck. Which in this case had run out.

The door gunner leaned over and tapped my shoulder. I looked up at him and he held up five outstretched fingers. A few minutes later, as the green-brown blur of the countryside flashed by, another tap. I stood up on the skid, one hand holding the strap connected to the bird and one hand on my CAR-15. The pilot started to flare the bird, bringing the nose up, putting us in landing position. I scanned the area in front of me and didn't see anything to keep me from stepping off the skid. It was my call. If I did, the team would step off the skid with me. If I didn't, the pilot would crank up the engine and get us out of there.

I stepped off and hit the ground a few feet below with a thump. I started to move away from the LZ with my weapon up, my eyes and the muzzle of the CAR-15 moved in unison. I knew that my point man, one of the Yards, was on my left. On the other side of the bird, my One-Two would be doing the same thing with another one of our Yards, our other two guys too. The second bird was right behind our bird, dropping off the rest of my heavily armed team.

After a short pause to listen for the enemy, deciding it was safe enough to move, we radioed in that we were OK. Then we started to move toward the wreckage of the O-2. It was uphill, and we began to push through thick vegetation. We pushed as much through the heat and humidity as we did through the greenery. It was hard, slow going, and it took us an hour to move several hundred meters up the slope before we came to the wrecked plane.

It had come through the triple canopy jungle above hard. One wing was sheared off, and the tail booms were bent up above the wing as though the plane had surrendered. The front prop was bent to hell and the rear prop was gone. The fuselage was riddled with bullet holes and was streaked with engine oil. The front engine cowling had popped open, probably from the crash. The windshield was a series of spiderweb cracks and missing puzzle pieces of glass.

The team spread out around the wreckage, and I went to look inside. The cabin was a mess of papers, broken glass and dangling wires where electronics had been ripped out. There were a couple of smallish patches of dried blood, flies buzzing over and around them.

My indigenous counterpart came up to me and pointed off to the west. The point man had picked up the trail; it looked like someone had crawled or dragged themselves away from the crash. We spread out and slowly followed it. It led downhill and then into a thicket. The pilot had dragged himself away into the nearest hidey-hole he could find, behind one of the larger boulders, so he had cover if he had to fight.

Off to one side of the boulder, my point man squatted on the balls of his feet. He stood up into a crouch and came over to me. He held out his hand and held up a couple of shell casings: 5.56-millimeter, US Army issue ammunition. Then he held up shorter, squatter, rounder shell casings. They were shell casings from an AK-47. He whispered to me, '*Baucoup* AK.' There had been a gunfight between the FAC and the NVA. He motioned me over to another set of tracks.

This one had lots of small footprints and some patches of dried blood. There had been a lot of NVA, and they had been dragging something heavy. We started to head downhill for an hour until the trail took a sharp turn down into a small canyon. The canyon led to the Ho Chi Minh Trail, and that meant the pilot was gone.

My point man stopped, and we all froze, dropping to one knee. I scooted up to him. He pointed down the trail and shook his head from side to side. He didn't like what he was looking at. He put his lips next to my ear and whispered, 'Ambush, *Trung Si.*' I motioned for the team to start moving back slowly. We backed up, covering the trail, waiting for the sound of gunfire, tense, sweating from more than just the heat and crushing humidity. We had spotted the ambush before they spotted us. We managed to back up a-ways when I heard a single rifle shot from up by the wreckage. An NVA trail watcher was signaling behind us.

I pointed off the trail, uphill to our side, and the team started to move into the thick brush, moving slowly uphill and away from the trail. We moved slowly and carefully, each step, each footfall deliberately placed. The NVA were behind us, stalking us. We got near the top of the hill and proceeded to work around it and away from the Ho Chi Minh Trail. We found a spot and I raised Covey on the radio.

'Pilot is either a prisoner or dead. NVA is on to us. Declaring Tactical Emergency. Need an LZ.' I told him a rough approximation of where we were, and he told me to move downhill east toward some bomb craters.

We started moving, pushing through the brush. A gunshot went off somewhere behind us. Another one off to the side of us answering the first shot. The NVA were letting us know, and each other, where they thought we were. Bracketing us and tightening an invisible net until they could bring a mass of soldiers to bear on us. They were good, and it wouldn't take them long to figure out we were going. We picked up the pace. We kept working our way down and around the hill, moving as quickly as we dared. There were more rifle shots, high-caliber call and responses.

We came to a riverbed with just a trickle of water and edged out to the tree line. It probably raged with white water during monsoon season. We crossed, point man first, then two at a time. Then we started trudging uphill, laboriously working our way up from bomb crater to bomb crater, the heat and humidity fighting us as much as the NVA would. We kept moving until we were up in the brush on the other side of the craters.

I heard a cough and swung round. Behind us were the khaki-uniformed NVA. Immediately, they started to shoot at us, rounds snapping by as we ducked into the jungle.

'Covey, this is Whiskey Six Six, we are taking fire from the streambed opposite bomb craters.'

'Hey Whiskey, roger that.'

'Do you have any Spads or Fast Movers who can lay some ordnance on the stream?'

'Standby, Whiskey.' I waited to watch the other side of the shallow stream as my men kept working their way uphill. The fire from the NVA side started to pick up. Soon there would be a lot of Communist soldiers in that valley.

'Whiskey Six Six?'

'Send it.'

'OK, I got a pair of Phantoms with some HE and napalm they'd like to use up before they head home. They are three minutes out.' High explosives and napalm would slow down the NVA.

We started pushing up the hill. We were already soaked with sweat. Trying to breathe was like breathing through a hot, wet towel. It seemed like forever, but then we heard the unmistakable whine of Pratt & Whitney-powered F-4 Phantom jets. Then explosions. The jungle was getting thicker, and that dampened a lot of the concussion from the bombs.

We made it to the LZ, which turned out to be a tiny clearing on the steep side of a hill. Calling it a clearing was an act of generosity. It was a hole in the jungle canopy on the side of a steep hill. There was no way to put a helicopter down in it, even if we blew some trees with det cord or C-4. I could see why Covey had picked it. It was the last place the NVA would think we would try to extract from.

The team fanned out to take up security positions. I motioned to my One-One, a happy-go-lucky kid from California who didn't look old enough to shave but was some sort of genius with explosives. He came over close enough that we could whisper to each other.

'What's up, Red?'

'Hey, man. This is the LZ. I think they are going to have to use ladders.' It would mean climbing up to the helicopter, which would take time. From the sound of it, the F-4s were working over the streambed with 20-millimeter cannons.

I pointed to the trees on the far side of the LZ, the downslope side.

'Can you take some of those down?'

'Sure, Red, I have C-4 and det cord. Lighter and faster than a chainsaw.' He grinned at me, and I nodded. That was all he needed. He took off his rucksack, opened it, and pulled out a wet-weather bag. He took the bag and his CAR-15 and went to blow up some trees. I got on the radio and let Covey know the deal.

'Choppers are ten minutes out. Keep your heads down.' Ten minutes. Shit. A lifetime away, but better than fifteen minutes.

The waiting was the worst – at least in a firefight you didn't have time to worry. I listened to the sounds of planes pounding the streambed with guns, bombs, and napalm. I had the radio handset stuck to my ear, listening intently into the static for Covey.

I alternated between watching the jungle, the team, and stealing glances at my Seiko. The minutes slowly ticked by. With a hair over two minutes to go, the childlike mad genius from California flopped down next to me. He held up the firing device and I nodded. It was faint, but off in the distance was the distinct WHUPWHUPWHUP of the Hueys. I watched the jungle intently and heard the crump of C-4. I looked back and our LZ had doubled in size from Tiny to Really Small. Covey came on the radio asking me to pop smoke so the choppers could find us.

I reached up and pulled the tape off the white phosphorus grenade taped to the left strap of my web gear. I pulled the pin and lobbed the soup-can-sized grenade into the clearing. It burst into a sudden, white-hot smoke octopus with white-hot ember tendrils of smoke. The smoke shot straight up in a thick column through the canopy of trees where the Huey pilots would see it.

'Whiskey Six Six, Whiskey Six Six, this is All City John.'

'All City, go ahead.'

'Roger that, Whiskey. All City John is here to bring you boys home. Gonna drop some ladders.'

'Roger that, All City.'

Then there was a UH-1, downwash and all, right above the clearing. The door gunners kicked two metal ladders out each side of the bird. My assistant team leader and three Yards moved to the ladders and started climbing while the rest of us covered them.

The Huey lifted straight up with my guys still climbing up the ladders. Then there was blue sky, and another Huey was overhead. Ladders rattled down toward us, and we ran for them. I grabbed mine, looked around, and the rest of the team were on theirs. We climbed, tired, fighting gravity, fighting the rucksack pulling against me. The bird started rising and then I was fighting the cold wind against my sweat-drenched uniform too. I made it to the skid and then the lip of the door frame and strong arms pulled me in. Safe, I collapsed on the deck, against my ruck. Tired but alive.

No one was hurt and that was rare, but there weren't any smiles. Based on the tracks, we had missed the pilot by almost a day. He had been alive after the crash. It was a kick in the guts to think that we might have gotten him out if we could have launched right away. We didn't and he was dead or on his way to the Hanoi Hilton.

I lay back against the deck of the helicopter, cold and exhausted. I was thinking about all the times we had sat around tables in the club after a mission botched by bureaucracy. Drunk and angry, each conversation beginning the same way: 'I am going up to Vientiane and frag that motherfucker of an ambassador.' He hated SOG, and tried hard to keep us on a leash.

Then, like that, I wasn't in Vietnam anymore. I was in Boston. Walking home to my apartment that I shared with the world's most contrary cat, Sir Leominster. It was over a decade and what seemed like a million light years from Vietnam. I had met the Ambassador, and the best I could manage after all of my angry talk was to turn down his job offer. Twenty-three-year-old me would have been disgusted with me. I wasn't sure I wasn't now.

THREE

The next morning had started out cool with a little mist when I had gone for a run. I was trying to do that more; I hadn't been successful at cutting back on cigarettes and whiskey, but I figured going for a run every other day balanced it out. I keep telling myself that.

By the time I walked to the office, the sun had come out. Soon, we would start to have more gray days, more rainy days than sunny ones. Then it would get cold, there would be snow and brutal cold. The streets would be filled with cold, wet slush, and every sidewalk would be a slippery obstacle course cursed by agile and clumsy alike. I liked the miserable weather just as much as the good.

My office above the video rental store was unusually neat. I had been on a cleaning jag lately, trying to live a more organized life. The last six months had put me through the wringer. I had lost two friends, had my earlobe shot off, almost been killed a couple of other ways and came to realize that maybe I needed to grow up a little. Make better life decisions.

Consequently, I was in my office eating a croissant and drinking an espresso from the machine Old Man Marconi had left me while I caught up on some paperwork. Marconi's had been the pizza joint that was now a video store. Marconi found out he had cancer and sold out to a national video rental chain so he could go home to bask in the Italian sun before he died. He left me his prized espresso machine. I hoped that the sun was warm and forgiving where he was.

I heard the outer office door open and – out of habit born from years of people trying to kill me – took the overbuilt Ruger .357 Magnum out of the drawer and put it under the papers I was looking through. They didn't do much to conceal the big revolver, but it was better than just putting the beast on the desk.

Brenda Watts walked into my office. Today she was wearing

a pantsuit, sensible shoes, carrying a large shoulder bag and packing a .38 on her hip. Even without makeup and heels, she was still something to see. Her honey-colored hair hung down in a ponytail, and the conservative cut of the pantsuit failed to entirely obscure the curves that lurked under it. She had pretty eyes that flashed at me in anger most of the time.

'Hello, Andy.' She plopped down in the visitor's chair opposite my desk, ending any further hints of the mysteries that might be hidden by the pantsuit.

'Hey, Brenda.'

'So, last night could have gone better.' For Brenda that was being subtle.

'I know, I know. You think I'm an asshole.'

'Well, history might lead me to that conclusion.'

'The Ambassador—'

She cut me off. 'He is a pompous ass and old lecher too.'

I looked at her in mild shock.

'He talks to my boobs and not my face.'

'Oh, I see.' It was odd realizing that the Ambassador and I might have some of the same flaws.

'Look, I don't know what your issue is with him, Andy. I know you well enough to know you probably have a good reason for it.' She stopped.

'But?' I asked.

'But I want you to take the case. I think that it might be someone who was in Vietnam, someone from SOG.'

'Well, if that is really the case, Stevenson is in a lot of trouble.'

'That's why I want you to take the case.'

'You Hoover types aren't exactly useless.'

'No, but our skill sets aren't like yours.' It was hard to picture Brenda in a pantsuit out in the jungle watching the Ho Chi Minh Trail.

'What do you mean by that?'

'When they put me on this, I was given clearance and access to a lot of stuff. I know what SOG was. I also got a look at your Two Oh One file.' That was the Army's equivalent of your permanent record: promotions, schools, awards, disciplinary actions, orders, that sort of thing.

'Oh.' It was weird to hear her say SOG. The Studies and Observation Group was ultra-secret. Those of us who were left didn't talk much about it, and when we did it was only to other guys who were in it.

'Andy, you and I both know that if it is an SOG guy behind these letters, the Ambassador is in trouble.' I couldn't argue with her about that. If it was one of the guys I knew, the guys I worked with, the Ambassador's death was a matter of *when* not *if*.

'Brenda . . .' I started to say something. I am not sure what, an excuse or some half-assed justification for not wanting to take the case, but she wasn't finished. 'Look, maybe it's nothing, a crank, whatever. But if it is an SOG guy, you are the best one to figure it out. Track him down so we can step in before this goes too far. I am not asking you to take a bullet for the old guy.' But that was the problem, wasn't it? You never knew if you were going to have to take a bullet. She continued, 'You know that none of the SOG guys left will talk to us. We can send agents all day long, and no one will say a thing.'

'Maybe, but there are still a few guys on active duty. You could call them in, clear them to talk and then order them to.'

She was shaking her head. 'You know that they won't. Even if one of them knows who it is, they won't talk. None of you would give up one of your brothers to save the Ambassador.' I had to admit that she had me there. 'I wouldn't, either,' I told her.

'I know you wouldn't.' She smiled at me in a sad sort of way. It was almost reassuring to see that I could still disappoint her. 'But you would take the case to try and keep an SOG out of prison. If you could figure out who it is, you might be able to dissuade him from acting on the threats . . . save two lives. His and the Ambassador's.'

'There is no way the Ambassador would go for it. There is no way the FBI would either.'

'The Ambassador doesn't like you, but sees the value of having you on the case.'

'I am sure he didn't have anything nice to say about me last night.'

'No, Andy, he didn't, but I don't think you can blame him.

If you weren't going to take the case, why did you even meet with him?' she asked, arching a moderately plucked eyebrow. Brenda had been blessed with the type of good looks that don't require much in the way of makeup or primping. I had a sadly untested theory that she looked just as good in the morning when she woke up as she did the night before.

'I'm between jobs and Sir Leominster hates budget cat food.' That was a lie. Sir Leominster never met a type of cat food he didn't like. The truth was I had planned to meet the Ambassador, and royally tell him off. Tell him off on behalf of all the guys whose names ended up on the wall in Washington, DC, because of those blown missions and stupid rules of engagement. I had practiced my short, eloquent speech in my head as I walked from my apartment to the Harvard Club. There were variations, but all of them ended with my telling the pompous ass to go to hell.

In the end, I just didn't have it in me. Staff Sergeant Roark, who at twenty-three would have fought anyone and anything, would be mighty disappointed at Andy Roark who was approaching thirty-six. The only difference was then I was sure I was right, and now I wasn't sure of anything much, except that my younger self would be disgusted with my current self.

'Andy, I know you think the guy is an asshole, but he is scared. He needs your help.'

'Well, you are right about that.'

'You'll help him?'

'No, I meant the asshole part.'

'Andy!'

'Yes, I'll take the case.' I tried to tell myself Stevenson's money was as green as anyone else's. That I was sick of divorce work, but that wasn't it. It wasn't even that Watts was asking. The truth was that I wanted to prove to Stevenson it wasn't an SOG guy. After everything we had survived, he wasn't worth it.

'Good.' She stood up and pulled a zippered vinyl document case out of her large shoulder bag. 'This should bring you up to speed.'

'What's this?'

'Copies of the letters he received, and police reports and

pictures of his house in Brookline. Some other pertinent stuff too.' She turned to go, then looked back. 'Andy, I really appreciate it.'

'So, now what?' I asked, following after her as she walked toward the office door.

'He is staying at the Harvard Club. He will be waiting for you at the bar at four.' She had been mighty confident that I was going to say yes.

'What if I had said no?'

'I was certain you wouldn't.'

'But if I had?'

'I would have reminded you that I had been very angry with you for good reason and that some might think you were obligated to me.'

'And I am the type of man who takes my obligations seriously.'

'Yes, you are.' She smiled at me. We had stopped at the office door. 'Call me later and tell me how it went with Stevenson.'

'Sure. Give me something to look forward to.' I watched the door close behind her and went back to my office. It had been a few months, but I was starting to make espressos in Marconi's old machine that weren't half bad. The machine made its noises and steam and then dark, rich espresso dripped into the little cup.

I picked up a pipe from the china bowl on the desk that I used as both a pipe stand and ashtray. I opened the office window, letting in the traffic noises from the street below, and to let out the smoke. I lit the pipe and drew on the stem, puffing out smoke until it caught. Satisfied it would reliably draw, I sat in my chair with the pipe and the tiny cup of espresso. I opened the document case and spread everything out on my desk.

I was half expecting to see letters cut out of a magazine and pasted on to the pages like you see in the movies. Instead, these were rather boring, typed pages. I picked them up and flipped through them, skimming them for the highlights. The message to the Ambassador could be summed up as, 'Your rules, your conduct led to the deaths of several good men. You have to pay for that. I will make you pay for what you did to my brothers in arms. You will pay. I will hunt you down and kill you.' There were a dozen letters, and the message was phrased differently in each one, but it was the same message overall. There were another few pages that were photocopies of the envelopes and postmarks. The postmarks were all from different cities and states.

I turned to the photos. They were black-and-white evidence photos. One showed a dog sleeping on some steps by a door. It might have been a golden retriever or an Irish setter. The next photo showed a close-up of the dog's mouth covered in foam and vomit.

I flipped through the next set of pictures. The next was a photo of an older Mercedes sedan with Washington, DC, license plates. The next photo showed a broken taillight with a wire leading from it to the gas tank. It wasn't the best way to blow up a car, but it was reasonably effective. My own beloved Karmen Ghia had been blown up six months ago. Fortunately, I hadn't been in it. But I had been cut up by some flying glass and was hard of hearing for a few days.

The last few photos were of a set of French doors that had some bullet holes through the panes of glass. They looked to be small-caliber holes that punched through the glass, leaving neat little circles and spiderweb cracks.

There were no pictures of shell casings and the police reports attached to the incidents were a great example of taking few words to say very little. The police seemed to approach it all as though it was some sort of series of pranks. I zippered everything back in the document case. I would look at it all more closely after I met with the Ambassador.

I wasn't looking forward to my upcoming meeting with Stevenson and less so working for him. Having to listen to him issue forth orders in his patrician tones. But Brenda wasn't one to ask favors lightly. I sipped the bitter brew and enjoyed the smoke from the mixture of Turkish and Virginia tobaccos burning in the bowl of the pipe.

The problem was the letters. It didn't feel like something any of the Recon guys would do. None of it did, neither poisoning the dog nor the gaff attempt at blowing up the car. The Special Forces guys that I knew wouldn't approach it this way. The guys I knew . . . if they wanted to kill the Ambassador, they would just set about doing it. No fucking around. No game of cat and mouse.

Once in Vietnam, I had been fuming about something that some REMF Master Sergeant had done while he was at our camp. He was some intel guy from Saigon. I forget now what the petty insult had been, but at the time I was fuming. Sergeant Major Billy Justice had come into the club where I was fuming and holding court. He sipped his Crown Royal on the rocks and, after listening to me sound off, he stood up and walked over.

'Red,' he addressed me.

'Yes, Sergeant Major.' My flowing and poetic diatribe was cut short by military courtesy.

'Red, you know this shit isn't that important.'

'But Sergeant Major, that asshole—'

Billy Justice cut me off. 'Red, if this shit was that important, you'd already be on your way to Saigon to kill that motherfucker.'

I stopped. He had me there.

'But you ain't. You're here in the club drinking and cussing.' His tone made it clear that my behavior was verging on unbecoming for a Recon man.

'Shit, Sergeant Major . . . shit, you're right.' Suddenly I wasn't even mad anymore.

'Usually am, young Sergeant . . . usually am.' With that, Billy Justice finished his drink and walked out of the club. That was how it was in my little patch of the Army in our little part of the war. It all boiled down to: is it important enough to kill for or not? The guys I knew weren't the type to send threatening letters or poison a dog. And if they were going to blow up a car, it was sure as hell going to get blown up, with the Ambassador in it!

Maybe there was a delicious irony to this situation. Stevenson had a reputation for being impatient with SOG. A lot of his policies had gotten a lot of us hurt or killed, and now he was turning to a former SOG man to protect him. My younger self would never have believed it.

I grabbed my denim jacket and locked up the office. It was sunny but breezy out. It was warm enough in the sunlight, but in the shadows caused by the buildings, it was chilly. I hadn't been to Brigham's in a while, and one of their cheeseburgers seemed like the perfect working man's lunch before my appointment. I would bet my next retainer the Ambassador had never willingly eaten at Brigham's. His loss.

It wasn't his fault. I didn't know much about him but enough to know that he had come from a family that had lost most of its fortune in 1929. He had manners and the right upbringing. He had gone to prep school, Saint George's, then Harvard. I had read that he had graduated Harvard in time to serve on a destroyer in the Pacific as a junior officer. After the war, it had been Yale and marriage to the first Mrs Stevenson. Somewhere along the way he made a pile of money, joined the State Department just before the Red Scare and ended up in Asia. He had worked in several countries and positions, rising to be the Ambassador of Laos.

I walked over to the Brigham's on Boylston Street. I walked in and was met with the smell of fried food and beef cooking on the grill. It was after the lunch rush, and I sat down the far end of the counter. I watched as the waitress was blending milkshakes in a stainless-steel version of a pint glass.

The waitress glided up and slid me a plastic-covered menu and put a small glass of water and a straw down in front of me.

'Want something to drink, hon?'

'Coffee,' I lied. I wanted a coffee frappé. A large one, the kind that you could only fit half of in your glass at one time. I didn't know anyone who didn't drink that first half impatiently so they could pour the rest in their glass. The kind that you drank so fast your head hurt but you wanted more anyway. But if I had a frappé now and a burger for lunch, I would be comatose for meeting the Ambassador.

I looked at the menu and toyed with the idea of getting something healthy, but I wasn't sincere. Instead, I decided on the patty melt. I am not sure what they did to their burgers that made them taste so much better than the competition's, but whatever it was it worked. I didn't eat at Brigham's often; if I did I would have to run a lot more.

She came back with my coffee, and I ordered the patty melt.

She left with a 'Thanks, hon' tossed over her shoulder. Maybe someday I would order a salad or at least a BLT.

I sipped coffee. If an SOG man was trying to kill Stevenson, that would greatly narrow down the field of suspects. Many Recon men had been killed or crippled in Vietnam. There were some still on Active Duty which would mean that their movements would be limited. That was even if it was an SOG man.

I am sure a man like Stevenson had made plenty of enemies in his life, not just guys from Vietnam. Though to be fair, I didn't know a Recon man who at some point or another didn't talk about killing Stevenson. Was it possible that one of those guys, now more than a decade later, was planning to make good on the idle, angry talk?

A few minutes later, the waitress was back, bringing my lunch and an end to my musings. The patty melt was essentially grilled cheese on rye bread with a hamburger and caramelized onions sealed inside. This one was cut on a diagonal and was a wonderful, greasy, tasty-looking mess. It came with coleslaw in a little paper cup, the kind with crimped sides that could be unfolded into a perfect paper circle, if one chose to. I shook some salt on to the fries and poured a small pile of ketchup at one end of my plate.

The first bite of the patty melt was fantastic. The charred burger combined with the creamy, greasy grilled cheese and caramelized onions was the perfect combination. My fingertips were immediately greasy, and I needed a napkin. I make no apologies for my actions. The French fries were good not great, but that is the magical thing about French fries: even OK ones are still great. The coleslaw was nothing special, but maybe nothing would seem that great on the same plate as a Brigham's patty melt.

I was pretty sure that there was nothing like a patty melt on the menu in the Harvard Club. Their loss. The waitress took my empty plate and came back to ask if I wanted dessert or ice cream. Brigham's is world famous in Boston for their ice cream, but I had to pass. She brought the check, and I left a five-dollar bill on the counter.

Outside on the street, it was warm in the sun, but there were definite hints that fall was going to exert its chill soon. I walked back to my apartment thinking about the problem at hand. Lunch had been a nice and necessary distraction, but my mind returned to the names of the men I knew who had been in SOG.

After stopping at my apartment to wash the remnants of the patty melt off my hands and face, I changed into more Harvard Club appropriate clothes. A light blue button-down shirt and khaki sport coat over it. I was still wearing jeans, and I wasn't going to wear a tie two days in a row. The sport coat was to give me the veneer of respectability, and to cover up the snub-nose revolver on my hip and knife in my pocket.

I walked the few blocks over to Commonwealth Avenue and took a right. Comm Ave is a pleasant place to walk. The street is lined with brownstones in their adjoining rows. Running down the middle of the avenue is a tree-lined median with a walking path. Thank god no overzealous city managers had ever tried to cut the trees down and pave it to make more lanes for cars. By Gloucester Street, I could see the large crimson flag with a big H in the middle hanging from a flagpole jutting from the second floor of the club.

I walked up the wide stone front steps and toward the two stone columns flanking the double doors. There was no doorman on duty, but an elderly couple pushed through the double oak and glass doors. I slipped inside in their wake.

I took a left into the bar, and even though it was a few minutes before the hour, Gordon Stevenson was sitting at the bar. He looked up from what looked like a scotch and soda and nodded once in my direction. I nodded back, and when I got to the bar, neither of us felt the need to offer the other his hand.

'Roark.' His tone left no doubt that I was a tradesman.

'Mr Ambassador?'

'Drink?'

'Scotch and soda, please.'

'Two more,' he said to the bartender, gesturing with his thumb to make it clear that he wasn't going to drink them both himself. 'I thought we might talk before my assistant joins us.'

'OK.' I had the sneaking suspicion that by 'talk' what he really meant was that he was going to tell me what he thought and wasn't expecting much input from me.

'Roark, I don't like cowboys. I didn't like cowboys like your outfit when I was in Laos, and I am certain that I like them even less now. I suspect that you are even more of a cowboy now than you were when you were in Vietnam. At least then you had a command structure to answer to, such as it was.' He might have a point there. He continued, 'I am hiring you to investigate because Special Agent Watts thinks this might involve someone from your former outfit. If that's the case then I need you, but if you step out of line, I won't have any compunction about firing you. Is that clear?' I should have been pissed off at his arrogant tone. I should have told him to fuck off and walked out. I should have but I didn't, because I realized something that my twenty-three-year-old self wouldn't have. All his arrogant posturing was a sign. The Ambassador, the one who had ruled over operations in Laos like he was some sort of tyrant, he was scared.

'Yes, sir. It is.'

'Good.' I was expecting him to say something else, but his assistant walked into the bar. He looked at the Ambassador, and we all moved to a small table to have a more discreet discussion. While I would trust a bartender at the Harvard Club almost as much as I would trust a priest in the confessional, I didn't have much of a reputation to worry about. We sat down and the Ivy League assistant took out a small leather document case, the kind that zippered shut, and laid it flat on the small table in front of us. It was the classier version of the one that Brenda had given me.

We all settled into our wing chairs and sipped our drinks.

'Mr Roark,' Bradley, the assistant said, having assumed some of his boss's authority, 'the Ambassador is being threatened.'

'So I heard. What makes you think this is a credible threat and not some kook just venting or fantasizing?' I asked Stevenson. He took a big swallow of scotch and soda while Bradley the assistant answered.

'There's more than just letters.'

I made a gesture with my hand to convey that the Ambassador should share.

'He poisoned my dog. Someone threw poisoned meat over the wall of the house in Brookline. Rat poison.'

'How's the dog?'

'Mercifully he is OK. The vet said Rex received just enough to make him sick but not kill him. He's staying with my housekeeper until this whole thing blows over. I take it you know about the car and the shooting?'

I nodded. I wasn't surprised, most people wouldn't know how much poison to use. It is a science, after all.

'The police thought it might be some sort of prank. When the letters started arriving, they filed a report, and after the attempt to blow up the car, they turned it over to the FBI.'

'That makes sense, the letters are postmarked from different states.' Sometimes I had to say things that made me sound like a competent detective.

'How do you plan to go about your investigation?' Bradley the assistant asked again.

'I will take a look at the letters, talk to the guys who were in SOG, and start by seeing if there are any living in or near where the letters were sent from.' It seemed like a logical starting point to me.

'Are you sure that is the best method? It sounds slipshod. Who's to say any of them will talk to you?'

'Bradley, have you ever conducted a criminal investigation?' I asked.

'No.'

'We don't have a lot to go on. I assume that the FBI has sent the letters to the lab and done all the analysis on them that they can. I am also assuming, because I am here having this discussion, that they haven't found anything.' Bradley nodded slowly, and Stevenson took a sip of his drink and looked at me appraisingly. 'The only real starting point we have are the letters, and they are anonymous. You don't have any shell casings or tangible evidence.' I paused. 'Was there any evidence from the car? Prints, tool marks, or anything unique about the wires used?'

'No.'

'The best thing you have is that it might be someone from SOG with a grudge. It isn't much, but it is what it is. If the men I served with think that there is an SOG man involved in this, they won't talk to anyone who wasn't in SOG. If it is an SOG man, then maybe I can talk some sense into him, and we can let this just be a stupid prank and nothing else.'

'Mr Roark, you have a better chance than the FBI or another investigator because of that very fact.' This from Stevenson. A vote of confidence. Maybe my attempts to seem more professional were paying off already.

'What is your fee, Mr Roark?' I told him, and also what I would need by way of a retainer. He nodded his head at his assistant who took a check out of the zippered case. It was already made out to me, and all Bradley did was fill in the right numbers. Like that, I was on the case that I had never wanted, working for a client I didn't like. I took the check, folding it in half and putting it in a pocket. Stevenson stood, as did Bradley and I; the meeting was over. No one offered me their hand and I didn't offer mine.

'We will be here at the club until Sunday then we are going back to the house in Vermont so the Ambassador can keep working on his memoirs. I have included the number of the Vermont house so that you can check in and make progress reports. If you incur expenses beyond the retainer, call and I will wire you more money.'

'Very good.'

Stevenson stood up and looked me in the eye. If I was expecting some sort of speech from the old tyrant, I was to be disappointed. He just nodded his head and said, 'Roark.' I nodded back. He turned and walked out, and Bradley followed closely behind.

When I got home, I took off my sport coat and poured myself a drink. I picked up the phone. I dialed Watts's number and she picked up on the third ring. We exchanged greetings then she said; 'How did it go with the Ambassador?'

'Better. We agreed on a price and we were civil to each other.'

'That is an improvement.'

'Yep, he cut me a fat check for a retainer and bought me a drink. I looked at the police reports and the crime scene photos you gave me.'

'They were a little underwhelming.'

'Was there anything from the lab concerning the letters?'

'Not much. I can get you copies of the reports.'

'That would be a help. Will that include the stuff from the Ambassador's house, the dog?'

'I can throw that in. Again, there isn't much.'

'I will take what I can get. Plus, anything you can tell me about the Ambassador.'

There was a little intake of breath and then she said carefully, 'Why?'

'Because this doesn't feel like a something a Recon man or an SF guy would do. If it isn't that, then maybe the motive has to do with the Ambassador himself.'

'Andy, right now, they need you to run down the Vietnam angle . . . not go off on one of your wild ass—'

I cut her off. 'Watts, I will look at the SOG guys, if for no other reason than to clear them, like you said.'

'Oh, OK. Good.' She sounded doubtful.

'But I still need to look at all the other options, too.'

'OK, I guess.'

'Good. Can we meet up so I can get the files from you?'

'Sure, can you meet for lunch tomorrow?'

'Sure, I can always eat.'

'Union Oyster House?' The Union Oyster House was the oldest continuously operating restaurant in America. It dated back to the Revolution, when it was a dry goods establishment that provisioned the Continental Army; sometime in the early nineteenth century it became a restaurant. The food was good, and it would be quiet. Who knows, I might be able to convince Watts to sit next to me in a booth.

'I haven't been there in months.' The last time I had been there with her, it was shortly before I went to California, chasing after my own version of the Maltese Falcon. When I got back, there was a gunfight with some Vietnamese gangsters. Watts knew I had been involved but kept it from the Bureau. She had been so mad that she had refused to answer my calls, much less return my cat, whom she had been watching. Now, months later, it was nice that things had thawed a little.

FOUR

I woke up with Sir Leominster sitting half on my head and half on the pillows. He meowed to let me know that he didn't appreciate being pushed off his perch. Maybe it was the indignity of being upended or maybe he just felt I should have been more accommodating.

The sky outside the window was gray, and rain pelted the glass. If I looked carefully through the right window, I had a view of the Charles River where it appeared between two buildings behind mine. When I was able to face the day, I put on clothes for running in, laced up my sneakers and left the apartment. It was chilly but not the 'knock the breath out of you' cold that January would bring.

I ran down to Storrow Drive and turned to the northeast. I passed the Hatch Shell with my feet slapping on the pathway next to the Charles River. I crossed the bridge into Cambridge and ran down Memorial Drive. I passed the Harvard Bridge with its carefully measured Smoots, ran another mile up to the more pedestrian Boston University Bridge, and crossed back into Boston. I ran down to Deerfield Street and from there I walked the few blocks back to my apartment.

After running a little over four and a half miles, the steam was rising off me. It had been a nice run and by that, I mean it hadn't rained much, I hadn't fallen, and it was over. In the Army we ran everywhere in boots, and now, years later, I could appreciate nice, light Nikes. Then we were preparing for war, now I was trying to stay fit.

Sir Leominster was waiting for me when I let myself in. He meowed at me a few times, no doubt wondering why he lived with a creature too stupid to understand him. I got a can of something that wanted you to think it was a classier brand of cat food than what the other guys sell. I opened it, and I was pretty sure it was little more than the ground-up castoffs from a fish-processing plant. The smell was predictably bad. The food didn't look much better, but who knows what Sir Leominster thought when I tucked into a steak or a pizza? I liked having the cat around. He was usually kind of wretched, which made me feel a lot better about myself.

I went into the kitchen. Ever since Marconi had left me his espresso machine, regular coffee just wasn't cutting it anymore. I had found a stove-top espresso maker in a small gourmet shop on Marlborough Street. Everything in the place seemed to come from France or Italy and cost a lot more than the pots and pans made here. I had spotted the stove-top espresso maker, sort of a fancier version of a percolator. It cost me as much as a decent bottle of scotch, but it made strong, dark coffee.

I filled the multifaceted bottom portion with water, packed fine ground coffee in the stemmed basket which went into the bottom of the pot. Then I twisted the top, with its black handle jutting off the side, on to the threaded base. When I was satisfied it was tight enough, I lit the burner and put it on top. While the coffee burbled, I made toast and got a yogurt from the fridge. It was the kind that was supposed to be French. When it was ready, I took my coffee and otherwise uninspiring breakfast to the table.

I sat down with the breakfast, coffee, and the letters. I wanted to take another look at them with a clear head and clear eyes, hoping that they might reveal something new. I munched on wheat toast and began going through them.

There were a dozen letters in all. They weren't dated, but someone had numbered each letter, and there seemed to be a corresponding number next to each envelope. The first envelope was postmarked in early June. It appeared that the letters were posted about one a week over a few months.

The letters from June and July seemed to follow a theme that I would sum up as, 'You know what you did in Vietnam. You are responsible for the deaths of many US soldiers. Their blood is on your hands. You will answer for it.'

The ones from July into August were variations on the following theme: 'Good men are dead because of you. I have lost brothers because of your decisions. You have blood on your hands. You have to answer for what you have done.'

The ones from September changed in tone. 'You can't hide. I will find you and you will pay . . . pay with your blood. You can't hide. You aren't safe and you can't keep anyone you love safe. I will find your spoor. I will gut you and leave you for dead. I will hunt you down and kill you for what you have done.'

The letters were typed, and there was nothing notable about them. I was curious as to what had made the tone of them escalate over the summer. Was the writer growing more unhinged? It is a bit of a step up from telling someone that they have blood on their hands to telling them that they are going to be gutted, that their loved ones weren't safe. Or that they were going to find their spore . . . was he saying that he was also targeting Stevenson's son? Was he using spore as a way of saying offspring? That was an odd way of conveying that message.

I got up to get a Honey Crisp apple. All of this self-improvement stuff left me wanting a cigarette and large whiskey. Or, at a minimum, a plate of corned beef hash and eggs, the size of Cleveland, from the local greasy spoon. Once the apple core was browning on the plate, I flipped through the pictures of the envelopes. The postmarks varied: Boston, Providence, Rhode Island; New York, New York; Buffalo, Springfield, Massachusetts; Colorado Springs, Raleigh, North Carolina; San Diego, Austin, Texas; and Saint Paul, Minnesota. They were mailed from all over the US, and that could mean anything.

There were Army bases near most of the places where the letters were posted from. That could mean something or nothing. Stevenson's own 'secret war' in Laos was hardly a secret. There were any number of military and CIA people who might have a grudge against him. The letters could be some sort of psychological warfare trick, the type of thing a CIA man might be into. Based on my two short meetings with the Ambassador and his stellar personality, he struck me as the type who might make enemies wherever he went.

There wasn't much more to be gleaned from the letters. I found my pack of Luckies and lit one to have while I finished the last of the espresso. I stood over the sink, ashing into it, and looked out the window. Between the buildings, there was a sliver of sky, a bit of green, and a tiny smidge of the Charles River. It wasn't much of a view, but it was mine.

I suspected that the Ambassador had a nice view from his kitchen, wherever he lived. I wasn't complaining about mine. But maybe that was what the American dream was all about, trying to work your way up to a better view?

I went to my desk and dug out my address book. This one was a battered brown plastic, made to look like leather, and nearing the end of its service life. In it, though, were the names and addresses of the guys I served with who I knew to still be alive. I took a felt-tip pen and a yellow legal pad and sat down to work.

I flipped to a clean page of yellow legal pad, took a blue felt-tip pen, and opened the address book. I started to write down the names of every Special Forces guy I knew on the legal pad. Most of the guys I served with I had lost touch with or were dead, but in the end, I had a reasonable list on the legal pad of nine names who had been in SOG and another two dozen or so who had been in Vietnam. It was a start.

There was always the Special Forces Association out of Fayetteville. I couldn't bring myself to call them to ask if they knew of any SF guys who could be sending threatening letters to the Ambassador. It just wasn't an option I could use. Even if I could, I am sure that they would tell me to pound sand. It was a moot point. It would have to be done by using the Jungle Telegraph of troops just gossiping.

I started to write out questions I had about the Ambassador. What happened to the first Mrs Stevenson? Had he always been in the State Department, or had he been in business before? How was he appointed to the Ambassadorship? Where did his money come from, and how much was there? What about his time in the service? Was there someone from as far back as college who harbored such a grudge that he would threaten to kill the Ambassador and those he loved? Was someone angry about him writing his memoirs?

I had nothing but questions and no idea where to begin to look. Most investigations involved finding a cheating spouse or someone who was committing insurance fraud. Or doing skip traces trying to find bail jumpers. The suspects, the motives, the crimes were all very clear. Or I got missing persons cases in which I had a point to start from.

In this case, I had some photos of sloppily executed crimes and a bunch of threatening letters that had no fingerprints or real clues. If that wasn't bad enough, I was investigating death threats against a man about whom I had on more than one occasion made drunk death threats myself. Oh, and he was an asshole, too. In short, this investigation was not starting well.

I started calling around, leaving messages on machines, or with wives or girlfriends. There were a couple of numbers that were out of service according to the mechanical voice on the end of the line. It wasn't exciting work, but TV and the movies would have you believe that most detective work is all car chases and shootouts. Mostly it is pure drudgery. I thought about calling Chris in San Francisco but he wouldn't be awake yet. His life was a bit chaotic.

FIVE

By the time I got out of the shower, the rain had gone from a light drizzle to a steady barrage of drops against the windows of my apartment. I put on a pair of old, faded blue jeans that I had, long enough to be comfortable but not so long that they were ratty-looking. Denim tended to make that change like flicking a switch. I pulled on a t-shirt and over that an off-white, loosely knit cotton sweater. It was only early fall. I made up for it by wearing thin wool socks and boat shoes. I completed my ensemble with a .38 snub-nose holstered on my hip and a speedloader in my left pants pocket. My old trench coat wasn't too worse for wear and my Red Sox ball cap was old enough that the 'B' was more pink than red.

I decided to walk to the Union Oyster house. It made more sense than fighting traffic and finding parking. I detoured to Old Stone Bank to deposit the Stevenson check. I made good time walking to the bank. The light rain helped motivate me. Inside, I endorsed the check and then got in line.

There were half a dozen people in front of me; of the eight or so teller windows, only two actually had tellers. The bank and the DMV both had that in common. My turn came, and I deposited the check and took out some cash for lunch. My bank account hadn't been this healthy in a long time.

I left the bank and headed toward the Public Garden. I crossed the bridge over the pond. The swan boats had been put away for the season. I crossed Charles Street and made my way along the Beacon Street side of the Common. When the city had been founded, it had been a public place to graze livestock, then during World War II it had been used to house a large number of Victory Gardens. The gold-domed state house loomed impressively over the Common.

I liked the Public Garden and the Common. They didn't have the grandeur of Central Park, but few parks did. I made my way down past old graveyards and churches. I passed the Suffolk

County Superior Court and cut through Government Center with its Brutalist architectural monstrosity. I managed to cut across Congress Street without getting killed, and, instead of heading toward Faneuil Hall, I took a hard left toward Union Street.

The Union Oyster House was on Union Street between North and Hanover Streets. It had been serving food there, under that name, since the 1820s. The location has so much history that it could boast that an exiled French king had lived above it for a time. At least he ate well, even if it wasn't what he was used to at home. There were some who said that it was he who gave the Oyster House its recipe for chocolate mousse. I don't know if it is true, but their chocolate mousse was good enough to have originated with French kings.

The brick front of the building was curved to match the curve of Union Street. The first floor was almost entirely made up of rows of brown-trimmed windows, and hanging from the third floor was a large brown sign which proclaimed the name of the restaurant in gold letters. The sign itself was as tall as a floor of the building, and if that wasn't enough to get customers' attention, the name of the restaurant was in red neon above the roof. That had been a recent addition, having been put up in 1958 to catch the eye of drivers on the new elevated highway that had been built.

Inside, it was warm and dry. There was a comforting quality in that it was exactly the same as it had been the first time I ate there, when my father had taken me after my first communion. It probably hadn't changed since the first time he had been there, either. The curved bar of wood with such a deep stain I could only assume it was mahogany contrasted the rows of colored liquor bottles behind it.

Watts was sitting in a booth that allowed her to have a view of the room. She was dressed for work in the office, business suit of blue and sensible shoes to match. I took off my damp trench coat, and hung it from the side of the booth.

'Hey, Watts,' I said.

'Andy.' She nodded her head in acknowledgement and smiled. I sat down and pulled the menu over to me. 'I am glad you took the case.'

'Well, you made a pretty good argument.'

'The case is important to me.'

'How come?'

'Andy, I am a woman in the Bureau. Most of the male agents think we should all be in the secretarial pool.'

'And if you screw this up you won't get anywhere near as good as this lemon of a case?'

'The Bureau isn't taking it too seriously, but I think there is something to it. I don't want anything to happen to Stevenson while this is my baby.'

'That makes sense. So far, it all looks pretty half-assed to me.'

'How so?' The waitress came and we ordered drinks. Brenda ordered a Perrier, and I ordered a beer. The waitress left and we went back to our discussion.

'It feels like amateur hour. Writing threatening letters, poisoning a dog, shooting the window, and the gaff attempt to rig the car to blow up; it isn't the type of work a vet would do, much less one of my guys.'

'Explain.'

'Well, Special Forces soldiers are well trained in small arms, all types, from all over the world. I don't think I ever met a guy who wasn't an expert shot. We are trained in basic demolition or at least are familiar with demolitions. Now, the Recon guys I knew in Vietnam, they were a cut above. We trained much more at those skills because we were much more likely to need them. The reality was we were operating on such tight margins. If one of us shot at the Ambassador, he'd be dead. If we wanted his car to blow up, then it would have been blown up, with him in it. I knew guys who could make a bomb out of the stuff under your kitchen sink. Wiring the brake light? Nah. To me, this all feels like some sort of gag or some type of psychological operation.'

'OK, fair point, but at the end of the day, we have to look at motive too. Disgruntled veterans who were affected by his policies have a grudge. We have to look into it.' She said the last sentence with extra emphasis.

'Watts, I will, you know that, but I am telling you this angle is a waste of time.'

The waitress came back with our drinks and took our orders. Watts ordered a shrimp cocktail and Caesar salad with grilled chicken in it. I ordered a cup of clam chowder and the broiled scrod. It was a New England institution. I skipped the baked beans that were supposed to come with the scrod. It was a house specialty but just didn't go with chowder or fish in my mind.

Watts frowned. 'It might be, but I don't want to find out when someone does succeed in doing a better job of killing him.'

I nodded; she had a fair point. 'What can you tell me about the letters?' I asked her.

'Not much. There were no prints on them other than his and his assistant's, which were consistent with them reading and handling them. There were no fibers or hairs either. They were typed on an IBM electric typewriter. The kind with the ball with the letters on it.'

'The Selectric,' I told her.

'What?'

'It's called an IBM Selectric.'

'Oh, sure. The postmarks correspond to different cities, and we are working on the theory that whoever is sending them has a blue-collar job that involves travel: a truck driver, bus driver, traveling salesman . . . that sort of thing.'

'Do they still exist?'

'What?'

'Traveling salesmen? Do you guys really think that Willy Loman is out there trying to off the Ambassador?' Sometimes the FBI was too clever for its own good.

'It's just a theory,' she said with the smallest hint of annoyance. The waitress brought my chowder and Watts's shrimp cocktail. The chowder was that off-white color that good chowder is, with a pat of butter melting in it. It was thick and rich. I added some Oyster crackers more out of tradition than any need to thicken the chowder up.

'Was there anything on the poisoned dog?'

'No, the vet thought it was rat poison. Stevenson was pretty upset. Man loves that dog like it's his child.'

'What can you tell me about him?'

'Stevenson?'

'No, the dog. Yes, Stevenson, what can you tell me about him?'

'Not too much. He was born in New York in 1920. His family had money, but in 1929 the family fortune disappeared with a lot of other fortunes in the stock-market crash. The family had enough money to send him to a private school in Newport, Rhode Island. He graduated a year early and went to Harvard in 1937. He joined the Navy in 1941 after Pearl Harbor and was a junior officer on destroyers in the Pacific. He was injured in 1943, and then in 1944 was seconded to the OSS. Apparently, he had a French nanny until the crash and then studied it in school. Someone somewhere figured that he could help the OSS and the British SOE with their efforts to kick the Japanese out of Southeast Asia.'

'So, that's how it all started.'

'More or less. He made contacts with a lot of the people who would grow up to be major players on both sides by the time you got to Vietnam. After the war, he went to law school, Yale this time. Graduated and bummed around a little. In 1949, he was prospecting for uranium in Canada with a friend when they hit a deposit. They staked a claim and sold it to a big mining concern. Apparently, the friend wasn't happy about the sale or the split, and he sued Stevenson, but it went nowhere. Stevenson did two smart things: one, he invested his share in the aerospace industry, and two, he took the Foreign Service exam.'

'Wait: Stevenson screwed over his business partner, and you don't think he's a suspect?'

'No one said he did anything underhand; but anyway the Canadians are looking into that angle. You worry about yours. He was hired by the State Department.'

'Let me guess, he ended up posted to an Asian country.'

'Actually, Paris. Then Algeria. He was in Hanoi when Dien Bien Phu fell. He kicked around a series of postings in Southeast Asia, and finally, in 1968, he was made Ambassador of Laos. In 1974, he rotated home to the States. He spent some time in Virginia and then was made Ambassador to Argentina in 1979. He did some tap dancing during the Falklands Crisis.'

'Yes, it sucks when two of your close allies go to war with each other. In some cases, fighting each other with weapons you sold them or intelligence you gave them.'

'He did a good job and called home a few months after the surrender. He retired in 1983, divorced three months later, and was remarried in the summer of 1984. He has been on a speaking tour the last few months to promote the upcoming release of his first book, in which he criticizes the US military policy in Vietnam. He is also working on his memoirs.'

'What can you tell me about the first wife?'

'Met her while he was in Canada prospecting. Her family wasn't rich, but, like his, had the right breeding and education. Her brother would go on to work for the aerospace industry, something to do with gyroscopes. He made a fortune, and a lot of Stevenson's investments were in companies he was working for or owned. Stevenson's uranium money doubled, tripled, and in no time, he was quietly worth a couple of million dollars.

'In 1960, much to everyone's surprise, the first Mrs Stevenson was pregnant with their first and only child. A son, Gordon Stevenson, Junior.'

'What's he like?'

'I don't know much about him. He went to Dartmouth, graduated after some academic bumps in the road. He has no criminal record, but that doesn't mean much. To be honest, I haven't looked too much at him.'

'And the new wife, Honey?'

'Her real name is Renee Jorgensen, now Stevenson, but everyone calls her Honey. No record. She is from San Diego, BA in visual arts from UC San Diego. They met at a gallery opening, whirlwind romance . . . you can guess the rest.'

'Gold-digger?'

'No, her family has money of its own. It doesn't look like she married him for his money.'

'True love?'

'Daddy issues, more like.' I didn't often get to see Watts's cynical side in terms of her discussing other women.

'How old is she?'

'Older than you think. Her birthday is 19 August 1955.'

'Thirty. That isn't old, but she doesn't look it.'

'No, she seems to come from a long line of beautiful Swedes with long legs.'

'Doesn't sound like such a bad family tree.'

'I thought you'd think that. Just keep your eyes on the case and not the wife, Romeo.' The way she said it was drier than Thanksgiving Turkey.

'Watts, you know I only have eyes for you.' I said it jokingly, but it had a grain of truth.

'You are a real paratrooper, Andy, jumping from bed to bed.'

'I just haven't found the right girl yet, and most of the time you don't return my phone calls.'

'You seem to be chasing a lot of skirts for a guy looking for Miss Right. As for returning your calls, you piss me off a lot.' She took some of the bite out of the last comment and smiled sadly at me.

'Can't blame a fella . . .'

'For barking up the wrong tree.' She finished my sentence. My witty retort was never to be, because the waitress arrived with my broiled scrod and Watts's salad. We ate in companionable silence for a few minutes. Watts wasn't the type to peck at her food and took real bites. I dug my fork into the baked scrod, flaking the meat apart and dipping a piece of it in the still molten butter it was baked in. I was pretty sure there was dill, garlic, shallot and white wine involved. The breadcrumbs on top of the fish had crisped nicely under the broiler and soaked up plenty of the butter. It gave the humble fish some texture and flavor.

'What about the assistant?' I asked between forkfuls.

'Bradley Lawrence, he's thirty. Been with the Ambassador since he retired from the diplomatic corps. He has no record, no military service. Graduated from Dartmouth a year or two ahead of Gordon Junior.'

'Another upper-crust type?'

'Nope, from some place in Ohio. Went to Dartmouth on a tennis scholarship. Looks like he got where he is through hard work.'

'OK, fair enough. Is there anyone else, disgruntled staff or someone he recently fired?'

'Nope. He has a cook/housekeeper and a gardener in Brookline, and he has a cook up in Vermont. They've been with him since he retired. He pays them well and they say he is a good boss.'

'Does he have any clay feet? Secret kinks? Anything?'

'No, Andy. Nothing we can see. If you are looking for suspects, the people in his life seem legitimate. That's why we think the vet angle might hold something.'

'Watts, I think the Canadian guy he screwed over is worth looking at.'

'Normally I would agree with you, but we are having a hard time finding him. The Canadians are looking into it, but we like the vet angle. That's why you're on this. It's a long shot, but it is all that we have left.'

'Jesus, you must be desperate if I am your last hope.' I said it jokingly, but a pained look crossed her face.

'Andy, I am. I don't think he is a great guy, but I think someone is trying to kill him. I can't let that happen.' There was an intensity to her voice that she rarely revealed around me.

'I get it. I do.' She had never said that I owed her. She had too much honor to do that. She had covered for me about a gun fight I had been in, but she had chosen that. She could have told her masters at the Bureau that I was involved in a gunfight in which four men were killed. She hadn't though. She had been angry with me for months, but it would have gone against her sense of honor to then use it to pressure me. But this case was serious enough to her that she had thought about it. I liked Watts for a lot of reasons, but the fact that she was tough and had principles were just a couple of them.

'So, what's your plan?'

'I've called a bunch of guys I was in country with. See if anyone has heard anything on the old Jungle Telegraph.'

'Jungle Telegraph?'

'GI gossip. Soldiers love to swap notes about what guys are doing now. Catch up, etc. I will ask around and see if there is anyone who has been sounding off about Stevenson or if anyone remembers or has heard of anyone from those days who had such a grudge against him that they might be doing stuff like this now.'

'That's it? That is what he hired you to do?'

'More or less. It is a start.'

'What happens if your few friends don't pan out?'

'Hey . . . who says I only have a few friends?'

'Andy, with your personality, you're lucky to have that many.'

'Well, after I will reach out to guys in the Special Forces Association and guys who were in Vietnam. Cold calling or dropping in is less than ideal, but it will do. Do you know if there was anyone from the State Department or CIA that he might have run afoul of?'

'We looked, but that world is hard to get any sort of view into. The CIA types will neither confirm nor deny anything, not even the time of day with a clock right in front of them. In a lot of ways, the guys from State are worse. They are just as bad about not answering questions, they just do it with a veneer of good manners. And least your guys in the Army just gave us an honest "fuck off". It was refreshing compared to the other two.'

'Yeah, I can see that.' I had limited dealings with both agencies, but it made sense to me. One was a group of honest men whose job it was to lie for their country while currying influence abroad. The other was a group of dishonest men doing dishonest things, all to protect their country or further its ambitions. Both were equally important. The nice thing about being a soldier was the simplicity and clarity of it all. Go find the enemy and do your best to kill them. No wonder Watts preferred dealing with us.

We finished our lunch. When the waitress came, we declined dessert, and I accepted the green check in its black, plastic tray. I peeled off enough bills to pay and leave a healthy tip. We got up and put on our not-quite-matching trench coats. Mine was a once proud gift from an old girlfriend and was showing its mileage. Watts's, on the other hand, was new and chic and probably came from Filenes or Jordan Marsh. Either way, they kept us dry and covered the .38 revolvers on our respective hips.

We stepped out in the light, misting rain and started to walk back toward Government Center. Watts said, 'Andy?'

'Yeah.'

'You volunteered, right?'

'For this case? You know I did.'

'No, the Army.'

'Yes.'

'And Special Forces?'

'It's all volunteer. Airborne, Special Forces, Rangers too.'

'Did you volunteer for Vietnam too?' I paused. It wasn't like Brenda to ask questions about my life, much less my past, and I was trying to figure out what new personal terrain we were navigating.

'Yes. In those days, the draft-era Army before "Be All You Can Be", you had to volunteer to go Airborne and Special Forces. Once in Special Forces, you could volunteer to go to Vietnam, and you *had* to volunteer to go into Recon.'

'How many tours did you do?'

'Three.'

'Why? I mean, there were other guys. Why volunteer for Vietnam, why do all that dangerous stuff? Why did you keep going back?'

'That is a question for the ages. I dunno. I guess because I grew up in Southie. My world was small, a few blocks in each direction. The first time I flew in an airplane, it was at Airborne school, and I jumped out of it. The first time I landed in an airplane was in Vietnam. Up until then, I had only ever taken off and jumped. That was it.

'My dad had been a paratrooper in World War II and had been in the thick of it. Normandy, Bastogne, all of it. But more than that, he had seen some of the world outside of the neighborhood. He had a taste of something else. He had been a part of history. He had picked up a taste for books and art. He wanted more than just working at the candy factory. More than anything, he wanted that for me too.

'I went to the University of Rhode Island, but it didn't take. It didn't take me long to get kicked out. I knew it was a matter of time before I got drafted. Instead, I enlisted. Infantry, Airborne, just like my old man.

'Right after graduating from jump school, my buddies and I were getting beers, and these dudes showed up in the bowling alley on post. They had their Airborne wings and green berets, and they just seemed like the masters of all they surveyed. The confidence dripped off them. Right then, I knew that I wanted to be one of them.

'They told us about Special Forces and how to apply for a shot if we were interested. They were there to recruit, but they did it the sneakiest way. They told us what Special Forces had to offer and they looked so cool, so different from the rest of the Army. They just dangled it out there. There were a bunch of us who listened to them. Half of that bunch applied. Four or five of us got off the bus at Fort Bragg, and when graduation came I was the only one from that group who made it.

'Then there was a lot of training. After training for almost two years to fight, it didn't make sense to go anyplace but Vietnam. That's where the war was, and that was where I wanted to be. I wanted to know if I was good enough. Then I ended up in Recon in this obscure, super-dangerous part of the war. I was working with the best men in Special Forces. I finally felt like I belonged somewhere. I finally felt like I was good at something. No, not good . . . exceptional. For the first time in my life, I was exceptional.'

'But why three tours?'

'It gets in your blood. Running the missions, the danger of it, but mostly because of the guys. At first, I just wanted to be on a team. To do my job, be the best team member I could be, learn and hone my skills. Then I was a team leader. I believed – you have to believe, fundamentally – that you are the best guy for the job. Better than the other guys. In the end, I didn't want to trust other guys to lead my team, my friends, my Yards on missions. They were my brothers, and I couldn't leave them to face the danger without me. I couldn't abandon them.'

'But you eventually came home?'

'Yes, I did. I have gone back and forth about that decision. I have certainly regretted it at times.' I didn't tell her how many times I wondered if it would have been better to stay. I knew if I had, I would have ended up a name on the black wall in DC. I am not sure if that would have been the worst thing. 'But toward the end, there weren't many guys left who I originally started with. I had seen friends – brothers – killed or badly hurt. I started considering taking more risks, more dangerous operations. I knew that if I stayed, I would eventually get killed.'

It was impossible to explain the reality of it. Running missions knowing every time you went out the odds of getting killed increased exponentially. Not wanting to give into that feeling. The adrenaline rush was a million times more powerful than heroin, but then crash and the need to party like Keith Richards just to burn it all off. I was reconciled to my own death, but seeing my guys get hurt . . . that was the worst.

'What happened?'

'Billy Justice happened.' She looked up at my apparent non-sequitur. 'He was my Sergeant Major. He had been there when I arrived and was there on the flight line when I left. He was timeless in his place in the war. There were rumors that he had been there since '62 as an advisor. But Billy Justice, he had been in Vietnam before me and stayed longer too. He knew that war the way a man knows his wife. His home was Special Forces, but he was married to that war.

'He saw that I was burnt out and moved me to a marginally less dangerous job. Then after that, he found me in the Recon club one day and bought me a Chivas and a beer. Told me it was time to either re-up, join up with the Company, or go home.'

'The Company?'

'The CIA. They liked to recruit SF guys, they were fighting the so-called secret war in Laos and were always looking for talent. It was a rabbit hole I wasn't sure I wanted to go down. I wasn't interested, and I had been in the Army long enough to know that I didn't like taking or giving orders.'

'Then why join the police?'

'Police work isn't like the Army. You work mostly alone, except when you don't. I didn't have to be in charge of anyone but myself.' I couldn't tell her that the thought of being out in the world unarmed was just too fucking scary. I had spent years training and then years in intense combat, armed to the teeth, and that had saved me. Boston was chaos . . . loud, traffic-filled, fucking chaos. I couldn't go out in the random world naked. Being a cop seemed like a good fit.

'You still had to take orders, though.'

'Sure, and at first it was OK. You know, it seemed worth it. But we both know how well that worked out.'

'And now you don't have to take or give orders.'

'Nope, it is just me and the cat, but he doesn't listen to anything I have to say.' We had arrived at Government Center. The Federal Building stood like an ugly concrete box on the edge of the plaza. Maybe it was a bureaucrat's dream, a building so ugly that people would instinctively want to stay away from it. We were now in the great brick expanse of City Hall Plaza, with its giant steps. Watts said goodbye and headed toward the Federal Building where her office and her orders awaited. I watched her walk away for a minute and then cut through the plaza on my way to my own office.

SIX

let myself into the office, opening the door gingerly. Six months ago, some angry Vietnamese war heroes had left me a present in the form of a fragmentation grenade, booby-trapped by a tripwire to my office door. No one had tried that same trick since then, but I was not about to whip open any doors that I was normally expected to go through.

I hung my trench coat on the coat tree, the blackjack in the pocket giving it a lean like a listing battleship that has taken a torpedo in its side. I went into the inner office and started the espresso machine. When it was filled, I took the scale model of a cup with its tiny saucer and sat down at my desk.

I tasted the espresso; it was still more bitter than the ones Marconi used to make me, but it wasn't bad. I was getting better at it. I pulled out a yellow legal pad and felt-tip pen, pulled the phone closer and started to dial. I decided to try some of the numbers that I had left messages on.

I ended up talking to a couple of guys who I hadn't talked to in years. They were good conversations, but, ultimately, I was just taking Stevenson's money to catch up with some old friends and make long-distance calls. They promised to ask around for me, and I told them I appreciated it. Last, I called Chris in California.

He picked up on the fourth ring. 'Hey, Andy, man, how are you?' he asked after I said hello. It was a fair question. When he had last seen me six months ago, I had a bullet hole in my left arm and a nasty infection as a result. He had patched me up and nursed me back to health enough to come back to Boston and get into some real trouble.

'I'm doing OK, man. How about you?' We made the usual small talk. Catching up about ourselves and guys we knew in common, had served with, the old Jungle Telegraph.

'Do you remember Ambassador Gordon Stevenson?'

'The asshole Ambassador from Laos . . . the one who

wouldn't let us operate outside of his precious box? That Ambassador Stevenson?'

'That's the one. He thinks that someone is trying to kill him. He thinks it might be one of us from Vietnam.'

'Bullshit!'

'How come?'

''Cause the fucker ain't dead, Andy.' In the passion of the moment, Chris had resorted to speaking in his native Alabama-ese.

'That's what I said, man, but he and the FBI aren't so sure.'

'How come?'

'He has, among other things, been receiving threatening letters, the tone of which makes it sound like a Vietnam-era grudge.'

'Do you believe that?'

'That someone hates him enough to kill him? Yes. That it's one of us? No. Have you heard any of the guys talking, or know of anyone who hates him enough to—'

'Kill him?' Chris interrupted. 'Sure, lots of dudes hate the SOB, but I don't see any of our guys sending letters. If they want him dead, they will just show up and zap him.'

'I know, but that was also a long time ago. Is it possible someone went off the deep end? Lost their shit and is doing it?' It didn't sound very likely even as I was saying it.

'Is it possible? Sure . . . is it likely? No.'

'What about someone who was there in another capacity, support type, or a Company man . . . maybe someone from Laos. You know, the Ambassador's secret war?'

'That could be, or maybe it is just someone writing letters to scare the old guy. You know, to mess with him.'

'Um, there's more stuff.'

'More?'

'Yeah.' I told him about the poisoned dog, the wired car, and the not-so-fatal shooting of a French door.

'Andy, there is no way it is an SF guy.'

'I know, but I have to ask, to look into it.'

'It's stupid.'

'It is, but he is the client, and I can't start looking for who is doing this until I rule out this theory of his.' I didn't tell him

that the FBI thought it was worth looking at, too. Since
Watergate, Chris hadn't had a real high opinion about the FBI
or the other acronym agencies.

'OK, I'll ask around, but I think you are barking up the
wrong tree.'

'I probably am, but that is what they are paying me to do.'

'Yeah, makes sense. How's the arm holding up?'

'No complaints. You did a good job patching me up.'

'Good. Glad to.' We hung up after a few more minutes of
catching up. Chris assured me that even though he thought it
was a fool's errand, he would make some calls. I filled my pipe
and lit it and pulled the legal pad over.

I looked at the scribbled notes that I had made over the course
of three phone conversations with the three SOG men who
answered. There were interesting tidbits of gossip about guys,
everyone had been pissed at Stevenson. But everyone I talked
to said the same thing; 'If it was an SOG guy, an SF soldier,
then Stevenson would be dead already.'

Outside the office window, the sky was darker, but it wasn't
night-time dark yet, that subtle time just before evening but
no longer afternoon. Lights had begun to twinkle in office
windows, streetlamps, and from the cars driving by. My back
was stiff, I couldn't drink any more espresso, and my pipe
had gone out a while ago. All of which were signs that it was
time to go home, make something to eat, pour a drink, and
see what was on the Movie Loft.

It was raining lightly when I stepped out on to the street.
The video rental place had a neon sign in its window that was
supposed to evoke thoughts of Hollywood. I thought it just
looked like a cheap imitation of something that was already a
cheap imitation. The problem was I couldn't figure out what.

I made my way home through the damp and darkening streets.
I stopped at the small market not far from my apartment. I
bought a couple days' worth of groceries and then stopped at
the package store next door for whiskey. I bought two bottles,
just in case the first one ran out. It was important to plan for
adverse situations.

I arrived home and let myself into the building, unlocked the
mailbox, and dumped the envelopes in the bag with everything

else. When I got in my apartment, I hung up my raincoat, still listing to starboard. I checked the machine, but the only message was from the wife of one of the SOG guys who I had left a message with. He was on a business trip and wouldn't be able to get back to me for several months. She couldn't say more, and she said she would let him know I called.

I unpacked the groceries and the mail. I unpacked some of the whiskey into a glass with some ice. The mail was mostly bills, the only notable exception was an official-looking letter from the American Association of Private Investigators imploring and inviting me to join them for a low annual fee that was about as much as a bottle of good scotch. I put it aside, took a sip of whiskey. I made a turkey sandwich and poured some potato chips on the plate next to it. I took the plate and my whiskey into my modest living room and put them on the coffee table in front of the TV.

I turned on the TV. It was still on WSBK TV 38 where I had last been watching. Dana Hersey came on and was telling me and the rest of the audience at home about tonight's movie, *The Deer Hunter*. I got up and switched the dial to WLVI TV 56. Most movies about Vietnam got everything wrong. I wasn't keen to watch someone else's vision of my war. Instead, Channel 56 had *The Mechanic*, with Charles Bronson as the steady and emotionless mob hitman.

I settled in to watch Charles Bronson mentor Jan-Michael Vincent in the art of dispatching people emotionlessly. Steely-eyed Bronson came up with elaborate methods that seemed to be a lot more trouble than just shooting the victim at close range. Maybe it was to prove to us viewers how good Bronson's character was at assassinating people. I don't know, I was just glad that Stevenson wasn't being chased around by Charles Bronson instead of an angry letter writer.

I ate my sandwich and watched Bronson elaborately research and plan each hit. There were no half-assed attempts to wire brake lights to gas tanks or shooting up innocent French doors. Nope, not for Charles Bronson. He certainly wasn't sending letters to warn his victims about what he was planning to do to them. No one who was serious about what they were doing would.

That was what was bothering me right off the bat. This whole thing seemed more like a publicity stunt or a practical joke than an actual threat to the former Ambassador. It was like something from the Hardy Boys or an attempt to make him look more heroic. Could he have come up with the whole thing to promote his upcoming memoirs? I wouldn't put it past him.

Sir Leominster was stretched out on the back of the couch. He had made out all right with a few scraps of turkey from my sandwich and was now luxuriating in his victory. I watched Bronson go to work with a sawed-off shotgun. I had been at both ends of one in my life and had a healthy respect for them as an unparalleled close-quarters weapon. Despite what the movies would have you believe, you do have to aim them. Bronson actually aimed his in the movie, and I was pleased by the small bit of attention to detail.

I am not saying that all the guys in SOG were steely-eyed, Charles Bronson types, but we were all NCOs in the Army. We ran, led, or conducted missions that required a great deal of planning and required a high degree of attention to detail. That, coupled with the ability to act and react, rejigger a plan in the blink of an eye. None of which fit with random letters, and half-assed attempts on Stevenson's life. I had been on the case for all of a day, and already it felt like I was spinning my wheels.

The movie ended with Bronson's car blowing up. That was a little bit too close to my recent history for my liking. I turned off the TV, topped off my whiskey, and turned on the radio. My local public radio station was playing jazz and uncharacteristically not asking its listeners to donate to support the station. Though they did play *Ellington at Newport*, and I would have paid good money to have been there, especially when Paul Gonsalves played his famous saxophone solo during 'Diminuendo in Blue' and 'Crescendo in Blue'. Almost thirty years later, the woman with platinum hair was the stuff of legend, her dancing in the crowd in Newport sent the crowd wild. The excitement and exuberance from almost three decades before poured out of my speakers, and I was almost transported to Newport for a moment.

I picked up the Nero Wolfe novel that I had been working my way through. It was much more innocent than hired killers and exploding cars. I sat reading about great food and appreciating Archie Goodwin's wisecracking ways. Maybe that is part of being a PI in New York. Boston was a town founded by Puritans trying to build some sort of city on a hill. In my experience, my jokes and wisecracks were met by Puritan stony silence. It had to be a holdover from colonial times more than a commentary about my sense of humor.

The next morning when I woke up, the weather was sunny. My mood wasn't. I had slept fitfully. I didn't dream about the jungle, the war, or exploding cars, which was nice, but I just hadn't slept well. I got out of bed, and before I could do anything other than stand there, Sir Leominster walked into the room and meowed plaintively at me. He had not-so-subtle ways of letting me know he was hungry.

I went to the kitchen and dug around for a can of the fancy cat food. I opened the can and dumped the vile-smelling mixture out into his dish. I put the saucer down in front of him and he seemed more than happy to tuck into it.

I filled the coffee maker and put it on the stove. I then went into the living room to do some push-ups and sit-ups. By the time my arms were wobbly and my stomach hurt, there was a thin sheen of sweat covering my torso. I was glad that I had the mustache because my arms were so shaky, I didn't trust myself to use a razor just under my favorite nose.

I walked back into the kitchen and turned the heat on under the espresso maker. I would need the espresso; I was facing a trip to the Boston Public Library research section. I wanted to go to the library and see if I could find any information about Stevenson or old newspaper articles that might offer a lead. It wasn't much, but neither was this case. I felt like I had been hired to prove a negative.

While the coffee was brewing, I made toast and got a yogurt out of the refrigerator, then turned on the TV to see what bad news had happened overnight. I ate my toast and yogurt, drank my strong coffee, and watched the newscaster read the stories with all of the polite detachment of a someone who worked in a funeral home.

After my uninspiring breakfast – the exception being the espresso – I went to shower and try to make myself look generally presentable. It was taking a little more work these days. My mustache needed to be reined in, I needed a haircut, and the missing earlobe – which had been shot off in a gunfight in Quincy – made my face seem a bit lopsided.

After the shower, I dressed like a man who wasn't going to have lunch at the Union Oyster House – jeans, running sneakers, a t-shirt, and grey hooded sweatshirt. Put my gun on my hip, bullets in one pocket and knife in the other. If I needed any of it in the Boston Public Library, then crime in the city had gotten a lot worse. I put on a blue windbreaker and headed out the door. I decided to stop at the office first.

It was still relatively early, which in Boston means the traffic is in full-on commute mode, inching down the highways and on to the city streets. The morning was pleasantly cool, and the walk gave me time to think about the case. The problem was that it wasn't much of a case. Sure, there were plenty of things to look at – letters, the dog, the shot-out window, and the car wired to blow – but there wasn't really much to any of it.

I was sure that when I started casting a wider net of guys who had been in Vietnam or part of the secret war in Laos, I might find a few people with enough of a grudge who might consider trying to kill the Ambassador; might even find a few with the skills to make it a real threat. But the pool of SOG guys who were left alive was small, and that kind of limited my options for suspects. Hopefully the public library's archives would offer some insight into Stevenson's life and not-so-hard times.

The light on the machine was blinking when I let myself into the office. I was eager to see if the messages were the fruit of my many phone calls yesterday. I opened the window over-looking the street to air out the office a little, and settled in at my desk with a legal pad and pen. They were as important to my trade as the camera or the gun.

There were three more messages from guys I knew who basically said what everyone else had about Stevenson. No surprises there. Then there was the last message.

'Red. It's Don Barry. I don't know if you remember me, we went through training at Bragg together. We ran into each other in country a couple of times in '69 or '70. Anyway, I heard that you were asking around about that asshole Stevenson and if there was anyone from those days who might have a grudge. I think I might know a guy. Give me a call at . . .' The felt-tip pen scratched across the yellow legal pad as I rushed to write down his number. I rewound the message and then listened to it again, as much to make sure I got his number right as to make sure that he said he might have a lead. I dialed the number that Barry had left on my machine.

'Hello.' As soon as I heard his voice, I could picture him. Tall, muscular, more running back than cross-country runner, with a shock of black hair. Barry had been a natural leader. When we were in training together at Fort Bragg, if there was mischief or trouble to be had, it was Barry who was in the thick of it. His love of practical jokes and rule bending were legendary.

'Don, it's Red Roark.' In the Army, I got the nickname Red because of what I looked like in the heat of North Carolina and later Vietnam – red face, sunburned.

'Hey, Red . . . good to hear from you, man.' We played catch-up on the phone, talking about jobs and families, guys we knew in common, stuff like that.

'I heard you were looking for a guy who might want to hurt that asshole Ambassador, Stevenson?'

'Yeah, someone is sending him threatening letters. He thinks it might be a Green Beret-type still angry about Vietnam. I don't. I think it is bullshit.'

'Probably is. The guy I am thinking of isn't Special Forces.'

'No?'

'No, when I was over there, I ran into this weird mother . . . a psychological warfare guy. You know.'

'Yeah.' I was trying to sound calm, but the prospect of having an actual lead made it hard.

'Yeah, guy's name was Arlo . . . no, Arno Kovach. He hated Stevenson.'

'What can you tell me about him?'

'Not too much. I ran into him in Bien Hoa or maybe up in CCN or when I was in CCC. I just remember he wasn't a big dude. He had been born in Romania or Hungary, one of those places behind the Iron Curtain. His family had made it out after the war, and he was a Lodge Act guy.' The Lodge Act had been passed to allow non-US citizens to join the Army. The only catch was that they couldn't be German nationals or from Marshall Plan or NATO countries. It was a very convenient way to get people who spoke the languages from behind the Iron Curtain in the Army. It didn't hurt that they already came with a built-in hatred for the Soviets. They got to fight the communists, and after five years of service and an honorable discharge, they emerged as US citizens.

'Yeah, he spoke with an accent. He moved around a lot, coming up with operations to try and convince the porters on the Ho Chi Minh Trail that their sweethearts were running off with Russian or Chinese advisors while poor Nguyen was humping rice and bullets down the trail. He even came up with a plan to buy Chicom and Rusky rubbers and have the CIA get someone to leave them all around in Hanoi, like the Chicoms and Ruskies were fucking like bunnies, just to make old Nguyen Cong depressed. Stuff like that.

'Anyway, he dropped out of sight for a while, then a few months later he was getting drunk in the club. Kind of crying in his beer. He looked rough, and I knew him a little and went to talk to him.'

'Went over to see if he'd sport you a couple of drinks, more like.' I liked Don, but he had mooched more than a few bourbons off me when I had been flush from a poker game.

'Ha!' Barry snorted, 'Yeah, probably. I was probably busted from playing poker. Anyway, I went over and started to chat with old Arno. He was sitting there, in a tough way, and had been at the Jim Beam for a while before I got there.' None of this was out of the ordinary for any of the scores of little bars and clubs in the Special Forces camps, FOBs, launch sites, or headquarters in the world of Special Forces in Vietnam.

'Well, the little dude was sitting there, looking like the saddest sack you've ever seen. There was a beat-up looking German Luger pistol on the table in front of him.' Again, not unusual at all. Guys tended to pick up weird, exotic weapons to carry around with them when not on a mission. On a mission, it was about stuff that worked, not a relic from the war to end all wars. It had been really funny to see guys put exotic weapons down at the poker table to cover a bet when they had run low on chips.

'He poured me a Jim Beam and offered me a smoke and clearly wanted someone to talk to. I didn't want to hear his sob story, but I was busted out of the poker game and couldn't afford to buy a drink without a loan. I didn't like the idea of waiting till the eagle shit and I could afford a drink again.' Guys could run tabs in their club or a club they were known in, but some guys like Don Barry had proven that not everyone should have a tab. For guys like Don Barry, it could be a long wait between pay days.

'He poured us each a shot and we toasted. Then he refilled our glasses, and we did another. Things were off to a good start. "Arno," I asked him, "why do you have an old German Luger out on the table, boy?"' Don Barry was from Lumberton, North Carolina, and was as country as country could be. 'He put his hand on the pistol, on the grip. No, that ain't exactly right, no sir. He kind of caressed the grip, the way you or I might caress a lady's naked thigh. It was a little weird. Then he said, "This gun, this Kraut gun, I am going to use it to kill the biggest backstabbing son of a bitch I ever met. Gonna use it to shoot him between the eyes." He was talking in his funny accent, you know, like from a war movie or something, so I asked him, "Who's that?" He looked up at me and smiled and said, "That son of bitch Ambassador in Laos. Stevenson. I'm going to kill him even if I have to follow him all the way back to the World."'

We all referred to America, not as 'back home', but as the 'World'. As in, 'When I get back to the World, I'm gonna . . .' It wasn't just home, but something else. Civilization, or not the jungle. The World was neat and clean with girls in miniskirts and ice-cold beer on tap and wide-open highways to drive your GTO down. That was the World. It was a place, and, for some, it was a dream of sorts. The dream of the World never quite lived up to the reality. Troops weren't welcome in the World, but in Vietnam, in the deadly game on the Ho Chi Minh Trail, we were always welcome. The more the merrier, bullets and bombs for all.

'Don, I don't remember this guy. Was he SF?'

Barry laughed. 'No. He wasn't a leg,' Legs were soldiers

who weren't Airborne qualified, 'but he didn't have a Greenie Beanie either, I am sure of that. I think he was an officer. He had just been doing all the weird Psywar stuff for so long that he was almost part of the background.' That was the other weird part of the secret war, there were lots of people who showed up but were in the background: supply guys, commo guys, CIA types. There were also USAID types, and the occasional missionary. There were journalists, but they were kept well away from us . . . our secret war wouldn't have stayed secret for very long otherwise.

'Do you have any idea where this guy Kovach is now?'

'Sure, I heard from a guy that he lives up near you, Taxachusetts. Fall Bedford or New River. Something like that.'

'Fall River and New Bedford,' I corrected automatically. They were two cities down on the south coast, wedged between Rhode Island and Cape Cod. Like many of the cities in the northeast, they had been important ports and vibrant centers of manufacturing once. After World War II, most of the manufacturing started moving to the south where wages, and therefore business expenses, were a lot less.

'Yeah, one of those places.'

'Did he ever say why he was so angry at Stevenson?'

'You know, that was over ten years ago, and a lot of bourbon got drunk that night. I got the feeling that Kovach was in Laos for a bit. Maybe he went native or something like that. Anyway, I don't remember much about that night, but I remember him sayin' that Stevenson had taken everything away from him. That, and Stevenson had to pay for it. Anyway, he was gettin' to be no fun, and I managed to borrow enough from him to buy into a poker game.'

'Bad investment on his part.'

'No, it wasn't. I won two hunnert bucks that night. I woulda paid him back too, but he was gone by the time I got up from the table.' There wasn't much more to his story. We chatted for a few minutes more and then we hung up, both agreeing that we shouldn't wait so long to talk again.

I sat back for a minute listening to the noises from the street outside. It was nice to have a name. Someone who definitely wasn't an SOG guy. The problem was that there were already a lot of suspects. Plus, I wanted to know more about the Canadian business partner.

I grabbed my old postman's bag and threw a couple legal pads and felt-tip pens in it. I left the office and walked to the public library, enjoying the architecture in town. Don't let the ugliness of Government Center fool you, Boston has some great architecture, the gold-domed Statehouse or the beautiful brick townhouses of Tremont Street come to mind. The Harvard Club isn't too shabby, and Symphony Hall is a work of art not just because of its architecture, but inside it is so well designed that the acoustics mean a cough from the audience can rival the timpani drum on stage.

For my money, though, the city's crown jewel among all the museums and restaurants and the fancy brownstones is the Boston Public Library in Copley Square. The Central Library consists of two buildings that are joined by a tunnel. When I think of the library, I think of the McKim Building, which was built in 1895. It is a stately looking building that belongs in Rome or Florence. The Johnson Building, which it is connected to, was built in 1972, and, while its architecture speaks of that time, it isn't soul-crushing like Government Center.

Inside the main hall was a large domed room with tables with green shaded bankers' lamps on them. There is also a beautiful courtyard with a fountain in the middle, but I wasn't there for any of that. I was there for the reference section. The whole of the McKim Building looks like it should have been a home for an Italian Renaissance prince, complete with art, instead of a library for the whole of the Commonwealth of Massachusetts.

I started with *Who's Who* and looked up Stevenson and jotted down notes. There wasn't much more there than what Brenda Watts had already provided. There was a little bit about his wartime service in the Navy, and he was a member of a couple of associations for those who did clandestine work during the war.

I was able to find records of incorporation for his mining concern. He and a Canadian man named Cecil Stanhope formed a prospecting outfit in 1949, named S&S Mining and Prospecting Services. No one said they had to be original when coming up with a company name. Stanhope was a pilot and amateur – emphasis on the amateur – geologist. I got the feeling, having met Stevenson, that Stanhope did the heavy lifting and Stevenson did the managing.

While the company operated in Canada, they had hedged their bets by each filing paperwork in their home countries. S&S was registered and bonified in both the US and Canada. The business address for S&S in the US was a post-office box in Boston. There was no indication of S&S doing much the first year or so it was in business. There was zero indication that it made any money. It staked a couple of claims, but there wasn't much else going on with it.

Then came the lawsuit. The short version was that after a year of flying around Canada in a beat-up Cessna, S&S was hemorrhaging money. Stevenson bought out Stanhope for about fifty dollars. The next day Stevenson sold S&S's claim to a chunk of land in a remote and barren part of Canada where the caribou outnumbered the people. Stevenson had sole owner-ship of a stake that he sold for a cool quarter of a million dollars. In 1950s money, at that. Stanhope sued but couldn't prove that Stevenson had done anything illegal. The suit was tossed out, and Stanhope couldn't have been happy at all.

Stevenson retired from the prospecting business and came home. Somewhere in all of that, he got married to a girl he met in Canada. Then he set about trying to make that pile of uranium money into an even bigger pile of money by investing in both Canadian and American aerospace companies. Usually, the ones his brother-in-law worked for.

Stevenson seemed to magically double his uranium money every few years. Stevenson might be an asshole, but he was a smart asshole. He was also, as far as I could tell, a millionaire a few times over again. It might have been his most likable quality.

Stanhope would have been a very likely candidate for the letters and other menacing hijinks but by 1965, he was dead. He died unmarried and childless, as far as the records from the great frozen north indicated. The microfiche of the Canadian newspapers didn't list the cause of death, but if one read between the lines, Stanhope drank himself to death.

Stevenson was in the Philippines at the time and likely never even heard about it. Would he have even cared? A short time later he ended up in Laos, where he fought his own secret war against the communists with his own private army. I suppose that was one of the few things we had in common – we had both, in our own way, tried to beat the communists. Neither of us had, but that was all a moot point now.

There were a few articles after that about Stevenson and his time after he left the State Department. He wrote a book and a series of op-ed pieces about the war and how it was immoral. He also opined that, had diplomats like him been allowed to function freely, the war would not have happened, and the wall in Vietnam would have thirty thousand fewer names on it. The war had happened the way it happened, and the names ended up on the wall.

He had turned into a fierce critic of the war in Vietnam, which endeared him to what had been the anti-war movement, now the left. His old pals in the establishment seemed not to appreciate his criticism. He had traded in cocktail parties in DC for speaking tours around the very liberal Ivy League. There were rumors that he might go into politics, possibly see if the Democrats would nominate him in 1988.

I was starting to get the idea that there might be a lot of people who might want him dead but not many who would try to kill him. It would stand to reason that if he had screwed over Stanhope then he had screwed over others along the way. I wanted to talk to Arno Kovach, as his was the only name that popped up.

I went back to the reference sections and found the phone books for Fall River and New Bedford. The phone books were thick, but not Boston thick. Both cities numbered in the tens of thousands and had long since seen their heydays. Both have large populations of Portuguese people who moved there looking for work in the mills. It is said that the longest bridge in the world stretches from Fall River to Portugal.

There were a lot of names in the 'K' section of the Fall River phone book, none of which was A. Kovach. The New Bedford phone book paid off, though. There was an A. Kovach who had an address in Fairhaven, which was a bedroom community of New Bedford. Fairhaven was right on Buzzards Bay. It was a weird mix of tough, violent fishing port and coastal affluence. Neither side had gained the upper hand, and instead the town managed a weird coexistence. I had to imagine it was a tough place to be a cop.

I wrote down Kovach's phone number and address on my legal pad. Then I went and tried to find out more about him. I wasn't sure that one drunken interaction from a club in Vietnam over a decade ago made him such a great suspect. Unlike the very public figure of Gordon Stevenson, there just wasn't much about Arno Kovach. I went through the volumes of membership lists in veterans' organizations, unit associations, and there was nothing. He wasn't on any of the property lists for the area. He hadn't incorporated any businesses in the area either.

By the time my stomach started to rumble in earnest, it was around three. I had spent hours in the library and gotten valuable background information about Stevenson. All I had to show for Kovach, other than an address and phone number that might not even belong to the guy I was looking for, was a kink in my neck. I packed my pens and notebooks into my bag and walked back to my office.

When I got there the light on the machine was flashing. Two more guys from Special Forces called and I called them back. Two more half-hour sessions catching up to get to the point that they didn't know anyone who would want to kill Stevenson. What they really said was anyone they knew, anyone who they had served with would have killed Stevenson if they were going to go to all the trouble of writing angry letters to him. I had expected as much; still, it was nice to catch up with the guys. After I hung up and sat for a while in the darkening office, it became clear that there was nothing left to be done there.

I started home through the darkening streets. Regular people – businesspeople, working people, people who were normal – were hurrying through the streets. The darker it got, the faster they seemed to move. Leaving their jobs, heading for the nearest T-station, heading for their apartments, their homes in the suburbs. Going home to wives, girlfriends, husbands, boyfriends, families, all those things that were foreign to me.

SEVEN

The next morning found me, after a run, breakfast, and a shower, on the road. The only good thing about the traffic was that it was all heading into the city when I was on the highway headed out of it. My Ford Maverick had a Holley carburetor and some other tricks under the hood, and the engine made a dissatisfied rumbling noise. It was meant to be driven fast, or at least it was after Carney the mechanic had gotten done with it.

I passed the Blue Hills, and by the time 93 hung a hard right at Braintree, I was able to open her up a little. By the time I got on Route 24 South, I was able to really open it up. I didn't see any Staties, and it was nice to listen to the engine growl and purr as my foot pushed down on the accelerator. Paul Revere and the Raiders were on the oldies station singing about a girl named Mo'Reen, and I found myself tapping my hand on the steering wheel in time to the song.

The night before I had called Watts to tell her about Kovach.

'I might have something,' I said after we had exchanged greetings.

'Go on.'

'I heard from a guy I knew from Special Forces. He was in Vietnam around the same time I was. He said he remembered a guy from Vietnam who seemed to have pretty big grudge against Stevenson.'

'A Green Beret?' she asked. She was the type to tell me she had told me so and was likely getting ready to do so.

'No, a Psyops guy.'

'Psyops?'

'Psychological Operations. The types who came up with all those pamphlets we dropped in villages, or the radio broadcasts. You know, the ones that would say things like "Surrender, and you will be well treated, stay with the NVA and your wife will be a widow." There hadn't been much use for them in

Recon, but other Special Forces units had used them or developed their own stuff.'

'That would fit with the letters.'

'Sure, might also explain the half-assed attempts to kill Stevenson.' Psyops guys were not known for their lethality.

'It might. What's next?'

'Well, that is the best part, he's local. I found an address in Fairhaven. I was going to take a ride down there tomorrow.' I didn't think he was much of a suspect, but he was the only name I had, and it wasn't far to drive.

As I was driving, I noticed that the leaves were beginning to show traces of reds and oranges. In a couple of weeks, green leaves would give way to a riot of red, yellow, and orange. Masses would take to the highways to drive north to get a good look at the fall foliage.

Route 24 brought me to New Bedford, once the whaling capital of the world back when whaling was a major industry. Before it was New Bedford, it had been Nantucket Island, which explained the whole beginning of Ishmael's journey in *Moby Dick*. New Bedford, like many cities in this part of the northeast, was just one more in a string of decaying industrial relics. They had been industrial giants in their time, but that time had passed decades ago.

I crossed the Acushnet River on Route 6. I was in Fairhaven now and near the waterfront. I had checked the road atlas from AAA last night and saw that Kovach's address was down on the waterfront near a shipyard and a couple of marinas. I pulled into the parking lot of a Cumberland Farms convenience store to check the atlas again.

I shook a Lucky out of the pack while I looked at the map. I was close enough to the water that I could hear seagulls crying out as they wheeled overhead, and I could smell the pervasive smell of fish. The marinas here catered to the fishing fleet more than the pleasure boat crowd. When I figured out how to get to Kovach's, I put the Maverick in gear and started off.

There are parts of Fairhaven that are high class, the type of places with ocean views, manicured lawns, and a Mercedes or two kicking around. This part of Fairhaven wasn't it. This part of Fairhaven was more like the battered ten-year-old Ford or Dodge part of town.

As I wound closer and closer to Kovach's address, the paint on the houses and buildings grew more faded. Eventually faded gave way to peeling. Instead of salt air, it was more like diesel and shellfish.

Kovach's apartment was above a diner that was between a ship chandlery and the offices for a boatyard. It was surrounded by a sea of tarred-over parking lot with spots denoted by almost completely faded white paint. A block or two down the street was what looked to be my favorite type of bar. A seedy dive bar.

I parked across the street from the diner and sat, listening to the engine ticking over. The diner was right on the water, with the narrow ends of the building facing out to the Acushnet River and Crow Island. The front door was on one long side, and on the other long side was a wooden staircase leading up to the second floor where Kovach lived.

In the boatyard I could see a forklift buzzing around. When he didn't have a load on the lift, the driver acted like he was Mario Andretti and the yellow forklift was a Ferrari. There were the sounds of machinery and grinders on metal deck plates, smoothing welded seams or getting barnacles off hulls.

I got out of the Maverick and crossed the street, heading toward the diner. A tractor-trailer rumbled by on its way to the shipyard. I could smell fried food from the diner, and it made me hungry. Some eggs and coffee couldn't hurt, and maybe someone could point Kovach out to me. High above, gulls wheeled and cried, and I was aware of the broken bits of shellfish on the pavement that they had dropped to get to the meal inside. The wind was coming in from the Atlantic, and my windbreaker did little to slow it down, much less stop it. It was one of those days that was warm until the wind blew.

I opened the door and went inside out of the wind. The door closed behind me with authority, pushed by the wind. There was a small counter with a cash register by the door. Opposite that there was a cigarette vending machine with its clear, plastic pull knobs.

There were booths along the walls, and the banquettes were

cushioned in green vinyl. There were tables in the center of the room with green vinyl-cushioned chairs. To the left of the door at the far end of the small building was a long Formica-topped counter with eight stools in front of it.

The waitress looked up and said, 'Sit anywhere ya want, hon.'

There were framed pictures of sports teams and pictures of boxers. Some were autographed, but none of the autographed ones were of boxers I recognized. The wallpaper around the pictures had faded years ago, and some of the linoleum tiles on the floor were cracked and chipped.

I took a seat at the counter, and the waitress slid a menu in a yellowing plastic sleeve over to me.

'Coffee, hon?'

'Please.'

One of the old-timers at the counter a few seats down was smoking a cigarette and telling his companion a story about a fish and a man named Howard. The waitress came back and put a ceramic mug of coffee down in front of me, as well as a glass silo of sugar, the kind with the metal top with the hinged spot, and small metal pitcher of cream.

'Need a minute, hon?' I nodded and she walked to the other end of the counter. She came back a few minutes later and I ordered a Western omelet with home fries and wheat toast.

I sipped the coffee, which was a fair specimen of diner coffee. Not good, not bad, just hot and caffeinated. Maybe I was getting spoiled by so much espresso. With the wind howling outside the way it was, I was happy to have the warm coffee.

The food came. The toast had been in the toaster too long and had been scraped off to make it look presentable. The home fries alternated between overcooked or soggy. The omelet had three pieces of green pepper, a lot of onion, and four cubes of SPAM. When *The Price Is Right* cut to commercial, the waitress came back and filled up my coffee.

'You want anything else, hon?'

'No thanks.' The wind howled and shook the building. 'Is it always this windy?'

'Nope, not usually. Usually it's worse.' She slid the check under my coffee mug.

'Say, maybe you can help me?'

'How's that, hon?' She was the type to call everyone 'hon' and used it the way most people use punctuation when they write.

'An old Army buddy of mine told me to look up a guy named Arno, Arno Kovach. He said I might find him here.'

'Are you a cop?' she asked suspiciously.

'Nope, just a guy looking to hire a guy like Arno.'

'What for?'

'For a job I need him to do. What are you, his manager?'

'No. Arno's not the type who likes strangers asking around about him.'

'Is he the type who likes making money? I need a guy who is discreet and willing to put some work in?' I leaned in and said it conspiratorially. I almost believed myself.

'He ain't around.'

'Know where he is?'

'Don't know. Out on the road, maybe.'

'Does he have a job?'

'Huh,' she snorted. 'He's a sometime truck driver when he ain't too drunk.'

'How often is that?'

'Not enough to afford to live anyplace nicer.'

'Does he drive for anyone in particular?'

'Nope, just goes where the money is.'

'Thanks.' I slid her a ten-dollar bill for a four-dollar breakfast. It was starting to look like maybe the Hoover boys, and girl, were on to something. Kovach was a Vietnam vet, SOG adjacent, and a truck driver too.

I went back out into the sun and wind. I walked over to the ship's chandlery. This was the type that catered to commercial fishermen and merchant sailors instead of the Yacht Club set. I browsed up and down the aisles. I didn't need foul weather gear, clevises, nor cleats. I didn't need anything they had to sell. The closest I ever came to fishing was ordering fish and chips or the occasional trip to the Clam Box down on Wollaston Beach. I didn't get to the Irish Riviera very often these days.

At one end of the building, there was a counter and a cash register. There was a woman who I took to be in her early forties behind the counter. She was thumbing through a marine equipment catalogue. Her hair was a light shade of blonde, and her face and hands spoke of a life outside on the water. She looked up as I approached her.

'Help you?' She had a pleasant smile, but after the waitress in the diner, it didn't take much to be friendlier.

'I hope so. I was looking to hire a guy to help me do some work for a few days. An old Army buddy of mine said I should come down here and talk to Arno Kovach.'

'Who?'

'Arno, guy in his late thirties, talks with an accent. Lives above the diner. Have you seen him around?' I smiled what I hoped was my best disarming smile.

'I don't know anyone named Arno.' Her smile had frozen. 'We aren't an employment agency either. If you are looking to hire a hand, this isn't the place to do it.' Her voice was frosty, and it didn't seem like it was all because of my winning personality.

'OK, thanks.' I walked out of the ship's chandlery and back into the wind. That left the boatyard and the bar. I decided to try the boatyard first. If I struck out with them, then I could console myself with a beer or two in the bar.

I walked across the street avoiding the potholes. The boatyard was surrounded by a large chain-link fence topped with coils of razor wire. There was a large chain-link gate that slid back and forth on metal wheels on a track. There was a small building that the gate butted up against when it was closed.

The gate was open, and the small building had a sign over the door that said, 'Office'. I walked up the three cement steps that had been rounded at the edges by decades of rain and salt. I opened the door and went in.

The room was warm and there was a long wooden counter that ran the width of the room. The end closest to the wall was hinged so that people could go behind it. There was a phone on the counter and a doorway leading to the rest of the building. I noticed the blinking red light on the camera mounted high in the corner facing downward at the door I had just walked through.

A tall man with salt and pepper hair walked through the door

I was facing and came up to the counter. He was wearing glasses, blue jeans, work boots, and a plaid flannel shirt. He looked at me skeptically over his glasses.

'Can I help you?' His voice gave away hints of Portugal.

'Yes, an old army buddy of mine said if I was on the east coast, I should look up Arno Kovach,' I said with more false warmth than one of the Santa Clauses at the mall at Christmas. 'He said old Arno drives trucks. I saw a whole bunch of trucks coming and going and figured, heck, old Arno might work there.'

'You're looking for guy named Arnold Kovaks?'

'Yep, I'm looking for a long-haul driver looking to make a little money taking a rig out to California for me.'

'Can't help you mister. Never heard of no guy named Kovaks.'

'Kovach, Arno Kovach. Buddy of mine was in Vietnam with him.'

'He might have been in Korea, too, but I still haven't heard of him. That all you want? We're kind of busy in here.'

'Yeah, thanks.' I let myself out, hoping that I would get a better reception at the bar. It was still windy and chilly outside but definitely a lot warmer than in the boatyard's office. I wondered idly why they needed a camera facing the door? Were they worried about being robbed? Did they keep a lot of cash on hand for things like payroll? Maybe he made a lot of enemies with his friendly demeanor and wanted to be able to record them telling him what an asshole he is?

I faced into the wind as I crossed the wide-open parking lots and streets, like some sort of black tar prairie land. The wind slicing through my ironically named windbreaker made it feel like the end of November, when winter is lurking like a mugger in a dark alley. I like winter, the stillness and quiet of it, the snow touching up the faded class of Boston like a fresh coat of paint on an old house.

The bar, when I got to it, was like everything else I had seen in this part of Fairhaven, run-down. It had a couple of bay windows on either side of the door. They had dark curtains strung across them, blocking the view of the inside. There were neon signs between the curtains and the windows advertising Budweiser and Michelob beers. Judging by the look of the place, those were probably their 'top shelf' beers. There was a faded sign swinging above the door with 'The Reef' painted on it.

The door was a color that might have been a faded black or an aggressive dark green once. In either case, it was faded and peeling too. I put my hand on the door. There was no question in my mind that the place would be open before lunchtime. The fishing fleet and the boatyard both could provide ample day drinkers. The door pulled open with the squeal of rusty hinges.

If the diner had forsaken the nautical theme, The Reef had doubled down on it. There were old fish nets hanging in the corners of the large room. There were pictures of all sorts of fishing boats and cargo ships on the walls. On one wall was a large clock made from a ship's wheel, and I counted no less than three brass barometers on three different walls.

The bar was long and made of dark wood that had once been shined to perfection. Affixed to the wall next to the bar was a weathered brass bell with a braided rope pull. If The Reef had been on Cape Cod, it would have been kitschy, almost cute. Here, it was what was left of someone's dream which had been kicked around by a shit economy and generations of despair.

There were half a dozen or so patrons scattered between the tables and the bar. According to the ship's wheel clock, it was just coming up on noon. Most of them were men, rough-looking types who worked on the fishing boats or in the boatyard. None of them was under forty, and they all looked as weathered as the building we were in.

I made my way to the bar and slid on to a stool by the wall with the bell. Beyond that was a small hallway where there were doors with signs reading, 'Sailors' or 'Mermaids'. If Watts were here, she might point out that women were 'Sailors' now too. The bartender came over, polishing a glass with a rag.

'What can I get you?'

'Pabst?' I asked.

'Sure.'

'And a shot of Wild Turkey, please.' I rubbed my hands. 'Cold out there with the wind.'

'Uh huh.' He was in his sixties, wearing faded khaki pants and plaid wool shirt. His face had the tracery of small, broken veins that spoke of more than a casual relationship with drink. There was a mirror behind the bar, and on stepped shelving in front of it were dusty bottles of liquor. The higher the shelf, the dustier the bottle, leading me to believe that no one was coming to The Reef looking for unpronounceable scotch.

The bartender came back and put a glass in front of me and a shot glass. He then took a bottle from in front of the mirror and poured a healthy slug of the bourbon into the chunky shot glass. I picked it up and made an almost toasting motion to him.

'Thanks.' He nodded to me. Behind him, next to the bottles, was a TV playing reruns of *Gunsmoke*. The sound was down, so James Arness was drawing silently, then a puff of smoke from the muzzle, and the bad guy would collapse silently. Bloodlessly. It would be nice if it was like that in real life.

I drank half of the bourbon in one draft, then turned my attention to the Pabst, which tasted as good as it always did. No one came or went, and I killed time watching James Arness and his silent duels.

By the time James Arness had shot the bad guy and the credits rolled, I had finished my beer and my shot. The bartender walked over and asked, 'You want another round?'

'Please.' He shuffled off to get my beer and was back a few seconds later. He reached back on to the shelf for the bottle of Wild Turkey. He poured more of the bourbon into my glass from the bottle topped with the ubiquitous metal spout. When he finished, I offered, 'You want one yourself? On me.'

'Sure, thanks.' He reached under the bar for a shot glass of his own, which he plunked down on the bar and poured some of the amber fluid into. He held his glass up toward me and I did the same. We drank.

'Hey, man, I'm looking for someone. Arno Kovach. An old Army buddy told me to look him up if I was ever in Fairhaven.'

'Yeah, sure you are.' He moved off without saying anything else. James Arness continued his silent rampage across the black-and-white television landscape in a new episode. A couple of guys came and went from the bar, but otherwise we all just sat there drinking in relative quiet. When my beer and shot were gone, the bartender drifted up.

'Time to settle your tab and be on your way.' His tone left no room for debate. I left a ten-dollar bill on the bar and went to the 'Sailors' room before leaving. It was almost an hour to Boston. Nothing had changed when I went back into the bar on my way out. No one said 'goodbye' or 'come again' as I pushed the squeaky door open.

The gulls were still wheeling and crying overhead. The clouds had moved in, and the sun was playing hide-and-seek behind them. The wind hadn't slackened at all. And to add to all that ambiance, there were two local lads leaning on the hood of my Maverick. By lads I mean big, brawny, tough-looking guys who were dressed like they worked in the shipyard and spent their spare time lifting weights. They were big enough that there wasn't much of my windshield showing behind them. I stopped ten feet from them.

'What can I do for you boys?'

'Do for us? Huh. Nothing. It's what we can do for you.'

'And what can you do for me?' The one talking was the bigger of the two. He was used to having the advantage of size and the willingness to do violence to people he had just met. I got the feeling that he rather enjoyed it. The other guy was slightly smaller but still big. He didn't say much but his eyes didn't miss anything. He was the more dangerous of the two.

'We can let you leave here with most of your teeth.' He smiled. Enjoying himself, confident in his size and strength. The playground may change as we get older, but the bullies only seem to get bigger.

'That's mighty generous of you.'

'Why are you looking for Arno Kovach . . .' this from the smaller guy, 'and don't try and sell me that bullshit about you're looking to hire him for some work.'

'You're right, I'm not looking to hire him.'

'Why are you looking for him?' I just shrugged, not saying anything. There wasn't any point, as this was only going to go down one way, whether I told them everything or nothing.

'Kid, you don't get it. We're asking you nice like. You tell us or we're going to mess you up.' This from the bigger guy.

'You always let him talk? Pretty sure he hasn't read *How to*

Make Friends and Influence People. Or any books for that matter.' The smaller guy shrugged.

'You're not gonna make this easy for us, are you?'

'Nope, not really my thing.'

'Shame.'

'No, it isn't,' I said to myself. The bigger guy shot off the hood of my car with more agility than I would have expected. He moved toward me with his fists balled and his arms up. I didn't want to try and box with him. It would be like trying to punch a small tank.

I stepped to my right, off his line of attack. I was not in the mood to fight fair with him. I pivoted on the ball of my left foot while raising my right foot, bending it at the knee, and I swung it at his leg in a scything motion. I threw the kick from my hips as I pivoted into him, bringing my leg in a downward arc toward his knee, simultaneously snapping my right arm down, following through the motion of the kick. My shin connected solidly with the side of his left knee, and I could feel it give.

His knee made a loud crunching noise and he screamed. He flailed his left fist at me, which hit my forehead, and I staggered back. It had been a glancing blow, but even a glancing blow from a bowling ball still hurts. His left leg gave out completely, and he crashed to the pavement with a cry of pain.

The second guy tackled me, and I hit the pavement hard enough to knock the wind out of me. I instinctively curled my shoulders and neck, and that saved my head from being smashed into the parking lot. The second guy was sitting astride of my hips, raining blows down on my arms which I was using to guard my face and body. With my fingers touching my temples and my hands protecting my face, this left my bent arms to protect my chest. His blows, while powerful, weren't doing much real damage.

I got my feet flat on the ground and arched my back then rolled hard to my right. I pushed off hard with my left foot and launched him off me. I rolled up into a crouch and he did too. We circled each other, and he reached under his shirt and came up with a vicious-looking filleting knife. I reached under mine and came up with my .38 snub-nose.

He looked at the gun in my hand, thinking. I shook my head side to side. He thought a half-second more and dropped the knife on the ground. 'Fuck it. It isn't worth it.'

'Almost never is.'

'You a cop?'

'No. I'm just a guy looking to talk to Arno, that's all.'

'He lives around here. Keeps to himself.'

'Then why all this nonsense?' In the background the big guy was rolling on the ground, crying, moaning. 'Seems to me this could have been avoided.'

'No one likes a stranger asking questions around here. It makes people nervous. Type of people who don't like cops.'

'Fair enough.'

'Did you have to break his knee?'

'No, but he is an asshole who likes pushing people around.'

'Yeah. You should go, more people are gonna be coming. You've done enough damage today.'

'Yeah, you too.' I could feel the various bruises beginning to take shape. I went back to the Maverick, never taking my eyes off him. The car started and in the rear-view mirror as I was already a block closer to Boston, I saw a group of hard cases from the shipyard around the big guy. I drove the speed limit through the neighborhoods of Fairhaven and eventually got on the highway out of town.

I didn't see any police cars flying lights and sirens by me. Nor were there any ambulances rushing by to help Thug 1. All I saw was Fairhaven going from seedy to nice as I made my way away from The Reef and shipyard. Everything grew less ocean industrial, and the foliage with its bright colors emerged more fully as I headed back to Boston.

EIGHT

My ride home turned out to be uneventful, which was just as well after my trip to Fairhaven. I wasn't sure why anyone would send two heavies to beat me up for asking questions about Arno. I couldn't tell if this made Arno a more or less likely suspect. According to Thug 2, Arno lived there and kept to himself. That didn't seem worth beating someone up over or possibly inviting unwanted police attention. Unless, of course, Arno didn't just quietly keep to himself. Maybe he was into something that no one wanted anyone poking into? But if he was into some heavy stuff, why risk exposure by sending letters to Stevenson, shooting up the house? It was all as clear as mud.

On the drive home I thought about getting off at the Furnace Brook Parkway in Quincy and taking the scenic route. I used to spend a fair bit of time in Quincy, but ever since a good friend had been killed in shootout there six months ago, I hadn't been back. Maybe it had something to do with the fact that I had survived that same gunfight, minus a bit of earlobe, and I couldn't face running into his family. Maybe they didn't blame me for his death, but I couldn't say the same.

Instead, I just rode the highway into town. I crossed over the Neponset River and past the Boston Gas tanks. The one with the picture of Ho Chi Minh on it always stood out, standing high above the neighborhoods that had sent poor kids like me from Boston to Vietnam. It probably hadn't been meant as an insult to us, but it felt like a big Fuck You that was wedged between the Old Colony and Dorchester Yacht Clubs.

I took the exit for Chinatown and made my way through the streets congested with people and cars. They were walking to and from class or work or late lunch. Just normal people leading normal lives. I skirted around the Combat Zone and made my way to my office and was lucky to find a parking spot in front, a little bit up from the video store. Other than a few bumps and bruises and breaking a guy's knee, the day was shaping up to be an OK one. When I got out of the car, I realized that the pocket of my windbreaker was ripped and hanging down, flapping. Another casualty of my chosen career.

I went up the stairs to my office. I unlocked the door and opened it slowly, but there were no hand grenades wired to the door. I wondered how long it would take me to get over that habit. I settled in, which amounted to ignoring the coat rack in the outer office and throwing my ripped windbreaker on the chair in front of my desk. It was a blue nylon one, and there were only a few million of them to choose from if I wanted to replace it.

I busied myself by making an espresso. When the demitasse cup was filled with a steaming shot of life-restoring juice, I took a sip. It was hot and bitter and good. It went a long way to easing the chill out of my bones from the wind down in Fairhaven, and was worlds better than the diner coffee I had there.

I settled at my desk with my espresso and took out the yellow legal pad with my case notes on it. I jotted down everything that I saw or did in blue felt-tip pen. Then I used a red pen and wrote down everyone I saw or met. I spent some extra time on the shipyard and The Reef. Almost an hour and three pages later, I put my pens down. I pulled the phone over and dialed Watts at the Federal Building. I was in luck because she answered. I listened to her say her name, rank, and all that other stuff they have to say pro forma. I said, 'Hi, Brenda, it's Andy.'

'You sound smug. Did you find something out?'

'I don't think you can sound smug. I think one can look smug, but I'm not sure smug is a sound.'

'What are you, an English teacher?'

'Good point. First, can you call around to the local hospitals around Fairhaven, probably New Bedford.'

'Oh god, did you shoot someone again?'

'No, no, nothing like that.'

'Good.'

'You're looking for a big guy with a lateral fracture of his left knee. Pretty sure he will have a criminal record.'

'You broke someone's knee?' She sounded mildly annoyed.

'You have to agree, it is better than shooting someone.'

'Marginally better. Are you going to tell me how all this went down?'

'Sure, over dinner or drinks?'

'Drinks. You drive me to drink. Anything else?'

'Can you look up a guy named Arno Kovach? He is a Vietnam vet, probably a naturalized citizen. I don't have DOB, but I can give you his current-ish address and phone number.' Which I did. We agreed to meet at the bar across the street from my apartment around six.

'You sure I can't interest you in dinner at the Café Budapest . . . very romantic this time of year. They even have a guy who comes around and plays the violin at your table.'

'I've been to the Budapest before. I wasn't that impressed with the violin player and no. I need a romantic dinner with you like I need a bullet in the head.' Maybe she had a point. I wasn't good for her career, and I was pretty sure that I wasn't much better for her romantically.

'You can't blame a guy for trying.'

'A guy, no. You . . .'

I said goodbye. Even I know when to quit when I'm ahead. I put the phone down in its cradle and sat back. She had only just started talking to me again. No point in screwing that up.

I got up, retrieving my tattered windbreaker, and left, locking the office behind me. I had enough time to head home, grab a quick shower, and a change of clothes. Between fighting and rolling around on the grime-covered parking lot, I could use it. Most people have never been in a real fight and don't appreciate how winded you get, how much of a sweat you work up. There is a reason why boxers do so much road work and jump so much rope.

By the time I walked into the bar across the street from my apartment building, I was freshly showered and didn't smell like I had been working out in a fish market. We must have rolled around on bunches of broken shellfish shells in the parking lot. The after-effects of the seagull version of fast food made for poor cologne.

Back at home, I had managed to find a Norwegian fisherman's sweater, not the kind with snowflake patterns, but the kind that was navy blue with white flecks of yarn woven in. It went well over a pair of jeans and boat shoes. Except for the ragged earlobe, slight scars on my face, longish hair, and my slightly too long mustache, I almost looked preppy.

Watts was already sitting at the bar and there was a businessman type standing next to her. He looked like he was trying to chat her up, and judging by the set of her spine, he was not doing a very good job. I made my way through the after-work crowd and the cloud of cigarette smoke to where she was sitting. I drifted up to them, catching Watts's eye in the mirror behind the bar. I heard the business type say to Watts, 'I am not bragging, but I do pretty well financially. I have a condo with a great view. You should come see it. We could go for a ride in my Porsche. I have some blow; we could do a few lines and party at my place.'

I leaned between them and said loudly, 'Dude, did you just offer an FBI agent *cocaine*? Man, I don't think that's a good idea.'

'FBI? You're putting me on,' he said, wanting it to be true.

'Nope, she's a real live FBI agent. Not just a pretty face.' Then to Watts, 'Show him your badge.' She started to reach for her handbag, and he grew visibly paler.

'I was just joking about the blow. I just remembered I have somewhere I have to be.' He got up from his stool at the bar and beat a hasty retreat. I slid on to the now vacated spot next to Watts.

'You're a poor excuse for a knight in shining armor.'

'He's gone, isn't he? You don't strike me as the type to be impressed by a Porsche, a nice condo, or some blow.'

'Nope, none of that holds much appeal.'

'You sure as hell aren't the type to need a knight in shining armor.'

'Also, very true. But you can make yourself useful, buy a girl a drink.' It wasn't a question. I motioned to the bartender who came over. Watts said, 'Bourbon, rocks.'

He nodded and looked at me. 'Löwenbräu, please.'

'So, what happened today?'

'I was following up on the lead, Arno Kovach, that I got from an SF buddy of mine. He remembered Kovach from

Vietnam, making threats toward Stevenson. It left enough of an impression that my friend remembered it fifteen years later.' I paused as the bartender put our drinks down in front of us. Hers came in a glass, and I ignored the Pilsner glass that came with mine. Watts raised her glass at me, not quite toasting.

'Here's how,' she said.

'And how,' I replied, raising the green bottle. Then I continued telling her about my exciting trip. 'My buddy said Kovach was local, Fall River, New Bedford, some place like that. I spent the better part of yesterday holed up in the public library looking up the name. I found a phone number and address in Fairhaven and drove down this morning.'

'Yes, I figured that was how you managed to be in Fairhaven and break a man's knee. Which I believe is a felony in the Commonwealth.'

'Only if he had a complaint. I bet that he didn't. He didn't want anything to do with the police, did he?'

'No, lucky for you, he claims to have hurt himself at work.'

'Well, he is partially correct about that.'

'What do you mean?'

'I was down in Kovach's neighborhood, charming little place down on the water, all peeling paint, depressed economy, and certain air of defeat about it.'

'Suddenly you're a critic?'

'Your sarcasm is noted. Anyway, while I was down there, I ate in a diner that wasn't very good. Kovach lives above it. According to the waitress, Kovach is a full-time drunk and part-time truck driver. I asked around at a dive bar called The Reef, a ship's chandlery, and the shipyard. The shipyard, by the way, had a lot of security: razor wires, camera facing the office door. Probably more than that, too.'

'Well, that's interesting. He fits the profile.'

'Sure, he does. After I left the dive bar, two goons were waiting for me, the one who went to the hospital and another guy. They made it clear that I was going to get hurt but that I was going to tell them why I was there. After a bit of tussle, the other guy told me I was making people nervous asking around down there. They were worried I was a cop.'

'Why do you think?'

'My guess is that the shipyard is involved in smuggling drugs or guns, something along those lines. The fishing industry has been getting harder and harder to make a living at. Lots of guys with boats looking to keep them out of the bank auctions. Owning a shipyard might be a good cover for smuggling, or a great way to alter ships to mule drugs. Or guns. Plenty of those heading to Northern Ireland these days. Who was the guy?'

'Frank Borges. Several arrests, mostly small-time stuff, simple assaults, things like that. Did three years on a felony assault, another couple for carrying a pistol without a license. Got out, picked up a couple more years for drugs. He's been in and out of the system. When he isn't in, he is a laborer down at the shipyard you mentioned. He's on probation and with five years hanging over his head.'

'That explains why no cops were involved.'

'So now what?' Watts asked.

'I will try to talk to Kovach.'

'What, are you going to camp out on his doorstep and beat up more felons?'

'I thought I might use the telephone this time.'

'Not a bad idea.'

'Thanks.'

'Does he have a typewriter?'

'How should I know?' I asked.

'Didn't you peep through a keyhole or a window or something?'

'No, he lives above the diner and the only way up is a set of wooden stairs. I was trying to be subtle.'

'Are you sure you know what that word means? I am sure that worked out just like you planned it.' She had a point there; I was a lot of things, but subtle usually wasn't one of them.

'Sure, I ended up ripping my favorite windbreaker.'

'Well, if you decide to do a B and E, keep me out of it.'

'Well, unlike the cokehead with the Porsche, if I am going to commit a felony, you are the last person I would tell.'

'Uh-huh.' It was funny how she could take two syllables and generate so much sarcasm with them. We both were conscious of the fact that she had only recently started talking to me again.

'Maybe he'll talk to me on the phone.'

'You're not going to go beat him up?'

'No, I thought I would appeal to him, veteran to veteran, that type of thing. Speaking of which, what did you find out about him?'

'Hang on.' She reached down into her voluminous handbag and pulled out some computer printouts. She spread them out on the bar. Seeing her bourbon was gone, I caught the bartender's eye and motioned for another round. He nodded. He was so cool; butter wouldn't melt in his mouth.

'Arno Kovach was born in Hungary in 1941. His family ended up in East Berlin in the late 1940s. In 1955, young Arno managed to slip into West Berlin and made it to the US in 1959. He was able to enlist in the Army as a Lodge Act soldier in 1961. Thanks.' This to the bartender who brought our drinks. 'Kovach enlisted in the Infantry. Then was detached in 1965 to attend Special Forces selection. He didn't make it and ended up in the Signal Corps. Instead of Special Forces, he ended up involved in psychological operations. He was one of those guys making taped broadcasts for the Voice of America, in both Hungarian and German. He gets promoted to sergeant and in May 1968 is sent to Saigon to Military Assistance Command Vietnam. He received an honorable discharge in December 1968, and in February of 1969 is working for the US Agency for International Development in Vientiane in Laos.'

'Sheep-dipped!' I said excitedly.

'What?'

'He was sheep-dipped. He was still in the Army but part of the secret war, so they sheep-dipped him, gave him a cover so he could be in Laos and not be part of the Army. He gets an honorable discharge then shows up in Laos, technically a civilian, but in reality working for the CIA or the Army.'

'Why bother going to the trouble?'

'The war in Laos was supposed to be a big secret. Everyone knew we were there. Everyone knew the Vietnamese and the Chinese were involved, but in order to maintain the illusion of neutrality, we all had to pretend it wasn't a war and we weren't involved. The belief at the time was that if the communists could prove that the Laotian government wasn't neutral, they could justify an invasion.'

'Were you there?'

'Was I in Laos? Part of that?'

'Yes.'

'No, I wasn't part of Ambassador Stevenson's secret war.' Fifteen years later my secret war was still classified, and I was still in the habit of keeping my government's secrets. Even with pretty FBI agents.

'But you were part of someone's secret war?' She was looking at me over the rim of her glass. Sometimes Watts could remind you that she was a woman with all the nuances and charms. Big eyes over the rim of a glass of bourbon were a potent reminder.

'I was a good soldier. I went where they sent me and did what I was told.'

'*Ha!* You? You don't strike me as the type to follow orders so much as the type who finds a way to do what he thinks is best by bending those orders. If not outright breaking them.'

'Sounds about right. Tell me more about Kovach.' I didn't need her to tell me how unsupervisable I was.

'By June of 1970, he is a sergeant in the US Army again. Back in Saigon. He rotates back to Fort Bragg and ends up getting out of the Army in 1975. His tax records have him showing up in Fall River in '76 and then Fairhaven in 1980. He has a couple of arrests for drunk and disorderly, but nothing else.'

'Huh, nothing too crazy, then.'

'No, the only thing of note is his request to get married.'

'What?'

'When he was in Saigon in 1971, he submitted a request to marry a local girl, Channa Chanthavong.'

'She wasn't local.'

'What?'

'She wasn't Vietnamese. That is a Lao name. He wanted to marry a girl he met in Laos. How'd it work out?'

'It didn't. The request was stamped DENIED in big red letters.'

'Sure, probably wasn't his first request. He probably met her in Laos, fell in love and tried to get married. The CIA or State or whoever probably didn't approve of the idea. Probably cut his time in lovely Laos short would be my guess.'

'Would the Ambassador have anything to do with it?'

'Don't know, maybe. Depends on what Kovach was really doing there and who he was really working for. But he might blame Stevenson for not being allowed to get married, and that certainly would make for a good motive.'

'That would be a hell of a motive.'

'Yes, it would, but for murder. Angry letters and half-assed attempts? I don't know. We don't know if he even knew Stevenson, or if Stevenson had anything to do with Kovach or the woman.'

'You said yourself, he fits the profile. He has a motive. What else do you think you need?'

'I don't know. I want to talk to him. Get a feel for him, make sure he is the right guy before we sic the weight of the Federal Bureau of Intimidation on him. It's a hell of a leap to make that he is the letter writer.'

'Why, because you have special insight? If Kovach walks like a duck and quacks like a duck . . .'

'Call it hubris. Or maybe I just want to make sure Kovach is a duck before I put the duck in the water.'

'What makes you think he will talk to you?'

'We were both in Vietnam, we were both part of a weird part of a small, unique part of the war.'

'Do you think that will be enough?'

'I hope so, but you never know. Maybe he has nothing to say to me. Maybe he isn't even the guy.'

'You promise you aren't going to try and beat it out of him if he doesn't want to talk to you?' She looked at me with a furrowed brow. Watts was the type to play by the rules, and she always seemed uncomfortable with the fact that I didn't always seem to play by the same set of rules she did.

'Hey, come on . . . that isn't how I do things,' I said, mildly aggrieved.

'Oh, really? Pretty sure there are a couple of guys who ran into you a few months ago who might think differently.'

'That was different.' It had been. I had been looking for a teenage runaway, the daughter of a friend who had saved my life in Vietnam. I owed him. That type of debt is impossible to repay.

'Pretzels, why can't they have anything decent to eat?' She rummaged in a half-full bowl of pretzels on the bar.

'Search me. You're the one who turned down dinner at the Budapest.'

'Dinner with you, wine, and romantic violins playing . . . no thanks. I'll stick to the pretzels.' She motioned to the bartender for another round. 'Don't get me wrong, you're good-looking in a scruffy, beat-up sort of way. You have this thing about you that probably makes most women want to take you home with them. Give you a bowl of milk and tuck you into bed.'

'Nothing wrong with that as long as we are talking in metaphors.'

'Of course, there is. It's hard enough being your friend.'

'Hey, come on. I'm a good friend.'

'That's not it.' The drinks arrived.

'Then what is it?'

'You aren't the type to grow old with.'

'That's not fair. For the right woman, I would settle down.'

'No, you idiot. That's not what I am talking about. It isn't about settling down.'

'OK, then what is it?'

'You don't have much of a future.'

'Ha, you never struck me as the type looking for Mr Dependable, nine-to-five.'

'No, I am not, but . . .' She took a big sip of bourbon. 'Andy, you aren't the type of guy who is going to grow old.'

'What the hell does that mean?'

'Since I've known you, you've been beaten up, shot, blown up, and god knows what else.'

'Hey, that's not fair. I wasn't blown up, that was my car. I was just explosion-adjacent.'

'Exactly. Not many people need to make that distinction.'

'Well, it comes with the territory,' I said defensively.

'Bullshit. Most private eyes don't get shot once in a career. You've been shot twice this year,' she had a point there, 'had a grenade booby-trapped to your door, had your car blown up while you were adjacent to it.'

'One of those two was just a flesh wound.' I took a pull on the newly arrived and mercifully cold Löwenbräu.

'That's my point. This is all so normal to you; this happens so often that one of these days your luck is going to run out. Instead of shooting off an earlobe, the next guy might have better aim and put one between your eyes. Or the next villain will do a better job planting a bomb, or maybe you'll be too slow on the draw. It doesn't matter; at some point your luck is going to run out, and I don't think I want to let a man into my life who probably won't live long enough to enjoy any of it with me.' Shit, she had a point.

'Well, when you put it that way . . .' I had never stopped long enough to think about it.

'Exactly.'

'Jeez, Watts, I have been turned down a lot of times, but that has to be about the nicest, most sincere way ever,' I said in my 'aw shucks, ma'am' voice. It was better to laugh about it than cry about it.

'Don't be a clown.' She smiled and I was relieved. I didn't have too many friends left these days and wasn't sure it was worth messing things up with Watts.

'Me? Never.'

'Good, now tell me more about the secret war in Laos that Stevenson was a part of.'

'Oh, he wasn't a part of it. He basically ran it.'

'Ooohhh.'

'Yeah, exactly. He wasn't the tactical guy, but he was the strategic commander. He let the Hmong do the fighting for him, with a guy named Vang Po leading the Hmong. He let the CIA train them, advise them and Air America supply them and provide air support. Sometimes the Air Force might slip in and bomb some stuff, but it was his show. It was his war. Napoleon without the accent, that was him.'

'Man like that must have made a lot of enemies,' she said quietly into her glass of bourbon.

'Exactly. He screwed over one business partner that I could find.' I proceeded to tell her about Stanhope and the uranium prospecting.

'Stanhope? Where is he now? Local? The RCMP is taking their sweet time getting back to me.'

'Nope, drank himself to death in the mid-sixties. Stevenson

also has an ex-wife. They usually have an axe to grind, and she probably wouldn't know much about blowing up a car.'

'We thought about her, sent an agent out to interview her. He came back and reported that she seemed quite happy to be the ex-Mrs Stevenson. Apparently, he is not a very easy man to be married to, but she wasn't complaining about her share of his millions.'

'Married to, he's hard enough to talk to without punching him in the face. I couldn't imagine being married to him.'

'He's hard to take. He tends to talk to my chest instead of my face.'

'Wow, that is foolish. I am pretty sure you can kick his ass.'

'Fortunately, there is no need. I guess the State Department at least taught him to keep his hands to himself.'

We finished our drinks and I walked her to her car. She had parked two blocks from the bar and occasionally our shoulders brushed while we walked. 'You don't have to walk me to my car.'

'I know.'

'I can take care of myself.'

'I know that too. I also know that you have a .38, and something tells me that you would have no problem shooting someone if the need arose.'

'Like I said, you don't need to walk me to my car.'

'Probably not, but I wouldn't be able to call myself a gentleman if I didn't.'

'Something tells me that most of the time when you walk a woman to her car, being a gentleman is the last thing on your mind.' She had a point there.

'Hey, this from the girl who wouldn't even accept my offer of a nice dinner.'

'Yeah, well . . .' We stopped at her red Saab, she unlocked the door and got in. I moved back a step as she started it up. Watts wasn't the type to have a bomb wired to her car and therefore wasn't the type to do the walk around hers before getting in it. She put it in gear, raised her hand, and pulled away from the curb. I watched her taillights for a few seconds and then walked the two blocks back to my apartment.

I poured myself a whiskey and sat down in front of the TV.

Thunderbolt and Lightfoot was on the Movie Loft. I had seen it a few times and liked the fact that it was a mix of buddy road trip and heist movie all in one. I went to bed after they pulled the job. I had to be up early, and the ending wasn't a happy one. I guess that was one way that art seemed to imitate life.

NINE

I was on the skid of the lead helicopter. I was the One-Zero, and we were coming into our LZ. The pilot flared and I jumped off the skid, landing hard in the tall grass. I got up and started to push toward the edge of the small clearing, but the elephant grass was high all around me. I kept trying to push through it, to fight my way to our rally point. The grass grew thicker and closer, pulling at my clothes and my gear. It pulled my CAR-15 out of my hands, pulled the grenades off my webbing. The grass kept pulling me until it pulled me down toward the red, clay earth. The grass kept pulling me down and finally into the red earth from which it grew, suffocating me in Vietnam itself.

The alarm clock on the bedside table was going off. I was twisted and tangled up in the sheets and blankets. My tossing and turning had turned into a fight against the elephant grass. I pushed the button to silence the alarm clock. It was one of those black, plastic, square travel ones.

It was three in the morning, and I had things to do. After brushing my teeth, I dressed in a pair of old jungle boots, old blue jeans, a dark turtleneck, and a Black Watch, wool, button-down shirt. The clothes were dark and subdued but wouldn't scream 'cat burglar' to a passing patrol car if there were any cops even awake. They were also warm enough for the wee hours of an early fall morning.

My .38 snub-nose went under my shirt in its holster inside my waistband. The extra speedloader of hollow points went in my left front pocket, the big Buck knife in the right. I put my trusty blackjack in my right back pocket and my wallet went in the left. I took a penlight with some electrical tape over the bulb and slid that into a pocket.

I took the navy-blue wool watch cap and my car keys and left Sir Leominster to his nightly assignations without me. Sometimes I would find him asleep next to me. Other times I would wake up and he would be in the window looking out at the street below. Good cat, standing watch in case the NVA or the Viet Cong infiltrated Back Bay, keeping me safe from enemies I hadn't had in over a decade. You can't buy that type of loyalty.

I got in the Maverick after taking a quick walk around it to make sure there were no bits of wire left underneath it. The engine started with its usual throaty rumble. It took me a few minutes to get out of the city and on to the expressway. I made it to Fairhaven in forty-five minutes. I had opened up the Maverick, enjoying the throaty purring of the engine. I assumed that any State Police cruisers I saw parked on the shoulder of the highway were occupied by a trooper diligently sleeping so he would be well-rested for his detail the next day.

When I got to Fairhaven, I parked a quarter-mile away from Arno Kovach's apartment. There was no place to hide my car in the wide-open parking lots all around the diner and his apartment. I was pretty sure that the boys in the shipyard would take notice, and if I was right about them, they'd have someone paying attention, even at four in the morning.

There was a phone booth a few blocks away from Kovach's. I stopped, put a quarter in, and dialed his number. It rang and rang and after ten rings I figured he wasn't home. I got my quarter back from the coin return slot and started toward Kovach's. Instead of walking directly in front of the shipyard across acres of black top, I skirted around all the wide-open space lit by streetlights. The longer route with more shadow that brought me around in a big arc, allowing me to approach the diner side of his building. That kept me as far from the shipyard as possible until I was at his building. The extra five minutes was well worth it.

I stopped at the corner of the building, keeping it between me and the shipyard. The diner was dark, which was not surprising given the hour. I peeked around the corner toward the shipyard. It was dark and nothing was moving. The big chain-link gate topped with razor wire was closed. I stepped around the corner and casually walked up the wooden stairs to Kovach's apartment. Guilty-looking people skulk. I was just a dude going home or going to see a friend.

There was a light above the door, a single bulb screwed into a fixture at the top of the door frame and off to one side. It didn't have a globe or cover. It was also off. I knocked on the door and waited. I knocked again, straining my ears for sounds of movement inside the apartment or from the shipyard. I was pretty exposed up on the landing. There was nowhere to hide and only one good way down.

Satisfied, I reached up and unscrewed the bulb partway just in case anyone was slow to wake up inside. Now, the fastest and easiest way to break in would be to kick the door open. The problem was that it would make a lot of noise and was very far from subtle. Kovach had a lock in the door handle and another lock above it, either a mortise or a deadbolt. I didn't want to mess around trying to pick two locks while hanging out on the exposed landing.

There was a window next to the door, maybe a foot away on the other side of the railing. If I leaned over the railing, I could reach it. I pushed on it and was pleased to find that decades of wind, rain, and landlord-level maintenance had left it loose. I took out my Buck knife, unfolded the blade, and pried up the screen. I pushed on the bottom window and slipped the blade of the knife up between the upper and lower windows, catching the latch, unlocking it. Then I put my knife away and slid the window open. I stepped on the middle board of the railing, the kind that is supposed to prevent people from falling through the railing, and I leaned over the top. My knees were braced against the top rail, and my torso was hanging out into space. I twisted my torso, reached my arms inside on either side of the window frame and pulled my body into Arno Kovach's apartment.

I slid over the windowsill and across a faucet and sink. I shoulder-rolled on to the floor, banging into a wooden dining table and chairs. I made a little noise but managed to get to my feet without making more. I stood still, listening for movement in the apartment or downstairs in the diner. That was one thing that I had learned in SOG, to listen, waiting patiently, being still, and waiting to see if the enemy was moving. I waited, listening to the wind outside, my own breathing, a clock some-where in the apartment ticking, and the slow, rhythmic drip of the faucet in the sink.

The apartment was dark, but light from the streetlights outside filtered in the curtain-less windows. The light fell in patches on the floor and walls. I was standing in a vinyl-floored kitchen. It smelled faintly of cooked cabbage and old grease. I was glad the lights were off because I was certain that Kovach was not the type to clean regularly. There were empty liquor bottles stacked next to the sink, and I was beginning to notice the smell of stale beer. There was an electric stove in one corner, and I could see pans piled on top of each other on top of the burners. I stepped further into the apartment and the vinyl flooring changed to shag carpet, which, in the light from the windows, looked dark brown and spotted. At least I hadn't seen anything small moving around yet. The night was still young.

There was a Salvation Army vintage couch and mismatched chair in the living-room area. There was a coffee table and another low table across from that which had a television on it. The coffee table had an old tuna can filled with cigarette butts resting on it. The tabletop had several burn marks on it from cigarettes that had missed the can/ashtray. Up against the walls were bookshelves made of boards and cinderblocks. I turned on my penlight and played it over the titles. Some were in a language with a lot of different accent marks over a collection of letters I could recognize that I took to be Hungarian. Others were about World War II, the Soviets, and a large selection were about Vietnam. There was a copy of *Small Arms of the 20th Century* and a couple of other books about guns. Kovach's apartment was beginning to remind me of a messier version of my own.

I went into the bedroom which smelled like stale sweat, stale whiskey, and little else. The bed was an unmade tangle of sheets. In one corner was a bureau with three drawers and in another was a closet. There was a bedside table which had a drawer and a shelf underneath it with a large copy of the collected works of William Shakespeare.

The drawer held a plastic flashlight and brown pill bottle with a few pills rattling around inside. Below that was a well-thumbed two-year-old copy of *Playboy* and a more recent copy of *Cherry* that looked like it had been worked over just as much. There was also a sheath knife inside, the kind that you can find in every Army Navy surplus store and are marketed as 'boot knives'. I slipped it out of its cheap, stiff leather sheath. The blade was sharp, and Kovach spent a good amount of time sharpening it. I slid it back in its sheath and put it back in the drawer.

I picked up the Shakespeare book and randomly flipped the pages. The first forty or fifty flipped freely, then the rest were glued together. They had been hollowed out in a square, inside of which was a large snub-nosed revolver, this one was a Smith & Wesson .357 Magnum. He had it loaded with full power hollow point rounds, the type that are half copper and half lead. They were nasty-looking rounds. There was a speedloader of the same ammunition in the book too. The bluing on the stubby revolver was deep and well-oiled. Someone had replaced the wooden grips with a chunky rubber one that would be easier on the hands when shooting it. I hadn't seen the whole apartment yet, but I was pretty sure that the revolver was the nicest thing in it.

I wiped the gun down and put it back in the book. I reluctantly turned my attention to the bed. There was nothing under the pillows and nothing between mattress and the box spring. There were a couple of pairs of shoes under the bed, and some of the biggest dust bunnies I had ever seen. There was nothing in the shoes, no stash of weed or anything exciting. Don't let anyone tell you private investigating isn't glamorous.

I got up and made my way to the bureau in the corner. I slid the drawers out and found what I expected to find. Underwear, socks, t-shirts in the top one, folded long-sleeve shirts in the middle one and folded blue jeans in the bottom drawer. Everything was neatly folded, and there was nothing hidden in the clothes in the drawers. Underneath the bureau were more dust bunnies. If Kovach were a dust bunny rancher, he would be a huge success.

I stood in the door of the closet facing jackets, shirts, and other clothes on hangers. There were shoes and boots neatly placed on the floor under the clothes. None of it was expensive, but they were all neat and well cared for. The pockets held neither secrets nor clues as I rifled through them. One sport coat felt off when I went through the pockets. When I took it off the hanger, I found a safety pin clipped under the left sleeve, which had been facing away from the door. There was a thread tied off to the safety pin, and when I pulled on it, I managed to fish out a small .25 caliber pistol. It was an FIE, a cheap knockoff of the Beretta .25. It was a low-budget but slick rig. Kovach could put the jacket on and have the small gun with him, or he could reach into the closet while it was on the hanger and retrieve it in a hurry. The thread would snap if one pulled on it hard enough.

On a hunch I gently slid my hand up over my head and ran it along the inside top of the door frame. I was rewarded with a cheap, Spanish copy of a Colt .38 hanging from a nail by the trigger guard. It had electrical tape wrapped around the grip with a little tab so it could be pulled off quickly. Inside the cylinder were six .38 Super Vel hollow points. The serial numbers had been scratched out, which in the Commonwealth is an extra couple of years in jail. Everything about the piece was hot, and I didn't like holding it. I wiped my fingerprints off it and carefully hung it back on its nail.

In the corner of the closet was a Ruger Mini-14 with a magazine in it. They were decent rifles, scaled down versions of the M-14, designed to fire the .223 or the M-16 round and therefore lighter. They didn't have a reputation for being very accurate, but it was a serviceable rifle. It had a full wooden stock and a blued barrel. On the floor, up against the butt of the rifle, was an old M-16 ammunition bandolier with seven curved magazines in it. Kovach had 240 rounds of rifle ammunition on tap.

When I went to bed at night, I put my .38 next to me on the bedside table. But Kovach was ready for something. His apartment was on top of a building that was surrounded by open parking lot or water on all sides. Good fields of fire and no one sneaking up on him.

In the back of the closet was an Army issue green duffle bag filled with old bits of uniform and memories. There was a battered suitcase, inside of which were boxes and boxes of ammunition for Kovach's guns. If Kovach was ready for someone to try and assault his defensive position, he had the ammunition to put a hurting on them. Maybe he was waiting for the NVA or the Pathet Lao to hit his position again? Or maybe he was just a guy who liked guns and liked to keep his at the ready?

I left the bedroom and went to see what wonders the bathroom would hold. The bathroom was surprisingly clean and there was a faint smell of bleach. The medicine cabinet had some cheap plastic razors, a can of shaving cream, aspirin, a couple of brown pill bottles with the labels missing. There were all the things that people have in their homes to keep themselves smelling and looking good. I found out that Kovach was an Old Spice man. There was a melted-looking bar of soap in the soap dish on the sink. Kovach used dandruff shampoo, and the soap in the shower was green and alleged to be Irish. There was nothing hiding in the toilet tank, but there was a switch blade taped with duct tape in a hollow at the back of the sink.

I went back to the kitchen. I pulled open the oven and shone the penlight in. There was nothing more exciting in it other than the wire rack. I quickly looked in the cabinets and drawers but was careful not to move anything. I unplugged the refrigerator – I didn't want the light inside to alert anyone to my presence – and swung the door open. There was a six-pack of Coors beer and a block of cheese that looked like it was made of hard plastic. There was half a can of corned-beef hash with a spoon sticking out of it.

I closed the refrigerator door and opened the freezer. There was a box of Sealtest vanilla ice cream and a couple of ice trays. There was a bottle of cheap vodka, the kind that comes in a plastic bottle. I put the penlight in my mouth, and, on a hunch, I picked up the rectangular box of ice cream. Half of it was gone, eaten or scooped out, I don't know. In the hollow was a plastic sandwich baggie filled with cash and a passport. I put the box of ice cream back and let the freezer door swing shut. There, in the faint light cast by my taped penlight, was the face of Ambassador Gordon R. Stevenson, asshole extraordinaire, my current client.

TEN

It was a picture in a newspaper article that Kovach had taped to the freezer door. The article was two years old and talked about Stevenson's desire to write his memoirs. In the article, it talked about Stevenson's accomplishments, his family, and his enjoying his retirement in one of Boston's more expensive bedroom communities. The picture showed Stevenson with his hand casually resting on the head of a dog outside on a patio near French doors. Another picture showed Stevenson in the driveway near his Mercedes sedan. Jesus! The article was like a road map to the crime-scene photos I had looked at.

It was time to go. I had been in the apartment for the better part of an hour, and dawn was going to be breaking. That meant the diner would be opening and the fishermen would be down in the area to start their day on the water. I bent down and plugged the refrigerator back in. I opened the window I had come through and pulled the screen back down, closed and latched the window. I did a quick look around to make sure that nothing seemed to be disturbed.

I undid the dead bolt and pulled my watch cap low on my head. I stepped out and pulled the door shut behind me, locking just the lock in the handle. There was no way for me to throw the deadbolt, but Kovach might figure he forgot to throw the bolt. He wouldn't if he saw all sorts of other signs of my having been in his apartment. I reached up and twisted the outside lightbulb back in. There were scuff marks on the railing, but there wasn't anything I could do about those.

I went down the wooden steps, not too quickly and not too slowly, just a guy not doing anything illegal. Nothing to see here. I got to the bottom, aware that my hearing was a little more dialed in and my heart was beating a touch faster than normal. I went around the corner away from the shipyard and retraced my way back to the car. The sky had gone from black with pinpoints of light to a dark, inky blue, and where the sun was starting to show, it was pinkish red. If the old saying about 'red sky in the morning' was to be believed, then the day promised some foul weather. I didn't care as long as I was well away from Fairhaven.

I got back to the Maverick, and this time there was no one waiting for me. I turned the engine over, enjoying the throaty roar, and aimed the car toward Boston. Joe Walsh was on the radio singing about the 'Rocky Mountain Way'. I turned the song up, feeling good. My B and E had paid off with a clue . . . a damned good clue at that. Kovach was a long shot, but it was a long shot that was looking a lot better.

I rode northeast on the highways and byways heading into Boston. It was early and there wasn't too much traffic. What little there was, was mostly delivery trucks finishing up their runs. There were few other cars heading in my direction. I got off the highway and nosed the Maverick into town. In another half an hour or so, traffic would be moving sluggishly along the ribbons of tar and concrete into Boston.

I got home and made my way upstairs to my apartment. Sir Leominster greeted me at the door. Mewing to let me know, not so much that he missed me, but that he missed my ability to open a can of food for him. He followed me into the kitchen and sat, twitching his tail impatiently while I found a can opener. I dumped the can on a saucer and put it down next to his bowl of water. He shut up long enough to plant his feline snout in the pile of foul-smelling meat-like stuff.

It was too early to call Watts, so I opted for a shower, clean clothes, and breakfast. Breakfast was uninspiring save the espresso. I found a banana that was more yellow than brown and ate that too. It wasn't what I wanted, but it was better than what I had in the diner below Kovach's apartment. That breakfast had shaken my faith in diner food. I picked up the phone, figuring that I could catch Watts at home before she left for the office.

'Hello,' she answered.

'Who's your favorite private eye?'

'I don't have one.'

'Ouch . . .'

'Why are you calling me so early? Shouldn't you still be hungover or something?'

'Hah, I'll have you know I have been up for several hours, and been quite productive, thank you.'

'You've been up for hours and very productive . . . oh, that sounds scary. Usually when you think you've been productive, people get hurt.'

'I took a trip to Fairhaven early this morning,' I said, ignoring her pointed comments.

'Andy . . . you didn't do anything illegal?'

'Other than a little B and E, no.'

'Burglary if it's at night.'

'No, burglary is the entering of a dwelling at night with the intent to commit a felony therein. I had no intention of committing a felony, and I didn't.'

'Semantics,' she countered.

'Well, they are important occasionally.'

'When?'

'At sentencing mostly,' I quipped.

'OK, hypothetically, what did you do?'

'I went to visit an old Army buddy in Fairhaven. When I got there and knocked on the door, it must have been poorly latched and swung open.'

'Ugh, have you ever heard of the poisoned fruit of the poisoned tree?'

'Yes, and I am not worried about testifying to anything right now. I don't think Stevenson is looking for a conviction.'

'No, probably not. What did you find?'

'My buddy Arno wasn't home, but I wanted to make sure no one had broken in. He lives alone, drinks a lot, and has guns and knives stashed around his apartment. Also, he isn't much of a housekeeper.'

'Andy, for all intents and purposes, you just described your own apartment.'

'Hey, that's not fair. My place is kind of clean.'

'Was there anything else?'

'No, not much . . .' I trailed off.

'Not worth the trip then.'

'. . . except a cut-out newspaper article about Stevenson taped to his refrigerator.' I enjoyed hearing the slight intake of breath at the other end of the line. I imagined her slightly biting her lower lip. It wasn't a bad thing to contemplate.

'It was a couple of years old. One of those "Meet the Writer" types of articles. Pictures of him with the dog, his Mercedes, and the French doors that got shot up. It was all in this one article.'

'Jesus.'

'It could still be a coincidence?'

'Not likely. You were productive this morning.'

'Yes, I was.'

'OK. Now what? I can't do much with this.' There was mild exasperation in Watts's voice.

'I don't know. I want to talk to Kovach. If he is on the road or something, it might be a while before he is around. I should probably tell Stevenson or that Pretty Boy who follows him around.'

'He is the type to like status updates.'

'Ha, there is nothing shocking about that.' My own voice betrayed how little I liked having a boss.

'OK. Good work, I guess. Keep me posted, but not too posted.'

Watts was never comfortable with my rare forays into felony land. 'Thanks, will do.'

She hung up and I listened to the dial tone, wondering if it might be worth shaping up enough to convince her to take a chance on me. I put the handset in the cradle, no closer to having an answer than I ever did before. Sir Leominster came over and rubbed up against my shins. His standards were a lot lower than Watts's.

The next order of the day was a trip to the office. I gathered up whatever yellow legal pads I had been writing case notes on at home and threw them in my old mail carrier's bag. The red sky in the morning had proven to be more than just a catchy rhyme, and now big fat raindrops were beating steadily against the windows of my apartment. This would be a great time to curl up on the couch and take a nap after my early morning adventures. It would be, except that after finding an actual clue I felt excited, and the thought of not following up on it was a non-starter.

I pulled on my old, battered trench coat and my old Red Sox cap. Like all the faithful, I held out hope that we'd win the World Series someday. And like all true believers, I knew it was a leap of faith to think that.

Boston was a town like that. It required a lot of faith to live here. Faith that you would find a parking spot close to your destination. Faith that your car wouldn't get crushed in a pothole. It required faith to get through long winters and then the false flag operation known as spring, where after a week or two of faint sunshine and near warm weather, we'd get buried by wet snow. Then, only a few months later, having to cope with the heat and humidity of summer's cruelty.

Sir Leominster had curled up on the couch with his snout under his paw, sleeping the sleep of the just. Outside on the street, the rain had slowed to a persistent drizzle. I walked to the office thinking about Kovach and what I had seen in his apartment. He seemed like a lonely man but not stupid. He clearly saw the world as a dangerous place and wanted to be prepared for it. He drank a lot, and the only thing that stood out was the clipping of the article.

If I did manage to get him to answer the phone, I needed to have something better to say to him than, 'Hey Arno, I broke into your apartment and I noticed that you like guns and whiskey too. Wanna hang out?' Something told me that would start the conversation off on the wrong foot. I could try to bluff him, but eventually I would have to tell him the truth about why I was calling, and I would most likely only squander whatever goodwill I might curry leading up to that. I could try the honesty dodge and scare him off right away. 'Hey Arno, my name is Andy, and I was hired to find out if you are writing threatening letters to the Ambassador. Oh, and by the way, are you trying to kill him too?' That didn't seem like a much better opening.

When I got to the office, the video store hadn't magically turned into anything else, but at least the place wasn't booby-trapped. I hung my wet trench coat on the coat rack and put my very damp baseball cap next to it. I put my postal bag on the desk and went about the business of cranking up the espresso machine. Then, because I didn't have enough vices that required a lot of small steps, I took out my favorite pipe. Packing the bowl wasn't unlike packing the basket of the espresso machine. By the time the espresso machine had built up a good head of steam, I had managed to get the pipe lit and drawing nicely. I opened the window a crack and then put the cup under the spigot, enjoying the sound of espresso filling the tiny cup.

I sat down and pulled the phone over. I dialed Kovach's number and listened to it ring and ring. I hung up for the first time today, but knowing that it was far from the last time. I pulled the legal pads over and began to consolidate my notes. I wrote down my observations about Kovach's apartment and the neighborhood – or, more accurately, industrial area – he lived in.

From Kovach's point of view, it was a pretty good set-up. He had food, booze, and employment all right there. He could see anyone coming or going for tens of yards in any direction. He also had paranoid neighbors in the shipyard, so that meant neighborhood security was taken care of.

From my point of view, it presented a lot of challenges. There weren't a lot of great places to lay up and watch Kovach's apartment from. If I showed up there again, I was likely to get into a fight, or worse if I was seen. I wasn't keen on breaking into Kovach's apartment again. I had used up my number of complimentary felonies from the FBI.

I started to catalogue the guns as I remembered them and where they were found. I added the knives too. I was surprised he didn't have a shotgun. They were unparalleled for close quarters, and Kovach seemed serious about stuff like that.

His books had mostly been history and some political science stuff. From what I saw, he was an anti-communist, which given his background wasn't surprising. The Lodge Act soldiers tended to have a grudge against the Soviets, and with good reason. The books he had about Vietnam were mostly historical, but a lot of the ones that had been written certainly had a political slant. America had only in the last year or so gotten to the point where it could talk about the war during holiday gatherings without it devolving into a fight.

Kovach had been in Vietnam and, more importantly, in Laos. He was a guy who requested through channels to marry a

Laotian girl and had his request denied. He had publicly made threats against the Ambassador. He fitted the FBI profile and he lived an hour from Stevenson. It was a lot of circumstantial stuff, but I didn't have to prove anything in a court of law. He looked good enough, and I didn't have a lot of other likely candidates at this point.

Still, there were things that bothered me. I hadn't seen a typewriter in Kovach's apartment. That didn't mean he didn't have one or didn't have access to one. Two, if you were going to shoot at Stevenson, the Ruger Mini-14 would have made a lot of noise on a suburban street. It would have attracted police attention pretty quickly. But if you were going to try and kill Stevenson, why would you use anything smaller if you had the Ruger available? Would a guy who has a small arsenal, stored ready for bear, be happy just writing letters or scaring Stevenson like that?

Mostly I couldn't shake the feeling that Kovach's apartment, and maybe Kovach himself, wasn't very organized. It was neat but not clean. Also, the odds bothered me. It seemed like a long shot that the one and only name that came up so far was the guy responsible. Stevenson had to have pissed off a lot more people than just Kovach.

I picked up the phone again. An hour had passed, my pipe had gone out, and the demitasse cup was dry. I dialed and listened to the phone ring and ring at the other end of the line. I was beginning to suspect that after my successful recon of Kovach's apartment, the rest of the day was going to turn out to be a lot of banging my head against the wall trying to reach him.

I decided to see if the Jungle Telegraph had anything to offer. I started calling guys I knew who had been in country around the time that Don Barry had said he had run into Kovach. Now that I had a lead, a name, I might be able to jar some memories, shake something useful loose. I started calling the names in my address book. I left messages about Kovach with wives, girl-friends, and answering machines. It wasn't much, but it was what I had to work with, unless I could get old Arno to answer his phone.

Every hour that I called and listened to it ring and ring, it seemed less likely to pan out. Between calls to his seemingly unanswerable phone, I added to my notes. Normally I would take pictures of Arno's apartment and points of interest around it, but something told me that wouldn't go over well with the boys from the shipyard.

I had spent most of the morning taking notes and listening to phones at the other end of my handset ring and ring. I was hungry, frustrated, and starting to feel the effects of not enough sleep. It was mid-afternoon and the pain in my lower back, on top of everything else, was telling me it was time to leave. I packed my legal pads and pens in the mail bag and put on my now-dry trench coat and baseball cap.

The rain had given way to sunny weather, and I regretted not having any sunglasses with me. Sunlight glinted off the windows in the buildings and the puddles of dirty water that were splashed around. Water was meandering in streams along the gutters, carrying with it a flotilla of paper cups and fast-food wrappers. The sidewalks looked a little cleaner, but it was Boston and that wouldn't last for very long.

I walked past the Eric Fuchs hobby shop, which fed the habits of model train builders and the military diorama types equally. If you needed a replica firearm or Airfix toy soldiers from England or an HO scale anything and all the glues, paints and brushes, Fuchs was the place. I passed under the giant gold teapot sign and made my way down a couple of blocks until I found myself at Provisions.

Provisions was a hidden gem down among the tall buildings near Government Center and the Courthouse. It was a small deli tucked between two larger buildings. Inside you could sit at one of the half a dozen tables, but good luck trying to get a seat between eleven thirty and two in the afternoon. The place was usually mobbed with business types, ties loosened and top button undone. You might find college kids or even the occasional tourist who stumbled in, slightly lost from the maze of streets that started their lives as winding cow paths a couple hundred years ago. They are the lucky ones.

I went inside and looked at the specials chalked on a blackboard. The muffuletta looked pretty exciting. I had spent a weekend I could barely remember in New Orleans once. On the other hand, the Roast Beast sandwich was enticing. The roast beef was roasted on the premises, every day, crusted in salt and black pepper, cooked to a perfect medium, and sliced very thin. Horseradish cream sauce was optional for everyone else, for me it was a must. They piled the roast beef on one side of the split loaf. On the other they laid down tomato slices, salted and peppered them, then added sliced black olives, sliced pepperoncini, and shredded iceberg lettuce. On top of the roast beef they laid slices of Havarti cheese with dill in it.

When I was able to get up to the counter, I ordered a small Roast Beast but kept thinking about the muffuletta the way you might think about the girl you almost chatted up in a bar. I added a bag of Cape Cod potato chips. They were kettle cooked and crunchy. In a world of flat, greasy chips, produced in factories that would have made Henry Ford proud, the Cape Cod potato chips were standouts.

I paid at the counter and waited for my order. I thought about Kovach. He looked like he might be good for menacing Stevenson. He was local, seemed to have reason to hate him, and didn't seem to have much else going on in his life. The college-aged kid at the counter called my number and I paid. I put the sandwich and chips in my mail bag. Case notes and a big sandwich made for strange companions.

Walking home as the fall afternoon light began the gradual dipping behind and between buildings, I kept thinking about Kovach. Was he that angry about events in Laos that happened over a decade ago? What type of person had the energy to make so much effort after a decade?

I knew guys who had a tough time moving on from Vietnam, but this seemed like a bit much. Or maybe Kovach was a nutter and his pressure cooker had finally blown a gasket? From my point of view, it probably didn't matter much. My job was to find the guy doing all of this, be it Kovach, an SOG guy, or someone Stevenson had wronged in the past. My job was to keep Stevenson safe by finding the guy threatening him, not to analyze motives.

I reached my apartment and let myself in. I took my case notes on their yellow legal pads out of my mail bag, the sandwich, and chips too. I poured a glass of water and sat down. I munched on the chips and the sandwich while I reviewed my notes. This was part of the process when I worked a case, go out and investigate, gather facts and talk to people, jot down notes, then try and tie it all together, summarize the notes, and attempt to make something coherent out of it all. I don't know how other investigators work, but this was how I did it.

I crunched on the salty chips and looked at the stuff about Kovach. He looked good for all of it, but I couldn't get over the feeling that Stevenson had screwed over a lot of people along the way to the nice house in Brookline, which came with the Mercedes and the young, leggy, blonde wife. The wife, I might add, who looked like she should be in a shampoo commercial. On the other hand, if I was right about Kovach wanting to marry a Laotian girl and Stevenson putting the kibosh on it . . . that was also someone from his past with a hell of a motive. Did all roads lead back to the war in Vietnam or, in this case, Laos?

Most of my cases were simple. Spouse A was sleeping with someone who wasn't Spouse B. Usually this occurred at a cheap motel or wherever. Or a guy claims an injury at work. Claims his back is hurt because of his employer's negligence and he can't work, he can barely walk. Then I find him down on the Irish Riviera, aka Wollaston Beach, playing beach volleyball with a couple of young ladies from Eastern Nazarene College. I can't prove it scientifically, but there seems to be a correlation between the size of the bikini and the religiousness of the college. That is the fun version of that type of case. More often it is the guy claiming a back injury lifting heavy stuff or doing construction. I watch and take pictures and don't think too much about any of it. Simple.

Most of my cases weren't mysteries, they were just a collection of people lying, cheating and/or committing low-level crimes. There were no supervillains with ambitious plans in my world, just human beings caught up in the drama of bad decisions and usually worse actions. Mostly it wasn't exciting, it was just sad.

Most of the time, most of my cases were not exotic. Now I was dealing with a small, shabby piece of my past, my war gone by, or at least the war next door. A name, a person, had popped up and I was questioning it. There weren't many more common motives than love lost, except for greed. Greed was universal. Maybe I just wanted a case involving the Ambassador to be more complex, more exciting than a lover who lost his love. It wouldn't be a stretch of the imagination to think that because I didn't like him, I wanted him to be the villain in this and not the victim.

If I had learned anything in the cops, I learned that you can't pick your victims. More than once I had to deal with people who I had fought with or arrested in the past, sometimes the recent past, who were now victims of assaults or thefts or had their kids run away. You couldn't hold it against them, you just had to deal with them like it was the first time you were meeting them.

My notes weren't offering any new insights, and I decided to put them away for the night. I got up, got a glass, put in a few ice cubes, and covered them with whiskey. I took my whiskey to the couch and pulled the phone over, putting it on the coffee table within easy reach. I then turned on the TV.

I clicked through the channels hoping for a fight or something, but there wasn't one to be found. It was getting harder and harder to find boxing on TV, as it was being pushed out in favor of TV shows with canned laugh tracks. Maybe like Marconi's being replaced by the video rental store, it was a form of progress. In the end, the Movie Loft came to the rescue. Dana Hersey was standing in front of the metal, spiral staircase, telling us about Sergio Leone's classic Western to end all Westerns, *Once Upon a Time in the West*. A slow, masterful epic that pit Charles Bronson's tight, restrained, quiet performance against Henry Fonda's even tighter, quieter turn as a psychopathic hired gun. Jason Robards was in it, delivering a touch of ragged and dusty nobility to the whole thing.

I sat, watching, enthralled at what had to be one of the dustiest-looking films in movie history. Its slow pacing was perfect for opportunities to call Kovach. I took sips of whiskey as Bronson, Robards and Fonda shot their way toward their inevitable showdowns. Every other commercial, I would pick up the phone and dial Kovach's number, which, after a day of trying to call him, I had memorized without meaning to.

I wasn't having any better luck this time but at least I was fortified by the very tasty sandwich, and whiskey. The movie was engrossing and took my mind off the disappointment of a phone that rang and rang but was never answered. The nice thing about the commercials, besides being able to call Kovach and feel like I was doing something to move the case forward, was that I was able to refill my whiskey glass as needed and not miss any of the movie.

By the time the credits were rolling to the distinct notes of the soundtrack, I was tired, and my eyelids were heavy. My belly was full, and I was a few whiskeys deep. I picked up the phone for one more attempt before bed. I listened to it ring and ring, bits of static crackling on the line between Fairhaven and Boston. Then, just like that, it stopped ringing and a voice said, 'Hello.'

ELEVEN

I sat up straighter.

'Hello,' he said again.

'Hi. Is this Arno?'

'Yes, and who is this?' His English was accented but not heavily so, and I got the feeling that his manner of speaking would be a little old fashioned. Formal and precise, the way Eastern Europeans tended to speak their adopted tongue.

'My name is Andy Roark. I'm a private investigator from Boston.'

'Are you the one who was asking my neighbors about me?'

'Yes.' There was little point in lying about that.

'Why do you want to talk to me, Mr Private Investigator?'

'I would rather talk to you in person.' I wanted to look into his eyes, gauge his body language, see all those tiny details that help divine the lies from the truth. It was hard enough to do that in person. It is impossible to do that on the phone.

'I am sure you would, Mr Andy Investigator,' it occurred to me that his words were just the tiniest bit slurred, 'but what about?'

'Well, it's a lot to go into over the phone . . .' I trailed off.

'It must be important if you are calling me this late at night.'

'You are a hard man to get in touch with.'

'Humph.'

'Can we meet tomorrow, Arno? Get a drink or something?'

'I heard you were in a fight with a couple of the men from the shipyard.'

'I wouldn't call it a fight, more of a misunderstanding, really.' There wasn't much point in going into the details. I was trying to be friendly Andy. The Andy you want to have a beer with, not combat Andy.

'I believe that one of them will be limping for a long time to come.'

'Again, a misunderstanding.'

'A painful one.'

'He seemed very intent upon hurting me. I don't care for that sort of thing.'

'And now you want to meet with me?'

'We don't have to meet down where you live.'

'How did you find out where I live?'

'We have a mutual friend from Vietnam, Don Barry.' That was sort of true, and I wouldn't mind if Kovach got the feeling that Don had given me his address and phone number. It seemed less sinister than my seeking out where he lived.

'Yes, I remember Don Barry. Good man, but a horrible poker player.'

'That sounds about right.' Things were looking up. 'What do you say? Would you like to get a drink and talk about the old days, Vietnam and all that?'

'Were you there?'

'Yes, mostly up in CCN. We could grab a drink and swap notes about Vietnam.'

'That is a generous offer, Investigator Andy. But I do not think that I like you.'

'How come?' Most people find me somewhat likeable. Well, some people.

'I came home today, and my door was only partially locked. My apartment felt different, things were out of place that should not be. It feels like someone has been going through my things. Now, a private investigator is calling me, I assume with questions . . . no, Andy, I think meeting you is a bad idea.' Then there was a click and the dial tone buzzed in my ear.

'But you haven't even heard about my self-improvement plan,' I said to the dead handset.

I thought about calling Watts and telling her about my conversation with Kovach, but I had one whiskey more than was advisable for trying to sound intelligent while speaking with pretty FBI agents. I was not sure I was ready to admit to her that I might have bungled things by having a peek in Kovach's apartment. I had, after all, impressed her with what I had found, and I didn't get to impress Watts often. I wanted to savor the feeling, at least until morning.

The next morning, I overslept by forty-five minutes but still went for a run. One of the advantages of being self-employed was that if I showed up at the office late, I wasn't going to be in trouble with me. The closest thing I had to a boss was the cat, and he was, frankly, not doing a great job of managing my work.

I went for my usual run, dodging the puddles left by last night's rain. I ran down Storrow Drive, enjoying the look of the Charles River with the morning sun glinting off it. Here and there a lone rower propelled a small wooden rowing shell on the river. Occasionally a large crew of rowers moved down the river, reminding me of small Viking long boats, minus sails and swords. I pounded up the steps to the Longfellow Bridge; while the breeze was more noticeable due to the excellent engineering of the structure, the threat of puddles was almost nonexistent.

I heard a car honk behind me. Looking over my shoulder I noticed an unremarkable brown sedan, maybe a Ford, maybe a Chevy, driving slowly down the bridge. Another car honked and the sedan shot ahead. I couldn't see the driver but noticed there were two men in it. I probably wouldn't have thought much more about it. Except that when I ran past the Harvard Bridge it was there again, a few cars back as I crossed over on to the Boston University Bridge heading back into Boston from Cambridge.

Was it a coincidence? Tan American-made sedans weren't exactly rarities in American cities. I hadn't seen the plate, just that there were two white men in it. It might not even be the same car. Just to be on the safe side I ran up a couple of blocks. With the morning traffic, the car never seemed able to get ahead of me, but it also didn't seem like it was trying too hard. If I was the type who tended toward paranoia, I might think that they were following me.

That was annoying. I liked my morning run. It was a part of the day when I could clear my head. Sometimes it was nice to go out in the world and pretend that I was just like every other normal person out there. The car was still behind me when Mountfort met Beacon Street, which I followed inbound toward my apartment. I cut over on to Newbury Street and turned left on to Mass Ave. The tan sedan was still behind me, aided by the sluggish traffic.

They were following me. The problem was who were they? Were they friends of Kovach and the two big dudes from the boatyard? Or were they associates of the local hoods I had pissed off in the Combat Zone a few months ago? Or were the Vietnamese gangsters having another go, six months later? Lately I had been pissing quite a few people off, and they were not the type to send angry letters.

Comm Ave. I would run to Commonwealth Avenue and take advantage of its central walking path to lose them. I could cut across the path and cross to the outbound side of Comm Ave and cross the street. If I did it right, they might have to go down a block or two to double around to stick with me.

I crossed Hereford Street, which was one way toward the Charles River, which meant they could turn on to it and follow me. I ran down to Gloucester Street which would be one way in the opposite direction. I turned left and lost them. I laughed watching them as they moved on down Commonwealth Ave. I followed the street down to Beacon Street. The light was against me when I got there and I jogged in place, sweaty and proud of myself. The light turned green, and I started to cross. I heard the sound of a big American-made engine revving and saw movement out of the corner of my eye.

I dived and rolled into the gutter, in a puddle. Looking up I saw the taillights of a tan sedan running through the light. I heard car horns blaring but I was all right. It had missed me. Was it someone trying to kill me or was this just another example of excellent Boston driving? I started back on my way, albeit a little bit scraped up and wet from the gutter.

I was almost home when a car dodging a pothole managed to splash me with a puddle of Boston's finest gutter water. My whole left side was drenched, but at least I didn't drink any of the oily, briny mixture. The day was going from bad to worse. I finished the last half of my run cold and with one foot that squished and slapped the pavement as I ran.

When I got home and inside the apartment, even Sir Leominster didn't want to rub up against me. I stepped out of my wet sneakers and stripped off my socks. I grabbed a towel and went back to the living room. Still wet, steam coming off me, I went to the phone to call Watts. She picked up on the third ring.

'What do you want, Andy?'

'How'd you know it was me?'

'No one else calls me as I am on the way out the door to the office in the morning.'

'Not even your mother?'

'Especially not her.'

'I spent yesterday going over my case notes, and when I wasn't doing that, I would call Kovach's phone and listen to it ring and ring.'

'Gee, Andy, that's great. Sounds like an exciting day.' Ma Bell must have a new feature that makes people sound very sarcastic. 'You called to tell me about your day doodling and making fruitless phone calls?'

'Last night he answered the phone.'

'Whaaat?'

'Yes, we talked for a few minutes. I asked to meet him, and he basically told me to pound sand.'

'OK, good to know. Anything else?'

'Nothing surprising. He sounded a little drunk and he is a very suspicious person.'

'Sounds like you two are a pair.' I wasn't sure that I liked being compared to Kovach.

'I can't exactly blame him.'

'OK, what's next?'

'I will put something together for Stevenson and see if he wants me to keep on looking for an SOG guy or if he wants me to stick with Kovach or stop all together.'

'Sounds good. I think he is up in Vermont.'

'What is he doing up there? It's too early for ski season.' Stevenson didn't strike me as someone with a secret passion for dairy farming.

'He's shacked up there in the mountains with his trophy wife, his assistant, and a ghostwriter so he can work on his memoirs.'

'Nice gig. Maybe I should write my memoirs.'

'No one needs another coloring book.' She hung up; I was

starting to wonder if that was her way of saying goodbye to me. I could only imagine what she would be like if she didn't find me mildly amusing.

I decided that my call to Stevenson's aide-de-camp could wait until after a shower and breakfast. That and I was starting to shiver; there is nothing quite like wet cotton to draw the heat right out of you. I stripped off my stuff, threw it in the hamper, and turned the shower on.

After I showered, toweled off and dressed, I felt a little warmer. In the kitchen, I started coffee in the stove-top espresso maker. I made a breakfast of wheat toast, an apple and yogurt. Self-improvement comes at a price, flavor being chief among them now. At least I felt ready to call Stevenson's ADC and report what little progress I had made so far.

I found the number the ADC had given me for Vermont when we were wrapping up the second meeting with Stevenson. I picked up the phone and dialed the 802 area code, listening to the clicks as the dial returned to zero after each number. I held the handset to my ear listening to it ring, and, unlike Kovach's phone, it was picked up on the third ring.

'Hello.' It was the ADC, Bradley.

'It's Andy Roark.'

'Oh, hello, Mr Roark. I was expecting you to call in a few days ago.'

'Yes, Bradley, I imagine you were.'

'Well, what do you have to report?'

'I have developed a person of interest and need to see how far the Ambassador wants me to pursue things?'

'Great, you have a suspect. Now maybe we can get this settled and behind us.'

'I don't have a suspect, I have found a person of interest, a person, who MIGHT' – I put extra emphasis on the might; I didn't want Bradley to call in an air strike on some poor SOB who might not be sending nasty letters and poisoning dogs – 'be a person of interest. That is a lot different than having a suspect.'

'I see. I suppose you want to talk to the Ambassador about it?'

'That seems sensible.'

'Hold on a moment.' I was trying to think of something pithy to say about his Ivy League accent and Ivy League manners, but winced instead as he dropped his handset on a table or desk. I had to assume that – with manners as nice as his – Bradley had done that on purpose. I waited, listening to the faint static from the phone. Then, 'Mr Roark, it's Bradley.'

'Yeah.'

'The Ambassador is busy working right now but wondered if you wouldn't mind coming up and briefing him in person?'

'To Vermont? Sure, I can do that.' It was a waste of time, but the foliage would be nice, and if Stevenson wanted to pay my mileage, who was I to argue?

'He was hoping you could come up today, brief him, and then you could head back in the morning?'

'Sure kid, it's his nickel.' I normally don't like to be so crass, but I had the feeling that Bradley found me annoying, and I had the childish impulse to encourage that.

'Good.' He didn't mean it. 'The Ambassador will be pleased.' Bradley then gave me directions through gritted teeth. I wrote them down and was very happy that I would be driving to central Vermont and not the Canadian border. Two hours in the Maverick was manageable. After Bradley confirmed that I had the directions properly written down, he said a curt goodbye and hung up.

I grabbed my postal bag and slid my case notes into it. From the bathroom I got my shaving kit in its canvas bag and added that to the mail bag. A change of clothes, a few extra items like socks and a couple extra speedloaders of .38 hollow points went in too. You never knew. On the other hand, what was I worried about in Vermont? An angry moose or black bear? I threw a paperback copy of an Eric Ambler novel in as well. I had an almost new bottle of whiskey and almost added it to my bag, but I was confident that Stevenson would have a lot of good hootch on hand.

I opened an extra can of food and put it out for Sir Leominster. I pulled on my preppy Norwegian sweater. I put my revolver, speedloader and knife in their respective places. I left the blackjack in the raincoat pocket. It wouldn't be much good against an angry moose. I laid my L.L. Bean's parka, the one that looks more like an army field jacket, over the mail bag and hoisted it on my shoulder.

Outside there were no bits of wire by the Maverick and no signs that anyone was trying to blow me up. The canvas postal bag and parka went on the seat on the passenger side, and I got in on my side. I started the car up and marveled at Carney's mechanical genius as it rumbled throatily, reminding me of the way some women laugh when they throw their heads back, showing off their necks.

I got on the highway and headed north. I drove over the Tobin Bridge, which I still thought of as the Mystic River Bridge. They had changed the name the year before I went to Vietnam, and I still had to make the switch in my mind when I thought about it.

The Maverick rolled ever northward, and the land became more dramatic and higher in elevation. The leaves on the trees were spectacular shades of red, yellow, and orange. About an hour into my trip, I saw a sign that said, 'Rest Area. New Hampshire State Liquor Store.'

I pulled off the highway into the rest area. There was a visitor center which had free maps and an information counter manned by people who looked as though they had been old when the highway had been built in the early 1970s. Kitty-corner to the information and latrine building was the State Liquor Store. Both buildings were built in the ski lodge school of architecture.

The State Liquor Store was where the State of New Hampshire proved to me that it was one of the most civilized of the New England states. The building was large, like a small airplane hangar or supermarket. There were rows and rows, shelves and shelves of liquor for sale. The best part of New Hampshire was that there was no sales tax. For the price of a bar tab at the place across the street from me, I walked out with not one, but two bottles of Powers Irish whiskey.

The Maverick's engine growled along as we went uphill, then down and then uphill again, each time bringing us to a higher elevation. Forty-five minutes later, we crested a hill, came out of the trees, and I was struck by a stunning valley opening up below me and to my left.

I crossed the Connecticut River and into Vermont. I drove through White River Junction where the White and Connecticut Rivers meet. It is also home to a railyard with a big carousel for turning railcars around. The further north I went, the more I had to hunt through the radio stations to try and keep good rock and roll on the radio. Which we all know is essential to any road trip.

I took the exit off the highway. I took a right and then an immediate left. The trees opened to a large field, and beyond that was a house. In the field a hundred yards from the road was a small, wooden building. Like something out of a German fairy tale.

The house was more like a European hunting lodge. The ground floor was white stucco, and the long side had no windows, but the short side had a row of Andersen windows that ran along its entire length. The second floor was dark, stained wood with a roof that hung over a few feet, no doubt to help with the winter snow. As I got closer, I realized there was a detached two-car garage and big mailbox by the road. There were a few large pines between the garage and the house. The garage was built almost to the wood line, which was never far from the house at all.

I turned off the road and bore to the right around the remnants of a stone wall. I circled around this impromptu traffic island and parked behind a newish-looking light blue Ford Mustang.

The house was built into the side of a hill. There was a covered porch which made sense in a place that saw a lot of snow in the winter. Under the porch, cords of firewood were stacked in orderly piles four feet high. To get to the house, I had to walk uphill to some granite steps. I took my mail bag and started up the steep incline.

There were fields sloping down to my right and, a few hundred meters away, a small building and the tree line consisting of oak, pine and birch trees. I turned and walked up the steps, which were large sheets of granite flagstones leading up to a flagstone patio that was thirty by twenty feet across and butted up against the wood line.

Facing the patio was a set of sliding glass doors. I walked down the porch to the glass storm door. I knocked on the door. The door on the other side of the storm door was half solid-looking wood and half glass. I guess that no one in Vermont was very worried about burglars.

Inside I could see a figure approaching the door. The light was wrong for me to see much more than the outline of a figure. It was a figure with hips, though; a woman, too curvy to be Honey. The door opened and I was staring at a woman who was tall as they go – by that I mean not much shorter than me. She had red hair pulled back in a sensible ponytail and freckles splashed across her nose and cheekbones. Her eyes were green and seemed to take in my slightly battered face, ragged earlobe, and generally sloppy appearance. She was wearing a cotton fisherman's sweater and blue jeans and tennis sneakers. She looked like the Ivory soap girl until she spoke.

'Are you our version of Sam Spade?' Her accent was English – not Cockney English and not Princess Di English, but definitely not 'on our side of the Revolution' English.

'Sure, if you don't mind being called Angel, Angel.' My Bogart imitation is pretty bad to begin with, but it was good enough to get a smile out of her. When she smiled her eyes crinkled, and I realized that she was in her thirties and not twenties.

'Well, aren't you a charmer?' She started to say more but a man appeared behind her. He was tall, with dark hair and a tan. He also had his hand down at his side, and I was pretty sure he was holding a pistol along his thigh.

'Maureen, who's this?'

'Relax, Baz, he's the private dick from Boston.' It might have been wishful thinking on my part, but I thought she put a little bit of extra emphasis on the second word of my job title.

'Who are you?' This was directed at me. He was in a bit of a pickle because if there was gun play, Maureen was between us.

'My name is Roark. I'm the investigator that the Ambassador hired in Boston.'

'Roger Basselman. Got anything to prove it?'

'You want to see a photostat of my license or didn't Bradley tell you to expect me? Or get the Ambassador or his wife. They both know who I am.'

'Well, let's see the license.' His accent was off, middle of America American, but that was under something foreign. Dutch, or maybe Afrikaner. He seemed intent, so I clawed my wallet from my back pocket and found the photostat of my license. Maureen held out her hand and I handed it to her. She studied it and spoke.

'Baz, this is from the Commonwealth of Massachusetts.' Then to me, 'Commonwealth?'

'Like a state but fancier. One of four in the country,' I said brightly.

'Oh, I see.' Then back over her shoulder to him, 'Says he is licensed by the Commonwealth as a private investigator and that he is duly authorized to carry a firearm too.'

'Do you have a gun?' This seemed to get his attention.

'Yes.'

'You'll have to give that to me.'

'No.'

'What? I just told you.'

'Listen, Base.'

'It's Baz.'

'I don't know you and I don't work for you and I sure as hell don't take orders from you.'

'My job is to protect the Ambassador and . . .'

'He's fine, Baz, you can trust Mr Roark with his gun. After all, we wouldn't want a cowboy roaming around without his six-gun.' Stevenson had appeared from somewhere beside Baz. He seemed to be in good spirits, and I was wondering if he had gotten into the scotch a little early.

'OK, Bass.' It sounded like he was trying to say 'Boss,' but his accent made it sound like a cross between the fish and management.

'Roark, I appreciate you making the trip up. I see you have met Baz and Maureen.'

'We haven't been formally introduced,' I said.

'Well, Baz is my bodyguard until this thing blows over. Good man, experienced, maybe almost as much as you, Roark. And

this is Maureen Kemp, she's helping me write my memoirs.'
She stuck her hand out to me.

'It's nice to meet you.' Her grip was firm, and I had the
impression that she had spent some time doing outdoorsy
things, like riding horses or wrestling alligators.

'My pleasure,' was the most impressive thing I could come
up with.

'Roark, stop flirting with my ghostwriter and come on in.' I
had been accepted into the Ambassador's private army, it
seemed. The Ambassador seemed much cheerier being on his
own turf. I stepped into a hallway with a door to my immediate
left, probably a closet. To my right was an open, airy living
room, and directly in front of me at the end of the hallway was
the kitchen. The hallway and the living room were separated
by a wall of brick that was so centrally located it could only
be the chimney. To the left was another open hallway and doors
that I assumed were bedrooms and a bathroom. There was a
stairwell leading downstairs that was surrounded by a railing
which gave the hallway a feeling of openness.

'Come on, we'll talk downstairs.' I dutifully followed him
downstairs into a ground floor. It was an interesting room with
highly polished floors and knotty pine walls but done with a
very light stain. There was a door to the right of the stairs and
a closet door in front of the stairs. To the left of the closet was
an old wooden desk and matching wooden office chair.

The only windows were facing the stairs, and they let in a
fair amount of light. There was a J-shaped sectional couch by
the windows, a small table with a lamp, and a chair that was
part of the matched set of the couch. There was a half wall with
shelves filled with books. The windowless wall had pictures of
Stevenson, his son, and his former wife all at varying ages. The
smiles seemed to grow tighter and smaller as they grew older.

The side of the bookshelf wall had a spear that was vertical
in a mount built into the wall. It looked to be from Africa.
There was a small alcove maybe six by ten that held another
bookshelf, a glass-fronted cabinet, and a wet bar. The bar was
well appointed with bottles of liquor and matched sets of
glasses. Across from the bar, in the alcove, was a bookshelf

with all sorts of books about recent history, and wedged between the bookshelf and the wall was a gun cabinet with some scoped rifles and shotguns in it. I had to give Stevenson credit for keeping the important things – guns, books and booze – in one convenient place.

There was a reclining chair that faced the room, and directly across from it and the bar/alcove was a battered couch. At the far end of the room was a massive fireplace of blue granite that looked like the stuff poking out of the ground in front of the house. To the left of the massive fireplace was a door.

The walls of the room were filled with pictures of the family, pictures of Stevenson in exotic, far-off places where he was ambassadoring, and the occasional mounted head of a stag or oil painting. The paintings were mostly landscapes or seascapes, and, unlike the cheap stuff in Kovach's local bar, these had been done by a real artist.

'Do you like them?'

'Yes,' I was surprised at the conviction in my own voice, 'yes, I do. Do you know the artist?'

'I hope so. I married her.' Show-off!

'Honey painted these? She's got talent.'

'Don't let her hear you sound so surprised.' He chuckled. 'Yes, she is very talented. I still haven't figured out what she is doing with a bum like me.' False modesty was about the only kind that I expected out of him.

'Drop your bag on the couch there. Get you a drink?'

I did as I was told, putting the bag down on the couch.

'Sure.'

'Scotch or bourbon? Business should never be discussed over clear liquors.'

'Bourbon on the rocks, please.'

'You and Sinatra . . . he likes two fingers over two cubes.' And then there was no modesty to be found. He went to the bar and retrieved a highball glass, which looked a lot like cut crystal. He opened a knotty pine cabinet door under the sink to reveal a small refrigerator and retrieved a couple of ice cubes. He took a bottle down from the shelf and poured some amber fluid into my glass. He poured some into a glass that had been on the counter with the remnants of an earlier bourbon in it.

'It's some special bottling that Honey got me for my birthday.'

'Thanks.' I took the glass he held out to me. He raised his glass to me, and we drank without touching glasses.

'Bradley said you have a suspect?'

'I have a person of interest.'

'Isn't that the same thing?'

'It's similar, just with a whole lot less evidence.'

'OK, do tell.'

I went to my bag and took out my yellow legal pad with case notes on it. To Stevenson, it probably looked busy with its bits of red ink and blue. I liked to list people in red. Narratives about the investigation were written in blue ink.

'After we last spoke at the Harvard Club, I started by calling around on the Jungle Telegraph.' I decided to leave out the bit about going to the library and doing research into his life.

'You Green Berets do like to get together and gossip.'

'Most of the guys from Vietnam who I reached couldn't think of anyone who would want to do you harm. The consensus was that if it was an SOG man who wanted you dead, then letters and half-assed attempts wouldn't be how he'd go about it.'

'Tell that to the dog. He didn't think it was half-assed.'

'A couple of days ago one of my Army buddies called me back. He remembered running into a guy he knew up at the club in CCN. The guy stood out to him because he'd been drunk, ranting about you and how you should pay.'

'Well, a lot of you cowboys seemed to blame me for everything that went wrong over there.' I had to resist the urge to punch him in the nose.

'This guy wasn't an SOG guy. He was some type who had been up in Laos, presumably part of your three-ring circus. His name is Kovach, Arno Kovach, a Hungarian Lodge Act soldier. Ring any bells?'

He thought for a second. 'No, I don't think it does.'

'Kovach kept applying for permission to marry a Laotian girl. He kept getting turned down. Sound familiar?'

'Could be. I don't know. There were a lot of guys that wanted to marry local girls. It was frowned upon. That was a long time ago.'

'It could be a pretty good reason to have a grudge against you.'

'Sure, it could. He could be anywhere now.'

'He lives in Fairhaven . . . that's about an hour from your home. Easy drive up, pop a few shots at the French doors, wire your car, poison the dog. Zip back down to Fairhaven. Hang out in his grimy Fortress of Solitude, in between banging out new letters on the old typewriter.'

'Still, that doesn't connect him to me.'

'No, but the newspaper clipping of an interview taped to his refrigerator door might.'

'Oh.' That got his attention.

'Yes, he has a small arsenal in his apartment; seems to live on cigarettes and alcohol.'

'You two have something in common then.'

'I like the occasional meal. I spoke to him on the phone last night. He knew someone had been in his apartment and put two and two together while we spoke. He seems a little paranoid, weapons hidden in his apartment. Probably puts hairs across doors to see if anyone has tampered with his stuff. That type of guy.'

'He looks good for all this?'

'He fits the FBI profile they worked up. He looks good, but I am not sure that he is the only person who might have a grudge against you. It is also just a bit coincidental his name popping up.'

'You seem skeptical.'

'Not skeptical, just open-minded. You are a rich man, and powerful for a time when you were in the State Department. I am sure that you made some enemies along the way.'

'I am comfortable, it's not like I am a Rockefeller or own IBM or anything. I mean, I've ruffled a few feathers along the way, but I can't see anyone who would hold a grudge like this.' Stanhope was twenty years dead so there was no point in bringing him up.

'You can't think of anyone who is angry enough at you to do these things?'

'No, not even my ex-wife is that angry at me.' Maybe she had been happy to be rid of him, but I hadn't met an ex-wife yet who didn't have some animosity toward her ex.

'OK, so far Kovach is the only lead we have.'

'What are you going to do about him?'

'Well, a lot of that is up to you. I can try and contact him and see if he will talk to me. But I doubt he will talk to me or stick around if I show up. I could go there and try to warn him off.' If he would stay in one place long enough for me to talk to him.

'Warn him off?'

'Reason with him, try and make him see the value of leaving well enough alone.'

'Coerce him? Beat him up?'

'No, Mr Ambassador, talk to him. I will bend some rules, break some laws, but there are limits. Beating a guy up to warn him off . . . that isn't my style. If that is what you are looking for, I am sure your hired gun is more than capable.'

'Baz, I am sure he is. He was a mercenary in Africa and has seen some stuff.'

'I am sure he has.' I wasn't super interested in his hired gun's résumé. 'I can also go back to Fairhaven, put Kovach under surveillance, which won't be easy, but it isn't impossible. It also won't be cheap.'

'Why not?'

'Kovach lives down by the water in Fairhaven. He lives above a diner, surrounded by acres of parking lot. This time of year, mostly empty parking lot. Parking a car there for any length of time would attract attention, and there is no place to surveil it from unless I had a boat or could rent a house nearby. Also, there is something shady going on at the nearby boatyard.'

'Shady how?'

'Not sure, probably drug related. They are very security conscious, cameras everywhere, high fences. The day I was down there asking around about Kovach, they sent some muscle out to rough me up.'

'How'd it work out?'

'One guy in the hospital with a broken knee. One guy who decided that he was at the losing end of the knife versus gun dilemma that has plagued man for centuries. Story as old as the hills.'

Stevenson laughed. It was deep and booming and shook the

house. 'Ha-ha, you are a son of a bitch. I was right about hiring
you. You must have been some cowboy in Vietnam. I wish I
had you with me in Laos.'

'You would have wanted to fire me for being insubordinate.'

'Probably . . . probably.'

'Sir, I know you are writing your memoirs. I am assuming
you have notes or journals that you are working from?'

'Yes, I kept diaries, and there are numerous other documents
I hung on to. Why?'

'I was wondering if you might skim through for any mention
of Kovach. There couldn't have been that many Hungarian
guys there. He would have stood out, and it might clarify his
anger toward you.'

'I can check, but I can't think of anyone like that.'

'Maybe for you it was an inconsequential incident, but for
him it might have had more significance.'

'All right. I guess I can do that. Tell me more about this
Kovach.'

I picked up my yellow legal pad and began to fill him in on
what I had found out about him. I told him about his apartment, the books he had on his shelves, and the guns he had
tucked away. There wasn't too much to tell, but it took the
better part of a half-hour and all the bourbon in my glass. By
the time I was done, the sun was starting to dip. It wasn't
twilight yet, but up in the high hills of Vermont, it got darker
just a little sooner than in the low country of Boston.

'Roark, are you in a rush to get back to Boston?'

'Not particularly.'

'You're going to stay the night. Why not stay for a couple,
go through the journals with me, and we can see if there is
anything in them. It's pretty nice up here. We've got acres of
woods and plenty of hunting if you are interested. It's close
enough to the season, and the locals won't tell if you bag one
out of season.' Suddenly I was all right in his book, and all it
took was my hurting someone, or maybe he just liked the idea
of having another hired gun around.

'I can stay for an extra day or two to go through your notes
and diaries.' I didn't feel like explaining that while I had nothing
against hunting, it just wasn't something I was interested in

doing. I'd had a bellyful of that type of thing in Vietnam, but at least the NVA was trying to kill me. I was pretty sure that Bambi didn't have an AK-47.

'Good, good. You'll have to sleep on the couch here. We'll get you sorted out, but between Maureen, Bradley, my son and Baz, we've run out of guest rooms. But the couch is more comfortable than it looks, and the booze is cheap.'

'The best kind.'

'Good. Good. I will let the cook know to set an extra plate. We have an old German lady who comes in from the village to cook dinner. It isn't haute cuisine, but it is good food, as long as you aren't a vegetarian.'

'I've been accused of a lot of things but never that.' As long as there was bourbon, it wasn't too hard to match Stevenson's bonhomie. He was casting himself as a Hemingwayesque character, and it seemed like I was to be in on the act. Some fees were harder earned than others.

'Do you want another drink?'

'Please.' I excused myself to use the bathroom and followed Stevenson's directions to a door to the left of the massive fire-place. I assumed it wasn't the closet door under the staircase. I went through the door and found myself in a washroom with a washer, dryer and chest freezer. There was a door with two steps to the right, leading to a sort of root cellar where the house was built into the raw granite of the hill. It was chilly and sloped upward, so that at the far end even a toddler would have trouble standing upright. The door to my left proved to be the bathroom.

Instead of heading back to Stevenson, I decided to poke around. There were more Andersen windows, the place was lousy with them, and a wash sink. There was another half glass door and beyond that, an identical glass storm door to the one upstairs. Outside there was a grassy hill that sloped downward, and the grass seemed to flow into a gap in the wall of trees in front of me. They were only thirty feet or so from the house.

There was another door to my left, and I opened it to find a sort of work room, a small table, some tools, a daybed against one wall, a closet and bureau. There was a duffle bag and a faded Army field jacket. This was where Baz was sleeping. I guess the hired guns slept on the first floor. I wanted to toss his kit just to see what he had or what he was about, but there wasn't time.

Prudence being the word of the day, I would let it keep. I closed the door and doubled back around to where Stevenson was waiting for me with a bourbon on the rocks. He handed it to me. 'Thanks. Nice place you've got here. Feels like a Bavarian hunting lodge.'

'That isn't an accident. I bought the land so I would have a place to hunt when I was home in the States. I used to camp out and then I had a little hunting shack. You know the type of thing, two rooms and a wood stove, not much else. But then they built the interstate and the off-ramp you took would run smack through it. My first wife didn't like to hunt, but she liked to ski, and so I built this place so we could both enjoy it.'

'It seems like a nice place to get away.'

'It is. It is close to everything, skiing. Hanover, you know, where Dartmouth College is, is across the river and twenty minutes south, which means that there are bookstores in town that have a wider selection than in most towns up here. There's plenty of good hiking, camping and hunting. All in all, it is a pretty good mix of culture and outdoor activities. If you ever get sick of the rat race in Boston, you should consider moving up here.' There was no point in telling him that there probably wasn't much use for private investigators this far north where the trees outnumber the people.

'Sounds nice. Me, I'm lucky if I can get to the Irish Riviera.'

'Ireland is nice. Many great rivers for fly fishing.' It wasn't that he was oblivious, it wasn't even his fault. He had been raised with money, and the closest he had been to Wollaston Beach was when he had sailed by it on his yacht.

'I'm sure. Don't get the chance to do much fly fishing.'

'No? Well, you should try it. It's getting close to dinner; we should head upstairs.'

I followed him, drink in hand, up the stairs. At the top of the stairs, there was a woman in her sixties in the kitchen. She was busy moving pots and pans around the stove. The aromas of cooking meat and cabbage reminded me that I hadn't eaten since breakfast. We avoided the kitchen and went into the living room, which turned out to be an open floor plan with the dining room tucked in the corner of the house between the living room and the kitchen.

The living room had a fireplace tucked into the brick wall/ chimney. There was an old Zenith TV and a Persian carpet. The couch faced the TV, and in the corner next to the sliding glass doors were two bookshelves making a corner of books. Between them and the couch was a card table covered in papers and journals, clearly Stevenson's research materials.

The dining room was denoted by a heavy beam in the ceiling and highly polished hardwood floors instead of Persian carpets. The wall separating the kitchen was taken up by a china cabinet. There was a table of oak in the center of the room with matching chairs. On the opposing wall was a matching oak sideboard. There were more Andersen windows, and the whole effect was a comfortable living space that was light and airy.

I turned to look through the living-room windows. Outside the sun was going down, and the road out in front of the house had a few streetlights twinkling on. They were few and far between, splashing puddles of light for people driving down into the river valley. Across Stevenson's field, beyond the little fairy-tale house, was the road, and across that was another field with a barn in the distance, all of it surrounded by a wall of green trees. The sky above the trees in the distance was turning reddish pink, and the infrequent cars driving down the road switched on their lights.

I picked up a pair of inexpensive binoculars that were perched on the windowsill and peered out at the land in front of the house. There was still enough light to see the terrain but not in much detail. Stevenson's front yard, for lack of a better term, was about two hundred yards from the house to the road, maybe two-fifty. Directly in front, it was mostly flat, and the land around it angled downhill toward the river valley and what seemed like a wall of trees, the usual mix of hemlocks, birches and pines. Across the road, the land started sloping up and the tree line by the highway off-ramp came almost to the road in front of the house. Years ago, it had been cleared and angled away to make grazing land, leaving a space of almost a kilometer.

I unconsciously started to calculate where and how many helicopters I could bring in. Where the North Vietnamese Army would set up likely ambushes or conceal 37-millimeter anti-aircraft cannons. I mentally plotted where I would move a team to maximize cover and to best fight the NVA from. You could take the boy out of the war, but you couldn't . . . well, you know the rest.

'I did the same thing when I was building this place.'

'Excuse me?'

'I started thinking about things like beaten zones and fields of fire. Where I would land helicopters and all of that.'

'I thought you spent all of your time in Vientiane?'

'Oh, I got out to see the troops when I could. I needed to see what was happening with Vang Pao and the Air America types, floating around with their ad hoc air force. They were like something out of *Terry and the Pirates*.'

'It must have been something,' I said, trying to sound sincere.

'Vang Pao was a magnificent leader. If we had ten more of him, we would never have lost the war. His men were brave, so brave. Did you know that the NVA and Pathet Lao tried to bring tanks up on to the Plain of Jars and we stopped them cold? Yes, we did.' I don't know if having more men like Vang Pao would have made a difference, but he was a good leader who had fought his noble lost cause with tenacity and courage. His men had been tough and loyal and deserved better treatment by the government.

'He was, and he was lucky to have the Hmong as his troops.' The Hmong were tough people from the highlands, like the Montagnards I worked with.

The table was set with simple china with a green and white motif on a plain white tablecloth. There were a variety of serving dishes, with steam rising from them, arranged in the center of the table. Two bottles of white wine were open, and the table had everything except candles, but it wasn't that type of dinner. There were six chairs, and Stevenson took his at the head of the table facing the living room.

People began to make their way to the table. Honey was first, all legs, in cowboy boots, tight jeans and a cream-colored silk blouse. She stuck her hand out to me. 'Mr Roark, I'm glad that you decided to join us.' I wasn't sure if she meant for dinner or if I had somehow gone off and enlisted again.

'No worries. Glad to help.' I tried to sound noble and heroic. Women like Honey bring that sort of behavior out in me. She went to the seat opposite Stevenson. I ended up sitting to his immediate left, and somehow Maureen ended up next to me. Bradley sat across the table from me, and next to him was a man in his twenties who was quite literally a pale reflection of Stevenson. Apparently, Baz was walking around the house making sure we were safe, and he would eat in the kitchen when he was done with his appointed rounds.

The meal was excellent, tenderloin of pork that had been rubbed with mustard and spices then roasted. One of the steaming serving dishes held boiled new potatoes that had been tossed with butter, garlic and dill. The last steaming dish held red cabbage that had been sliced thin, with bits of apple mixed in, then braised in beer. The wine turned out to be a very dry white Rhine wine which complemented the pork and cabbage quite nicely.

The dinner conversation was mostly taken up by Stevenson holding court and regaling us with stories he planned to include in his memoirs. He had been so used to being the focus of attention for so long that he couldn't switch it off at the dinner table. I couldn't imagine that it made him easy to live with.

Honey ate in small bites and beamed at him. When she wasn't taking small bites of food and beaming, she took minute sips of wine. His son didn't say much of anything and ate his food mechanically. Bradley made supportive comments that fell just shy of kissing Stevenson's ambassadorial ass. Maureen and I managed to fit in a bit of quiet small talk when Stevenson wasn't asking me questions that were worded in such a way that made it clear he was looking to validate his point of view on matters.

By the time the apple cobbler was put on the table, after second glasses of wine had been had, I noticed that Maureen's elbow kept brushing up against mine. I became dimly aware of her hip and thigh close to my own. I wanted to believe that I could faintly smell perfume, something like honeysuckle. Maybe the trip to Vermont hadn't been such a bad idea after all.

TWELVE

After dinner Stevenson said, 'Let's go downstairs and have a snort.' Since he didn't seem like the type to do coke, I figured he meant a drink.

'Sure, why not.'

'Bradley, bring the mail down. Honey, Maureen, come on down for a drink.'

Maureen said she would, and Honey begged off. We trooped downstairs into the land of lightly stained knotty pine and mementos of Stevenson's glory. He flipped lights on as he went, and when he turned on the light in the bar, I realized that it was made from a bazooka round. Jesus, this guy took himself seriously.

'What does everyone want to drink? Roark, another bourbon? Maureen, bourbon or a beer?'

'Beer, please,' she said in her accented voice. Years of watching PBS had given me a slight bias toward women with English accents.

'Bourbon would be great,' I said. Stevenson set about getting us our drinks, and Bradley came downstairs with some mail in hand. Stevenson offered him a beer and Bradley accepted. He took out two St Pauli Girls and popped off the caps. I liked the lady on the label, but not so much that I splurged on it over Löwenbräu. When everyone had a drink and had taken seats, or in my case, leaned against the wall by the spear, Stevenson spoke. 'Bradley, show Mr Roark the letter.'

Bradley quickly riffled through the pile of correspondence he had with him and handed me an envelope that had already been opened. I put my drink down on the edge of the bookshelf and slid the letter out. It was like the others, typed and to the point. This variant said, 'You know what you've done. You took everything from me. You have to pay! Either with Treasure or Blood you will pay!'

'Short and to the point,' I said, for want of anything more clever.

'Yes, it looks like Mr Kovach is at it again,' Stevenson said.

'You have to stop him, Mr Roark.' Bradley seemed quite earnest in his worry for his boss.

'Exactly, Gordon, you need to take this seriously . . . this Kovach sounds dangerous. Pay him if you must.' This from Maureen.

'Pay him,' Stevenson spluttered out, 'pay him? Never. I won't give in to threats. This isn't something that can be bought and paid for.'

'Did you tell me that part of your job had been bribing your country's allies to stay allied with you? Didn't you deal with mercenaries and warlords? How is this any different?'

'Maureen does have a point, sir. If this can be resolved financially that might be best, save us potential embarrassment before your memoirs come out.'

'Roark, what do you think?' He pointed an index finger at me while the rest of his meaty hand was wrapped around his glass of bourbon.

'First, we don't know if it is Kovach. He looks good, but I haven't proven he is our letter writer.' And dog poisoner, window shooter, and would-be car blower-upper. 'Second, if it is Kovach, there is nothing to say that paying him off will make him stop. He might take the money and keep coming back to the well as many times as he wants.'

'Come on, man. It has to be Kovach. He is the most promising thing that you or the FBI have managed to come up with.'

'Like I said, Mr Ambassador, he looks good for it, but I am not one hundred percent certain he is our guy.' I didn't add, as much as I was tempted to, 'A prick like you has probably pissed off a lot of people.'

'Mr Roark, who else could it be?' Bradley asked in his earnest, Ivy League-accented voice.

'Bradley, I don't know. I do know that powerful men, like the Ambassador here, tend to make enemies. Kovach looks good. He may even have a grudge against the Ambassador, but that doesn't necessarily mean he is doing this stuff.'

'Well, you need to find out, and fast.' More earnestness.

'Yes, I do. Has there been anything else or any indication that he is escalating?'

'No, just this latest letter.'

'OK, tomorrow the Ambassador and I are going to go through his old journals and see if anyone else pops out. If nothing does, then I will go back to Boston and figure out a way to watch Kovach. Does all that sound reasonable?'

'What if he isn't at his apartment? What if he went to ground after your, frankly, amateurish attempts to date?' Bradley asked.

'Bradley, I am sure that you are a good lapdog,' I enjoyed the angry look on his face, 'but I am pretty sure your knowledge of investigating people begins and ends with you watching detective shows on TV.' Bradley started to fluster when Maureen chimed in.

'Oh, Andy . . . don't pick on Bradley. He's just concerned about the Ambassador. We all are . . . I think we are all worried that this Kovach could be out there somewhere, waiting to hurt Gordon.'

'Sir, maybe Roark is right, maybe Baz should handle this? He's tough and Roark . . . Roark clearly has his limitations.'

'That's fine by me. I can't say that I was very eager to take this case to begin with.'

'Roark, don't be silly . . . and Bradley, I will decide who I want doing what on my behalf. Is that clear?'

'Yes, sir.' The lapdog knew how close to the doghouse he was.

'I asked for Roark because he came highly recommended by Special Agent Watts. I also know for a fact that he is tough and resourceful because I know what he did in the war. He stays until he or I decide otherwise.' In a flash I had insight into what had made him the right man in Laos. I didn't like how he ran his war because of how it impacted mine, but he was a general through and through, just without the uniform and the stars. He then turned to me, 'That suit you?'

'Yes, it does.' I turned to Bradley, 'I want to make sure that Kovach is our man because if he isn't, I can waste a lot of time and resources, and if there is someone else out there who is a threat to the Ambassador, I will be that much further behind the curve. I understand that you want results and that everyone is worried about the Ambassador, but my job is to find the person threatening him, and I am pretty good at what I do.'

'OK, it's just . . . it's . . .' He was trying to find the right words.

'It's scary. It's scary when someone you care about, look up to, is in danger. It's scary to feel like there isn't much you can do, and it's frustrating too.'

'Yes, that's it.'

'Well, look at it this way. The boss has done a couple of smart things. One, he has hired Baz to protect him. Two, he is here, and this place is hard to approach without being noticed.' I was lying to him about that bit. On three sides the house had nice clear views where you could see anyone coming, and it was higher than most of the ground around it. The problem was that it was too close to the tree line on one side, and even someone who wasn't particularly skilled could get close without being seen. 'Last, he hired me to find the guy. The Ambassador is doing all the right things. It will work out.' I wasn't sure I believed it, but I said it with confidence.

'Well, you have my vote, but I'm a sucker for the tall, take-charge types.' This from Maureen, who was smiling at me with more than a bit of mischief. I was starting to wonder if she was having unprofessional thoughts too.

'Thank you, ma'am,' I said, smiling at her, doing my best imitation of John Wayne. It was only a lot worse than my Bogie imitation.

'Roark, stop flirting with my ghostwriter long enough to have another bourbon.' I wasn't keen to stop, but a bourbon would cushion the blow a little. It was, after all, pretty good bourbon, and flirting was hard enough under normal circumstances.

Stevenson held court and we were to be his audience. It was his dime and his bourbon, so when Bradley politely excused himself, I managed a seat on the couch next to Maureen. As the stories wore on and more liquor was poured out, we went from having a polite six inches of air between us to sitting quite comfortably together. She was warm and felt nice leaning against me. I could smell honeysuckle and made a mental note to thank Watts for talking me into the job.

Gordon Junior came in at some point and sat listening, like the rest of us, to his father regaling us with tales of his greatness. Baz came in to report that the cook had left for the night and that the house was secure. He looked over at me on the couch and I threw him a mock salute. I thought he'd pull a sour face, but instead he smiled and returned it with equal comic flair. Maybe he just liked me better after I'd had a few bourbons. Most people do.

Honey came downstairs in sweatpants and an old Rolling Stones t-shirt. She had a stack of sheets with an old Army wool blanket and a pillow in her hands. She put them down on the couch on the side of me that I wasn't trying to press into the cute redhead with the English accent.

'Mr Roark, I assumed that Gordon wasn't going to remember that you might need bedding,' then she smiled, looking at Maureen and me, 'or maybe you've already made arrangements for bedding?'

'No, he definitely needs those,' Maureen said, blushing, wriggling away from me on the couch and then she was standing. Damn! 'I think this is my cue to go turn in for the night. Goodnight.' With that, Maureen was away and up the stairs, tennis shoes slapping on the wooden steps.

'Oh, Mr Roark . . . I'm sorry. Did I ruin your plans?' I had been done ugly, but there was nothing to be done about it.

'No worries, Mrs Stevenson. You might as well call me Andy.'

'Honey,' she said in reply. 'Now it is time to take the Ambassador to bed. C'mon you, you have a big day tomorrow.'

'Goodnight, Roark,' he said as he got up. 'I have found there is no sense arguing with her. She gets what she wants by hook or by crook.'

'Goodnight.'

They went upstairs, and I made a bed of sorts on the couch. It wasn't much, but I had slept on worse. I helped myself to more of Stevenson's whiskey, took the .38 out of my waistband, and slipped it under the pillow. I dug my book out and read for a while before drifting off to sleep with the faint scent of honeysuckle tickling my nose.

I slept fitfully, the way you do in a strange place with strange sounds, sleeping just below the surface, floating up now and again. Baz seemed to wake up at intervals to check the house. The first time I woke up fully, the .38 was in my hand but held low. He saw me and said, 'Sorry, mate . . . rounds.' I listened to his footsteps as he went upstairs and then moved around the floor above. There was a faint moon out, and I got up and looked out the windows toward the garage and trees. No cars or people were moving around. It was too late or too early for the deer, who tend to move around near dusk and dawn. I went and lay back down, the revolver a comforting lump of metal under my pillow.

I woke up early. The world outside the windows was misty and grey. My mouth was dry, and my head felt like I'd had one bourbon too many after one bourbon too many. I could hear Baz snoring away on the other side of the door. I couldn't blame him. Waking up to check the perimeter means that you only ever get broken-up sleep.

I pulled on my jeans and t-shirt and slipped the gun back in its holster. I padded upstairs, enjoying the house while it was quiet and still. Upstairs, with a chance to look out the windows, I could appreciate the architect's vision. The idea of putting the main living space on the second floor was brilliant. The windows combined with the height to offer a spectacular view of the front lawn – front field, more accurately – and the rolling land beyond the road. To the south the tree line was just emerging from the mist on Stevenson's patch, and there wasn't much to be seen on the other side of the road as everything on that side had been swallowed by the mist. Occasionally a car's headlights would slowly lead the way down toward the river valley or up away from it, the good men and women of central Vermont on their way to work or school.

I made my way past the dining table and into the kitchen. I took a glass from the dishrack and filled it with some cold tap water. The kitchen was darker than the other rooms, being basically a box with doors at opposite ends and just a pair of windows over the sink, facing north.

I rummaged around in the cabinets until I found a percolator and some coffee in a blue can. I poured water into the bottom of the percolator, put the basket in, and filled it with ground coffee. I put the cover on the basket and the lid on the percolator and it all went on a burner. I wasn't sure I was able to wait for the cook.

I went back downstairs and dug my shaving kit out of my bag. I at least wanted to brush my teeth and splash some cold water on my face to help me wake up. I toweled my face off and was back in the kitchen a minute or two before the percolator started to percolate. Maureen walked in from the door that led to the hallway and the bedrooms beyond it. She was wearing flannel pajama bottoms and a Brown University t-shirt. I didn't think much of Brown, but I might have been distracted by the fact that Maureen wasn't wearing a bra.

'I thought I smelled coffee. Good.'

'I wasn't sure what the protocol was, and I wanted a cup of coffee.'

'A little too much bourbon last night?'

'The Ambassador has a heavy pour.'

'You don't look like the type to complain about something like that.'

'No, I don't suppose I am.'

'How did you end up a private investigator?'

'I was in the Army, went to Vietnam. I came home and tried the cops for a while but that didn't take. I wasn't the type to end up working in an office and I needed a job, so I got my license and here I am. How about you? How did you end up as a writer?'

'Oh, I lived on a farm, and when I got older my parents sent me to boarding school. I spent holidays and summers on the farm. I loved it. Then came time for university, and I found out very quickly that I was not smart enough to be a veterinarian, but I liked writing. I was able to find work as long as I wasn't trying to make money. I built up a reasonable résumé and a friend told me about the Ambassador wanting to write his memoirs. He arranged it, and here I am.'

'Not a bad gig.'

'No, it isn't, but the company can be a little bit dull.'

'Present company excluded, I hope?' I wasn't one to let such an opportunity pass by.

'Present company excluded.' She laughed. 'It's just that we have all been spending so much time together, and we've all grown so used to each other. So familiar.' I was about to make the obvious clichéd comment about what familiarity breeds, but we were interrupted by the Ambassador.

'Morning, Roark, is that coffee I smell?'

'Yes, sir. I wasn't sure what the protocol was, so I put a pot on.'

'Well, Frieda will be here in a little while. I wouldn't own up to messing around in her kitchen without her permission. I may own the house, but it is her kitchen.'

'Gotcha.'

'No, you don't want to run afoul of Frieda in her kingdom,' Maureen said, laughing a little. The percolator started making its tell-tale burbling noises. I started to look around the kitchen for mugs. Stevenson pointed to a cabinet, and I handed him one, another to Maureen, and I took one for myself. I poured them each a cup. They both thanked me. She added cream and sugar to hers. He just added cream. I took a sip of mine. It was hot and it resembled coffee.

There was a knock on the front door; it was the elderly woman, Frieda, who cooked dinner the night before. It was a courtesy knock at best, because she used her own key to unlock it. She let herself in, then closed and locked the door behind her. She took off her coat and hung it up in the closet by the door. She walked down the short hall and stopped in the kitchen, looking at us.

'Good morning, Herr Ambassador. Oh, I see you have made your coffee already.' Everything after the greeting dripped with not-too-subtle disapproval. 'I wish you had waited for me. I have a system.'

'Good morning, Frieda. I am afraid that Mr Roark couldn't wait and took the initiative.'

What a rat, I thought.

'Don't hold it against him,' the Ambassador went on. 'He learned such behavior in the Army, I'm sure.'

'Oh, I see.' She rounded to me. 'Mr Roark. I am Frieda, the cook.' She wasn't so much describing her job as making sure that I knew both of our positions in the house. 'I will see to the kitchen. If you are by nature an early riser, I will make sure you have coffee waiting for you.' She didn't end it with 'understood?' and I resisted the urge to click my heels and say '*Jawohl*, Frau Frieda!' like they do in the war movies. Instead, I smiled at her and said, 'Oh, I don't want to be any trouble.'

'Humpf.' She turned to Maureen and said, pointedly looking at her chest, 'Aren't you cold, miss? Perhaps you would like a sweater?'

Maureen smiled sweetly and said, 'No, I am fine, thank you.'

'As you like, miss. If you don't mind, I would like to start breakfast.' We all took the hint and left the kitchen. Stevenson took his coffee and went off to shave or something like that, while Maureen and I made our way into the living room.

'Do you like it?' she asked.

'The coffee? No, it's wretched.'

'No, being a private investigator. They are all over the TV right now, like—' I cut her off before she could say Magnum PI.

'I do. At first, I was doing it half-heartedly and then I began to enjoy it.'

'What do you like about it?'

'I don't have a boss. I don't have to take the cases I don't want, unless I am short of funds. Sometimes the work is interesting and sometimes it is boring.'

'Which is this case?'

'Mostly boring, to be honest. Today, my big investigative effort will be to go through his journals with the Ambassador. Does that strike you as exciting?'

'No, I guess not. Are you any good at it?'

'Going through journals?'

'No, investigating.'

'No, not very,' I said, laughing. It was too early in the morning to take myself seriously. After all, I had just made a mortal enemy of Frieda the cook.

'Oh,' she said awkwardly, 'that's, um, refreshing.'

'I am probably stubborn more than talented,' I said truthfully.

'At least you're honest.'

'I am that. Listen, have you come across anything while working with him that might point to someone with a grudge?'

She thought for a moment then answered slowly. 'He isn't

always the easiest man to work with and I am sure he has angered some people along the way. But enough to want him dead? No, I don't think so.'

Outside the windows, the mist wasn't so much burning off as receding into the tree line a foot at a time. Off in the distance I saw a speck of brown and then another. Deer. They were eating and stopped. Their tails went up and they scampered back into the woods. Then a car appeared on the road to the south, moving slowly down the hill. It all played out like a silent movie in front of me.

'I think I will take a quick shower before breakfast.' She walked away before I could say anything witty. I went into the kitchen and, dodging Frieda who was studiously poaching eggs, I topped up my coffee. I went downstairs and put on my sneakers, took out my pack of Luckies and my lighter. I was pretty sure that Frieda was not OK with an interloper like me smoking in the house. I pulled on my sweater and took the cup of coffee upstairs.

I unlocked the front door and stepped out on to the veranda. It was damp and chilly, the way Vermont in October is, hinting at the snow and cold of winter to come. I liked Vermont – the air was clean and the land dramatic – but I wasn't sure I would love it up here in the middle of February. I put a Lucky between my lips, lit it with my Zippo and inhaled, enjoying the first smoke of the day.

I walked over the veranda and down the steps. There was a ten-year-old green Plymouth Duster in front of the blue Mustang, which was in front of the Maverick. I walked south away from the house and then turned to the left, downhill. There was a small log cabin – more of a shed – tucked into the trees a few yards in front of me. Off to my left was more lawn, and a wide path leading into the forest. Out of habit I went over to the log cabin/shed and opened the door. Inside the shed was a lawn mower, rakes, a scythe, and other lawn implements and tools.

I closed the door and turned to the path into the woods. As I walked, I looked over at the granite cliff that was part of the hill the house was built into. I was fifteen or twenty feet below the top of it and the house seemed even higher. The ground sloped up to the granite but then it turned into a vertical wall. I could see why Stevenson thought this was good defensive terrain.

I followed the path north, down into the woods, realizing that it was a logging trail. The trees here were thirty or forty feet high. The granite hill rose on my left, and while the road was level the terrain to my right sloped downward. I kept on the road, and ten yards further down the tree cover began to block the sky. Each step further into the woods, they grew darker and cooler.

With the receding mist and darkness, it reminded me of Vietnam. It was always dark under the triple canopy jungle, and often the mornings were misty and relatively cool. While it would be difficult to mistake the pine-needle- and moss-strewn forest of central Vermont for the Central Highlands or any other part of Vietnam or Laos, for a brief second, I did. It wasn't a fully developed memory or a vivid nightmare, just enough similarity and overlap to put me in two times and places at once.

I was walking down the trail in Vermont, slowly and quietly, as is my habit in woods. I wasn't on the Ho Chi Minh Trail, where I would have moved glacially and silently. There, stealth was our best defense, and that was achieved by moving very slowly, sometimes moving only hundreds of meters in a day.

Here and now, I just didn't want to disturb the quiet peacefulness of the woods. I wanted to slow down and listen. Somewhere, a mourning dove called out to its mate. Everything in the forest was preparing for the fall. Down on the sloping ground to my right, I saw a deer, its fawn-colored coat glistening with dew as it ate from a bush.

We had been moving down the jungle one time. We could hear the NVA trail-watchers signaling to each other with rifles and looking for our tracks. I was trying to erase marks of our passing, bending twigs back that we had brushed against or fluffing up tufts of grass. I put out a couple of toe popper mines, as much to warn us if the NVA was getting closer as to slow them down.

I turned and started to follow my teammates. I had gotten ten meters when I heard them go off behind me. I pivoted, my CAR-15 sweeping, pointing everywhere I was looking. I could slow down the NVA so the team could make a little distance. I couldn't hear anyone moving but I could hear ragged, gasping breaths. I waited. Still no movement.

I started back up my trail to see if the NVA might have some documents or if he could be taken as a prisoner. I moved slowly, ready to shoot. As I got closer, I saw him. It was a deer, a buck. They were different from the ones back home; smaller, and they made an odd barking noise.

This one was the unluckiest in country filled with nothing but unlucky creatures. Somehow, he had stepped on a toe popper and fallen on his side on to the other. His foreleg was gone and his stomach had been blown open, ruptured by a mine designed to maim humans. His stomach was the part that caught my attention. Ruptured and steaming, intestines splashed about. There were two distinct piles of partially eaten vegetation steaming on the ground where they lay.

I should have shot him or at least used my knife. As much as I felt it my fault, and as much as I wanted to put him out of his misery, I couldn't. When the NVA got here they might think he had been blown up by some old munitions. The country was awash with them. But a bullet or knife wound would confirm we had been there. 'I'm sorry. You deserved a better death, certainly better than this,' I whispered to him, all too aware of my part in his end. I turned and started back down the trail to my team.

Back in Vermont, the deer turned, blissfully unaware of me or my history with his Asian cousins, and moved off deeper into the woods. I kept walking north down the pine-needle-strewn trail another hundred yards or so and the ground slanted down even more. There was a secondary trail to my immediate left which seemed to go east around the base of the granite hill that the house was built into. This trail should take me back to the house. The other trail would take me deeper into the woods.

My coffee cup was empty, and my cigarette had been out for a good five minutes or so. I opted to head back to the house and see what Frieda had made for breakfast. I turned left, following the secondary trail as it sloped gently upwards. In thirty or forty meters, it opened into the small clearing that was behind the house. The angle of the hill was more pronounced on the back side of the house. I walked around the house to the front, passing by some large pines between the house and the garage.

I walked around to the front of the house, passing the parked cars by the driveway. I walked up the hill and then up the steps and went to the edge of the patio, the side facing the valley. Between the house and the tree line was the backyard, a grassy hill that sloped steeply down to the woods and the road beyond that.

I went inside and was treated to the smell of bacon cooking and coffee brewing. I grinned to myself as I pictured Frieda pouring my offensive attempts to percolate down the drain. I walked into the living room to find Honey and Stevenson already at the table.

'Roark, come have something to eat. Breakfast is a pretty informal affair here.' Stevenson was in gregarious host mode.

'Yes, Mr Roark, do.' Honey was the soul of politeness.

'Sounds great.'

As with dinner the night before, there were serving dishes in the middle of the table. One held eggs that were scrambled with green peppers, onions, and cubes of Virginia ham. Another held breakfast potatoes that had been uniformly cubed as only an elderly German lady could. They were brown and I would bet a little crunchy but soft inside. There was a plate with bacon laid out on it. It was cooked perfectly, with a little life left in it and some fat at the ends. The Army had convinced me that it was OK to eat bacon cooked to the point of fossilization. It had taken me years to readjust.

There was a plate with toasted English muffins, pre-buttered. However, in the Stevenson house you could pick from a variety of jams and jellies in fancy jars and labels. Every one was French or English, no Smucker's grape jelly here. Both tea and coffee could be had from either the teapot or the electric coffee pot on the table.

I picked up a plate, covered it with food, and then filled my coffee cup.

'Mr Roark, how was your walk?'

'Very pleasant. I was enjoying your woods. I saw a deer.'

'Yes, do be careful. It will be hunting season soon, and you shouldn't go out in the woods without something orange on to let the hunters know you aren't a deer. Some of the locals like to take them out of season,' Honey said.

'Ha. Honey, I bet Roark would be fine. Hell, the best soldiers in the North Vietnamese Army couldn't kill him when they were hunting him. I think he'd be fine with a couple of local yokels in the woods.' I didn't feel like pointing out to Stevenson that the NVA had managed to shoot me, just not kill me.

'Thanks. I don't want to get shot.'

'Again?' Honey added unnecessarily.

'Well, I can't say that it is a pleasant experience. Plus, I bruise easily.'

'Hahaha, see that, Honey. What a tough guy. He even jokes about being shot.'

'Well, it is better to laugh than cry,' I said.

'You've been shot before?' Maureen had appeared in the living room from around the big brick chimney/wall.

'One of the hazards of being in the Army, I guess.'

'That's right. Vietnam?'

'Yes, I was too young for the other wars, even the Dominican Republic thing.'

'Is that what happened to your ear?'

'Similar people, wrong war.'

'Communists?'

'No, Vietnamese gangsters, here in America, several months ago.' It had been long enough ago that my earlobe only itched occasionally.

'Oh, I thought you said you weren't a very good detective?'

'If I had been a better detective, I wouldn't have been in the situation to begin with.'

'Did you at least get the girl?' Maureen asked.

'No, and I lost my car too.' It had been a rough month.

Bradley and Gordon Junior walked in, said their 'good mornings', filled plates and sat down. Maureen turned to Bradley and said, 'Mr Roark was just telling us that he isn't a very good detective.'

'Oh, I hope that isn't the case.' Bradley looked queasy.

'Unfortunately, it was. I really liked that car too.'

'I meant the part about your being a poor detective.'

'Only my finances . . . the rest of me is A-OK.'

'Mr Roark, can I ask you a question?' This from Gordon Junior.

'Sure.'

'How did you end up in Vietnam? I mean were you, like, drafted and had to go or . . .'

'I grew up in South Boston, Southie. I screwed off and got kicked out of university. I didn't want to go back home to Southie or a dead-end job in a mill. The Army offered me a way to avoid that, so I enlisted and eventually ended up in the pearl of the Orient.'

'You enlisted knowing you'd go to Vietnam?' he asked incredulously.

'Yes.' I didn't blame him. Everyone who went to college from the late sixties on had been taught to believe that the war was wrong, and the government was wrong, and that those of us who volunteered were wrong too.

'Did you kill anyone?' It seemed a question more suited to a ten-year-old than a man in his late twenties.

'Gordon!' Honey exclaimed. I guess that wasn't her idea of polite breakfast conversation.

'Yes, I did.' It wasn't something I was particularly proud of, nor was I guilt-ridden about it. It had been part of the game. It didn't matter if it was with a gun or a radio calling in air strikes, dead was dead, and I had killed.

'But the war was wrong. It was immoral,' he said indignantly.

'Never had the time to really think about it. We were too busy trying to stay alive in our little section of it.'

'Roark, don't hold it against the boy. They get indoctrinated in the schools these days. It isn't his fault he went to Dartmouth.'

'I should go shower.' I stood up. There was no point arguing with the boy. There was no way to explain it to him. He didn't have the context to understand anything more about it other than what he had been taught. There was no explaining that very quickly war becomes about your team, your brothers, and not much else. I picked up my plate and cup and went into the kitchen. Frieda was sitting at the plain oak kitchen table with Baz, who was eating breakfast.

'You were in Nam, mate?'

'Yes.'

'Me too. I was in the 25th.'

'Funny, I didn't take you for an American, much less a veteran.'

'I am, well, sort of. My mum was Rhodesian, my dad American. I lived in Rhodesia until I was thirteen then I moved to California.'

'When were you there?'

'Sixty-nine and seventy. Then I went home and joined up with the Rhodesian Light Infantry. Now that was some shit. You thought fighting the communists was bad . . . nothing like Rhodesia. Fought at home until there wasn't a home to fight for anymore. Then moved back to the US and realized I could make money being a bodyguard. You?'

'I was there in sixty-nine, in the northern part of the country. Went home, was a cop for a while and decided that I didn't like taking orders anymore. That is how I ended up here.' I was leaving a lot out, but I wasn't in the mood to swap war stories with Baz. After Gordon Junior's comments and Gordon Senior's big, loud show of bonhomie, I needed a little break from everyone else's opinion about the war.

'Yeah, we can swap notes sometime,' I said with absolutely no conviction.

I walked out of the kitchen and then down the stairs into the land of knotty pine and Stevenson's memorial to his career. I took my .38 out of my waist and put it behind a copy of Bernard Fall's outstanding *Street Without Joy* on the bookshelf in the bar. Then I took my shaving kit and clean clothes to the shower.

The bathroom was small, and the tile-covered shower was dark and mildly claustrophobic. The water was hot, and I washed, trying as much to clean myself as rub away the mild annoyance that the morning had offered me already. I was about to turn the water off when Maureen pulled the shower curtain back. She put a hand on my chest and pushed me back into the shower.

'You missed a spot,' she said teasingly.

'Where is that?'

'Let me show you.' And she did. She showed me one or two more while she was at it. I kissed her deeply and ran my hands over her body. The shower was a tight fit, but we managed to make it work, and there were advantages to being with a woman who was only a few inches shorter than I was. Several minutes later, she had finished showing me the spots I had missed, the water was going from hot to tepid, and we got out.

Fortunately, our breathing was no longer the ragged breathing of sprinters. I enjoyed watching her as she toweled off. She wasn't a slim woman, but she had curves and wore them well. She looked as though she had spent time riding horses around the farm. I dried myself off, aware of her watching me too.

'That was nice,' she said, smiling.

'I am glad to hear it. I would say the day is off to a good start.'

'You're staring.'

'I'd be a fool not to.'

'I'll blush.'

'It's a bit late for that, don't you think? And you are staring too.'

'I am. I am sorry. Are those bullet wounds?'

'The scars? A couple. Some are from shrapnel.' There was a pretty gnarly one from a piece of white phosphorus that one of my Yards had to dig out with the tip of his knife.

'You seem to have been wounded a lot?'

'Well, most of it is from Vietnam.'

'God. Why? It can't be worth it, the war, the cops, this?' she said, looking up at me from an odd angle while she dried her red hair with a towel.

'I don't know. I have never thought about it. It is just what I did, what I do.'

'Well, I am glad that I write books. I don't think I could do what you do.'

'It isn't for everybody,' I said lightly, hoping to turn it into a joke.

We dressed and she slipped out after giving me a light kiss on the lips.

I wanted a cigarette, but it was a bit of a cliché, and I wasn't in the mood for that. I also wanted a nap, but that wasn't in the cards either. I quickly folded up my bedding and put it in a neat stack on the end of the couch. After I put on my sneakers and retrieved my .38, I went back upstairs to find Stevenson and start going through his journals. As I passed by the kitchen, I heard Frieda complaining in German about the lack of hot water for her to wash the dishes. The little grandmotherly lady used language that would have made a sailor blush.

Stevenson was sitting at the dining-room table with the coffeepot and stacks of old journals piled around him like he was in some sandbagged defensive position. In many ways he was, given that Kovach or somebody was out there sending threatening notes and making half-hearted attempts to kill him.

'Roark, pull up a chair. Grab an ashtray, you look like you could use a smoke.'

'I don't want to run afoul of Frieda.'

'Nonsense, just crack a window.' I did as I was told. I took a fresh cup and filled it with coffee from the pot and settled in with Stevenson to go through his journals.

It felt strange, sitting down to read the intimate thoughts of a man who was a part of history and who had played such a significant role in my part of the war. It was mildly uncomfortable and felt a little bit voyeuristic.

'Where do you want to begin?' he asked me.

'How far back do these go?'

'College, but those are mostly sentimental and philosophical musings and observations.'

'After that?'

'The war and the OSS.'

'Seems like a good place to make an enemy. Let's start with those.'

THIRTEEN

I t took us two days to go through his journals. The first day was boring and, except for Bradley and Frieda, we didn't see anyone. That night at dinner it was just Honey, Bradley, Stevenson and me. I had no complaints because the excellent roast duck was stuffed with apples and buckwheat was not something I wanted to share with anyone I didn't have to. Stevenson had again managed to pair it with an excellent bottle, this time of red wine. Thankfully Honey only had a half-glass, leaving all the more for us.

Later the Ambassador and I adjourned to the lower floor, and I listened to his stories about Washington and his various postings. The stories had the feel of often-repeated cocktail party fare. They were interesting enough, but not as interesting as his journal entries about his time in the war.

His early months in the Navy, when he described going through his initial training, were not unlike the college journal entries we went through the day before. But it was fascinating to hear about his time on destroyers, and it reaffirmed my belief that I was not cut out for the Navy or life aboard ship. I did all right on the ferry to Nantucket, but that was as much time as I wanted to spend at sea.

There wasn't much of interest between his time on the ship and when he ended up in the OSS. Stevenson's ability to speak French made him quite valuable to the OSS. He was sent to work with a small team operating in and around French Indochina, which was occupied by the Japanese. His time in the OSS was fascinating, as he had been in Indochina twenty-five years before I got there. He had worked with the communists at times, fighting the Japanese. Those stories were the stuff of adventure novels. Stevenson had acquitted himself well and, by war's end, was a lieutenant commander with a chest full of medals.

We drank too much bourbon. Stevenson was the type who

liked having an audience and that led him to have a heavy pour. I went to bed wondering what type of shape I would be in in the morning. Waking feeling better than I had any right to. Breakfast was the same every morning and after a post-breakfast cigarette we would set to work.

It was interesting seeing his take on events that had turned up in my research at the Boston Public Library. Then there were things that hadn't made it into the BPL research, like a trip to Africa to hunt big game with a friend from the OSS. It was right out of Hemingway but not as well written.

From Africa, it was off to Canada and his days prospecting for uranium. His journals made mention of the fact that Stanhope was a drunk but a decent enough pilot when he was sober. His description of their big find and his sale of it was oddly lacking in detail.

That was quickly overshadowed by his courtship and marriage to his first wife. He was married and in the State Department. He was investing wisely with the help of his brother-in-law, and Gordon Junior was born. Then he was posted to Asia. He was leaving the Philippines for his role as head of mission in Laos by the time we decided to break for lunch.

Lunch was a simple affair. Frieda brought us a basket of bread and a plate piled with slices of fancy Serrano ham from Spain. There were slices of cheese on the plate too, and a small pot of mustard. Stevenson opted for sweetened iced tea, and I just had a glass of water. We made small open-faced sandwiches; the Serrano ham was unlike anything I had ever tasted. I knew I would never be able to afford it on my earnings.

'Is anyone leaping out at you?' he asked me.

'The only person, other than your ex-wife, would be Stanhope.'

'Stanhope?'

'There is an argument to be made that he might view your good fortune with some jealousy.'

'Sure, sure . . . he might. But he has been dead for years now.'

'I know. That is why I ruled him out. What happened there?'

'You mean, did I cheat my friend?'

'Yes, exactly.'

'Stanhope was a drunk, not a bad man, but he drank his money away. The business wasn't going well, and he was worried about it going under. I found out that one of our claims was the big one. He was trying to sell it for pennies to keep his plane up in the air.'

'What did you do?'

'Oh, I gave him a bottle of rye, and several drinks later he signed everything over to me. It wasn't a nice thing to do, but it was better than having him sell our claim for pennies.'

'What happened?'

'I skipped out and sold the claim to a big Canadian mining concern. I wired Stanhope a few hundred dollars so he could join me in the States. He sent me a telegram that told me where to go. I met my first wife and sometime later I heard or read that he died in a crash. I wish it had worked out better. If he were alive, he would make the perfect suspect for all of this.'

'Not very convenient of him,' I said dryly.

'No, but your Kovach looks good too.' I didn't bother to point out that Arno Kovach wasn't mine.

'He does,' I said reluctantly.

'But you have doubts?'

'Yes, but I am not entirely sure why. Maybe motive.'

'Motive?'

'Whoever is doing this is going to a lot of effort to get under your skin. Whoever it is has a grudge, but you don't remember Kovach.'

'You think that if it is him, did I do something so bad to him that I should remember it?'

'Maybe, you were responsible for a lot of people. Did you have a policy about GIs marrying local girls?'

'It was heavily discouraged. If they were attached to the embassy, or USAID, which in reality most Americans were, then it was up to me. If they were with the Company, then that was up to their chain of command to deal with. But if I had anything to say about it, the answer was no.'

'Did it come up a lot?'

'Not often. Most of the people we ended up with were older, more mature. Once in a while you might get an Air America guy, usually a sheep-dipped Air Force type who might fall in love. But it wasn't very common.'

'OK, well, do you remember any Lodge Act guys in your outfit? Kovach is Hungarian, with an accent.'

'Sure, we had some, but the ones that stand out really stand out. I know them, I know their names. I don't remember anyone named Kovach. He might have been there. We were fighting our own war. He might have been at a camp somewhere or with Vang Pao's people.'

'So, it's possible he was there, and not inconceivable that he wanted to marry a local girl and you kiboshed it?'

'Sure. That is possible.'

'OK, makes sense. Let's do our due diligence and see what there is to see in your journals.'

'Then what?'

'I will head back down to Boston. Figure out a way to watch his place and have a conversation with him.'

'What will you say?'

'I'll try and reason with him or get him to incriminate himself.'

'And if that doesn't work?'

'I'll come up with something.' I wasn't sure what that would be, and I was pretty sure that there was a lot of stuff I wouldn't do.

'Well, we have a plan of sorts.' He didn't sound very confident, but I have that effect on my clients. The only thing that had been missing from the lunch was good beer to go with it. All the case was missing was a better suspect.

We went back to the journals and notes and began working through his time in Laos. His youthful enthusiasm and Pollyannaish worldview had given way to realpolitik, and it made for dry, if pragmatic reading.

Stevenson had been in Laos right up to the end. After that, he had bumped around to different ambassadorships. Somewhere along the way he ran afoul of the head office in Washington, and that led to his retirement. If he screwed over anyone along the way who would bear a grudge, it certainly wasn't recorded in his journals. Somewhere along the way he had ceased recording his true feelings, and had begun writing for posterity's sake instead.

We knocked off in the late afternoon as the sun was easing its way down. I could hear Frieda banging about in the kitchen and muttering in German. I stood up and stretched and then said to Stevenson, 'I could use some fresh air.' I nodded my head toward the veranda.

I let myself out. I pulled a Lucky from the pack and, by the time I had it lit with the Zippo, cupping my hand to shield the flame, Stevenson had joined me. He had pulled on an old, OD green Army wool shirt. Not a bad idea as it was chilly out, and it felt like there would be a frost. We walked down the steps and on to the lawn.

The large pine in the front yard was throwing a long shadow.

'Sir, I wanted to just talk to you away from the house for a minute.'

'Why?'

'Well, sir, I have to ask you some questions that might be uncomfortable, and I felt you might answer me more freely if we had a little privacy.'

'You mean, I might talk if I wasn't around my family and the people who work for me?'

'Exactly.'

'I don't have anything to say to you that I can't . . .'

'Sir, you and I both know that isn't true. You've been around, you've amassed a small fortune, you've done your country's bidding . . . Somewhere along the way you made an enemy. Maybe it's Kovach, maybe it isn't.'

'OK, Roark, I get it. Ask your questions.'

'OK, other than Stanhope, did you have similar business dealings with anyone?' I phrased the question carefully; I didn't want to accuse him of anything or he wouldn't talk.

'You mean did I fuck anyone else over?'

'Exactly.'

'No. My former brother-in-law provided me with information about the aerospace industry, but we both made a pile of money on that. His sister cleaned up nicely in the divorce settlement, and was happy to see the last of me.'

'Were you faithful to her?'

'No, but she wasn't particularly faithful to me either. Infidelity is a rite of passage among people from our set.' He meant the

boarding school to Ivy League to CEO set. I didn't bother to
tell him that there was plenty of it among the more modest
classes too. It helped pay my rent.

'Any jealous husbands out there?'

'No, once I met Honey, I hung up my spurs, so to speak.
Anyone who felt wronged by me . . . well, the statute of limitations has long run out.'

'Anyone out there who might have figured out that they've
been raising a kid they thought was theirs but in reality is
yours?'

'Crude. But no. As far as I know, Gordy is my only child.'

'Anyone from the State Department days?'

'No. I don't fish off the company dock. The ladies in
the typing pool were off-limits and so were the wives and
daughters.'

'Anyone you might have competed with professionally?'

'You mean, fucked over to get ahead?'

'Yes.'

'No, I made it the old-fashioned way – family connections,
a little money, and some talent. And if there was anyone I
fucked over, that was decades ago. I think they would have
tried something long ago.'

'Other than Kovach, is there anyone or anything from your
time in Laos?'

'You mean, besides all you SOG cowboys? No.' I ignored
the dig. He was irritated, which was understandable given the
questions I was asking him. I had yet to meet anyone who
didn't get irritated when I questioned them about the parts
of their lives that they had glossed over so they could believe
they were the best versions of themselves.

'OK. Let me ask you this . . . how well do you trust
the people around you?'

'You mean like Bradley or Baz?'

'Sure, isn't it always the butler who did it?'

'I don't have a butler. I just have Frieda, and the only grudge
she would have is when I mess about in her kitchen.'

'Bradley?'

'He and Gordon went to Dartmouth together. They were
friends. He, frankly, always seemed more interested in my work

than Gordon ever has. Gordon wants to be a filmmaker. I wanted him to be a lawyer, or a diplomat.'

'What about Baz?'

'He's a mercenary, pure and simple. I needed a bodyguard, and he had the right résumé. Vietnam, Rhodesia, and a couple other hot spots in Africa. If there is to be shooting, I want it done by someone who is good at it.'

'OK, what about Maureen?'

'I needed a ghostwriter and Bradley found her. Just like he found me Baz, that's what Bradley does.'

'OK, and you trust them?'

'Yes, I do. In their own ways, they are both mercenaries, working for me. If something happens to me, they won't get paid.'

'What about the current Mrs Stevenson?'

'Honey?' He laughed. 'I doubt it. She definitely married down. Her family is worth a lot more than I am.'

'How about anyone whose nose might have been put out of joint by you marrying her?'

'Other than her father? Ex-boyfriends, that sort of thing? None that I know of.'

'All right. I guess that's it.'

'So, Kovach then?'

'So far, he seems the most likely.'

The sun had dipped below the trees. It was October in Vermont; when the sun was no longer up, it cooled down fast. We had walked a good way from the house and were almost at the little fairy-tale house in the front yard.

'What is that for?' I asked.

'Pump house. We have a spring-fed well and that holds the pump and electronics that feed water into the house. Take a look.' He turned a wooden latch and revealed that the house was just a cover for a small foundation with a ladder leading down ten feet. Inside, I could see pink insulation, a circuit panel, heavy gauge wire, and a pump. There was a bare bulb and a chain hanging from the roof of the pump house.

'Neat, looks well-thought-out.'

'It has to be well-insulated for the winters up here, but it is worth it.'

'Where's the spring?' I hadn't seen any water in the pump house.

'Just through those trees. There is a small house over it.' He pointed to the tree line at the edge of the field running downhill. Everything was technically downhill from the house. The ground was uneven with small dips and rises, all evidence of glaciers past.

'C'mon, it's getting dark and neither of us wants to face Frieda's wrath if we are late for dinner.' He motioned to the house with his arm like he was John Wayne encouraging the Marines to hit the beach. We headed up the gentle slope toward the hunting lodge, whose windows were lit with warm light that spilled out on to the yard and the terrace. I could almost imagine the smells coming from Frieda's kitchen.

I wasn't wrong. The house was warm and the smells coming from the kitchen were fantastic.

'There you two are. I was about to send Baz out to find you.' Honey was standing in the living room. She was dressed simply in white tennis sneakers, jeans that were tight but not too tight, and a cream-colored silk blouse with the top two buttons undone. Diamonds glinted in her earlobes and a simple cross of gold was visible at her open collar.

'Roark wanted to ask me a bunch of embarrassing questions and felt I would be more likely to talk if I was out the house.' So much for subtlety.

'And did he talk?'

'No, he didn't crack under questioning,' I joked.

'See that, he is disappointed that there is no dirt on me.'

'No, not disappointed. In a lot of ways, having just one person to look at makes it a lot easier.'

'As long as it isn't one of you SOG cowboys?' His voice had a needling quality to it that made me once more contemplate punching him in the nose, but that is usually bad for business.

'Mr Ambassador, I'm a hired gun, just like Baz and the lady writer. You hired me to investigate and I am. If that leads me to an SOG guy, then so be it.' My voice had the old familiar steel in it.

'OK boys, separate corners. Gordon, why don't you go see

if you can find a nice wine to go with dinner? Mr Roark, why
don't you go wash up?' While both were phrased in the form
of a question, there was no mistaking them for what they were.
Orders.

'Yes, ma'am.' I gave a mock salute and went downstairs to
do as I was told.

By the time I had returned, the table was set and there was
a place for me. We were all seated where we had been the night
before, except for Bradley who was downstairs on the phone
to the West Coast. He was allowed to skip dinner to try and
sell the rights to Stevenson's memoirs to Hollywood. Even
Stevenson wouldn't mind that type of money coming in.

I had wondered if I was going to have to join Baz and Frieda
in the kitchen. Dinner in either place would have been fantastic.
It was a roast; Frieda had put the meat on a bed of carrots and
onions and then put peeled Yukon Gold potatoes around so that
they took on some of the meat's flavor as it all roasted. There
was a large wooden bowl filled with salad and homemade
dressing that wasn't shy with either the garlic or the dill.

Stevenson also followed his orders well. He had produced a
couple of bottles of Bordeaux that had been bottled in the
middle of the Carter presidency. I don't know enough about
wine to tell the difference between a good bottle and a really
good bottle. I do know a bit about cheap wine, and this was
far from it. Stevenson carved the meat, and Frieda was to be
commended. It was a perfect medium to medium rare.

Maureen joined Honey, Stevenson and me for dinner, while
Baz again ate in the kitchen with Frieda. Maureen chatted with
me and, when she thought no one was looking, she slid her
hand under the tablecloth and gave my thigh a squeeze.

'Andy, what did you do during Vietnam?'

'I was a clerk.' This warranted a pinch instead of a squeeze
on my thigh, a little higher than was entirely comfortable.

'No, really.'

'I was in Special Forces.' That answer was usually enough
for most people.

'Doing what?'

'Yes, Andy, doing what?' Stevenson asked, parodying
Maureen.

'Oh, working with indigenous soldiers, that sort of thing.'

'Working on what, exactly?' She was like a terrier ferreting out a rodent.

'Nothing too exciting, just helping to train them.'

We went back and forth like that for a bit until Stevenson said, 'Maureen, he can't tell you.'

'What, doesn't he know what he did during the war?'

'No, Maureen, it's classified. He could go to jail for telling you about it. You can bat your pretty eyes at him and grope him under the table all you want. He won't tell you anything.'

'Is that true?' This to me.

'There isn't anything to tell, really. I went to a war, I worked with indigenous people. I came home and then the war was over.'

'Haha, see, Maureen, he is an infuriating prick.' Stevenson laughed but he wasn't very far off.

'Most people who don't like me don't really know me that well. Once you get to know me, I'm a real peach.' That got a laugh from everyone, and we were able to pay attention to the excellent meal and wine instead of rehashing my war record.

When the main meal was done, Bradley came upstairs to join us. Frieda cleared the table and brought brandy and strudel for dessert. She made no mention of coffee, and no one seemed interested in it. Stevenson poured a large snifter of brandy for both of us. Maureen was poured a more ladylike measure and Honey declined.

'Roark, you were a team leader over there, weren't you?' Stevenson was back in Hemingway mode.

'Yes.' It was still classified, and I wasn't the type to talk about it. The problem was that Stevenson knew all about it and I didn't want him to lay it all out in front of everyone.

'You were responsible for what . . . five, maybe eight other men?'

'Something like that.'

'And you SOG guys always blamed me for putting restrictions on your operations.'

'It was frustrating.' That was the world's biggest understatement.

'You guys . . . that's the problem, no perspective.'

'Perspective, sir?'

'Yeah, sure. In World War II, I was responsible for a hundred men. In Laos, I was fighting a war.'

'So were we, sir.'

'Yes, but I was responsible for trying to keep the communists from overrunning the country by attempting to maintain the illusion of its neutrality. We were able to tie up thousands of NVA. Keep them out of Vietnam and off the Trail. I had an army of forty thousand men that I was responsible for. You had eight. You're mad because I wouldn't let you go after one or two downed pilots.'

'Yes, sir. Yes, I am. We owed those guys. They saved my hide on numerous occasions.'

'They did and they deserved better, but war is a messy business. I occasionally had to sacrifice one or two to protect thousands. I had to protect an army, a country; you had to worry about a squad.' His face was flushed and the veins in his cheeks from years of hard drinking were a little more prominent.

'Bass,' Baz poked his head in from the kitchen. 'I'm going to go do my rounds. Everything OK?'

'Yes, yeah, sure. Sure, they are. Aren't they, Roark?'

'Just ducky.' I could have brought up the fact that his responsibilities and sacrificing a pilot or two would be cold fucking comfort to their widows. Instead, I uncharacteristically kept my mouth shut. Baz nodded at us and then left to go on his rounds. I watched him through the Andersen windows as he walked along the veranda on his way to the front yard. I turned back to the table when his head disappeared down the steps.

Stevenson topped off his brandy, and I shook my head when he offered to do the same to mine. He ignored me and poured more. Everyone else was quiet, picking at their strudel and wondering what the hell had happened to their nice dinner.

'Oh, come on, Roark, have a drink with me. I know I'm a bastard. I do. It's just hard to sit here having you ask me all these questions. Judging me about my life, my war. Come on, man, let's bury the hatchet.' It wasn't a bad idea, but I think he meant something different from what I was thinking.

'Sure, why not.'

'Well, good. Good for you. Hell, let's move this downstairs.

Ladies, boys, come on.' Life of the party Stevenson was back. We all got up and moved away from the table. Bradley looked a little green around the gills and Gordon Junior looked flushed.

I stood by Maureen, pulling her chair back, pretending to be some sort of gentleman. Glancing out the window by the part of the terrace that touched the woods, I saw fireflies. Except there are no fireflies in Vermont in October. It's too cold.

I wrapped an arm around Maureen's shoulders and dived, pulling her to the floor with me. Stevenson, decades from his time in the OSS, half in the bag as he was, hit the floor too. His cries of 'get down!' were lost as the windows began to shatter and the reports of the rifle reached us. They were loud and close, someone firing fast on semi-auto, tearing up the windows, the walls, and the china hutch opposite the windows.

Plaster dust was starting to fill the room from where the rounds were punching through everything. I rolled on my side and saw light switches above the phone on the sideboard by the mercifully untouched sliding glass doors. I reached up and flicked them off and the room went dark.

'Crawl into the kitchen or hallway. Get behind the chimney,' I heard myself yell. Then I stood up like a fool, my .38 in hand, and ripped five rounds into the wood line where I thought I had seen the muzzle flashes. Each of my five rounds exploded into a ball of orange flame as hot gasses escaped from the muzzle and the cylinder in the darkened room.

I dropped to the floor, cordite in my nose and ringing in my ears. They were all moving away slowly and carefully on their bellies. I emptied the cylinder on the floor then dug a speed-loader out of my pocket. I fitted the rounds into the cylinder, tossing the empty speedloader away.

Because I hadn't done enough stupid stuff that night, I stood up, back to the wall, and unlocked the sliding glass door. I slid it open, took a couple of deep breaths, then stepped out into the night and the screen door. I got tangled up and went down, hitting the terrace, but was quickly up and free of the screen and moving into the wood line, toward where I thought Kovach was. I could hear something or someone big moving through the brush.

I started moving forward and promptly smacked into a branch.

Shit. The flash from my own shooting had wiped out my night vision. I put my left hand out in front of me and pointed my .38 in front of me with a bent arm. I took a couple of steps, but it was slow going. I heard footsteps behind me, and I heard heavy breathing. I pivoted when the beam from a flashlight hit me square in the eyes.

'Roark, don't shoot. It's me, Baz.' At least I could still hear.

'Where the hell have you been?' I asked angrily, as much needing to vent as being genuinely curious.

'I was down by the garage. I thought I saw something. I heard the gunfire and came running. I hit the ground when you opened up. Then I saw you charge in here and stop. I figured you couldn't see anything after ripping off rounds at night with that snub-nose.'

'You are right about that.'

'Jesus!'

'What?'

'Look at that.' He shone the light on a tree in front of me. There was a note pinned to it with one of those cheap, Rambo-type survival knives that popped up in droves after the movie came out. There was also something twinkling in the pine needles near my feet. I picked it up; a warm .223 shell casing. The ejected rounds from rapid firing must have bounced all around and off the trees that were closely situated. 'What is it?'

'A shell casing. .223. I know a guy who has a Ruger that shoots these.' Actually, I knew a few guys who shot them, but I only had one in mind.

'Who's that?'

'Kovach.'

We stepped closer to the note which read, 'Next time I won't aim high. I wanted you to know I can reach you any time I choose to. If you want to live, you will pay me half a million dollars. Cash, or next time I won't miss. I will be in touch.'

'So, he's buggered off then?' Baz said.

'Yes, it looks like it. I don't think this guy is subtle enough to shoot up a house and leave a note as some sort of feint.'

'No, likely not,' Baz said, as he slid the Spanish Star 9mm he was holding into his waistband. The Star was a not-too-exact knock-off of the Colt .45. They were the pistol of choice for the Rhodesians and South Africans in their bush wars.

I slid my .38 back into its holster. We went back to the house. Baz had to check on the Bass, and I had to call the Vermont State Police – and Brenda Watts. Fortunately, no one inside was hurt, which, between the bullets and broken glass, was nothing short of miraculous. I wish I could have said the same for my pride.

FOURTEEN

As calmly as I could, with ears still ringing, I explained to the Vermont State Police that someone had shot into the house and could they send an officer by to take the report. When they asked, I assured them that no one was hurt. Frieda had fainted but was all right now, and there was no need to share that with them. They said they would send the next available car, but he was coming from Barre so it would be a bit.

Next, I called Brenda Watts. After exchanging greetings, I said, 'Someone just shot up the house and left another note.'

'Shot up the house?'

'Yeah, fired a magazine of .223 into the dining room as we were getting up from dinner.'

'Jesus. Was anybody hurt?'

'No, just my pride. We were lucky because he fired about thirty rounds. He was aiming high.'

'Kovach?'

'Probably, he has a semi-automatic .223. So, yeah, it could be him.'

'OK.'

'There was a note too. Pinned to a tree with one of those survival knives. He is asking for five hundred thousand dollars.'

'OK. That's new.'

'Yes, it's typed, but I can't tell you much more than that.'

'OK, did you call the police?'

'Yes, they are on the way.'

'All right. I'll call them and I will be up there in the morning.'

'Good.'

True to their word, a Green Mountains green Chevy Caprice rolled into the driveway. Unlike TV and the movies, he didn't come tear-assing into the driveway, lights and sirens blaring. A very tall and earnest-looking trooper in his Smokey the Bear hat and OD green uniform, reminiscent of what my dad must have worn in World War II, got out of the boxy green Chevy. He had a large .357 holstered on his Sam Browne belt on his hip.

'Roark, you were a cop, c'mon.' Stevenson was back in Ambassador mode again. 'You speak his language.' I wasn't so sure of that, but I followed the Ambassador to the front door. Stevenson opened the door and greeted the trooper from the veranda, like he was addressing his adoring public.

'Good evening, Trooper,' he boomed. Had he been any louder, I am sure he would have startled the trooper into whipping out his revolver and finishing what Kovach had started tonight.

'Evening, sir. Trooper Scott. We received a call that someone shot your home, sir.'

'That'd be Roark here.'

'He shot your house?'

'No, I called to report the shooting.' I managed to edge around the Ambassador. 'Someone in the woods by the terrace shot the house.' Scott had made his way up the steps to the terrace, and, in the harsh light from the outside spotlights, saw the damage to the corner of the house with the dining room.

'Jesus.'

'My thoughts exactly,' Stevenson added.

'I'm a licensed private investigator from Boston. My name is Roark. I was hired by Ambassador Stevenson to investigate matters on his behalf. The FBI is involved in the investigation, and they will be calling your headquarters if they haven't already.'

'Wait, what? Investigation? FBI? What is this all about?' Clearly this wasn't in the normal day-to-day of the Vermont State Police. I glanced over at Stevenson who nodded.

'Somebody has been threatening the Ambassador.'

'OK, so what happened tonight?' I told him about the shooting, not bothering to mention that Stevenson had been angry with me. I mentioned my return fire, and when I got to the part about the screen door, Scott shone his Maglite at the crumpled remains of the screen on the ground. We went inside as the sound of sirens began to slice through the night from a distance.

When Scott stepped inside and saw the carnage to the china

hutch and the dining room in general, he whistled softly. 'Mister, I think that someone really doesn't like you.' Scott took a small notebook and a silver Cross pen out of his breast pocket and began to take notes.

He copied down my license information and my particulars as well. He wrote down the names of everyone in the house. When Baz was introduced to him, Trooper Scott raised an eyebrow. Clearly Rhodesian mercenaries turned bodyguards were new territory. He was just starting to ask Baz questions when the cavalry arrived, bathing the house in flashing blue lights.

For the next two hours things were a little hectic. State troopers and detectives descended on the hunting lodge, intent on interviewing everyone and taking pictures of everything that couldn't talk. They carefully collected the shell casings and took pictures of the note pinned to the tree. They bagged the note for the FBI, and my license information was taken down three times by three different troopers: Trooper Scott, his sergeant, and a sleepy-looking detective whose sideburns I slightly envied. When I was a cop in Boston, I had been to homicides that had gotten less attention.

They took my gun, after I told them that I had fired it. Collected the shell casings where I had dumped them. Then, agreeing that my .38 wasn't what shot up the house and that I had, in essence, done nothing illegal, immoral, or just plain old wrong, gave me my .38 back. Then, when things were really winding down, Baz and I were able to go to the garage to get some scrap plywood to cover the windows.

On the way to the garage Baz said, 'Come look at this.' He led me around the side and for the first time I realized that the garage was built on earth that had been pushed in place to level it. The earth formed a three-foot-wide path then fell away four feet on the north- and west-facing sides of the garage.

'There.' He pointed his flashlight beam at a bush by the back corner of the garage. Tied to it, fluttering in the evening breeze, were two strips of silvery Mylar. The reflective material would catch a person's attention at twilight. 'That's what I was looking at when he opened up on you guys.'

'Looks like someone tied it there intentionally. Is this part of your regular rounds?'

'Yes. I make sure the cars aren't tampered with. Wouldn't do if the Bass got in his car and it went boom, eh?' He had a point there.

'OK, so is it possible that he's been watching us? Gets to know your routine. Sets up a passive distraction device so he can work his way up to his firing position.'

'Could be, plenty of bush out there to watch the house from.'

We went into the garage and found plywood, a couple of hammers, and a jar of nails. We carried the plywood like a stretcher between us back up to the house. We nailed the sheets over the shot-out windows. It wasn't fine carpentry, but it would keep the weather out and most of the cold. Walking back to put the hammers away, Baz bent down and scooped up the discarded screen.

'Your handiwork? Wanna keep it as a trophy?'

'No, thanks. Not my proudest moment, but at least it was over quickly.'

'Haha. I'm sure that the drinks the Ambassador poured didn't hurt.'

'Nope, helped my injured pride,' I told him.

Baz laughed a short, barking laugh as we walked past the two State Police cars parked driver's door to driver's door. They were to spend the night and allegedly were also going to walk around the house to make sure that no one snuck up on us. I was betting that after one walk around they would catnap until their relief arrived just in time to take their own naps. I didn't care. Just having them parked out front was a deterrent.

The house was still by the time I went downstairs. I made my camp bed on the couch with sheets and wool blankets. Then I went to Stevenson's bar and poured myself a healthy bourbon on the rocks. I picked a bottle of the stuff that looked very expensive and took a deep gulp of it. Then I opened the gun cabinet.

His taste in guns was like his taste in bourbon and women: expensive. There were any number of scoped, bolt-action hunting rifles. There were plenty of shotguns from Italy for hunting birds. I was hoping for a plain old riot shotgun or an M-1 carbine, but the closest thing I could find was a Browning Model 81 lever-action rifle.

I popped the four-round magazine out. It was empty, but I found a box of .243 caliber 100 grain soft point ammunition for it. I thumbed four rounds into the magazine, put it in the rifle and jacked one into the chamber. I popped the magazine out and topped it off, then reinserted it. I made sure the safety was on and put it on the floor by the couch so I would be able to reach down with my left hand and pick it up. I put my .38 under the pillow.

I tried to read but was too keyed up. The bourbon helped take some of the edge off, and I turned out the light and went to sleep. I hadn't been in bed long when I heard someone coming quietly down the stairs. A sliver of moonlight made its way through the window. I could see feminine curves. The best kind. Maureen stood by the side of my makeshift bed.

'Got room in there for company?' she whispered.

'For you? Always. But you might be overdressed.' She was wearing a t-shirt and, as far as I could tell, not much else. I pulled the blanket aside. It turned out that I was right about what she had on under the t-shirt. She straddled me, kissed me hard on the mouth, and I was left with newfound respect for equestrian pursuits.

Later, breathing hard in my ear she said; 'You were magnificent.'

'Thank you, that is nice to hear.' The whole thing left me feeling like the Roger Moore James Bond.

'No, not just now. I mean that was nice, but you should have seen yourself. Standing up and blazing away at the night. Face lit up by the muzzle flash. Amazing. Like some sort of cowboy.' In reality it had been a foolhardy thing to do, but I had been angry and feeling useless. In the end, firing into the woods had been sort of like jousting a windmill.

I drifted off to sleep. I woke up alone in the middle of the night. I put my hand down, and the rifle was still there. The .38 was still under the pillow, and I relaxed a little. I fell back asleep on the narrow couch, wondering how comfortable Maureen's bed was.

When I woke up again, it was morning and sunny out. I got up and took the rifle over to the gun cabinet. I dropped the magazine and cleared the round from the chamber. I left the loaded magazine and spare round next to a box of .243 soft point hunting rounds. Then I put the .38 behind the books on the bookshelf and went to take a shower.

I was out of the shower, dressed, and had my bag packed by the time coffee was ready. I went upstairs and said good morning to Frieda, who seemed to be more kindly disposed to me today. She handed me a cup of black coffee, and I thanked her. Then I went out on to the veranda with it and lit a Lucky.

There were two boxy State Police cars in the driveway. They seemed to be in different spots from the last two. Exhaust trickled out of their idling engines, and I noticed there was frost on the ground. I walked down the steps, waved to the trooper who looked up from his nap at me, walked down the slope, and turned a sharp left into the woods.

There wasn't much mist this time, but under the canopy it grew quickly dark, and the morning's chill seemed to run a little deeper. I followed the logging road north, downslope into the woods. The forest was coming alive with the sounds of birds and creatures. I turned left at the secondary cut just like the day before, except this time I stopped at the base of the hill. I was looking for broken twigs and tree branches and, in a few minutes, found one at chest height and then another. They were freshly broken, within the last day or so.

I started to follow the trail, marked by the broken twigs up the hill. I slipped a couple of times on the bed of pine needles and had to make my way around a couple of small boulders. In about two minutes I was standing just behind the tree that the note had been pinned to. I was looking at the east side of the house and had a great view of the plywood Baz and I had tacked up.

It had only taken a few seconds to empty the rifle into the house. If Kovach's goal was to send a message, then it wouldn't have taken long. I turned around and started back down the hill. Without going fast, I made it to the base and the logging road in about a minute. I started walking deeper into the woods, and I noticed that – in a few places – I could see the blacktop road twenty or thirty yards away, through the trees. The ground between the logging cut and the blacktop looked like the type of mud that shoes got swallowed whole by, never to be seen again. In warm weather it was the type of place that had mosquitos by the swarm.

I followed the logging cut further into the woods. It gently veered away from the road, which quickly disappeared amongst the pines and hemlocks. Then it turned sharply to the east and away from the road. I stopped, put a fresh Lucky in my mouth to replace the one long since gone, and lit it with my Zippo. Enjoying the smoke filling my lungs, I just stood still, listening to the woods.

Kovach could easily have ripped through his thirty-round magazine, hustled down the hill, and into the woods before I had switched the lights off. Then he could have hustled down the trail while I was blazing away at some innocent pines and hemlocks. While I was crashing through the screen door, he could have made his way out to the hardtop road and driven off into the night. He could have been on the road, laughing at my stupid response, by the time Baz and I found the note. The thought of that irked me.

I turned back toward the lodge, and it occurred to me how well the Ambassador had chosen the location. The slope wasn't gentle but not so steep that I had to lean into it. He had picked a spot that, if the wood line had been cleared and concertina wire had been strung, would have made for a formidable defensive position.

When I came to the base of the hill, I took the secondary trail and ended up at the back of the house. I was able to get within ten yards of the house before I was exposed. It took me a few seconds to cross, and I was at the back door. The storm door was locked, but I kept an expired Diners Club card in my wallet for just that purpose. I used it to jimmy the lock on the door and was inside in a few seconds. The Ambassador had picked the perfect location to build an armed camp but hadn't thought about installing deadbolts.

I slipped inside, quietly closing the doors behind me. I could hear voices coming from Baz's room. I couldn't make out what they were saying, but I could tell that one of them was female. The only thing I could tell for sure was that it wasn't Frieda. The voice was too young and not nearly as harsh as hers.

I went the other way, opened the door, and stepped into Stevenson's lair. Brenda Watts was standing by the couch holding something in her hand. She turned to me and held up what turned out to be a long red hair.

'Glad to see you aren't wasting time up here.' Watts could have gotten a PhD in Sarcasm from Harvard.

'Things got . . . emotional last night.' I shrugged.

'Ha, is that what we are calling it now? The redhead with the hips?'

'Pretty sure you all have hips.'

'True, but we don't all use them the same.' She had me there.

'A gentleman never tells.'

'Since when do you consider yourself a gentleman?'

'It's a new thing I am trying, part of my self-improvement program.'

'How is that working out for you?'

'You know. Good days and bad.'

'You and me both. What the fuck happened last night?'

'It was a dark and stormy night . . .'

'Don't be a clown.'

'OK, the short version is that someone, probably Kovach, emptied a whole magazine of .223 ammunition into the east side of the house where the dining room is just as we finished dinner.' I filled her in on what happened, trying to make the part where I got tangled up in the screen sound somewhat heroic. I had been trying to impress Watts for years with little or no effect.

'Where do you think he went to after shooting the place up?'

'Down the hill, through the woods from his firing point. I found his trail down there. I couldn't find any tracks from there. My guess is that he hustled through the woods, cut across the swampy area out to the road that runs by the garage side of the house. From there he could have gone anywhere.'

'Any ideas?'

'Well, if he's nearby, he is probably shacked up at a motel in the area. Based on what I saw of his apartment, it will be of the No Tell Motel variety. My guess would be near the interstate, maybe within thirty-mile radius.'

'Thirty miles?'

'Close enough to get here conveniently but not so close as to stand out.'

'OK, that makes more sense than going back to Fairhaven.'

'Sure. He will want to be close enough to pick up the money once he sets up the drop.'

'That could be at any time though.'

'I think he is getting itchy. This seems like a bit of an escalation, or like he is moving toward resolution of some sort.'

'Five hundred thousand dollars is a lot of resolution.'

'You are starting to sound like me. So, what now?'

'Right now, I have a couple of agents on their way to see a friendly judge about a warrant.'

'Do you have enough probable cause?'

'Friendly judge who wears very thick glasses.'

'Aha . . . I get it.'

'I may have written the affidavit based on the information gained by a confidential informant.'

'That would be me as a result of my B and E?'

'One and the same.'

'I do try to be useful.'

We walked upstairs to survey the damage, which didn't look much better during the day. The plywood clashed with the nice, stained trim around the windows and the china hutch would never be the same. The .223 rounds were nearly identical to the small, high-velocity 5.56mm round that the Army used. It punched through things and tumbled and left a lot of damage behind.

Bradley and Stevenson were sitting at the table, deep in conversation.

'We don't need him. Baz is more useful than he is.'

'Bradley, I don't . . .' He stopped, seeing Watts and me. 'Roark, where have you been?'

'I went for a walk in the woods and then I had to bring Special Agent Watts up to speed.'

'Did you find anything?'

'Nothing of use.' There was no point in my offering up theories about where Kovach shot from or how he fled.

'Mr Roark, how did he find the Ambassador?' Bradley asked.

'I'm not sure. He isn't exactly keeping his head down.'

'What do you mean by that?'

'Speaking engagements, newspaper articles. It wouldn't be hard to find the Ambassador if one wanted to.'

'I think he followed you. Followed you up here from Boston.'

'Nope.'

'How else would he get here?'

'Bradley, it's a two-hour drive from Boston, almost all of it on the highway. I would have noticed the same car following me the whole time.'

'What about a tracking device?'

'You've been watching too much TV. They are expensive, which is why the federal drug boys are about the only ones who use them. They can afford them. Kovach makes cheap beer money at best.'

'Bradley, leave it alone. Roark is right,' Stevenson admonished.

'What is the plan?' I asked, hoping that someone other than me would come up with one.

'He has two choices: wait for the drop and we will grab Kovach then or we will turn him up eventually. The choices are whether you want to stay here or go back to Brookline. Either way, you will need protection.'

'I will stay here. I can hire a couple more men, and between them and Baz that should be enough to deter Kovach until you arrest him.'

'I can have the State Police keep a car posted here for a couple of days too.' Watts wasn't going to be able to convince the State Police to do much more than that, but it was better than nothing.

'Roark, what about you?'

'I will head back to Boston. I have a couple of things about Kovach that I need to look into. I can come back up after that.'

'That would be good. I want you around for the drop.'

'Sure. I can be back tomorrow or the day after. It is only a couple of hours' drive.'

'OK.'

I picked up my bag. Watts walked me to my car.

'What are you up to?'

'Nothing. I need a change of clothes, and I would like to sleep in a bed that isn't a couch by day. Also, I still have some guys who I want to touch base with about Kovach.' I didn't add that I was thinking that the .38 might not be enough gun for this job.

'Still convinced we are barking up the wrong tree?'

'No, just doing my due diligence, making sure the Ambassador gets his money's worth.'

'Very conscientious of you.'

'Let me know if the search warrant turns up anything of interest.'

'Will do.' There wasn't much more to say. We were too much of something and not enough of something else to each other to hug our goodbyes. I unlocked the Maverick and threw the postman's bag on the passenger seat. The car started with a rumble, and I watched her get smaller in the rear-view mirror and then she turned to go back into the house. By the time I got on the highway on-ramp, Joan Jett was singing about her opinion about her reputation, and I had stopped wondering what Watts thought of mine.

FIFTEEN

I f the ride had been dramatic heading north to the Ambassador's hunting lodge, it was even more so going south, past rolling hills dappled with fall-colored leaves. The two-lane blacktop highway was occasionally marred by patched frost heaves, giving the whole thing a Frankensteinian effect. Interstate 91-South led downhill toward the White River and offered views of pastures and farms on the lower hills. I passed through White River Junction and took the ramp on to 89-South. The highway climbed back up into the hills and curved around them, rising up and, when I wasn't in a corridor of trees, offered dramatic views of the valley.

By the time I left the state liquor store with another bottle of Powers, the scenery was transitioning from rolling hills and foliage to wider highways and suburban sprawl. Going through the journals with Stevenson had only convinced me that – while there were a lot of people over the years who might have a grudge – there couldn't be that many alive now, or able to act on it. Kovach was looking better to me as a suspect by the time the grittiness of the city started to overwhelm the semi-nature of the highway. He had the right type of rifle, seemed to have a motive.

I followed the highway into the city, took my exit and made my way through the early afternoon traffic to my office. I pulled up behind the building. Now that Marconi's Pizza place had given way to a video rental store, the big dumpster behind the building was gone. There was a greasy spot left from decades of leaks. Parking behind the building was a lot easier, and in Boston that was kind of a big deal.

Taking my bag, I locked the car and went into the building. Months ago, I would have let myself into Marconi's warm kitchen, redolent with the scent of sauce and cooking pizza, hoping to get an espresso from Marconi. Instead I just went up the stairs to my office.

That was the problem with the past, it was nothing more than memories. There was no way to go back to those times and places. Maybe that was what this case was all about. Kovach couldn't go back, so maybe he was trying to take control of what was to happen next. This was a case of Stevenson's past coming back to haunt him. He said he didn't remember Kovach, but this was very personal.

I let myself into my office. There were no booby traps, but it was dusty and smelled like stale pipe smoke. I opened the window and went through the equally cumbersome processes of making espresso and filling a pipe. I figured fresh pipe smoke would cover the stale stuff. I checked in with the answering service and the machine I kept in the office. There wasn't much. An old client wanted to hire me to make sure the guys at his shipping company weren't stealing. A local insurance company thought that they could offer me better rates. When the espresso was in the demitasse cup and the pipe was drawing nicely, I dug out my case notes.

They were looking a little battered and smudged; apparently legal pads don't travel well. I went over the notes I had taken going through the journals, which didn't amount to much more than a few distant maybes for suspects. I wrote about the house being shot up; there wasn't much to say. I omitted my time with Maureen. While memorable, that didn't seem gentlemanly, nor relevant to the case. While I was musing about Maureen the phone rang.

'Andy.' It was Watts.

'Watts, what's up?'

'I just got a call from the office.'

'And?' I am not often accused of verbal brevity but this time it seemed appropriate.

'They just searched Kovach's apartment.'

'What did they find?'

'It's what they didn't find.'

'What's that?' Confident that she would say a Ruger Mini-14.

'The Mini-14 was missing, that and the .357 Magnum revolver in the book.'

'I'm assuming all the ammo and magazines too.'

'Yep, he took all that with him. That's a lot.'

'Yeah, he can do a lot of damage with what he had there.'

'Also, we found the typewriter.' They must be some crack investigators to find it when I couldn't. Maybe I was losing my touch.

'Where was it?'

'On the coffee table. Sheet of paper in it, half-written message.'

'Is it the same one?'

'The lab boys will have to confirm it, but based on the page in it, yeah, it looks good. One of those IBM Selectrics.' She sounded a little breathy . . . Watts loved the hunt.

'Watts?'

'Yeah?'

'Do me a favor. See if you can find out where the typewriter comes from? You know, who sold it?'

'Oh, no need. There is a little plate on the back. It comes from a typewriter shop in Hanover, New Hampshire.'

'Thanks. Any chance of finding out who bought it or when?' My mind was already turning over and over.

'We're working on it. Andy, we'll find him. We have a BOLO out for his car.' A Be On the Look-Out for his car meant that every cop in New England at every roll call was alerted. 'And two more hired guns will be there by tonight.'

'Great, that will help. Keep me in the loop.'

'Sure thing.' She hung up and I leaned back in my old wooden office chair. Hanover, New Hampshire, was a nice town. Not too big and not too small. It had a village green and was overloaded with New England charm. Most of all, it was home to Dartmouth College, where both Bradley and Gordon Junior had gone. If I had learned anything from reading mysteries, it's that the butler did it. Stevenson didn't have a butler, but he had a Bradley.

I updated my notes and sat puffing on the pipe. I took sips of the espresso and looked out the office window at the people moving around outside. They were busily going about their business, unconcerned that Kovach was moving around the great state of Vermont with a Mini-14 and a revolver. Or that he had shot up a house to send a message and that he wanted half a million dollars.

I had searched the apartment well. An IBM electric typewriter wasn't small, and I hadn't seen one. He could have had it with him in his car or truck if he was working. It seemed odd that the one in his apartment had come from a typewriter shop in Hanover, New Hampshire. I doubt that Kovach had gone to Dartmouth, but it is possible that his job had taken him to Hanover. That was one of the great advantages of being a truck driver. Travel. The ability to write menacing letters on your IBM and then mail them from all over the country.

I picked up the phone, but I had already called everyone I could think of about Kovach. I had gotten about as much information as there was. I put the phone back in its cradle. What was I doing? Kovach wasn't SOG so I had done what I had set out to do. He was in the wind, armed with a Mini-14. He had shot up the hunting lodge in Vermont. How much more did I want? Or was it my old need to solve the case? All I had was a vague, ever-diminishing sense of doubt that it was Kovach. Even less so since the house was shot up.

I knocked the ashes from the pipe into my palm and dumped them into the wastebasket. I put the pipe back in the rack, gathered up my notes, and put the bottle of Powers in the desk drawer. I was annoyed with myself. There was a reason why I didn't read Agatha Christie novels. Most of the time the butler didn't do it or there wasn't a butler.

I was being distracted by Bradley because I didn't like him. I was part of a culture of tough guys and drunks who looked at someone with his Ivy League manners and good diction with disdain. I was from a group of people who put greater value on how well you held your liquor than how well you spoke. I was looking at the closest thing to a butler because of my hang-ups and not based on the evidence. Maybe my self-improvement plan needed some improvement?

I packed up and went home. I was hungry and needed a drink. I wanted a change of clothes and, even though I had only fired five rounds through it, I wanted to clean my revolver. If the Army had taught me anything, it was the value of a clean weapon. The Army had turned weapons maintenance into a virtue since the adoption of the M-16.

Sir Leominster was waiting for me when I unlocked the door.

He meowed at me in a scolding tone that let me know what he thought of my lack of attentiveness in the cat food area. After quickly unpacking I went into the kitchen to attend to Sir Leominster's dinner needs. My own dinner would not have impressed Frieda, but I hadn't been to the market in a few days. I settled for macaroni and cheese, the kind that comes in a slim, blue cardboard box.

While I waited for the water to boil, I put an old section of the *Globe* down on the table. I got my gun cleaning supplies out and unloaded my .38. I dipped the copper wire brush into the jar of Hoppe's No. 9 and ran the brush back and forth in the barrel and then in the chambers of the cylinder. Hoppe's has a pleasant, albeit chemical, smell. When that was done, I pushed a few patches through the gun to dry up the Hoppe's. Then I ran some patches with gun oil through it. I finished by wiping a thin coat of oil all over the gun.

When it was done, I took the macaroni and cheese over to the TV along with my whiskey. The newly cleaned and oiled .38 went on the table next to the food and drink. I turned on the Movie Loft and was in luck. Dana Hersey was showing *The Yakuza*. It was always fun to watch Robert Mitchum in anything, and Richard Jordan had graduated from Harvard, so he was kind of local. The movie was a nice mix of private eye story, past loves lost, and samurai film. I was grateful that Mitchum stuck to guns and fists instead of trying to be an instant samurai.

I went to bed after the movie. I put the .38 on the bedside table next to me. I tried to read but my eyes grew heavy, and I switched out the light. My sleep was fitful, and, at some point, the cat jumped up on the bed, circling and kneading with his paws until he settled in.

I dreamed that I was on a helicopter going into an LZ. We were taking fire and the door gunner was laying down some impressive heat. When I looked at him it was Bradley in a flight suit and helmet with the dark visor down over his eyes. Instead of laying the heat down with an M60, he was banging away, touch typing, on an IBM Selectric. The Huey flared and I jumped off the skid into the tall elephant grass. I was in the bush, moving quietly, and then there was the deer, blown up, half-eaten grass, still steaming, blown out from its destroyed stomach.

Its mouth moved convulsively and, even though it had no words, I knew what it was saying. 'You killed me.'

I woke up, and a cold rain was falling outside of the window. Even though I didn't feel like it, I went for a run. I pushed myself the last mile back to the apartment, lungs straining and my knee aching, as if to remind me that my twenties were long gone. I was beating myself up, angry about a deer that died, accidently, in the jungle a long time ago. The fact that it had been an accident made it worse.

I got back to the apartment and stretched out. I wanted a Lucky Strike, running did that to me. Maybe there was something to the typewriter. Maybe Bradley was in on it? Is it possible that he was in it with Kovach? I went over to the phone and dialed Watts's office number. They took my number and told me she would call me back shortly. She did a few minutes later.

'Good morning,' she said.

'Where are you? You aren't staying in the hunting lodge?'

'No, I am staying in the Lyme Inn.'

'The Lyme Inn?'

'It's just across the river in Lyme, New Hampshire. It's nice, reminds me of Newhart.'

'Hey, you said the typewriter came from a shop in Hanover, New Hampshire?'

'Yes. Why?'

'Didn't the Ambassador's assistant Bradley go to Dartmouth?'

'Sure, he met Gordon Junior there. That was how he got the job with the Ambassador.'

'When you looked at him, was there anything that might give him a motive?'

'Nothing leapt out but I can take another look.'

'I'm probably clutching at straws, but the typewriter being sold in Hanover, and Bradley going to school there, Gordon Junior too . . . well, it just seems a bit coincidental.'

'I will take another look.'

'Thank you.'

'Are you going back up there?'

'Yeah, I am going to head back up there this morning.'

We hung up and I went to shower. After I dressed and had

breakfast I went to the closet in the bedroom and moved the hangers of clothes out of the way. On the short wall I pushed on the top and bottom corners on one side. The magnets gave way and the panel slid open on a hinge. I had gotten the idea from a fancy glass-fronted stereo system. I unlocked the gun cabinet on the other side and put the .38 on the shelf. I took out my Browning Hi-Power.

I had gotten it a few years ago, one of the new Mark IIs. I had sent it to a gunsmith who had worked his magic on it. Now the magazine dropped free, the trigger was actually decent, and it would feed hollow points. It was a good gun made better. The magazines held thirteen rounds of 9mm ammunition, and with good hollow point ammunition, it was a formidable weapon.

If Kovach came by the house again with his Mini-14, I wanted a little more in hand than a five-shot .38 snub-nose. The .38 usually served me well, but this time I wanted a little more. I took a couple of extra magazines and a box of expensive hollow point ammunition. I closed the gun locker and hid it behind the panel again.

I stood over the bed and thumbed 9mm rounds into the magazines. Then I put one in the gun and racked a round into the chamber. I popped the magazine out and topped that off. The remainder of the box of ammunition went in my bag, along with clean clothes and my shaving kit. I put a pair of sneakers in the bag too.

I threaded my leather belt through the slots in the leather holster. It was the type that canted forward slightly and had a thumb break that went over the back of the pistol when it was holstered. I double-checked the chamber of the Hi-Power, made sure the safety was on, and slid it in the holster.

The gunsmith had replaced the rear sight with the adjustable sight from a Smith & Wesson Model 19 and had made me a front sight with a bright orange insert. He had Parkerized the gun and bobbed a quarter-inch off of the hammer so that it wouldn't bite my hand. To that he added a pair of custom-made slim wood grips that were well-checkered. The whole thing had been expensive, but I had ended up with an excellent handgun for gunfighting. I slipped a thirteen-round magazine in my left front pocket. I reached into the closet and pulled out a British

paratrooper smock in that funky camouflage pattern they like. I
dropped the other magazine in the left front pocket.

I made sure that I packed an old surplus wool commando
sweater in my bag. I pulled the smock on over the flannel shirt
I was wearing. I left some food for the cat and let myself out. I
thought about stopping by Carney's on the way out of town.
Instead of going to Carney's, I steered the Maverick through
the city streets and up on to the freeway.

I pulled off the highway and turned on to the road by the
hunting lodge a little over two hours later. Once I got over
the Tobin Bridge, I was able to open the Maverick up. It was
a fun car to drive on the highway. Out of habit I had watched
my rear-view, checking it often. Despite what Bradley had
suggested about Kovach following me, I did take precautions
as a matter of course. The ride had been uneventful, save the
steady rain that beat down on the Maverick's roof, keeping time
to the Rolling Stones songs on the radio.

As I approached the house, I could see the light blue
Mustang was parked in front, as was an AMC Eagle with New
York plates and the unmistakable green Vermont State Police
car. I pulled in the driveway at a gentle speed so as not to alarm
the trooper. He got out of his car, and I pulled up to him, rolling
down my window. I was about to tell him who I was when he
waved me on and got back in his car.

I guess someone was on top of things and told him that I
was OK. I parked behind the AMC, which looked like a station
wagon with an overactive growth hormone. They were supposed
to be four-wheel drive, and I didn't know much about AMCs,
but I have heard good things about the Javelin.

I got my postman's bag out of the car and walked up the hill
to the house. There was a man standing on the terrace. He had
on an old Army field jacket, blue jeans and combat boots. His
hair was on the long side, but he was far from being a hippie.
The silver antenna from a walkie-talkie stuck out of the pocket
of his field jacket. He was holding the ugliest-looking gun I
have ever seen. It looked like the Doctor Frankenstein of
gunsmiths had gotten ahold of Mac-10 parts, leftovers from a
sheet metal factory, then cobbled together the Weaver Nighthawk.
It was a semi-automatic 9mm carbine.

He said something into the walkie-talkie while not quite pointing the Weaver at me. He nodded to himself and then I heard the door to the veranda open. Another man walked out wearing a commando sweater, a dark blue one, blue jeans, sneakers; he was also carrying a Nighthawk which he wasn't quite pointing at me either. Jesus, these guys were a matched set. I walked forward slowly. The last thing I wanted was to get shot by some trigger-happy hired help.

'You Roark?'

'Yep.'

'OK, they're expecting you. Baz says you're a private eye and you have a gun on you.'

'I am and I do.'

'Baz also says you are touchy about giving it up.'

'What else does Baz say?'

'That you're a wiseass but cool under fire.' He rested the gun, front pistol grip in his left elbow, muzzle down and stuck out his right hand. 'I'm Smith. That's Jones over there.'

'Smith and Jones, huh? At least you guys are original.'

'Those actually are our last names.'

'No shit,' I said cleverly.

'No shit,' Smith replied.

We went in the house, and I went downstairs to find both the Ambassador and Honey. There was also a neat pile of bedding at one end of the couch.

'Roark. Glad you're back.'

'Thank you, sir.'

'Yes, Andy. It's good to see you. We have Baz and the two others.'

'Frick and Frack,' Stevenson added.

'But Gordon and I both feel better having you here.'

'Where did they come from?' I asked, putting my bag down beside the couch.

'Baz found them. Said he knew them from a job that he did.'

'OK. Where did you find Baz?'

'Bradley found him. I'm not sure where. Why?'

'Curious, that's all. Did Watts tell you about the search warrant?'

'Yes, they found his typewriter.'

'That and his rifle is missing. It's a semi-automatic that shoots the same round as lit up the house the other night. That and he has a .357 magnum revolver with him.'

'Well, that is why I have three hired guns and you.'

'Are they any good?'

'They seem to be. They are using radios and the three of them are working in shifts. Two men on duty at all times. That, and there is a state trooper parked out front. I have to think that will give Kovach some pause.'

'Has he been in contact?'

'No, not since the other night. I have been in touch with my bank, and they will arrange for me to get the money from a local bank in Hanover or White River Junction.'

'What does Watts say?'

'Not much other than don't make a move without her. I get the feeling that the FBI is not happy about this.'

'Probably not. They don't like extortion and they really don't like things they can't control.'

'And this is both of those.'

'Pretty much.'

'Do you think he will stop when he gets the money?' Honey asked.

'I don't know. On one hand, he knows that the FBI will forever be hunting him and that might mean he is planning on this being a one-time deal. It's enough money that Kovach could leave the country and go live in someplace like Thailand, where he could live like a king. On the other hand, there is nothing to stop him from starting up again if he runs out of money.' I wasn't offering much comfort, but there was no point in lying.

'Jesus, Roark, don't be such a depressive. This man Kovach wants to make some money at my expense and then be on his way. I'm certain of it.' He went to the bar and poured himself a drink without offering one to anyone else. It was early afternoon, not that I am one to judge.

'We are a little jumpy, Mr Roark.' I was Mr Roark again. 'Gordon and I are both nervous, and we just want this ordeal to be over so we can move on with our lives. You can understand that, can't you?'

'Of course.' Anyone would, really.

'It's the waiting. Gordon isn't used to waiting, to not being in charge.'

'That's true, and Gordon is right here in the room, dear.'

'Yes, you are, but Mr Roark is just trying to help, and you are being rude.'

'Roark's a mercenary, just like the rest of them. He's here to help because he is getting paid to be. It isn't like he cares about us, just the money.'

'Gordon!'

'It's OK, Mrs Stevenson. The Ambassador is right, I am being paid to help you, and he is right that I wouldn't be here otherwise.'

'Thank you, Roark. See, Honey, he is a professional, not some sort of knight errant. He knows the score and he isn't here out of chivalry.'

'Yes, Gordon, I am sure that's all it is,' she said sarcastically and went upstairs, leaving us with a heavy, uncomfortable silence between us.

'Aw, Jesus! Women. No, that woman. Lately she's been more sensitive than . . . well, I don't know what.'

'It might have something to do with the death threats and the house being shot up,' I offered dryly. He shot me a look and I thought he was going to want to have a fistfight over it, but instead he drank his drink.

'Whatever the deal is, you'll work it out,' I said. I wasn't sure I believed it, but I said it with all the confidence I could muster. I was only lying a little less than your average used-car salesman. 'I'm going to grab a smoke outside.'

'Sure, sure,' he said, lost in his thoughts. He had a lot to worry about, and I couldn't blame him. It would just be easier if he was less of a prick about it all.

I went upstairs and poked my head in the kitchen. Frieda gave me a nod, which, given her demeanor after my invasion of her kitchen the other morning, could be regarded as considerable warming. In the living room I found Maureen and Bradley standing over the card table. They were discussing a passage from the Ambassador's memoirs.

'Andy, you're back,' she said brightly.

'Roark,' Bradley said, with considerably less enthusiasm.

'Yes, couldn't keep me away.'

'Have there been any developments?' Bradley seemed to have no interest in my witty repartee. His loss.

'The FBI searched Kovach's apartment. He's gone, his car too. Also, he took a semi-automatic rifle and a revolver with him. He left the typewriter behind, though.'

'Well, that's hardly a surprise, he did shoot up the place with something,' Bradley said sarcastically.

I shrugged. My desire to talk to Bradley was a hell of a lot less than my desire for a cigarette. I nodded to Maureen. I would have loved a few minutes alone with her, but went outside instead.

Jones was still walking circuits around the patio with his carbine slung across his chest. I could see Smith walking along the edge of the field by the road a few hundred yards away. He also carried his Mac-10-meets-sheet-metal-ray-gun carbine slung across his chest. I wondered what passing motorists thought of that. On the other hand, maybe that didn't raise eyebrows in Vermont. I dug a Lucky out of the pack and lit it with my battered Zippo lighter.

I walked down the steps and away from Jones. I didn't really want to talk to Smith or the state trooper, so I headed to the garage. I hadn't looked inside it yet. I wasn't doing my due diligence with Baz and the hired guns around. There was a side door and, high up, centered on the wall, was a single horizontal window with a matching one on the opposite wall. I opted for the door, which was locked. Under the watchful eye of the trooper, I took out my old Diners Club card and jimmied the lock.

I was in a small room with shelves on the wall to my right, a door immediately in front of me, and one to my left. The shelves held things like potting soil, pots and gardening supplies. The door in front of me led to a smallish room that held two lawn mowers and various landscaping tools. There was a three-gallon gas can on the floor and a couple of sharp-toothed handsaws on the wall.

I doubled back, and the last door opened into the garage itself. Stevenson's Mercedes was on one side and an older Ford Bronco on the other. It was small, metallic green, with a white hard top, stubby and boxy but good off-road. The garage was well-appointed with hand tools, a couple of five-ton jacks, and a chain lift for engine work. There was a worktable with all sorts of hand tools, not just automotive ones, on it. There were cans of motor oil, brake fluid, transmission fluid, and boxes of spark plugs. I would never have figured Stevenson for a shade tree mechanic. Two sets of mechanics' coveralls were hanging from pegs on the wall.

I checked in the cars. Under the cars. Under the worktable. Kovach wasn't hiding anywhere in the garage. He wasn't hanging out in the rafters. Satisfied that Kovach wasn't lurking, I went outside, locking the door behind me. I wanted to take a walk through the woods, but with Smith and Jones out and about, I wasn't eager to find out if they startled easy. Part of my self-improvement plan included not getting shot by hired guns with shitty 9mm carbines. I was setting the bar pretty low, but I was trying.

SIXTEEN

spent some time walking around the property and checking the other outbuilding, but nothing leapt out at me. The only vulnerable point I could see was the one that Kovach had already used, the tree line at the back of the house. Smith and Jones, with their patrolling, were certainly a deterrent. It was obvious from the way they carried themselves that they were ex-military.

To my surprise, dinner that night was a sit-down affair at the dining-room table. Stevenson's influence or money had been enough to get the windows replaced while I was in Boston. This provided a view of either Smith, Jones or Baz roaming around the terrace. I wondered if they were patrolling through the woods at the base of the hill at night as well, or were they just sticking close to the house?

People get weird about being in the woods in the dark; they feel the tug of some old childhood fear, some bit of fairy tale told to them to keep them in line. In most cases, the only boogeyman in the woods is man; all it takes is an enemy who is more comfortable in them than you are. For those who can get beyond it, the woods at night, in the dark, confers a huge advantage. It offers a place to hide, to observe and provides comparative safety.

Part of me wanted to be out there with them, protecting the family with my shitty carbine, using the skills I had learned in the Army and had refined in Vietnam. Gliding quietly on jungle-booted feet through the woods, ignoring the bugs and listening intently for anything out of the ordinary. I was good in the woods. I knew, no matter how motivated he was, Kovach was no match for me out there. But that wasn't where I was being paid to be.

Instead, I was at Stevenson's table, sitting close enough to Maureen to feel the heat from her shapely thigh. Frieda had made Jaegerschnitzel, basically a pork chop, pounded thin, breaded, and pan fried with a mushroom sauce to go on top. She made spaetzle, and by made, I mean handmade. Lastly, she had made braised cabbage with sour apples. I was beginning to think that she owned stock in a cabbage farm somewhere.

It was fantastic in the way that only homemade meals can be. The German food complemented the chill of the fall night in New England. Stevenson had opened yet another bottle of good wine. This one was a very dry white from some part of France that I couldn't properly pronounce on my best day. Conversation that night was sparse. Most of them had never been in any real danger before. It was odd to think that Stevenson and I were the only ones at the table who had been.

We were rewarded by a dessert of poached pears with a dollop of hand-beaten whipped cream. Stevenson also brought out a bottle of apple schnapps to complement dessert. Afterwards everyone went their separate ways. Honey had started it by excusing herself. The rest followed quickly.

Downstairs, I opened my bag and took out my notes and went over them. It still shook out the same. Someone, most likely Kovach, was threatening and trying to extort the Ambassador. I didn't like that the typewriter came from a shop near Dartmouth where Bradley had, by all accounts, met Gordon Junior and weaseled his way into a job with the old man. Now the Ambassador had to come up with a cool half a million. I just didn't like it. Didn't like any of it.

I heard Stevenson's heavy tread on the stairs. He looked tired, and much of the bluster seemed to have left him for the night.

'Roark, fancy a bourbon?'

'I certainly wouldn't say no to one.'

He poured us each one on the rocks, but these were double Sinatra's. He held out his glass. 'Here's how.'

'And how.' We touched glasses.

'You think I am a fool to pay the money.'

'No, no, sir, I don't. I can see where it makes sense.'

'But you don't think it is a good idea.' It wasn't a question.

'I can see the appeal, but it doesn't guarantee he'll stop or that he won't come back again when the money runs out.'

'But he might be satisfied with the money?'

'Sure. He might get hit by a bus too. He has planned a lot, has built this up a lot. This is personal, very personal. This doesn't strike me as an average shakedown. I don't think he will be satisfied with the money.' I didn't like Stevenson, but someone had to be straight with him.

'For god's sakes, I don't even remember this . . . this Kovach!' Stevenson bellowed angrily. 'How in the hell can he do this to me?'

'I don't know. But somehow, he feels you've wronged him. Wronged him enough that he wants you to pay financially, to suffer as well.'

'I don't care. It's not important. I'll pay him, I'll do anything to keep my family safe.'

'Of course,' I said placatingly.

'No, you don't understand.'

'It isn't that hard, sir. You want to keep your family safe, and this seems the best way.'

'You don't get it. Honey is pregnant.' He sat there looking at me like I was the slow kid in class.

'Congratulations,' Maureen had come quietly down the stairs – not that it would have been hard with Stevenson's going on, 'that is excellent news.'

'Oh, thank you, Maureen.' Her presence seemed to take a lot of wind out of his sails.

'We should have a congratulatory drink. Can you spare a gal a splash of bourbon? I am pretty sure Roark wouldn't say no to another.'

'No, Roark wouldn't,' I assured them.

Stevenson got Maureen a glass and offered her ice, which she declined by saying in her prim English way, 'No thank you. I prefer my whiskey neither cold nor diluted,' instantly making us question our tough guy standing. Stevenson poured her a bourbon, and she raised her glass. Maureen said, 'To fatherhood.' We echoed her and we all clinked glasses.

'Do you have any children, Andy?' she asked.

'Yes, Roark, are there little commandos running around out there that look like you?'

'No,' I laughed at the thought. 'I have a cat. It is all I can do to take care of him.'

'Really, after all the fleshpots, all the adventures and damsels in distress, you've never?' Maureen was grinning wickedly.

'Just my inner child.' I smiled back. I couldn't even imagine being married, let alone having my shit together enough to be a father.

'You should do it. You will never really know who you are, never really be a man, until you're a father,' Stevenson assured me. I was pretty sure that I knew who I was as a man, but I definitely had no idea what it meant to be a father.

Later, after he left, in the dark, naked on the couch under the old Army blankets, Maureen was again astride me. She seemed more urgent, more purposeful in her efforts. Other than a few scratches and a stray bite mark on my chest, I had no complaints. We fell asleep in each other's arms the way you do after. That deep, almost narcotic sleep.

Later still, I woke with the moon streaming in. The night had grown chilly. Maureen was again astride of me, but this time we weren't making love. She was tracing gentle fingers over my face.

'Hey,' I said, trying to impress her with my witty repartee.

'Hey back at ya.'

'What are you doing?'

'I woke up, feeling good. I wanted to look at you. Remember this moment. This one perfect moment all for myself.'

'That's nice to hear.'

'I like you, Andy. You're not like the rest of them.'

'Thanks. I like you too.'

'I wish we had more than a few stolen moments in this house.'

'There is nothing to say that we can't see more of each other. Boston is a big town, planes land there, trains roll in there, buses pull up all the time, and there are a lot of roads to drive in on.'

'Emmn.'

'Also, I have a car and I am not afraid of flying. I can meet you wherever you are.'

'Can you?'

'Sure, sweetheart,' I said in my bad Bogie imitation, which

was a lot better than my attempt to raise one eyebrow like Magnum.

We fell back asleep, and when I woke up again it was morning, and she was gone. The sun was shining outside, and I had to resist the urge to whistle. Upstairs, I could hear Frieda moving about, and I could smell the two best smells in the world – brewing coffee and frying bacon. I stashed my Browning behind the books in the bookcase and went to shower.

Breakfast was laid out at the table by the time I got there. Bradley, the Ambassador and Honey were all tucking into bacon, eggs, toast and coffee. Honey also had a glass of orange juice and the Ambassador had what looked like a Bloody Mary in front of him. Outside, Jones was walking around the patio with his ugly Franken-Mac-10-ray-gun carbine. I could see Baz's head moving around the back of the house doing his rounds too.

I sat across from Bradley, in part because it was a chair without arms, and few things are more embarrassing than standing up and having the pistol holstered on your belt catch the chair arm. I also wanted to get a look at him. I couldn't quite shake the feeling that the butler had done it or at least was involved in it.

'Morning, Bradley.'

'Good morning, Roark.' I got the feeling that in his mind there was a pecking order to the hired help. He was junior management, and I was not. Little did he know that Frieda was at the top of the heap.

'Hey, you went to Dartmouth, right?'

'Yes, and where did you go to school?'

'A couple of semesters at the University of Rhode Island, a few years in Vietnam, and then I finished my degree in night school.'

'Oh.'

'Yeah, it wasn't what I had planned, but it worked out.'

'Good for you.'

'Hey, when you were at Dartmouth, do you remember there being a place that sold typewriters there? You know the place, new and used typewriters and repair, that type of thing?'

'Yes, I remember the place.'

'Did you buy a typewriter there?'

'Yes, I did. Why?'

'Oh, I was curious, Kovach got his typewriter from the same shop.'

'So what?'

'It just struck me as coincidental, that's all.'

'It is. Lots of people got typewriters there. I did. Gordy did. Pretty much anyone who bought a typewriter at Dartmouth got it there.'

'OK, that makes sense. I was just trying to piece together how Kovach came by his. He doesn't strike me as the Ivy League type.'

'Well, it takes one to know one.' Bradley got up from the table and left. Score one asshole point, Bradley. Gordon Junior walked in, looking sleepy, with tousled hair and a surly expression. He said good morning to his father, ignored Honey, and grunted at me. I think he was trying to impress me with how tough he was. That was all I needed. Between Stevenson Senior, Baz, and the two matching mercenaries, this place was overflowing with testosterone. Now Junior wanted in on the action.

Maureen came in a bit later, damp red hair and scrubbed skin. She wore pale blue jeans and a Dartmouth sweatshirt that was too big for her. I guess, when in Rome, wear the colors of the local college. She said good morning to everyone and sat down next to me.

I was about to say something witty when Baz strode down the veranda and into the house. He walked across the living room to us. Instead of an ugly 9mm carbine slung across his chest, he had his own Mini-14 slung on his shoulder, muzzle down. They weren't great rifles but certainly a more practical choice than the Nighthawk 9mm. He was holding an envelope and he handed it to Stevenson. Everybody held their breath while Stevenson read it. He frowned and then handed it to me. It was short and sweet.

'Put the money in an Army issue duffle bag. Have your big bodyguard and the private dick drive the money up to Thetford Hill and then down Academy Road to the covered bridge tonight at 2300 hours. The bodyguard will park at the ranger station and the private dick will take the money up to the middle of the Union Village Dam. Leave the money in the middle of the dam and leave. I will be watching. No tricks. Double-cross me and I will come for you.'

'Well, Roark, are you up for being the bagman?'

'Sure, why not. I don't have anything else going on.'

'Good.'

'Do you have any maps of the area?'

'Sure. All you want.'

'OK, I will want to look at them. Maybe drive by the area to get a feel for it. Right now, I should call Special Agent Watts.'

'Do we have to?'

'It's too late now not to involve the FBI in this. They take things like extortion very seriously.' I walked over to the white phone on the sideboard by the sliding glass doors that I had gracelessly exited through a few nights before. I picked up the phone and dialed the Lyme Inn, and the front desk connected me to Watts's room. She picked up after a few rings.

'Watts, we've gotten a letter with instructions about the drop.'

'Oh, OK. What are they?'

'It's probably better if you come here and read the note yourself.'

'Roark, we don't—'

'Know who's listening at the front desk.' I cut her off.

'Right. I'll be there in fifteen minutes.'

'I'll let the Ambassador know.'

'Right.' She hung up and I put the handset in its cradle, thinking that a white phone was a little bit ridiculous.

'The FBI will be here in fifteen minutes,' I told Stevenson.

'Good.'

'You mentioned that you had maps?'

'Sure, they're downstairs. Come on.' He beckoned with one hand, and I followed him downstairs. Next to the old wooden desk was a narrow, wooden box in which paper tubes were stacked. He pulled a few of the tubes out, checking notations written on the back of the map in pencil.

'These are the ones. Come on, we can lay them out on the table upstairs.' I followed him back upstairs, marveling at the change. A few minutes ago, he was sullen and drinking his breakfast, now he was energized, focused. He had a mission again. It had to be hard for him to be a hostage to Kovach's machinations. To have to wait. And now that there was movement, he could plan, which was almost as good as action.

Frieda had cleared the dining-room table of everything save the coffee pot and cups. Stevenson unrolled one of the maps, using an ashtray, salt and pepper shakers, and an empty coffee cup to hold the corners of the map down.

'I bought these when I was planning to build this place. They are US Geological Survey maps. Similar to what you used in the Army.' And indeed, they were. Black squares for buildings, red or red and white hash marks for roads, lines with perpendicular dashes for railroads, green for vegetation, blue for water, and red, tightly packed lines for contour intervals.

'We're here.' He tapped a black box in the green right angle formed between the juncture of the two roads out in front. I noticed the contour intervals around the house were closely packed, indicating a steep angle of ascent for our little hill. He traced a finger on the map, following the road and very tightly packed, squiggly, red contour lines, indicating a steep uphill from here.

'This is Thetford Hill.' He traced a finger downslope. 'This is Academy Road,' then following down to a blue patch with the symbol for a bridge. 'That's the covered bridge in Union Village.' His finger doubled back on the path it had just traced on the other side of the Ompompanoosuc River, then back up a circuitous bit of road that doubled back on itself leading to a straight line across the river. I was reminded of our Land Navigation instructor in the Army telling us, 'There is no such thing as a naturally occurring straight line in nature. If you see a straight line on a map or in the woods . . . it's man-made.' Stevenson tapped a finger on it. 'This is the dam. It rises about a hundred feet above the valley floor. The Corps of Engineers built it to prevent the spring floods damaging the towns downriver.'

'I take it that it's wide open there. How far across is it?'

'About a thousand feet long, give or take. The side you are coming in from is completely exposed. The side you will be facing has a two-story brick building that houses machinery and controls, a road and a lot of trees. The dam itself is made of earth and has riprap, you know, loose rock piled on it.'

'Shit.'

'Yes, you will be exposed out there. Probably not the first time your ass will be hanging out in the breeze.' We both knew it wasn't.

If we wanted to discuss my life and hard times in more depth, it would have to be another time. Watts pulled into the driveway in her boxy government-issue Ford. She got out of her car, and the mercenary stood a little straighter. Even the trooper got out of his car, put his Smokey the Bear hat on, and showed Watts due deference. I couldn't blame them; Watts was probably the most captivating woman in the whole state of Vermont. The fact that she was a fed and commanded respect were icing on the proverbial cake.

'FBI's here,' I said unnecessarily. I noticed that Stevenson was watching her walk across the uneven ground to the house. Even in sensible shoes, there was something about the way she walked.

When she had made it through the door and accepted a cup of Frieda's coffee, which sadly was nowhere near as good as her cooking, Watts got down to business. 'Let me see the note.' She read it once, and then again for good measure. She handed it back to Stevenson and looked at me. 'You're OK with this?'

I shrugged in what I hoped looked modest yet heroic to her. 'I'm as good as anyone.'

'It could be that he is pissed off at you too.'

'Probably is, but it is a lot of money. He wants the money.'

'What's to prevent him from taking a shot at you?'

'Not much . . . unless, of course, you don't plan on being there.'

'The Manchester and Boston offices are already scrambling to get some agents up here. VSP also has a couple of troopers who are marksmen. I have been told they can shoot the ass out of a gnat at five hundred yards.'

'Don't you guys have any of your own sharpshooters?'

'Sure, two are down at Quantico training, and one is on vacation in the Virgin Islands.'

'Probably better off with the boys from the State Police. I am sure they have been out in these woods bagging deer every year of their lives since they were old enough to hold a rifle.'

'Those the maps?' She thrust her chin at the table with the maps on it.

'Yep, wanna take a look?' We huddled around the map as Stevenson went through it all again. He pointed out where we were, the route, and the dam.

'So, he has locked you into a preplanned route, and he could be anywhere on it, watching you at any time.'

'Pretty much.'

'What about the bodyguard, is he in?'

'We haven't asked him yet.'

'Let's get that nailed down.'

'I'll go check with him,' Stevenson said, and wandered off in search of Baz.

'What do you think of it?' Watts asked.

'I think it sucks. There is a lot of open terrain to cover; there are plenty of places for him to hide or to take a shot from. This feels off, and there are no guarantees that we'll get him or if he will stop when he has the money.'

'That is our concern too. There are a lot of places he could go with the money. We won't be able to cover the woods. Between us and the VSP, we can cover the roads reasonably well. We'll also have a helicopter on standby, but that will be down in White River Junction. We don't want to scare him off.'

'Did you look deeper into the assistant, Bradley?'

'Yes, he is squeaky clean, never been arrested, pays his bills early, not so much as a speeding ticket.'

'Of course.'

'Except that his parents are about to lose the family farm in Ohio to the bank.'

'Oh, that would be a lot of incentive to turn to extortion.'

'Sure would be.'

Stevenson came back in. 'Baz says he'll do it. He's a good man.'

'Good. I'd like to take a ride over and see the place firsthand,' I said.

'We'll take my car.' Then to the Ambassador, 'When will the money be ready?'

'The bank will be driving it over later in the morning.'

'Good. We'll be back in a while.'

'Let me grab my jacket.' I ran downstairs and grabbed my British para smock and then went out to join Watts at her car. She didn't say anything until we were on our way up to Thetford Hill.

'I wanted to talk to you away from the house.'

'OK, makes sense.'

'Do you think there is an inside man?'

'Bradley looks kinda good for it. But it is just a suspicion at this point.'

'But you don't think that Kovach is acting alone.'

'No, I don't. He seems to know too much about the house and the people. He would have to be a master at surveillance and to have watched them for weeks on end. I just don't get the feeling that he is that patient or that skilled.'

'He is smart and patient enough to terrorize Stevenson into coughing up half a million bucks.'

'His new wife is pregnant, and he is scared.'

'Ooohh . . . OK. Yeah, that makes sense.' She nosed the boxy, American-made government car up the hill. At the top there was a little white clapboard church and a village green that was a couple of city blocks long and encircled by blacktop. Across the green there was a library. She turned left on to Academy Road.

We drove by quaint, old New England houses of either red brick or white clapboard, some of which had been here since before the Revolutionary War. We passed Thetford Academy, and the road tracked steadily downhill. Off on the left was a small cemetery, and to the right was a road that I knew from the maps was Buzzell Bridge Road and would lead up to the dam. Instead, we kept driving down to the river.

We drove under the old wooden covered bridge, on which there was only room for a single car at a time. I wondered how many young couples over the years had stopped under the bridge to steal a kiss.

'Could this be anymore stinking, bucolic New England?' Watts asked.

'Only if it were late fall and we were on a hayride.'

'With some hot cider and plaid blankets.' She was getting into the spirit of things.

We turned right once we exited the bridge and started to climb back uphill. I caught my first sight of the dam. If I was expecting the Vermont version of the Hoover Dam, I was out of luck. Instead of an Art Deco cement monstrosity, I was faced with a giant dirt and rock wall that rose above and across the river floor. We followed the road up as it snaked to the left, and Watts pulled over by the flagpole.

We got out and walked across the dam. It seemed high up and awfully exposed. To our front left was two-story brick building that seemed to rise out of the dam like an afterthought. The view was magnificent and, at the midpoint of the dam, I got an idea of just how much my ass was going to be out in the breeze. I made a mental note of where the middle of the dam was and then kept walking over to the other side. The Corps of Engineers had gated off both sides of Buzzell Bridge Road so that there was no driving through.

'I don't like it, Andy.'

'Nope, me neither.'

'Your ass is going to be hanging out here if it goes bad.' She had a point. There was no cover, and jumping over the side probably wouldn't kill me, but it wouldn't be fun either. 'There's no cover or concealment, you will be exposed the whole way.'

'Yep.' There wasn't much to say. She had a point. 'On the plus side, Kovach wants to get paid. He can't do that if he starts shooting at me. He'll have to figure that there will be some type of FBI or police on the dam. I just don't see how he hopes to get away with it.'

We walked down by the brick building and the two gates at the other end of the dam. 'We will coordinate with the Corps of Engineers and see if we can put one of the sharpshooters in there.'

'OK, that should give me some cover.'

'There's a scenic overlook on Route 132 behind us. We could put the other Green Mountain Boy there. You would be covered front and back.'

'They'd be pointing at each other. Also, that looks like it would be up to a thousand-foot shot to cover the dam from there.'

'So, sharpshooters in the building then?'

'How about a surveillance team at the scenic overlook and maybe an arrest team in the brick building?'

'You don't want sharpshooters to cover you?'

'No. Not guys I don't know or haven't worked with. Guys who might have to make a thousand-foot shot, at night, across a river valley. Nope, that sounds like a good way to get clipped. I have given up getting shot for Lent.'

'Lent has come and gone. But I see your point.'

We ducked under one of the metal gates that was painted yellow and started to walk down Buzzell Bridge Road toward Academy Road. The road was a ribbon of blacktop through a tunnel of pines that rose high on either side. It sloped dramatically upward to Thetford Hill, and it was perfect ambush country. We didn't say much on the walk down, which took all of ten minutes. We got down to the bottom and decided against walking Academy Road and doubled back up to the dam.

It was a steep enough walk back uphill that we were both breathing a little harder and my calves ached. Fortunately, the morning was cool and there were no bugs to annoy us. Back at the yellow gates and the brick building, we had seen enough. There were only so many ways in or out.

'What do you think?' Watts asked, standing again in the middle of the dam.

'I think it's a shitty set-up.'

'Yeah, no cover.'

'Nope, not just that. How is Kovach going to get the money and get out again? There are only three roads to come in on, but even if that weren't the case, there are only two ways on or off the dam.'

'OK, so what would you do?'

'If I didn't have a helicopter?'

'Yes, no rappelling.'

'I'd ambush the delivery car en route. Either up on Thetford Hill or down by the on-ramps to the highway. Hit the car, snatch the money, and take off on the highway.'

'OK, so what do we do? Follow you with a chase car?'

'Yes, at a distance. No sense making him nervous. You'll need agents to cover the dam, the roads in and out, and maybe have a couple of cars of agents or troopers ready to roll in if

it starts to go to shit. Or just to grab him with the money if
he runs.'

'We can do that. We have about ten agents, and VSP can
provide twenty troopers, so that should give us a lot of options.
Plus, the Vermont National Guard will put a helicopter at our
disposal. But at the end of the day, you will still have to walk
the money up on to the dam and out to the midpoint.'

'Great,' I said dryly. I wasn't over-reassured because the
whole thing stunk. The plan, the drop, the instructions, all of it.

'Let's head back.'

'Sure.'

We walked back to the car. It was a nice fall day in New
England. The leaves were spectacular, the view from the dam
was truly impressive. I was walking next to Watts, and in other
circumstances, this would be the stuff that dates were made of.
Except that it wasn't. We got back to her government car and
headed back to the Ambassador's hunting lodge.

SEVENTEEN

We pulled into the driveway as a blue Audi was pulling out.

'I wonder who that could be?' I asked.

'That's probably the money from the bank.'

'They deliver?'

'When enough money is involved, they do.'

'I don't think that is a problem I will ever have.'

'Not at your rates.'

We got out and walked past the trooper in his green Chevrolet. Smith and Jones were circling the house with the ugly carbines. Inside we found Baz, Stevenson, and Bradley standing over the dining-room table. When we got close, we realized they were standing over a pile of money. Literally standing over hundreds of packets of dollars that were banded together with currency bands. Each band had '$2,000' printed on it in mirror image between the colored stripes on each side of the band.

'Ah, Roark, Watts, glad you're back. How did the recon go?' Stevenson was back in his element, in command of an operation again.

'It went as well as can be expected,' Watts said deliberately. Stevenson may have reawakened the feeling of conducting operations again, but he would be sorely mistaken if he thought he was in charge of Brenda Watts or her case.

'Roark, what do you think?'

'I think it stinks.'

'See,' Bradley interjected, 'I told you he isn't up to this. Baz can drop the money. He's experienced enough for the job and he's always sober.'

'Easy there, sonny. This job isn't a good one and, frankly, being drunk wouldn't make it any worse.'

'Don't call me sonny.'

'When I meet someone who is so rude, I assume that they

didn't have good parenting. Usually that is followed by an offer to teach them some manners, sonny.'

Bradley began to splutter and took a step back.

'Knock it off, you two. Roark, you don't have to fight with everyone. Bradley, don't be stupid. A fight with Roark won't be like fisticuffs on the lawn of the frat house. He's a killer.' That was probably the nicest thing Stevenson had ever said about me. 'Roark, why does the set-up stink?'

'There are realistically two roads leading to the dam. One comes up from Academy Road but is blocked at two ends by locked metal gates. The other is the winding, switchback road that comes up from the ranger station. The dam is a hundred or more feet above the river valley. Only two ways on or off. There are plenty of places to watch but, at the end of the day, Kovach still has to get to the middle of the dam to get his money.'

'That strikes me as his problem, not ours,' Stevenson said.

'I agree. I'm just trying to figure out his game.'

'You're still going to make the drop, right?'

'I don't have anything else on my dance card tonight.'

'Baz, you still in?'

'Yes, Bass.' His accent seemed more Rhodesian when he talked to Stevenson.

'Good. You said you have an Army surplus duffle bag?'

'Yes, Bass.'

'OK, go get it and we'll load it up.' Baz left and Stevenson started to ask Watts about the plan. She generically outlined where the surveillance teams would be, and what assets would be available. He nodded and smiled when Watts mentioned the Vermont National Guard helicopter. Everyone likes helicopters.

'Roark, you'll be armed right?'

'I have my pistol.'

'You don't want something bigger?'

Of course I did. Instead I said, 'Handgun will be fine.'

'OK.' Baz had returned with an Army issue duffle bag which he and Bradley proceeded to fill. Each packet was about an inch thick, and there were two hundred and fifty of them. They filled the bag three quarters full, and when I picked it up, it weighed as much as a bag of cement. I handed the bag back to Baz.

'Baz, take that downstairs and watch it. Try to get some rest, but you stick with that bag until it gets handed over to Roark. Got it?'

'Sure, Bass.' He shouldered the duffle and headed downstairs. I watched Baz walk away and wondered what would keep him from walking out the back door with the money.

'Roark, I have to go meet with the agents and the boys from the State Police. They have a command post set up in the elementary school. Get some rest. The last thing any of us needs is a sleepy bagman out there.'

'Sure, sure. Don't worry about me, I'll be fine.'

'Give the redhead a rest and stay away from the booze.'

'I'll have a salad and cottage cheese for dinner, so I am light on my feet.'

'Good idea. I like it when you are thinking.' She left to go meet with her task force, and I went downstairs to get some peace. I poured myself a glass of water and dug out the yellow legal pads. I noted the details about the note and the drop. I went back upstairs and grabbed one of the maps of Thetford Hill, Union Village, and the dam and went back downstairs.

I sat at the old wooden office desk and out of habit wrote down the map section and the approximate grid coordinates for the dam and the drop. I noted the roads in and out and generally tried to figure out which way Kovach would come from. It was a moot point. The drop was all at once very simple, one long stretch of open blacktop with a road at either end that had to be covered. The sides of the dam were too steep for Kovach to hike up them. Which meant he would have to stop us on the road, but where? The 'how' part was pretty obvious.

There were plenty of places to ambush us and grab the money. Academy Road snaked and curved toward the bottom, which was perfect ambush territory. Kovach would have to contend with both me and Baz. We'd be armed with handguns at a minimum. For Kovach, the best bet would be to get us on the covered bridge, stop the car we were in, and hose it down with the Mini-14. The problem with that was it would make a lot of noise. The FBI and State Police would come a-running, and there was only one way out from there, which was the road to Norwich.

Or he could wait for the wee hours and try to sneak in and grab the duffle bag. I wasn't sure how long the FBI was prepared to wait. There wouldn't be any traffic on the dam at night. There had to be a reason why he wanted the money dropped off at eleven o'clock at night.

I sketched out the dam and the area around it. I added a bunch of different arrows, mostly so it seemed like I was working on a problem, but there wasn't much to work out. There were only two possible places he could come from; both could be easily watched. It was a problem that was so simple, it was complex.

I wanted to look at the map and try to memorize as much of the terrain as possible. If something went down, I wouldn't have time for a map or a compass. I would have to know the major bits of terrain from memory. It would also be dark, and old mission prep habits die hard.

After an hour I couldn't look at the map anymore without all the lines and colors running into squiggles and blurs. I folded up the map and went to lie down on the couch. There was nothing wrong with taking a nap before a dangerous mission.

I woke up when Watts came back to brief Baz and me about the plan. There would be a six-man team watching from the brick building at the edge of the dam. They would also be the primary arrest team. She would also have agents and troopers watching the roads in and out who would act as secondary teams. There would be cars in the area with agents as well, all talking to each other on their state or federal government radios. That was almost reassuring. We'd have a radio in our car in case Kovach tried anything sneaky.

Baz would drive me to the ranger station at the base of the dam, and I would walk up to the drop with the money. Drop it in the middle of the dam and then walk back down again. She left out the part about trying not to get shot in the process.

Dinner that night was roast chicken with roast potatoes and carrots in some sort of cream sauce. I picked at mine and did my best to answer the unending stream of nervous questions that Stevenson came up with. Honey was polite and solicitous. Maureen rubbed my thigh under the table, and Bradley looked at me as though he hoped something would go wrong and I'd get shot in the process. Gordon Junior just stared sullenly at his plate.

Later I went downstairs, and would have tried to get some rest, but I heard footsteps on the stairs. I wasn't in the mood for drinks with Stevenson but was treated instead to the sight of Maureen.

'Hey there.'

'Hey yourself, cowboy.' She smiled a funny smile and I realized that one of her eye teeth was a little crooked.

'What brings you down here?'

'Oh, you know,' she said with mock evasiveness. She sat down next to me on the couch and rested her head on my shoulder. 'Andy, you asked if I could drive down to Boston when this is all over?'

'Yes.' I held her hand in mine, fingers intertwined.

'Did you mean it?'

'Of course.'

'Andy, this may sound crazy, but this feels like the beginning of something.'

'I'd like it to be.' I wasn't sure I meant the words until I heard myself saying them.

'Me too. We just have to get through this.'

'Well, it does seem to be hogging a lot of everyone's attention.'

'OK, after this is done, I will come down to Boston and we'll have a proper date.'

'I can't complain about our efforts so far.' Smooth, Andy, very smooth.

'No, nor can I.' She actually said nor . . . maybe that was the difference between English girls and American ones. 'Tell me, what you were like as a boy?'

'Umn . . . a little too tall and lanky. I got in trouble a lot at school. The nuns didn't care for my sense of humor.'

'Did your father get mad at home about it?'

'No, he understood. He rebelled in his own way and wanted to do other things with his life.'

'Like what?'

'He wanted to write, but after the war, he had a wife to take care of, and shortly after that a son. Poetry doesn't pay enough to support a family, so he went to work for the New England Confectionery Company.'

'Making confections?' She laughed and it was a bright, tinkling sound.

'No, an Army buddy of his – who he'd been in the Airborne with – got him an office job.'

'You were raised in a happy family?'

'It was happy enough.' I didn't feel like bringing up my mother's leaving or my father's slow, alcoholic retreat inward. 'How about you? You said you grew up on a farm?'

'My grandparents' farm in the country. My parents were killed in a motoring accident and my grandparents raised me. They sent me to a boarding school because they thought I should be raised a proper English lady. Then to uni in London. I spent every holiday and free moment on their farm.'

'It sounds very nice.'

'It was there that I learned to ride, to shoot, and to take care of the animals. I treasured those moments on the farm.'

'I can see why you would. They must be very proud of you.'

'They were.' I kissed her softly on the lips, and that probably would have led to more satisfying activities, but Watts had arrived upstairs. Watts wasn't the type to put off a pre-mission briefing for a few minutes to let the sacrificial bagman enjoy one last roll around under the sheets.

'You'd better go upstairs. We can always resume this conversation when you come back safely.'

'Well, that is the best motivation to come back from a mission I have ever had.' Not that still being alive wasn't a great motivator, but in Vietnam there was no hero's welcome waiting from a pretty, curvy redhead. Instead, it was debrief, clean gear and weapons, get a steak dinner and get drunk at the club.

She kissed me lightly on the lips, and I went upstairs to see Watts. She was dressed in blue jeans, cute work boots that had never been anywhere near a construction site, a black turtleneck and flannel shirt. Her .38 was holstered on her hip. I assumed that she had left her raid jacket with 'FBI' in big yellow letters in the car. Smart. If Kovach was watching the house, make him wonder who she was and not announce it.

She saw me and smiled. Stevenson, ever used to being in charge, was pestering her with questions. I walked over and he stopped. 'Roark, how are you?'

'As good as can be, sir.'

'Rested?'

'Yes, sir.'

'Good.'

'Sober?' This from Bradley, who didn't bother to hide his dislike. I ignored him and turned to Watts.

'Everything set?'

'Yes. I brought you these.' She held out two radios, one large walkie-talkie, and a much smaller pocket-sized one.

'Good. One for the car, and I assume the smaller one is for me up on the dam?'

'Yes. The range on the small one isn't great and will be worse if you are down in the valley, but it is better than nothing. The bigger one should let you stay in contact with us and vice versa. If Kovach tries to ambush you, just squawk and we will be there in no time.'

'Good.' I didn't tell her that if Kovach opened up on us with the Mini-14, we probably wouldn't be in much shape to use the radio. I kept my mouth shut. No one likes negativity before a mission.

'Do you think he will try that?' Honey had quietly entered the room and now had a very serious look on her otherwise beautiful face.

'Mrs Stevenson, we have to try and cover every angle, no matter how unlikely.' Watts said it in her professional FBI voice. She sounded so confident I was almost reassured myself.

'Baz and I are both armed, both experienced soldiers. It probably wouldn't be a very good idea.' I smiled my second-most cocky smile at her. As a rule, I didn't use my cockiest smile on married women. She smiled back with evident relief.

'OK, it's just that you are taking such risks for us. I know you like to say you're a hired gun, but still this goes beyond the investigating that Gordon hired you to do.' I shrugged, trying to do it the way I thought Bogie would in *Casablanca*.

'Andy, I brought this for you too.' Watts held up a blue lump of nylon and Velcro the size of a man's torso. I shook my head no. 'Andy, the SAC wants you to wear this. What if there is shooting up on the dam?'

'Watts, if the Special Agent in Charge wants to do the drop, he is welcome to wear whatever he wants. But for me, no thanks. I'm all set.'

'Andy, this is no time to act macho or to try and impress the ladies.'

'Watts, if I want to impress the ladies, I'll hum a few bars of "Camptown Races" and tap-dance my ass around the floor while doing it.'

'Andy, you piss people off, and they tend to shoot at you. One of these days their aim won't be so sloppy,' she said, pointing to my ragged earlobe.

'Watts, that vest is bulky and heavy. If Kovach is intent on gunplay, then I need to be able to move, to shoot.'

'What if he is good?'

'Watts, even if he is great, he isn't in my league.' I said it with no trace of ego. The Army had taught me how to shoot, spent a lot of time and money doing it. Then, years later, I went out to Arizona and the Colonel really taught me how to use a pistol. He would disapprove of my Hi-Power. In his mind the 9mm was a near useless cartridge compared to the .45 APC.

'Andy . . .' It was odd to see an exasperated Watts.

'Brenda, I might have to move and move quick. This thing will get in the way. If he has his Mini-14, those rounds will punch through this vest like it is made of tissue paper. Speed and violence of action will be all I can bring to the table. No vest.'

'Fine,' she said tightly between pursed lips. 'OK, I have to get in position. You need to be at the ranger station at quarter of.'

'We'll be there.' She left and I killed time waiting for Baz by going over the map with Stevenson. I pointed out where I thought the FBI and the state cops would be positioned. It reminded me of pre-mission briefings when I was in SOG.

Then it was time to get ready. I went downstairs and switched from running sneakers to my old jungle boots. The Hi-Power was fully loaded with hollow points and a round in the chamber. I pulled the old commando sweater on over my shirt, put a spare magazine in my pants pocket, and pulled on my para smock. The weight of another thirteen-round magazine in the front pocket was comforting. I put the radio in the left chest pocket of the smock.

I slipped out the back door. I didn't feel like saying goodbye to Stevenson or Honey or any of them. Not even Maureen. My stomach was starting to tighten, and I just wanted to go and do the job and get it done. Baz had the Bronco waiting by the garage. He was leaning against the tailgate smoking a cigarette.

'Hey, mate.'

'Hey, Baz.'

'Take a look at this.' He had taken the rear bench seat out of the back, and in its place was a lump covered by a blanket. He lifted a blanket and pulled the top of the duffle bag over. He undid the clasp and opened it up to show me the stacks of twenty-dollar bills in the weak light shining from the Bronco's interior light. Banded stacks of two thousand dollars each.

'That's a lot of dough.'

'Sure, it is. Want to run to Canada with it?' he joked.

'Tempting, but then I'd have Special Agent Watts hunting me for the rest of my life. It's a lot easier to do the drop.'

'Right, good on ya.' He laughed and closed the duffle bag up, clasping it, and shoving it under the blanket. 'C'mon, let's go.' We got in. He had his own Mini-14 with two curved thirty-round magazines taped together. The whole thing lying across the dashboard. He saw me and nodded. 'Just in case Kovach doesn't want us to make it to the dam.'

'Probably more useful than this,' I said as I turned on the big FBI radio and put it down between our bucket seats. Baz put the Bronco in gear, and we headed up to Thetford Hill. My stomach was tightening the way it used to when we got on the helicopters. My stomach would tighten and tighten until we were approaching the LZ and I would step on the skid.

Baz drove carefully and we both kept our eyes peeled for any sign, any indication that Kovach was going to try and ambush us. We made it up the hill, Baz turned left, and we started the twisting decent to the floor of the river valley. Each curve forced us to slow down, making us an easier target for Kovach. We passed the small cemetery to our left and then Buzzell Bridge Road which led up to the dam.

Then we were in front of the wooden covered bridge. Baz had stopped short and put the Bronco in neutral. He looked at me. 'Well, mate, if it hasn't happened yet, this is where it is most likely to happen.'

'Yep.' I couldn't see anything in the dark opening. 'If we're gonna do it, let's get to it.'

'Sure thing, Bass.' He grinned in the darkness and put the Bronco in first gear and then second as our wheels touched the wooden floor of the bridge. I had my hand on the butt of my Hi-Power and the holster unsnapped. We cleared the bridge and Baz turned right, and we headed uphill to the ranger station at the base of the dam. He pulled into the little parking area and we both got out. I paused to snap my holster closed over the Hi-Power and readjust the smock over it.

At the rear of the Bronco, Baz had lowered the tailgate and raised the rear window. He reached in and pulled out the olive drab duffle bag, the same type that GIs had been schlepping their kit in from war to war since World War II. He grunted slightly as he humped it off the tailgate and on to my shoulder. I slid my hand through the other shoulder strap, settling the almost sixty pounds of money on my back.

'Don't go running off into the bush with that, or the lovely FBI agent will be on your spoor for sure.'

'Ha, I wouldn't even know what to do with the money.'

'Haha, I would. Good luck, mate.' He sat on the tailgate and lit a cigarette.

I nodded to him. 'See you in a few.' Then I turned and started up the road with the scent of fresh, burning tobacco in my nostrils. It made me want a cigarette, but now wasn't the time.

The gradient was steep and the money in the duffle bag didn't help. The duffle was soft-sided, and it pulled at my shoulders uncomfortably. By the time I had gone a hundred yards, I was sweating and unzipped the para smock. I had entered a small copse of trees that rose on either side of me. Fortunately, there was a full moon and no clouds. I could see the pinprick of lights in the night sky and could tell the night was going to be one of the cold ones.

This would be the perfect place to brace me and take the money. If he was quiet enough about it, he could walk the money out through the woods. The only good news was that he probably wasn't going to light me up with a bunch of .223 caliber rifle rounds. I kept walking. If the Army had taught me anything other than how to wait in line, it was marching, putting one foot in front of the other, eating up the distance.

I kept winding my way up the road and, in a few minutes, I was next to the turnaround at the flagpole where Watts had parked her car hours earlier. The breeze was more noticeable at the top. It smelled of pines and wet leaves, and the smell of tobacco smoke wafted on the breeze too.

I stepped on to the dam and paused, listening. I could hear wind rustling the trees and, far off in the distance, a car droned by. I started forward, aware of how exposed I was. There was no cover, and if there was any type of gunplay, my only option was to shoot back. Jumping over the side of the dam seemed like a great recipe for several broken bones, at best. While I was contemplating all of this, I had reached the middle of the dam.

I knew Watts was in the brick building in front of me, watching with a bunch of other keyed-up agents, eyes straining to see Kovach out there in the night. I slid the straps of the duffle bag off my shoulders and put it down in the middle of the dam. Five hundred thousand dollars in used twenty-dollar notes. That could buy someone a nice retirement. I looked around then turned back the way I came.

The walk back didn't take as long and wasn't as tense. I was a little chilled from the sweat that I had worked up, and I zipped up the para smock to conserve some warmth. It felt weird walking down the middle of a road at night in the woods. I had spent two years of intense combat avoiding even walking on a trail unless there was literally no other option. The weight of the Hi-Power on my hip was comforting, and, in a few minutes, I was back at the Bronco with Baz, who was still sitting on the tailgate.

'I didn't hear any gunfire, so it went off all right?'

'Our part is done. The bag's sitting in the middle of the dam waiting for Kovach to come get it.'

'FBI all around?'

'Of course.' I shook a Lucky out of the soft pack and offered him one. He shook his head, and I cupped my hand over the flare of the lighter while I lit the cigarette. The tar and nicotine were a welcome change from all the fresh, pine-scented air.

'We should get out of here. If Kovach is watching, he will think we are lying in wait for him.'

'OK, let's head up the hill and park in the parking lot of the school.' We'd be close enough to be able to hear on the radio if anything went down. We'd also be close enough to get involved in it.

We got in the Bronco. Baz started it up, and we again crossed the covered wooden bridge and made our way uphill. In a few minutes we were parked, lights out, facing Academy Road, waiting anxiously for something to happen. We sat there, not saying much, listening to the radio that wasn't broadcasting. We smoked with the windows cracked and our hands cupped around the glowing tip of the cigarettes.

'The Bass said you were a Green Beret in Nam.'

'Yes.'

'Where were you?'

'Mostly up north,' I said vaguely. Stevenson might know all about it, but I still wasn't going to talk about it with anyone who wasn't in SOG. 'How about you?'

'Spent some time in the Central Highlands and the A Shau. How long were you there?'

'When all was said and done, I was there for almost three years.' My Army career had been short, a little over five years, a quarter of the way to a pension.

'Jesus.'

'Yeah, well, it seemed like the thing to do at the time. You were a mercenary in Africa.' Small talk on a tough-guy man date. Give us something to drink and we might start comparing old scars. Thankfully, I was sober.

'Yeah, in Rhodesia.'

'What was that like?'

'Hairy. The whites were in the minority but felt the country was theirs. The blacks were in the majority and thought the same thing. You can guess how that worked out, and the commies just saw another war to fuel. It was weird.'

'How so?'

'Well in the Green Machine, we had everything we needed, right? Helicopters, close air support, resupply. In the rear, you had cold beers and ice cream and the Donut Dollies might come visit. There was a PX on every base and USO tours. Bob Hope, his golf club, and Ann-Margret.'

'Oooh, Ann-Margret.' A lot of guys were partial to Raquel Welsh, but Ann-Margret had a special place in my heart.

'In Rhodesia we didn't have many helicopters, certainly no Hueys. We used to fly in old Dakotas and jump in on operations because that was the fastest way to get troops to a hotspot. Or we'd be out in the bush, tracking some rebels' spoor for days at a time. The firefights were brutal, but we had the advantage. The blacks we fought, they weren't like the VC or the NVA. Most of them didn't have the training or skills we had. The Cuban advisors, that was a different story.'

'So, what happened?'

'The Vote happened. For all our skill on the battlefield, the politicians gave it all away and Rhodesia was voted out of existence. We fought and toiled to preserve what our ancestors had built from nothing, and they just turned it all over to the blacks. They didn't waste any time tearing it all down.'

I didn't know much about Rhodesia or the history of the area, but I was pretty sure that his characterizing it that way might have glossed over a lot of colonial real-estate snatching and brutal violence. We smoked in silence for a while, and I watched the glowing hands of my Seiko dive watch click in their circular arc. When they showed a little past one in the morning, the radio crackled.

'Roark, are you on?'

'Yes.'

'Watts here.' Even through the tinny speaker I could tell it was her. 'Kovach hasn't shown up yet. I am guessing you guys are nearby.'

'Roger that.'

'This is going to turn into a long night, maybe morning too.

You guys should head back to the lodge and get some rest.' I looked over at Baz who nodded and started the Bronco.

'OK. We're on our way back. Touch base with you in the morning.'

'Watts out.' And the radio was just soft static.

Baz put the Bronco in gear and steered us downhill toward the hunting lodge. The trip was a short one. We pulled into the driveway and Baz dropped me in front of the house, then went to put the Bronco in the garage. The trooper was readjusting himself in his seat after we woke him up with our lights. I started toward the house and the outside floodlight snapped on, blinding me. Smith or Jones said, 'Oh, it's you.'

'Yep, the one and only. Baz is parking the Bronco.'

'Got it.' I walked past him into the quiet house and made my way downstairs. Something was niggling at the back of my brain. An annoying itch, and I couldn't figure out how to scratch it. Downstairs it was dark, save for the moonlight coming in through the windows. I put Watts's FBI radios down on the bar. I didn't bother turning on the lights but took off my para smock, dropping it on Stevenson's chair, the commando sweater too.

I helped myself to a large glass of Stevenson's good bourbon and some ice. I undid my jungle boots, pausing to take big sips of the bourbon. I had been keyed up going up to the dam and then kept it at a low simmer while we were waiting in the Bronco. Now my nerves were jangling with unspent adrenaline, and my mind was trying to undo some knot that I couldn't figure out. I dropped my jeans – holster, Hi-Power and all – on the chair and took off my t-shirt too. I was about to unholster the pistol to put under my pillow when Maureen said, 'Leave the damned gun and come to bed. I've been waiting in here forever.' I wasn't one to argue. She was naked and warm. After reacquainting ourselves, I fell into a deep sleep.

I was in the jungle again. Moving carefully and quietly I am a green ghost, camouflage paint on my face, slipping through the morning mists. My CAR-15 is pointed in front of me, looking for an enemy.

The morning is misty and cool, and I can smell the jungle, all the rotting vegetation. It is a paradox that a place teeming with so much life also smells so much of decomposition. Then the acrid smell of ammonia from explosives rides the morning mist into my nasal passages. It is quickly overwhelmed by the smell of coppery blood and death. Twitching in front of me on the ground is the deer.

The deer is moving its mouth, but no sounds are coming out. It kicks its legs in a futile attempt to right itself. Piles of chewed-up grass lie on the ground in front of it, steam rising off them in the cool morning. I have killed in Vietnam. That is the job, but the deer is different. The deer was just trying to have breakfast.

'Andy,' Maureen's voice was just a whisper, and her face was close to mine. Her hand on my shoulder was strong and she shook me hard to wake me up. 'Andy.'

'What?' I whispered back to her. I opened my eyes and my mind registered that it was around dawn. It was gray outside, and I struggled to shake the few hours of sleepy cobwebs out of my brain.

'It's Baz. I heard him moving around. He went out to the garage.'

'What?'

'Yes, I heard him moving around. It woke me up. I looked out the window and he was going into the garage. He has his rifle.'

'A Mini-14,' I said automatically. For too long, guns had been a part of my life. I got up and pulled on my clothes and quickly laced up my jungle boots. I pulled on my smock, went to the window, and was rewarded by the sight of Baz coming out of the garage with an Army issue duffle bag slung on his shoulders and the rifle with its curved magazines slung across his chest. He had an Army issue intrenching tool in his hand that he was swinging aimlessly back and forth.

A green Army issue duffle bag. I remember one of my drill sergeants bellowing at us.

'DO NOT DESCRIBE YOUR DUFFLE BAG AS ALL DUFFLE BAGS LOOK THE SAME. NOW DO PUSH-UPS MOTHERFUCKERS! ONE TROOP FORGETS HIS GEAR, EVERYONE PAYS. IN VIETNAM FUCKS-UPS ARE PAID FOR IN BLOOD NOT A LITTLE SWEAT.' One severely unlucky private, without his duffle bag, and the rest of us soon to be just a little less unlucky.

'Do not describe your duffle bags . . .' I started to say.

'What?' she asked. I opened the door to Baz's room and saw through the window that instead of coming back to the house, he was heading into the woods. I went back to the bar and to the gun cabinet. I took the Browning out of the case and jacked a round into the chamber then put another cartridge in the magazine, which I then put back in the rifle. I dropped the box of cartridges in the pocket of my smock. I grabbed the radio and switched on as I was going up the steps two at a time.

'Watts, Roark . . . check the duffle bag! Check the duffle bag!' I dropped the radio on the couch next to a snoring Smith or Jones. I opened the sliding glass door and stepped out on the patio. Baz had about a minute's head start on me, but he was going around the base of the hill and he didn't know he was being chased.

I stepped into the woods, moving as quickly and quietly as I could without crashing through the brush. As the slope got steeper near the bottom, the morning mist grew thicker. There was frost on the pine needles, leaves, and on the ground. I made it down to the main trail and saw Baz and the duffle bag disappear around a corner. I started after him and too late heard the flushing of birds above me. I stepped on a piece of granite sticking out and slid, stumbling but not falling.

Baz broke into a run a hundred yards ahead of me. I started after him, jungle boots slapping on the soft forest floor. I had the advantage by not having to haul almost sixty pounds of twenty-dollar bills. Baz turned right down the bend in the trail where I had stopped last time I was in these woods. I neared the bend and stepped off the trail and into the woods heading parallel to the trail, deeper into the forest.

I heard the rounds cracking by my head and the reports from the rifle. I dove into a pile of ferns and crawled through some mud and pine needles until I was behind a downed tree. The tree had snapped at the base during some storm or another and I was near the top of it. He fired a couple of rounds and I saw muzzle flashes in the mist. I poked the rifle through the branches of the top of the tree and ripped five rounds off in his general direction, then dropped down on to frost-hardened ground.

The .243 was a little bigger than the .223 bullets he was shooting at me, and it was nice to be armed with something other than a handgun for a change. It was nice to think of the rounds snapping by Baz, to think of him scrambling for cover.

I was rewarded for my efforts by more rounds snapping over my head. I rolled on to my back and pushed myself along with my heels, wriggling my shoulder blades, while Baz was turning the top of the tree into woodchips. The mud was hard and dug uncomfortably in my back. I paused and dug the box of shells out of my pocket. I opened the action and fed a round into the breach and then popped out the magazine and pushed four rounds into it. I popped the magazine back into the rifle and kept wriggling on my back toward the thicker part of the tree. There was a little bit of space under the tree where it had snapped and the base of it was propped up on the splintered trunk.

I turned my head and saw movement. Baz was kneeling against a tree, scanning with the rifle fifty or sixty yards away. I wriggled back some more and then quietly rolled over on to my stomach, sticking the barrel of the Browning under the downed tree. He had been obscured by the mist in the short time I was moving. I fired a spoiler round into the tree above where I thought he was. He started firing at me as fast as he could pull the trigger, rounds slapping into the three-foot-thick tree above me.

I lined the sights up on the muzzle flashes in the mist and fired the remaining four shots in rapid succession, the stock punching into my shoulder, hand working the lever, the smell of burnt powder hanging in the air. I rolled over and dropped the rifle in the mud. I sprang up and ran to a thick hemlock tree, drawing my Hi-Power. Then, safety off, pistol in hand, I slowly worked from tree to tree, trying to get behind Baz.

It didn't take long, a minute or two that seemed like a short lifetime. He was sitting up against a tree. There was blood on his chest and the Mini-14 was across his lap. I could see a partially ejected shell casing stove-piped in the chamber. He coughed; pinkish mist came out of his mouth. He was alive and he had a sucking chest wound. One of my rounds had punched through a lung. There was also blood coming from his abdomen.

'Fuck, that hurts,' he spoke, more pink foam.

'Yeah, probably does.'

'Hard fucking way to make your fortune, mate.'

'You mean steal someone else's.'

'Well, it's a living for a gentleman of fortune.' I was amused that he used an arcane term to describe pirates, instead of 'soldier of fortune'.

'How long have you been gaslighting Stevenson for?'

'Ha, since the beginning.'

'And Kovach?'

'Never heard of him till you turned up with his name.'

'It was you who shot up the house. What, did you get the Mini-14 after finding out Kovach had one?'

'Hahaha,' he laughed weakly.

'Why did you do it? Why Stevenson?'

'Me? I'm a mercenary, mate.' Like that explained it all.

I had more questions but there was no point. The life had gone out of him. He was as dead as any I'd seen.

The duffle bag was at his side. He had opened it and a couple of banded bundles of money had spilled out. I sat down on a nearby stump and lit a cigarette. I sat smoking, contemplating the man who I had just killed while I waited for Watts and the FBI to arrive. I heard myself telling Baz, 'Do not describe your duffle bag, as all duffle bags look the same.' He didn't have a witty retort. I couldn't blame him.

EIGHTEEN

I was on my second cigarette when the state trooper who had been parked out in front of the house found me. He pointed his giant stainless steel .357 Magnum revolver at me and yelled commands that I couldn't really hear. Gunfire tends to do that to me. I put my hands up and did my best to comply while he handcuffed me. He wasn't gentle when he slapped the handcuffs on my wrists. He frisked me, taking my pistol, which he stuffed into his belt. It annoyed me – like watching another man dance with your girl.

Watts and the FBI/Vermont State Police task force descended on the scene before my hands started to throb too badly from the too-tight handcuffs. When the trooper uncuffed them, there were hints of pins and needles. He handed my Hi-Power back to me butt first, and I awkwardly reholstered it.

'Jesus, you're a sight.' That was about as much sympathy as I could expect from Watts.

'Good to see you too. What was in the duffle bag on the dam?'

'Well, you know what wasn't,' she said, gesturing to the one on the ground. 'Old *Newsweek* magazines. I guess Stevenson hung on to his subscription, tied them up with string and stored them in the garage for posterity.'

'Of course, he would.'

'Sure, he's a man of greatness. What happened?' I told her the story pretty much as it happened. I didn't feel the need to mention that Maureen had woken me up, or why she was in my bed to begin with.

'You just woke up?'

'Sure.'

'You still smell like bourbon and sex,' she said, with only a little vinegar in her voice.

'A gentleman never tells.'

'Since when are you a gentleman?'

'Ha. Flattery will get you nowhere. Anything linking Baz to Kovach?'

'Not much. We found Kovach's car at the rest stop off the interstate in New Hampshire. You know, the one with the liquor store.'

'I've driven by it.' I felt no need to add my other deviant behaviors to her list. She was doing fine on her own.

'A New Hampshire state trooper noticed that the car had been there for a couple of days. When he got out to check, he noticed some blood on the back seat.'

'Kovach?'

'We think so. No body yet, but they are checking the area around the rest stop and will bring in the dogs if they need to.'

'I wonder if that is Kovach's rifle?' I gestured to the Mini-14.

'We'll have to print it. None of his weapons were registered, so that doesn't help, but you never know.'

'Baz said he never heard of Kovach until I showed up.'

'Do you believe him?'

'I don't know. He was on death's door, and I think he had it in him to make up a lie.'

'OK, the State Police crime-scene boys will be here in a little while. Did you use your pistol?'

'No, just Stevenson's rifle.'

'OK, the State Police will want a statement from you. Once everything is photographed, we'll count the money and get it back to Stevenson.'

'OK. Sounds good.'

'Andy, you did good.'

'Thanks.' I wish it felt like I had.

'Let's go back to the house. You look like you need a cup of coffee, and you smell like you need a shower.' She wrinkled her nose, and if she hadn't had a .38 holstered on her hip, I would've told her she looked cute. One gunfight a morning is my limit.

I was able to get a cup of coffee and a quick shower in before I had to give my statement. The Vermont State Police detective was in his forties, with an iron-gray brush cut and K-mart suit. I couldn't blame him; polyester is affordable and stands up well to wrinkles. He had all the personality of a Styrofoam cup, and his last name was Lyndgarten. He had me write out what happened and then read it into a black, push-button tape recorder.

I shouldn't complain, he saved me a trip to the nearest barracks to do it. When they woke up, Smith and Jones both said the last thing they remembered was Baz bringing them cups of coffee. He had thoughtfully put in milk and sugar and a few sleeping pills. It had been enough to knock them out but not kill them. He was a considerate SOB.

Watts came back in from the woods around noon. They had taken pictures of every shell casing and bullet hole they could find. They had bagged the rifles, Baz's pistol, and a bunch of shell casings as evidence.

The troopers had hauled a body bag out to the waiting ambulance that would transport Baz's body to the morgue in Saint Johnsbury. The now thoroughly photographed duffle bag was brought inside and the money counted and recounted in front of Stevenson, who was beaming. Who could blame him? Tired FBI agents were searching Baz's room. The whole house was a hive of activity.

'They found a body in some trees on the far side of the parking lot of the rest stop,' Watts pulled me aside to tell me.

'Kovach?' I asked.

'His wallet was in the body's pants, but small animals have been at the face and soft tissue.'

'Ugh. Any idea how he died?'

'Shot through the temple. Maybe a .38 or a 9-millimeter. Close range.'

'Baz had a 9-millimeter.'

'OK. The boys from the lab will check it out.'

'Is there anything that connects Stevenson's aide Bradley to either Baz or Kovach?'

'Still on the "butler did it" angle?'

'Well, one butler certainly, but what if there were two? Baz didn't end up here by accident.'

'Nothing. I know you don't like the guy, but don't let that cloud your judgment.'

'Hmph.'

'You got the bad guy. We don't know all the details yet, his motive, but you got the guy. Stevenson and his family are safe because of you. You can feel good about that.'

'Watts, maybe Baz was smart enough to put together the scheme. Maybe he was able to work it out so that he could drive down to Fairhaven and plant the typewriter, steal some guns, all of that, but Baz didn't strike me as the type to come up with this type of thing.'

'You said it yourself that this was pretty half-assed.'

'How did he guarantee that he got hired?'

'Andy, I don't know. We may never know. We have the guy. We have the gun. We have the money. No one other than that asshole got hurt. That's what we in the Bureau call a win.' She left me to go back to the investigation.

I only caught fleeting glimpses of Watts the rest of the day. Maureen was even more scarce. Stevenson was tied up with the FBI, going over their questions about Baz. Bradley hovered close by Stevenson but didn't say much to me. Gordon Junior was almost as scarce as Maureen. Amid all the investigative dog-and-pony show, Honey came in and sat down next to me on the couch.

'Hello.'

'Hi.'

'I wanted to thank you.'

'No need. I was just doing my job.'

'You might act like it isn't a big deal, all "Aw shucks ma'am, tweren't nothing",' she mocked gently, 'but to Gordon and me, it is everything.'

'I am glad to help,' I said lamely.

'Mr Roark, he was terrorizing us. It was never about the money. Gordon and I have plenty between us and we would have paid ten times that to be free from the constant worry of this thing. Now we have a chance to have our baby and raise it in safety. Gordon looks better than I have seen him in weeks.' It was true; it seemed as though a weight had been lifted from Stevenson's shoulders.

'I am glad to have helped.'

'You did. Thank you.' Then she leaned over and kissed me quite chastely on the cheek. She stood up and walked over to her husband. Well, how about that?

I watched the FBI agents carry box after cardboard box of stuff up from Baz's room. I saw another agent walk out with a brown leather duffle bag, more the L.L. Bean style than Army issue. It had an evidence tag tied to one of the leather handles. When the parade of boxes and luggage stopped, I went down-stairs. Watts was in Baz's room, holding a notebook and a pen in hand.

'Find anything interesting?'

'Not much. Clothes, passport, a small vial of coke, a bottle of uppers and ten one-hundred-dollar bills in his shaving kit.'

'That's a lot more than I keep in my shaving kit. I usually just keep it to shaving stuff.'

'There is a bunch of stuff to go through. We found a receipt from an Army Navy surplus store in Providence, Rhode Island. He bought a survival knife and two army duffle bags back at the end of September.'

'So, he was planning this for a while.'

'Looks like it.'

'Funny, last night he showed me the money in the duffle bag. He opened it up and made a point of showing me and then made a joke about running away with it.'

'He must have had the other bag in the back and made the switch.'

'Yeah, the bag was under a blanket. I thought he was being cautious pulling the blanket over it. Then he joked about me running away with the money, and I made a joke about you hunting me down.' Slowly, through the lack of sleep and the sheer exhaustion that comes after shooting someone, some memory, some itch was working its way to the surface of my consciousness. 'Then he said . . . something about me not wanting you on my spoor.'

'What is your spore?'

'Spoor. It's a Cape Dutch term, derived from Old English. It means animal tracks or footprints, something that can be followed. Like a trail.' Maureen had appeared, and was leaning one hip against the door frame. 'It's not spore with an "e", but spoor with two "o"s. You hear it a lot in South Africa, Rhodesia, places like that. You might hear it in England, but when you guys left the Empire, it fell out of favor.'

'Ah, yes. Thank you, Ms Kemp.' Watts was all FBI professional.

'I'm a lot more than just a pretty face.' As if I needed to be reminded. She smiled at me, and then headed off upstairs again.

'She has a high opinion of herself.' I was beginning to think that Watts wasn't a fan.

'Anyway, that's what Baz said. He said I wouldn't want you on my spoor.'

'No, you wouldn't. So what?'

'It's in one of the early notes. I thought it was spore and he was threatening Stevenson's family.'

'That's good. It ties him into this that much more.'

'Kovach was Hungarian and probably learned his English from Americans somewhere along the way. He probably wouldn't use a word like spoor.'

'OK, well, he might still be an accomplice, even if he didn't write the letters.'

'Sure, or he was some poor schmuck who had nothing to do with any of this until I found him. Maybe I handed Baz a ready-made patsy for this job.'

'We don't know enough yet. Baz chose this. No one made him do any of this. Certainly not you.'

'I know, I know.' I felt tired and suddenly I was feeling very sick of being in the hunting lodge. Intellectually I knew she was right. I was tired and worn down. I had probably been right not to want to take this case.

'When can I head back to Boston?' I had a cat to feed.

'I will check with the State Police, but you should be good to go.'

'Good.' I went over to where my bag was and packed the few things in it that I had brought with me. I still had the Hi-Power on my hip. Watts went upstairs, and when I heard footsteps coming down a few minutes later, I was surprised to see Maureen.

'You weren't going to leave without saying goodbye, were ya, cowboy?'

'No ma'am. I was most definitely going to say goodbye.' I put my bag down and stepped closer to her as she stepped into my arms. We kissed for a long minute and then I leaned back. 'The offer of a place to stay in Boston is a standing one.'

'Emmnn, I'd be a fool not to take you up on that offer.'

'I can cook, too.'

'I could certainly get used to a man who can cook, too.' We kissed again and then she slipped away upstairs.

I walked around, looking at the purpose-built sanctuary that Stevenson had created for himself. The books, his awards, the Masai spear, Honey's rather good artwork. All trophies. A small monument to a career, an ego. There were steps on the stairs, and this time it was Watts.

'The State Police are OK with your heading back to Boston. They said you will probably have to come back for an inquest.'

'That makes sense.'

I didn't mind. The case was over, and I just wanted some fresh air. I went upstairs to let Stevenson and Honey know I was leaving. The State cops were interviewing Smith and Jones, who couldn't tell them much more, other than that Baz had brought them coffee and they fell asleep.

I found Stevenson and Honey in the kitchen with Frieda, who was peeling vegetables with a paring knife. Her hands were strong but showing the signs of arthritis. Stevenson looked up at me, taking in the smock and the postal bag slung on my shoulder.

'Going somewhere?'

'I have things I need to see to in Boston.'

'Roark, you did a fine job out there. Thank you.'

'All part of the service. I'll send you a report in a week or so.'

'Sure, sure. Whatever you need. Bradley will take care of it.'

'Mr Roark, thank you. You were very brave, and we appreciate what you have done for us.' Honey smiled warmly and I gave her a lopsided grin in return. I gave a mock salute, touching my hand to my eyebrow, and said, 'Goodbye.'

Outside the air was crisp and cool, and I realized it was the first of November. Somehow, in all the noise and machinations, I had missed Halloween. It wouldn't be long before Stevenson and company would be dealing with snow. I got in the Maverick and started it up. I got on the highway, pointed the car toward Boston and pushed down on the gas pedal.

*   *   *

The drive had been uneventful but tiring. Sir Leominster was waiting for me at the door when I let myself in. He ran back and forth, tail sticking straight up while he meowed at me, airing his many grievances. He did rub up against my shins and consented to have his ears scratched. I shut the door, dropped my bag, and went to open him a can of cat food.

After that was done, I poured myself a whiskey on the rocks and went to unpack my bag. I put the holstered Hi-Power down on the bedside table, the two loaded magazines next to it. I could switch back to my normal .38 snub-nose in the morning. I went back to the kitchen.

I put a pot of salted water on to boil and took out a box of elbow macaroni. I also found a can of Dinty Moore stew. I was glad that Maureen wasn't here to see what dinner was going to be, because she would have reason to doubt my claims that I could cook. When the macaroni had been drained, I used the same pot to heat up the canned stew. When it was heated, I poured it over the macaroni, which I had put in a large bowl.

I added more whiskey and ice to my glass and took it all to the couch. I turned on the TV and Dana Hersey started to talk to me about *The Conversation*, Gene Hackman's tightly acted masterpiece of paranoia and wiretapping. It was slowly paced but perfectly acted and executed. In a lot of ways, I felt like Hackman's lonely character. With my belly full and whiskey working its way into my body, my eyelids grew heavy, and I went to bed.

I slept heavily and dreamt about being in the woods. I was dressed in my old sterile jungle fatigues and wearing a Howdy Doody-style toy cowboy hat. Baz was there dressed in a khaki North Vietnamese Army uniform. He was leading an NVA human wave assault. I stood up and realized I was wearing flip-flops instead of boots. I pulled two pearl-handled cap guns from cheap plastic holsters on my hips. I fired at Baz and the NVA bayonet charge, the red paper caps unfurling and smoking as I pulled the trigger. It was the absurd last stand of Staff Sergeant Roark. They overwhelmed me, running over me, pushing me deeper and deeper into the mud of a hemlock forest.

I woke up with Sir Leominster on my chest. He was kneading my chest with his front paws, the way cats do. He meowed at me when I opened my eyes and, for a second or two, I had no idea where I was.

In the bathroom I splashed cold water on my face. The bruises that I had picked up in the woods were starting to make themselves known. I had scratches I didn't remember getting. Just reacting, moving, careening off things and not feeling them because of the adrenaline, the focus on the gunfight. There was a bite mark on my chest, but that had nothing to do with any gunfight.

It was raining outside, and the wind rattled the apartment windows. The rain was coming down hard enough to make me abandon the thought of going for a run. Fall in Boston was either woodsmoke on crisp air, fall foliage and hot chocolate, or it was a storm. There never seemed to be any middle ground.

I found an old dressing gown that had been a gift from an old girlfriend. It was a little thin at the elbows these days, but it was perfect for lazing about in. After all, I had earned it after tangling with Baz in the woods. I couldn't decide if I had been lucky in the woods or just more skilled. Or whether he had just been unlucky. Luck counts as much as skill in a fight. It didn't much matter now.

I made an espresso on the stove-top and contemplated my day. I wanted to start typing up my case files so that I could send Stevenson a report of the investigation. More importantly, I wanted to send him a bill. When I had lazed about enough and had enough espresso and cigarettes, it was time for a shave and a shower.

When I was showered and dressed, I gathered up my notes and put them in my trusty mail bag. I dressed for the fall chill and topped it off with my old trench coat, which still repelled some water. I went back to carrying my revolver holstered on my hip.

The rain let up enough that I was just damp from the walk. When I got to the office, there was the faint smell of pipe tobacco in the background, like the bass in a John Coltrane number. There was something to be said for the quiet days. I hung my trench coat on the coat rack, appreciating the simple nuances involved in not being dead.

I cracked the window open, letting in a cool, damp draft. I

pulled out my notes and a mostly clean legal pad. I packed a pipe and managed to get it lit with only two matches. I have heard that people who really know what they are doing can get a pipe lit and drawing with one match. I wasn't one of them.

I went through my case notes methodically, and on the mostly new legal pad turned them into some sort of coherent narrative. I stuck to the facts and the indicators that had led the investigation in the direction it had gone in. Putting it all down on paper, Kovach seemed like a very thin lead to follow. Baz seemed obvious – the butler did it. Butler, bodyguard, whatever.

It still nagged me how Baz had gotten Bradley to recommend him to Stevenson. It was awfully convenient for Baz to get that close. How had Bradley come up with Baz's name? He didn't strike me as the type to read *Soldier of Fortune* magazine.

Was there anyone else who had a reason to get involved in the scheme? Stevenson was obviously out. Honey, having a lot of money of her own, didn't seem likely. Gordon Junior just didn't strike me as having enough get-up-and-go to do much more than sponge off the old man. That left Maureen and Frieda, and I couldn't see either of them having the motive or the knowledge to plan something like this. That left Bradley, the aide-de-camp, Stevenson's loyal assistant, whose parents were about to lose the farm in Ohio. He had the brains and he certainly had motive. He also had opportunity and he hired Baz.

The problem was that this was all speculation, and I wasn't going to put any of it into a report to Stevenson. I had been paid to investigate, not type up a bunch of assumption and conjecture. I stuck to the facts and tried to write up a neat, clean report and nothing else. When I had written it out long-hand, I took a break and went to the deli around the corner for lunch.

Later, back at the office, I dug out my own typewriter and, thanking my freshman year typing teacher, I started to type up my findings. My typewriter was a Brother Correct-O-Riter, which, compared to an IBM, seemed positively petite. After an hour and a half and a bit of cursing, it was done. I typed up a bill and it all went into an envelope that I addressed to Stevenson's hunting lodge. I put two stamps on it and popped it in the blue mailbox on my way home.

NINETEEN

The next week was taken up with an insurance fraud case that came my way. It wasn't the most exciting case, but most of them weren't. It had meant spending a little time following a guy around. A little digging and it turned out he was working under the table for his cousin who was in construction.

My client was happy, which was good for me. It has been my experience that the insurance companies paid faster when they liked the results. It also helped that they might need me for a deposition, and prompt payment always kept me in a good mood.

A week after I sent the Ambassador his case report and bill, I opened the mailbox to find a cream-colored envelope of thick paper. It was embossed with Stevenson's name and title. Inside was a note of thanks. It also explained that he had included a bonus. He had added five hundred dollars to what I had billed. I thought that was rather sporting of him.

A few days after that, I was at a loose end again. I had sent the insurance company their report, complete with pictures. I had spoken to Watts a couple of times, but she didn't have anything more to tell me other than the body they found by the highway was Kovach.

Later that night my phone rang, and I had only had one whiskey, so I answered.

'Roark. Stevenson here. Listen, Honey and I were wondering if you'd come up to the house over the weekend.'

'Is everything all right?'

'Yes, things are great. Honey just felt that, you know, we should thank you. That money wasn't enough. Come up for the weekend.'

'Umn.' I wasn't sure that I wanted to spend a weekend listening to Stevenson talk about himself.

'Come on. It's only a couple of hours away. Honey insists.

You don't want me to be in Dutch with the wife, do you?' I personally didn't care, but I didn't have anything else to do and Maureen might be there. That possibility made the thought of another trip to Vermont much more interesting than sleeping alone in Boston.

'I can drive up Saturday morning,' I said, hoping that an urgent case would come up.

'Good, good. I will tell Frieda to make her world-famous Sauerbraten.'

'That sounds great.' I have a well-known love of Sauerbraten, which I can only get at the Wursthaus in Cambridge. They had it at the Café Budapest, but I could hardly ever afford to eat there.

Saturday mid-morning found me driving north again. The fall colors had faded from the trees. And there was a bright, brittle kind of sunlight shining through their bare branches. In spite of the lack of foliage, I enjoyed the ride through the hills.

I had stopped at the New Hampshire State Liquor Store off the highway. You couldn't tell that – a few weeks before – a man had been murdered there. I am sure it wasn't the first and was confident it wouldn't be the last. The radio was playing 'Rock and Roll' by the Velvet Underground and I tapped my fingers to it against the Maverick's steering wheel. By the time I pulled up to the hunting lodge, I was feeling pretty good.

Maureen's light blue Mustang was parked next to the house, and I swung my own Ford in behind hers. I got out and was greeted with crisp fall air and the smell of woodsmoke from the chimney. It was nice to see the place without bodyguards or State Police hanging around.

Stevenson was waiting for me at the door.

'Roark. Glad you could make it.'

'Thank you, sir.'

'Come on in out of the chill.' It was colder than the last time I had been here. I was glad that I had my old pea jacket on.

'Sure thing.'

'I am glad that you made it. Honey would have had my hide if you hadn't.'

'We can't have that. It was nice of her to invite me up.'

'I think she has some romantic vision of you as our savior. She said you didn't have to chase Baz into the woods and get into a gunfight with him. You could have just let the authorities handle it.'

'Never even occurred to me. Either way, it is nice of you to invite me up.'

'Sure, let's get you settled. Bradley is in Brookline, so there is an open guest room. Unless you'd prefer the couch downstairs?'

'Guest room is fine. How are the memoirs coming?'

'Much better now. It is funny how not having a murderer threatening your family helps.'

'I can see where that would be a weight lifted off your shoulders.' I followed him into the house and had to keep myself from instinctively going downstairs when he turned left down the hallway. He showed me a corner bedroom that gave me a view of the garage and front field by the road.

'Come downstairs for a drink after you've settled in.' He left and I put my bag down on the wing chair in one corner by the closet. The room was furnished simply but tastefully, with a queen-sized bed, a wooden night table with a brass lamp, and an antique bureau in addition to the chair. There were a few watercolors, landscapes of varying sizes, on the wall.

After washing up, I stepped out to the unmistakable smell of Frieda's Sauerbraten. It smelled fantastic. I poked my head into the kitchen where Frieda was peeling potatoes with a paring knife. '*Guten Tag.*'

'*Guten Tag*, Herr Roark.' I was rewarded with a smile.

I jerked my head in the direction of the stairs and said, 'Herr Ambassador?'

She nodded and went back to her potatoes. I walked downstairs and joined Stevenson in his inner sanctum.

'What do you want to drink?'

'Scotch and soda?'

He made my drink and handed it to me.

'Cheers.' We ritually clinked glasses. I took a sip and admired Honey's paintings.

'They're something. Even I can't get over how talented she is.'

'They are.' Then something occurred to me. 'Did anything hang here before?'

'Trophies. I used to do a fair bit of hunting and had a few heads mounted on the wall. Honey wasn't a fan of them, and these went up in their place.'

'I think you made out on the deal.'

'Yes, you're right, but I was proud of them. I used to have a bearskin in front of the fireplace, from a brown bear I bagged.'

I looked over at the polished bit of floor in front of the fireplace.

'Was that your biggest kill?'

'No, I did some big game hunting in Africa . . . now, that was exhilarating. I haven't done much in the last few years.'

'No? It seems like this is the perfect area for deer.'

'I was going to get back into it but, you know . . .'

'What happened?'

'Honey happened. She has views about killing defenseless animals.'

'Ah . . .'

'Roark, why do you think he did it?'

'Baz?'

'Yes.'

'He said it best himself. He was a mercenary. He had half a million reasons why.'

'Yes, but why me? Why did he choose us to terrorize?'

'I don't know. I have wondered that myself.'

'Would you look into it for us?'

'I don't think I could do anything in this case that the FBI can't do better.'

'You don't want to make more money?'

'It isn't that.'

'Then what?'

'When you first hired me, it was because you thought it was an SOG guy doing it.'

'Sure, that was the theory.'

'I was the right guy for that job, for obvious reasons.'

'You were. You caught Baz.'

'I got lucky. If I was a heavier sleeper, you'd be out half a million.'

'But you weren't.'

'No, to try and find out why Baz did it, that might involve a lot of things that are just a little bit beyond my skill sets.'

'Like what?'

'Like getting the State Department to give us an idea of his movements in and out of the country, or getting his service records from Vietnam, and there is no way I would be able to get any details about him from his time in Rhodesia. No, sir, I think this is a case for the FBI.'

'Are you sure I can't persuade you?'

'Special Agent Watts is good. If she can't find out why, then it can't be found out.'

'OK. Come on, let's go upstairs and say hi to Honey and Maureen.'

'Sure.'

Upstairs there was a fire in the living-room fireplace. Honey was sitting on the couch with her feet tucked under her. She was dressed casually, jeans and sweater, hair behind her ears, and I understood why Stevenson had given up hunting. She put down her book, stood up and walked over.

'Mr Roark, it was so good of you to come. I wanted to say thank you.'

'Mrs Stevenson, of course. I am glad to be here.' I was lying. I wanted to be just about anywhere else, but here I was.

'I know you think you were just doing your job, but we think you were exceptional. Don't we, Gordon?'

'I was just downstairs trying to tell him that, but he was more interested in your paintings.'

'Do you like them, Mr Roark?'

'Yes, they are quite good. I mean, I'm no art critic, but I like them.'

'I am so glad.'

I saw Maureen walk in from the kitchen with a cup of tea in her hand. She saw me and smiled ruefully, 'I heard that the cowboy was coming back for a weekend appearance.'

'Well, I was told that there would be Sauerbraten.'

'Silly me, I thought you came up for the conversation.'

'That too. That too.'

Later over dinner, it was just the four of us. It was like a weird double date, but with homemade Sauerbraten, potato dumplings the size of tennis balls and braised red cabbage, all of it served with a generous amount of brown gravy. It was fantastic, and Stevenson paired it with a very dry German Riesling.

Dinner was followed by Bienenstich, or bee-sting cake. I dug a fork into the cake, which consisted of two bread layers that had vanilla custard between them and were covered with a crunchy almond and honey topping. It was to die for. It was one of the best meals I have ever had.

Stevenson was better too. He was more relaxed and less of a caricature. He told funny stories about his time in the OSS and the diplomatic corps. Honey beamed at him, and it was easy to see that she loved him. Maureen told funny stories about her time staying on her grandparents' farm, tending to the animals, learning to ride, and nice stories of life in the country.

Later that night, after everyone had gone to bed, my door opened, and Maureen slipped into the room and then into my bed. We made love slowly and sweetly, falling asleep next to each other. It had been a very good day.

The next morning, I woke up alone. I took my shaving kit and went downstairs. I went to Baz's room and tossed it, but there was nothing to be found that the FBI hadn't already taken away. Something about the case was bothering me still though, but I couldn't put my finger on it. Giving up, I went to shower.

Breakfast was coffee and the rest of the cake. Being a god-fearing woman, Frieda didn't work on Sundays. It was just Stevenson, Honey and me at the table. Maureen was sleeping in. It was still early, and there was frost outside on the grass.

'Are you heading back today, Mr Roark?'

'Yes, but first I might take a walk in the woods.'

'I wouldn't do that, Roark,' Stevenson said.

'I don't think it will bring back any flashbacks or nightmares.'

'Oh no, not that. It's hunting season. The locals will be out with high-powered rifles shooting at anything that moves. You think the NVA were dangerous? These boys . . .'

'That bad?'

'Oh yes, Mr Roark. This time of year, I take my morning

walk around the field. I stay out of the woods and don't even walk on the road,' Honey said.

We finished breakfast and I went to pack. I stopped at Maureen's door, opening it a crack. She was still asleep, snoring softly, and I didn't want to wake her. She knew how to find me if she ever wanted to come to Boston. I went to say goodbye to Stevenson.

'I don't suppose you'll reconsider?'

'No, sir. I have taken this case as far as I can. Anything more would just be taking your money.'

'I see. Well, thanks again.' He stuck his hand out and I took it.

'You're welcome.'

'Honey is outside, walking around the field. Don't leave without saying goodbye to her. She thinks you're a good egg.'

'Well, there's no accounting for taste.'

I put on my pea jacket and shouldered my bag. Outside, I put the bag on the Maverick's passenger seat and spied Honey walking down by the tree line on the low side of the field. I called her name and she stopped, turning my way. I walked the forty yards downhill to her. She smiled when she saw me, and I understood what people meant when they describe pregnant women as 'glowing'.

'Mr Roark, I'm glad you came up to see us.'

'It was my pleasure.'

'It was a nice time?'

'Yes, very.'

'We can't thank you enough.'

'It's OK. Really. I am glad to have helped.' She leaned in and kissed my cheek again.

'Thank you. I do hope you will come and see us again. Gordon likes you. He doesn't meet many people who stand up to him. He is a good man, though.'

'I know he is. Goodbye, Mrs Stevenson.'

'Goodbye Andy.' She turned to continue her walk, and I turned back toward the Maverick. There was a bite in the air that hinted of a cold winter just around the corner. The smell of woodsmoke offered the only sense of comfort regarding the coming of ice and snow. I was halfway back to my car when

I heard a shot from somewhere in the woods. Stevenson was right, the hunters were reckless. I looked over my shoulder, expecting to share a grin with Honey.

Except she wasn't there to smile back. She was lying on the ground. As I ran toward her, I could see the blood on the ground. Steam was rising up from her. I got to her, and her lips were moving but only a gurgling noise came out. She had been shot in the abdomen, just a couple of inches below her sternum.

Please, please let it be a through-and-through, I thought. She could live with a gut shot if we got her to the hospital quickly. I ran my hand under her and felt a lot of blood. I rolled her gently on her side and I saw her back.

The entrance wound was about the size of a pencil eraser, but the exit wound was the size of a large grapefruit. The wound was a gaping mess of blood, bone fragments and flesh. All I could smell was ammonia and blood. Her wound was horrific, easily one of the worst I had ever seen. The breath rattled out of her lungs and her eyes lost all of the light in them. She died in my arms.

I had her blood on my hands, my clothes. A rough hand at my shoulder pulled me away. Stevenson gave out a tortured scream of pure anguish. He was a man suddenly and irrevocably dipped in the fire of hell. Maureen ran up a few seconds later, barefoot and wearing flannel pajamas.

I was looking at the deer again. The wounds, the smells, the steam rising from the ground. Except I wasn't in Laos. I was in central Vermont. Gordon Junior walked up, dressed in sweatpants and a t-shirt. He took one look at all of it and promptly vomited on the grass. I stood up and ran back to the house.

I called the Vermont State Police and told them there had been a shooting and a woman was dead. I gave them the address and hung up on the dispatcher. I dialed Watts's number, and I noticed that I left bloody fingerprints on the white phone where I had touched it. Watts finally answered. It was, after all, a Sunday.

'Hello.'

'Watts.'

'Roark, isn't it a little early for you on a Sunday?'

'I'm up at the Ambassador's place in Vermont. Stevenson's wife is dead.'

'Dead how?'

'Shot. From the tree line.'

'OK, I'm on my way.'

'Brenda?'

'Yes.'

'Can you stop by my place? My clothes . . . my clothes have her blood all over them.'

'Sure. You OK?'

'No. Not by a long shot,' I said to the dial tone after Watts hung up. Honey had been a beautiful, talented woman looking forward to motherhood, and now she was dead. Horribly dead. People like her aren't supposed to die like that. That is reserved for people like me and guys like Baz. Not her.

I put the phone down in its cradle and went outside. There was nothing to be done. I stood there watching Stevenson, whose life had been blown apart in a millisecond, clutching his wife's corpse. Gordon Junior looked queasy, hungover and shocked. Maureen looked flat, in shock and just flat.

'Maureen. Your feet. You must be cold.'

She looked up at me.

'Maureen, go put some shoes on, get a coat.'

'Oh, OK.'

Gordon Junior looked up at me without saying anything and followed Maureen. I stood there, useless, Honey's blood on me growing tacky and cold. In the distance I heard the wail of the siren. It had nothing on Stevenson's anguished howls.

TWENTY

The Vermont State Police came in droves. My old friend Detective Lyndgarten arrived, this time in a warm jacket over his polyester K-mart suit, his feet sensibly tucked into duck boots. He pulled me aside and I told him what happened. He listened, nodding.

'Sounds like some careless hunter. We get 'em up here every season. Usually from down south, idiots from New York or Connecticut. Sometimes they try and stave off the cold with a little liquid fortification. They get too close to homes, roads, and shoot at anything that moves.'

'What about the exit wound? It was huge.'

'Some of 'em use guns that are way too big. Had a fella up here one time with a .458 Magnum. Hunting deer, can you imagine? Just reckless.'

'I smelled ammonia.' It was gone now, just the smell of blood and death remained.

'I don't smell anything now, but who knows what some of the yahoos do to their ammo.'

The ambulance arrived, and they took Honey away in a body bag. I felt sick. Not like Gordon Junior, but sick as in 'with the world'. Nothing about this made sense. That type of sick. I watched as a big state trooper led Stevenson back to the house. Stevenson looked dazed and in shock.

Watts showed up while I was sitting downstairs looking at Honey's paintings. I was on my second, maybe third bourbon, which wasn't bad for eleven fifteen in the morning. She softly said, 'Hey.'

'Hey.'

'Andy, what happened?'

'They invited me up yesterday for dinner. We had a nice time, ate Sauerbraten, drank good wine, laughed and told stories. You know, like normal people do. I woke up this morning and wanted to get an early start.'

'Why? Traffic shouldn't be bad today, it's Sunday.'

'They asked me to investigate Baz Basselman and figure out why he did it. It wasn't my type of investigation.'

'That's why you wanted to leave early?'

'No, they were fawning over me. They acted like I had done something special, like I was some sort of hero. It made me wicked uncomfortable.'

'So, you decided to leave.'

'Yes, after breakfast. Stevenson told me not to leave without saying goodbye to Honey.'

'That's when it happened.'

'Yep, I said goodbye and turned to walk back to my car. I got about ten or twenty yards away when I heard the shot. I thought it was just, you know, a hunter too close to the house. Then I turned to look, and she was down. I ran over, but . . .'

'It was too late.'

'Watts, the bullet really messed her up. I don't know if it was a large caliber or a dumdum or what, but it blew a huge hole in her.'

'Jesus.'

'Watts, she was pregnant.'

'I know.' Watts knew there was nothing else to be said.

'I need to get cleaned up.' I had dried blood on my hands and on my clothes. Watts handed me the duffle bag of clothes she had gathered up at my apartment. I went to the bathroom. I pulled my clothes off while the shower heated up, filling the small room with steam. I scrubbed my hands and arms. Lathered and washed away the blood that soaked through my clothes. I lathered my hair, face, and then stuck my head under the stream of hot water.

When I was as clean as I could possibly get under the circumstances, I turned the water from hot to very cold, the spray stinging me with cold drops. I put my face in it and stayed under until I was shivering. I turned the water off and stepped out. I toweled off and dressed in clean clothes. My blood-soaked clothes just went in a trash bag. They would never be clean enough to wear again.

Watts was upstairs in the living room. She was standing over the white phone. As I grew closer, I saw that she was wiping it down with a rag. She was wiping away Honey's blood that I had gotten all over the phone. She looked up.

'I couldn't leave it on the phone.'

'It's OK. I know what you mean.' It didn't have any value as evidence, and I wasn't even sure if anyone was looking at this as a crime. Even if they were, it still wouldn't be evidence of anything other than that I had held her after she had been shot.

'You look better.'

'Bourbon and a shower helped.'

'Good. You looked rough.'

'That was bad. I have seen some things . . . but that . . .'

'I can see that. Doesn't make much sense after Basselman's little game. She gets through all that and gets hit by a stray round.'

'Is that it? I'm not so sure.'

'Andy, the State Police said it happens a few times a year up here. It's bad luck but not unheard of.'

'I don't know.'

I looked outside. The morning had warmed in the pale sunlight and the frost was gone. 'The timing seems coincidental.'

'Sure, it is. It would be more so if Basselman or Kovach were still in the picture. But they are gone.'

'I know, I know. It just doesn't feel right.' I couldn't bring myself to say it 'didn't add up', like they might on TV.

'Maybe you're too close to it. You liked them. I don't know if you know this, but you are bad at feeling useless.'

'You have a point there. Where's everyone?'

'Stevenson changed and went with the troopers. There is a lot of paperwork and there are arrangements to be made. Gordon Junior went with him. Maureen called Bradley; I assume to get him back here. She's kicking around here somewhere.'

'Probably dealing with it. Not an easy thing to see.'

'No, I imagine not. What are you going to do?'

'I don't know. I will hang around till Stevenson gets back. Make sure he is OK and then head back to Boston.'

'That sounds like a plan. I called my boss and let him know what happened.'

'What did he say about it?'

'If it is a hunting accident, head back home and work on my caseload. If it is a murder, stay and advise the State Police.'

'That sounds reasonable.'

I realized that I was standing looking at the tree line, across the field toward the road. On the other side of the road was another field and four or five hundred meters away was another wall of trees. In my head I was mentally calculating things like velocity and bullet drop. I was going through the index of different bullets, different calibers, trying to make the math add up to the wound I saw. Nothing did. Maybe Lyndgarten was right; maybe it was some yahoo trying out an experimental round.

In the early afternoon, Bradley arrived. Watts filled him in on what happened, sparing me from having to go over it again. Later Watts got a phone call and took it downstairs. Bradley came over to me.

'How was the Ambassador?'

'Bad.' His anguished, grieving howl still echoed in my mind. 'It was just bad.'

'Jesus. Poor man.' He would have said more but Watts came back upstairs.

'That was the State Police. They combed the woods adjacent to the field and found some beer cans. Right now, they are leaning toward it being an accidental shooting. The shooter, if they were aware that they shot someone, probably took off.'

'So that's it?' I asked.

'For now, yes. They won't release preliminary findings for weeks, but the reality of it is that it is an accident as far as they are concerned.'

'OK, it is what it is.' I didn't like it, but that was the way it seemed to be going, whether I believed it was an accident or not.

The Ambassador, son in tow, returned home a little while later. Neither of them looked good. The elder Stevenson was pale and moved in a bit of a daze. The younger looked like he was going to throw up some more. Without being asked or told, we all followed Stevenson downstairs to the bar.

He poured himself a large bourbon and drank a couple of inches off it in one draft. Then he topped it off and sat heavily in his chair. He waved his hand at the bar and said, 'I'm not up to playing host. Help yourselves.'

I took his advice and poured myself a large bourbon. Fortunately, all that time in the diplomatic corps had taught him well and I knew he bought the stuff by the case. Bradley got himself a beer from the refrigerator, which hardly seemed strong enough considering recent events. Gordon Junior poured himself a couple of fingers of vodka. Maybe there was hope for the kid yet. Watts didn't have anything; she was going to head back to Boston soon.

Stevenson finished his bourbon and made to rise, but Bradley got up and poured him another one, adding a few ice cubes. Stevenson took it, mumbling an absentminded, 'Thanks.' Bradley didn't say anything. Gordon Junior poured himself another two fingers of vodka without saying anything. Maureen came downstairs wearing jeans and her Dartmouth sweatshirt, hair pulled back in a ponytail.

'Gordon, I'm so sorry.'

'Thank you.'

Watts stood up. 'Mr Ambassador, I'm leaving. I am sorry for your loss, sir.' She said the same inadequate words that we all say. Stevenson nodded and said, 'Thank you,' his voice coming from light years away.

Bourbon in hand, I walked Watts to her car. When we got to her red Saab, she said, 'Are you going to stay up here for a couple of days? Keep an eye on the old guy?'

'I think so.'

'Good, I think he needs someone who will look out for him.'

'You don't trust the others?'

'His assistant is too much of a yes man. His son is on something, and that redhead is a cold fish.' It didn't seem like the time to point out to Watts that I had firsthand knowledge to the contrary.

'Look in on Sir Leominster for me for the next couple of days?'

'Sure, take care of yourself.' She got in her car and drove off. I watched her taillights until they disappeared into the twilight. I got my bag out of my car and went back into the somber house.

We sat with Stevenson, rotating in and out. Bradley had been given his marching orders and was making phone calls on behalf of the Ambassador. Gordon Junior came and went. I wondered what he was ingesting, besides vodka.

Later I went up to the kitchen and dug around in the refrigerator and found some cold cuts. I made sandwiches for everyone. They weren't great but they were good enough. Even Stevenson managed to mechanically eat one. At least it would help soak up some of the bourbon. I sat with Stevenson, who described to me what the earlier phone call to his dead wife's parents had been like. You didn't have to be a detective to figure out that it had been bad.

Later, when he passed out snoring in the chair, I went and found some bedding by rummaging in the upstairs closets. The house was quiet and still, making me feel even more like an interloper. I bedded down on the couch, my .38 under my pillow. At some point I woke up and heard Stevenson sobbing. There was nothing to say or do. Later I woke up again and he had gone.

The next couple of days came and went much the same. The only difference was that Frieda had arrived Monday morning and she took charge of the domestic affairs. Food was served and we were expected to eat at the table. Stevenson maintained a healthy amount of bourbon in his system, and I only drank at night.

Maureen had stopped coming to my bed at night. It wasn't anything we discussed but we didn't have to. Honey's death was still too recent. Everyone was very polite to each other. Bradley was kept busy trying to make arrangements, working around the fact that the coroner hadn't yet released the body. Stevenson drank enormous quantities of bourbon trying to stay numb. Gordon Junior was like a wraith, only to be seen sparingly and even more rarely in the sunlight.

On the third day, the walls felt like they were closing in. I paced the living room, staring out at the woods and thinking about stray rifle rounds. The NVA – with all their skill, experience, and intent – had managed to wound me a bunch of times with very deliberate fire. Honey was killed by some asshole who just fired a round without any thought for where it might end up. The world wasn't fair, and there was no point in expecting it to be.

I had packed and put my bags in the Maverick. I was thankful for my sweater because the blood-soaked pea jacket had gone in the trash. I went back to the house and ran into Bradley. 'Leaving, Mr Roark?'

'Yes, I'm not much help here.' He nodded. No one seemed very talkative anymore.

I went downstairs to say goodbye to Stevenson. He had been spending more and more time in his recliner. Sinking into himself, sinking in his grief, pickling himself in expensive bourbon. He hadn't showered or shaved since he had washed his wife's blood away that morning. In the few short days, he had aged considerably.

'I came to say goodbye, sir.' He didn't look up, and I turned to go but turned back. 'I didn't know her well, but I liked her. There was a sort of grace about her.'

I turned to leave when he said, 'She was luminescent, Roark.' I turned back. 'When I first saw her, I fell in love with her. I had only ever been in love with two other women. A woman I met after the war and Gordon's mother. Neither one compared to Honey.'

'I can see that.'

'Goodbye, Roark.'

'Goodbye, sir.'

I walked upstairs and out the door of the hunting lodge. It had gone from being a place of happiness and conversation to having all the warmth of a mausoleum. Every time I closed my eyes I could see Honey on the ground, blinking at me with a total lack of comprehension. I got in the Maverick and drove to Boston in a foul mood.

The mood slackened as mid-November slid inevitably toward Thanksgiving. I don't much care for the holiday. I don't like turkey and I detest stuffing. Besides, it was a family holiday and, except for some guys I was in Vietnam with, I don't have any family anymore.

In the last couple of weeks, I had spent time going over the case again and again in my head. I hadn't really figured it out so much as I got lucky seeing Baz leaving the garage. When we shot it out in the woods, the case had closed. Which had been neat and tidy.

Then Honey got shot by a hunter. I couldn't get over the wound channel his round had caused. I know a lot about guns. The Army had spent a lot of time and money teaching me about guns and ballistics. Yet, shy of a .50 caliber, I couldn't think of a round that would do that much damage. It kept nagging at me.

The Saturday after Thanksgiving, I'd had enough. I got out my address book and thumbed to the Vs. I found Hank Vogel's number in Pennsylvania. The first couple of tries were met with the phone just ringing. Later in the afternoon he picked up. He said 'Hello' in his heavy German accent.

'Herr Vogel. Zis is zee quartermaster . . . you still owe zee Reich for the uniforms, equipment and rifle you lost on zee Eastern Front.' Hank Vogel had been Heinrich Voegel when he had been in the Wehrmacht. When he came to America and joined the Army to fight against communism, he became Hank Vogel.

'Ach Andy, it's you, yes?'

'*Ja,* Hank, it's me.' Hank was funny, if I tried to speak to him in German, he insisted that we speak English. If we were drunk, he'd let me speak German but would correct my grammar so much that it wasn't any fun. I had met Hank in weapons training where he had been a small arms instructor, and then again on my second tour in Vietnam. Years after the war, I ran into him at Fort Devens at the Class Six store, where I was trying to score some of the cheap but good German brandy. He was there chatting up a German dependent, trying to score his third Mrs Vogel. It had worked, but she had insisted they move to Pennsylvania to be closer to her sister. Not a bad life if you like scrapple, I guess.

'Herr Oberfeldwebel Roark, to what do I owe the pleasure of your calling?' he asked after we had spent a few minutes catching up and talking about mutual friends, alive and dead.

'I had a question about bullets.' Hank knew more about small arms and ammunition than anyone I knew.

'*Ja,* what is it?'

'I saw someone shot recently. The entrance wound looked

normal, maybe 7.62 millimeter.' The downside of talking to Hank about this stuff was his Germanic love of the metric system. 'The exit wound looked like a large grapefruit with a lot of damage.' I could still see it in my mind. 'That, and I swear I could smell something like ammonia.'

'Ach, again.' I repeated what I had just said. '*Ja, ja*, it sounds like the Tropish Patron.'

'Tropish Patron?' I repeated.

'*Ja*, the tropical round, tropical bullet, the B-Patrone.'

'What is that?'

'It was a 7.9 millimeter bullet. It was designed for sighting aircraft machine guns.'

'Like a tracer?'

'Not exactly. It was fired at a steel target and was used to adjust the machine gun sights. For airplane machine guns.'

'If it wasn't a tracer, how did it work?'

'It would explode. There was a small explosive charge in the bullet.'

'Excuse me?'

'*Ja*, the Tropish bullet had a small amount of explosive in it. Very nasty.'

'Jesus.'

'Our snipers on the Eastern Front used them against the Ivans. They had their own that they shot us with. We only used them against the Russians. They were animals. We would never have used them against the Tommies or the Yanks.'

'Well, that was very sporting of you all.'

'If we had to surrender, we wanted it to be to the Americans or English.'

'How common is this bullet here in America?'

'The Russian version is impossible to get here. There might be some of the B-Patrone here. You captured a great deal of weapons and ammunition from the Wehrmacht.'

'What would someone shoot it from?'

'That is simple, a K-98, any 7.92 Mauser, or an MG 42.'

'No, this was a single round, not a burst.'

'K-98 then.' That would make sense. The Mauser Karabiner 98 had been the German Army's weapon of choice. It was an excellent rifle, and we had captured tens of thousands of them.

They had been brought home as war trophies, and many had been turned into more traditional rifles by a process called 'sporterizing'. Sporterizing meant that a home or professional gunsmith nipped off bits of wood and metal to turn the rifle into something that resembled a more traditional hunting rifle.

'If I was near the target, would I smell ammonia?'

'*Ja*, definitely.'

'Were the rounds marked in any way? How would I recognize one if I saw it?'

'The box would have B-Patrone written on it. The bullet itself will have a copper tip, a green painted ring around it. Below that it will be painted black, and the top of the cartridge case too.'

'Thank you, Hank.'

'My pleasure, Andy. Always good to talk to you. Oh, and Andy . . .'

'Yeah?'

'Don't get shot with them. They were horrific tools of war. Usually fatal and, if not, they always maimed.'

'Thanks. I don't plan on it.' But then again, I never had.

TWENTY-ONE

Sometimes when you have an itch and you scratch it, the itch goes away. Anyone who's ever had poison ivy knows, sometimes you scratch an itch, and it just itches worse. My conversation with Vogel was like the poison ivy itch. I couldn't sleep. When I did sleep, I either dreamt of the dead deer on the Trail, or of Honey. Neither was particularly pleasant.

Finally, at three in the morning, I threw back the covers. Sir Leominster meowed at me in the dark. I didn't have to speak cat to know he was telling me that I was an idiot. I dressed warmly and holstered my .38 in its holster inside my waistband, put a speedloader of hollow points in my front pocket and my folding Buck knife in the other front pocket. This was a reconnaissance mission. I wasn't going looking for a fight.

A trip to the Army Navy surplus store had equipped me with a new pea coat, and I had leather gloves with a fur liner and a wool watch cap. I was dressed for the cold weather. I made some regular coffee and poured it in my battered Thermos. I dropped an apple in my coat pocket for the road. No point in being hungry and cold. I made sure I had my Zippo and a fresh pack of Luckies. Then I headed out to my car.

There was almost no traffic leaving the city and even less on the highway north. I headed over the Charles River Bridge; you can call it the Tobin if you want. I put the Thermos between my thighs and unscrewed the cup. I undid the cap and then, keeping the wheel straight with my knees, I poured a cup of hot coffee. I recapped the Thermos and drank my coffee as Aerosmith sang 'Sweet Emotion'.

The roads were wide open, and I pushed the pedal down. The needle on the speedometer was steady at eighty. I crossed into New Hampshire and drove through the low parts. I came to the toll booth and threw my quarters into the basket. The light turned green, and I kept driving, ignoring the rest stop and the liquor store. Then I was on I-89, climbing up into the hills,

when the snowflakes started coming at my windshield, like
angry moths in my headlights.

The windshield wipers fought against the snow. The roads
winding through the hills were slippery and there was no more
pouring and drinking cups of coffee. The Maverick's heater
pumped a stream of warm air at the windshield. I contemplated
the foolishness of being obsessive about my work. Surely there
was nothing I could do that couldn't be done better during
the day. Could there?

I took the ramp for 91 North at White River Junction and
drove over the bridge spanning the White River. The road rose
up through the granite hills, leveled off, and a few minutes later,
I was getting off the highway. There was no traffic, and I turned
the Maverick's lights off as I turned toward the hunting lodge.
Everything had a white coating of snow. I shifted into neutral,
turned the engine off and glided into the driveway, stopping in
front of the garage.

I reached up and made sure my dome light was off. I unhol-
stered the .38 and slipped it into the pea coat's right pocket. I
took my penlight out of the glove box and dropped it into my
left pocket. I put my watch cap on, pulled on my gloves, and
got out of the car. I gently pushed the door closed. The wind
was whipping snow everywhere, and I waited, listening. All I
heard was the wind in the tops of the trees, reminding me of
the ocean. I slowly walked over to the side door of the garage.
I dug my old Diners Club card out of my wallet and the door
quickly popped open. I stepped inside the garage and pushed
the door closed behind me, locking it. I stood still, listening
to the garage, getting a feel for what sounded normal as the
wind shook it.

I took my penlight out and turned it on. The beam wasn't
very strong which was good. That meant that it wouldn't be
obvious to anyone outside. I was looking for a Mauser K-98
rifle. Stevenson didn't have one in the gun cabinet. I would
have noticed.

I searched the hallway. Fortunately, there weren't too many
places to hide three-plus feet of rifle. Next was the small room
right in front of me. Ten minutes later, I was certain there was
nothing. There was nothing in the rafters.

I went into the main part of the garage, my breath coming out in clouds of steam. I checked the garage, the area around the workbench. I searched the Mercedes and the Bronco thoroughly. Nothing. Nada. Zip. Bupkis. Those were all professional investigative terms, in case you wondered.

I had been at it for forty-five fruitless minutes. Then I looked over and saw the coveralls hanging on their hooks. Kovach had hidden guns in his clothes. Maybe he wasn't the only one. The larger of the two was nearest to me. There was nothing in it, nothing in the pockets, no clues of any sort.

The smaller one. The smaller one was a treasure trove of seemingly inconsequential things. Singularly they were nothing, but taken together they were an arrow of sorts. That is how clues tended to work. There was nothing inside the coveralls. There was nothing in the pockets. But the pant legs were rolled up.

The wind blew, rattling the garage doors. The breeze from the small gap between the bottom of the door and the floor made something twitch. I bent down and saw it was a piece of brown grass caught in the cuff of the rolled pant leg. It was a detail I would have missed except for the wind. Then I noticed a bit of dirt ground into the knees and elbows of the coveralls.

But the true gold was on the right arm of the coverall. In this case the gold was pink fuzz. On the wrist of the right sleeve, in the faint light from my penlight, were pink fibers. I plucked one away and rolled it between my thumb and forefinger. It was soft and a bit itchy. Fiberglass insulation.

I wiped it off on the coverall and went to the side door. I clicked off my penlight, dropping it back in my left pocket. I readjusted my watch cap and pulled my gloves back on. I cracked the door and peeked out. Dawn was coming and the snow was swirling in lazy wisps. The storm, it seemed, was over.

I stepped outside and pulled the door shut behind me. The sky had turned from black to inky blue. The sun would be up soon, and I didn't have a lot of time. I started in a straight line across the lawn, by the big hemlock and into the field.

My feet crunched on the three scant inches of snow. I was

leaving tracks, but I didn't care. It took me five minutes to reach the pump house. The wind had died down but would occasionally gust, reminding me that it was still fall in Boston, but winter had arrived in central Vermont.

I reached the quaint-looking pump house. I pulled the door open against the scant snowfall. I got down on my knees in the cold snow and flicked on my penlight. I panned around the interior of the pump house. Most of the insulation was uniformly pressed into the studs, but there was one corner, one small corner, that was sticking out at the bottom.

I shone the light on it and leaned in to carefully pull it back. There was an off-white cardboard box. My flashlight was dim, but not so dim that I couldn't read the printing in German that told me it was a box of 7.92mm B-Patrone ammunition. I picked up the box, pulled a glove off with my teeth. I opened the box and shook a round out. It was everything Hank Vogel had told me about. The green circle around the bullet was clear. I dropped the round in my pocket; it was too cold to bother fitting it back in the box. I dropped the box of rounds in my pocket too, then put my glove back on and peeled back the rest of the insulation.

Standing on its butt, held in place by the pink fiberglass insulation with its brown paper backing, was a rifle. It was a hunting rifle with a scope. I pulled it out and played the light on it. The markings were in German, to include the eagle and swastika, a sporterized Mauser.

The wind died down and I heard footsteps in the snow. I stood up and stepped back from the pump house. I slung the Mauser muzzle down over my left shoulder and stepped to the side.

'Hello, Andy.'

'Hello, Maureen.' She was standing there, wind blowing strands of her red hair around. She was wearing duck boots and a warm-looking winter jacket. She also had a thick snub-nose revolver pointed at me. It looked like a .357 Magnum. 'Is that Kovach's?'

'Yes. It was.'

'And the Mini-14 that Baz used.'

'Also, his,' she said pleasantly.

'Did you shoot him with his own gun?'

'Why, are you sentimental about these things?'

'No, just curious.'

'I did. I am assuming you have a pistol?'

'Yes.'

'Where is it?'

'In my pocket.'

'Carefully take it out with two fingers by the butt.'

'OK.' I did as I was told, letting it dangle while I pinched the wooden grip between my thumb and index finger.

'Throw it over there.' She thrust her chin toward the woods. I did as I was told, albeit without much enthusiasm. I heard it land in the snow several feet away. 'Good. Now, carefully point the rifle at the ground, without touching the trigger, eject the rounds.' I slowly and carefully did as I was told, making a small pile of brass bullets in the snow. I gently pushed the bolt forward, not actually closing it.

'Here.' I held the rifle out to her.

'No thank you, Andy. I am not going to get close to you. Certainly not close enough for you to hit me with a rifle. I think you should carry it for me.'

'OK, whatever you want.'

'Andy, the box of bullets with it?'

'In my pocket.'

'Take them out.' I did. Holding the box up for her to see. 'Here.'

'Drop them on the ground.'

I did.

'Take your gloves off and drop them on the ground, your hat too.'

'Doll, it's a little cold out here for that.'

'I think I want your hands to be a bit clumsy.'

'Sure, whatever you want.'

'Andy, let's go back to the house.'

'I can leave the rifle here if you like.'

'No, you carry it. Slung. Stay six feet ahead of me. If you try anything I will shoot you at the base of the spine.'

'OK, you're the boss, lady. Why are we bringing the rifle back to the house?'

'Walk.' I started forward. 'I want to give it to Stevenson. Give him the rifle I shot his precious Honey with.'

'How did you do it?'

'It was elegant, Andy. I had suggested to her that with the hunters she would be safer walking around the yard in the mornings. I put on a pair of mechanics coveralls over my pajamas. Coveralls from the garage, duck boots over bare feet. I was watching her; I was letting my breath out and my finger was on the trigger. I had the special German bullets Baz had gotten for me.'

'Then I walked out to say goodbye.'

'Then you walked out to say goodbye. I let the tension off the trigger. You turned away and started to walk back to the house. My uncle taught me to hunt. I lined up the sights, took some of the slack out of the trigger, let my breath out and squeezed the trigger.'

'Weren't you taking a risk shooting her with me right there?'

'Oh, you mean was I afraid that the great Andy Roark would get me . . . no. It was satisfying to shoot her right under your nose. Especially after watching you lap up all that fawning they did over you.'

'Then what?'

'Then when you ran over, you were so focused on her. I low-crawled along the low spot. I knew you couldn't see me. I low-crawled to the pump house. I quickly put the rifle and bullets in. By then Stevenson was with you. I low-crawled to the big hemlock. Both of you were so focused on her, you never saw me go into the garage. I took off the coveralls and my boots. I stepped out and came over. Oh Andy, you were so concerned for my poor, cold feet. I was so exhilarated.'

'Why? I mean why kill Honey?'

'I wanted to hurt Stevenson. I could have killed Bradley, but that would have just inconvenienced him. I was going to kill Gordy, but when I found out Honey was carrying Stevenson's child . . . I knew it had to be her.'

'Why do any of it? '

'He took everything from me.'

'How?'

'My name isn't Kemp, it's Steinkemp.'

'German?'

'Dutch. My grandparents moved from South Africa to Rhodesia before the war.'

'Oh.' It was clear as mud.

'He changed it when he went to Canada. He figured it would hurt his business to sound too German. All the Canadians who had fought in the war might not want to do business with him.'

'Let me guess, he changed it to Stanhope.'

'Exactly. He married my mother during the war, before he changed his name. After the war, he came home with his friend who wanted to hunt big game.'

'Stevenson.'

'Yes.'

'What happened next?'

'They went off prospecting in Canada. They hit the big claim and Stevenson cheated him. After that, he came home for a bit. My mother got pregnant, and my father went back to Canada. He thought he'd find another claim to make his fortune.'

'He drank himself to death in Canada.'

'Which is why he wasn't home during the Bush War. We were living on my uncle's farm when they came. My mother hid me, but the blacks killed them all. Later, the Army came, and my grandparents sent me to school in England to keep me away from it all. Then Rhodesia went away. Our country was gone. Next they came for my grandparents, killed them and burned the farm to the ground.'

'That is horrible. But that isn't all Stevenson's fault.'

'If my father had been there, everything might have been different.' She sounded angry. We were near the spot where Honey had died.

'So, you wanted him to pay?'

'At first, I thought money might be enough. I researched Stevenson and found out he had retired. I arranged to meet his son. It wasn't hard, he liked night clubs and cocaine. It didn't take much to make him my lover. When he told me his father was looking for a writer to help with his memoirs, I convinced him to introduce me to Bradley.'

'Who was impressed with your nice accent and your résumé. You hatched the letter-writing scheme.'

'You are clever, Andy. Yes, I used Gordon Junior's typewriter. The shot-out window, poisoned dog, the car – that was all me.'

'Why? Weren't you worried about getting caught?'

'Not really. You and Stevenson are the same. You see a girl, a pretty enough girl, and you see tits and ass, nice eyes, nice hair but not much else. You're like the detectives in books or TV. For you, the women who come into your life are just supporting characters. In your story we aren't the hero, we aren't the villain. We're just here to make your story more interesting. A little generic love interest to move the story along. Stevenson is no different. I used that to my advantage.'

'Jesus.' It was a harsh bit of criticism that I hadn't been expecting.

'Yes, for all your talk of "come down to Boston, spend time with me", after the sex you weren't really interested in me. You were worried about your case. I was just something to round out the story.'

'Maureen, it might not have been love, but it wasn't like that. I meant what I said about coming to Boston, seeing if there was anything to this.'

'Maybe you did, Andy, but I didn't.'

'What about Baz?'

'I knew him from home. He wasn't bright but he served a purpose.'

'What happened?'

'I wasn't interested in the money. I had developed the scheme to get him interested. I was already shifting gears when he came up with the last few notes. He wanted to kill you. Put you in your car and hide it so that the FBI would think you took it.'

'But you woke me up and told me he was in the garage. Why?'

'If the money was off the table, if Baz was dead, then I would have more room to operate. Everyone let their guard down. The bodyguards and the police all left. Even you left.'

'And that first morning in the shower?'

She laughed. 'Oh, that wasn't the plan. I was reading your case notes. Honey was coming downstairs, and I stepped into the hallway outside the shower. I heard it turn off and I heard Honey coming. I took my clothes off and stepped into the shower. Your face was priceless. After that, you never looked at me as anything other than a piece of ass. I used that to my advantage.'

'OK, now what?' We had reached the house.

'Inside. Walk slowly. Don't be stupid. I don't have to tell you what a .357 Magnum loaded with hollow points can do.' She didn't.

We walked down the veranda and I pulled the door open.

'Living room,' she said.

'Answer a question for me.'

'What?'

'Was Kovach involved?'

'No, I got his name out of your notes. Those days when I wasn't here, I drove down to Fairhaven. He was in the bar by his apartment, and I let him pick me up. We went to his place. After he got what he wanted, he was amenable to my job offer. He even carried Gordy's old typewriter into his apartment for me.

'I told him I needed a man who could use a rifle to do some work up north. I made sure he took the rifle and this revolver. He followed me to New Hampshire – me in my car, Kovach in his. We stopped at the rest stop and I convinced him we should step into the wooded glen for a few moments. I undid his pants, and while he was distracted, I took the revolver out of his waistband. I shot him in the head when a loud truck went by.'

'Jesus. Why kill him?'

'I knew he would get picked up by the FBI and it wouldn't take long for anyone to figure out that he wasn't involved. Killing him meant that you all were looking for a villain you could never catch. I took his guns and ammunition. I gave the rifle to Baz. He was the one who shot up the house at dinner. You looked ridiculous tangled up in the screen you fell through. Brave but ridiculous.'

When we were inside, I asked. 'Now what?'

'Dining room. Put the rifle on the table and put your hands on your head. Stand in front of me, off to my right side.' I did what she told me to do. She stood with her back to the sliding glass doors.

'Why are you doing all this?'

'He has to pay. I want to see him suffer the way I did.' I didn't point out that Stevenson hadn't killed her spouse or unborn child. Something told me she wouldn't listen anyway. 'I want him to see me and to know I did it to him,' she finished.

'Got it, you're Ahab and he's the white whale. Now what?' If I remembered my senior year English class that book didn't end well for any of them.

'Now we wake up Gordon.' She fired a round into the glass shade of one of the overhead lights on the ceiling. The report was like a small explosion going off, and I felt the heat from the muzzle blast on my neck. The round going off startled me and I ducked down, turning away from it, my hand sliding into my pocket. A sharp stabbing pain in my kidney from Maureen jamming the muzzle of the pistol into my side got my attention.

'Hands on your head.' I did as I was told, cupping the exploding bullet in my right hand against my head.

Bradley came running into the living room and stopped when he saw me with my hands on my head. Then he saw her with the big revolver pointing at him. She shot him and he howled. The round hit his pelvic bowl, dropping him like a box of rocks. Stevenson and Gordon Junior were next.

Both were slightly addled, one by drugs and one by alcohol. There wasn't much difference.

'Roark. What are you doing here?' from the elder.

'Maureen,' plaintively from the younger.

'Gordon, do you remember Cecil Stanhope?' Maureen asked.

'Yes, my old partner.'

'He was my father. Because of you, he wasn't there when my mother and I needed him.'

'Cecil's *daughter*? He never said anything about a daughter.' Then, almost pleading: 'That was just business.'

'I know. That is all it ever is with men like you. That's why I shot Honey, so it wouldn't be "just business".' She cocked the gun and pivoted, shooting Gordon Junior in the stomach. Stevenson let out a roar and rushed her in a fit of rage.

I stepped to the table, grabbing the Mauser, pulling it to me by the butt, clawing the action open and feeding the B-Patrone bullet into the chamber. Maureen shot Stevenson, but he was a big man and kept coming at her. She fired again and I closed the bolt on the round, pivoting, holding the rifle in two hands at the hip like in the old training films about snap shooting. She saw me out of the corner of her eye and spun, firing. Her round went wide, flame and hot gasses in my face. I fired and the round plowed into her stomach from three feet away.

My ears rang. My nose was filled with cordite and the smell of ammonia. Maureen was sitting on the floor, her back against the couch. Her eyes wide, her mouth moving, reminding me of the dead deer. Her hand was still wrapped around the butt of the revolver, twitching. She fell over on her side. I didn't need to see the wound in her back.

I kicked the gun out of her hand, sending it skittering across the floor. When I looked back, her face was slack and her eyes were glassy marbles, nothing more. The Ambassador had taken two rounds to the chest but, somehow, he was still breathing. He might as well be dead. He was dead when a B-Patrone bullet from World War II killed his wife and child-to-be. That and seeing Maureen kill his son. Stevenson was alive, but what sort of life would it be? I had done my job and found out who was behind it all. What good had it done?

I went over to the white phone and dialed the State Police. I told the dispatcher that four people had been shot and we needed an ambulance. 'Call Detective Lyndgarten too. He'll want in on this.' I hung up and then dialed Watts in Boston.

I stared at the carnage and my eyes settled on Maureen's lifeless eyes. I couldn't believe one person's rage had caused so much devastation. The phone rang and rang till finally Watts answered.

'Roark, it's early even for you.'

'Brenda. You'd better get up to Vermont again as soon as you can.' I know she was talking but my ears began to ring. I put the phone down in the cradle and put the rifle on the floor. I went into the kitchen, stopped to light a Lucky. I needed the nicotine. I found some clean dish towels and went back to help Bradley and the Ambassador.

I looked up when Frieda, who had let herself in, screamed. Then there was a big state trooper pointing a giant, stainless steel Magnum revolver at me. I wish they'd stop doing that. I was getting sick of people pointing guns at me. One of these days I might end up getting shot.